Sudhindra Nath Ghose (1899–1965)—best known as Sudhin Ghose—was born in Bardhaman in Bengal. He moved to Europe as a student in the 1920s where he first studied science and art history before completing a doctorate in literature. Though he spent his entire writing career in the West, Sudhin Ghose, like his contemporaries Mulk Raj Anand, R.K. Narayan and Raja Rao, based his work on India, drawing material from the villages and towns of Bengal. An impeccable prose stylist and a master of sprawling narratives which draw inspiration from myths, fables, legends and epics, Sudhin Ghose is among the greatest writers in Indian English literature.

Sudhin Ghose wrote journalistic pieces, a scholarly tract, and three volumes of Indian folktales apart from the work for which he is best remembered: a quartet of novels comprising *And Gazelles Leaping* (1949), *Cradle of the Clouds* (1951), *The Vermilion Boat* (1953) and *The Flame of the Forest* (1955).

THE VERMILION BOAT

SUDHIN N. GHOSE

SPEAKING TIGER

SPEAKING TIGER PUBLISHING PVT. LTD
4381/4 Ansari Road, Daryaganj,
New Delhi–110002, India

First published by Michael Joseph, London 1953

ISBN: 978-93-86338-58-7
e-ISBN: 978-93-86338-59-4

10 9 8 7 6 5 4 3 2 1

Typeset in Adobe Jenson Pro by Jojy Philip
Printed at Thomson Press India Ltd.

PART ONE

Behold the Idols

I

'Remember, you are going to Calcutta.' Jogin-Da spoke as though he were addressing a child and I knew nothing of my destination or of Calcutta! 'And Calcutta's railway terminus,' he continued, 'is not called Calcutta.'

'It is Howrah,' I murmured.

'Don't argue,' Jogin-Da scowled. 'There is also Sealdah. What do you know of Calcutta? Just listen to what I say.'

I listened, standing at the door of the railway coach and watching the excited, swirling crowd on the platform.

'You will get off at Howrah, and take a cab. A horse-drawn cab, and not a taxi. Nor a rickshaw. Nor a bus. Nor a tram. But a *gharee*—a horse-drawn cab, and drive straight to the Hostel of the Teachers' Training College. There you will be staying: at *Masters' Mess* and nowhere else.'

I thought it rather odd that he should repeat the obvious for the hundredth time.

'Remember, you are a scholar. And you should behave as such: as a true scholar.'

I demurred: I was a mere scholarship-holder, a future teacher. What claim had I to be called a scholar?

'Don't answer me back. A scholarship-holder is as good as a scholar. And a scholar should behave with dignity. Never allow yourself to be browbeaten. You must never allow yourself to be imposed upon. Let others do whatever they will, but you should keep yourself pure. Pure in words. Pure in thoughts. And pure in deed.'

What was on his mind? I wondered if he was going to give another lecture on *ahimsa* and the doctrines of his spiritual master, Prem Swami.

'You may be a scholar,' Jogin-Da went on. 'But railway travelling all by yourself is no joke.' He laid special stress on the words 'all by yourself.'

I readily agreed and repeated for the third time that it was nice of him to come to Asansole solely to see me off.

~

Some thought Jogin-Da was crazy—a perfect lunatic, but harmless. Others considered him to be simply queer—somewhat feeble-minded, but amiable all the same. To me, however, my legal guardian was nothing short of a miracle-man: an ever-bubbling fountain of living wisdom in spite of his occasional fits of tiresomeness.

'He has gathered much practical knowledge,' I was told, 'from his solitary peregrinations.' Certainly he was not like the other villagers who did their travelling in big parties: 'Moving in hordes,' to use Jogin-Da's language, 'from one unholy pilgrimage station to another more unholy and allowing themselves to be bullied and badgered by railway inspectors, ticket collectors, guards, guides, porters, hawkers, coolies, *goondas* (professional hooligans), *pundahs* (temple touts), and priests: all soliciting bribes or tips.'

Jogin-Da preferred travelling alone or in the company of the disciples of Prem Swami: people who did not believe in pilgrimages. It was rumoured that he had a special pass entitling him to free travel to any part of the world. This belief was widespread on account of an aphorism attributed to him: 'Only fools bother about buying tickets.'

'Jogin-Da,' I once ventured to remark, 'you must have some sort of a pass. What does it look like?'

'A pass!' Jogin-Da chuckled. 'Who cares two pins for a pass? Once I had a big dog with me. That was my railway pass as well as my voucher for all the meals I enjoyed during the journey at the expense of the Government.'

That was the occasion when he travelled from Calcutta to Simla and then to Kasauli and finally back to Calcutta by an infinitely longer route via the Bengal Nagpur Railway. The whole trip lasted, I understood, a fortnight or three weeks, and it cost Jogin-Da just one copper coin. His travelling companion was a huge mastiff that was looking for its master, 'So he took charge of it,' the villagers gossiped. 'And to make the animal comfortable he got a whole first-class coach all to himself. "It is the Governor-General's pet," he declared at the Howrah station. "It has been bitten by a mad cur." The rest was quite simple. Some of the smaller fry at Howrah muttered something about getting the mastiff shot, but Jogin-Da silenced them with a growl: "You can't get rid of the Governor-General's favourite dog like a common mongrel. This is the last British-born mastiff in the world. Everything must be done to save it." Of course, Jogin-Da had to invent a post for himself; he claimed to be the Director of the Veterinary Department of the Pasteur Institute at Kasauli. The mastiff was a big animal, about the size of a six-month-old bull-elephant. Jogin-Da wept when he parted with it.'

It was noised abroad by the more spiteful—he had quite a few detractors on account of his profound veneration for Prem Swami—that he had made a handsome sum by selling this stolen mastiff to a dog-fancier from Colombo, who was also an amateur 'bioscopist.' (I never discovered for sure whether this wealthy traveller from Ceylon turned the handle of a film-projector without being paid, or took moving pictures for his own pleasure.) However at the most the dog-loving Singhalese could not have had the animal in his possession for more than an hour when Jogin-Da collected the reward offered by the advertiser who had lost the mastiff: a widow owning the Torulata Soap Factory at Budge-Budge near Calcutta.

The profits of this double deal may not have been much. For Jogin-Da often complained of the expenses he had incurred—on account of the dog—in buying a platform ticket at Howrah. 'All due to inexperience,' he lamented. 'The railway inspector did not even bother to look at the platform ticket! He, and later the guards of the Simla Express, were hypnotized by the sight of the big mastiff. I got straight into a first-class coach which emptied by itself to make room for the dog. The deference they showed to me made me feel as though I were the Governor-General himself. Had I known all this beforehand I could have spared myself the trouble of buying that platform ticket. It was money thrown away. All due to inexperience. A good copper coin wasted.'

~

'Don't jingle your coins when travelling,' Jogin-Da enjoined. 'And don't talk to your fellow travellers. Just ignore them. Don't listen to their drivel. Shut your ears to dirty stories and silly twaddle.'

I nodded and tried to smile. Inwardly I was getting alarmed: the coach was full of people; though they were not much concerned with Jogin-Da's counsels they were not deaf. What opinion were they forming about me? I felt positively uncomfortable.

'Pretend to be deaf. That's the best thing to do when you are travelling alone. And be dumb as well.'

'Why?' The question escaped from my lips quite inadvertently.

'You are inexperienced. If you open your mouth you will be lost. The man next to you may be a commercial traveller, and he will try to sell you a gold mine which does not exist. Or perhaps he is an insurance agent, and will make you sign a piece of paper. And that will land you in gaol. You may be a minor, but that is no plea for mercy in a law court. Your age will not save you if you allow yourself to be egged on by a secret agent to commit a bomb outrage. Who knows? Your neighbour may be a C.I.D. officer in search of an escaped convict, and whatever you say might be taken down in evidence against you.'

I looked at the station clock. It was time, I thought, to shut the door of my coach. 'Perhaps,' I remarked in a timid way, 'I am in the way of other passengers.'

But Jogin-Da refused to take my hint: he was not concerned with my embarrassment, nor with what others thought of his counsels. He was a puny man, but his voice was definitely high-pitched. Instead of speaking he was shrieking. Every word of his reached the farthest corner of the carriage: it was one of those old-fashioned coaches with sitting accommodation for fifty and standing room for two hundred.

'If anyone offers you a paper to read,' he went on as before, 'pretend to be illiterate. It may be a seditious journal, or an obscene magazine, or an illegal publication. Who knows? If someone offers you a drink, refuse it. Just shake your head. The drink may be drugged, and you will end by becoming a drug-addict. Remember, only crooks try to contact fellow-travellers. I was once fooled in that way at Kidderpore.'

'When was that?'

'Long before you were born. I was then a greenhorn like you. I had nobody to give me good advice. In that way you are lucky. You have me as your guardian and counsellor.'

I tried to lure him into telling me what happened at Kidderpore. It must have been a very disturbing experience, and its memory evoked unpleasant thoughts in Jogin-Da.

'Don't ask silly questions,' Jogin-Da frowned. 'Don't be too curious—especially in the hearing of strangers. Let me tell you plainly that in my time I have been a commercial traveller, an insurance agent, and an amateur detective as well. I know what I am talking about. If you follow my advice it will be all to your good.'

Many stories were current about Jogin-Da's adventures and misadventures. There was, however, no knowing if they were true or just made up. About his disagreeable transaction at Kidderpore all that I had heard was mere gossip.

Once, I gathered, a travelling circus missed its performing seal at the same time as Jogin-Da's mother lost her casket of jewellery containing the family heirloom: she found in the place of her precious coffer a cryptic message enjoining her to give up luxury and to show charity to dumb creatures; there was also Jogin-Da's future address—c/o the Police Headquarters, Mombasa. How the disappearance of a seal and the loss of a jewel-casket were interlinked no one ever explained to me. But I did hear that the boat scheduled to carry a stowaway of below middle height—a would-be guardian of law and order in East Africa—left the Kidderpore Docks without him: the circus company eventually recovered its seal, and the box of jewellery found its way back to its rightful owner, emptied of its contents. 'The misadventure at the Kidderpore Docks,' Jogin-Da's detractors said as they chatted among themselves, 'has added a new page to Jogin's volume of practical wisdom.'

I may mention here that Jogin-Da was fond of exotic animals. He simply adored them. Once he went to Karachi by the sea route—a pretty long and tiresome journey—simply to examine some alligators kept in a huge pond under the supervision of a pious fakir; for these were said to be sacred, though by no means tame. Jogin-Da obtained the permission of their keeper to look after them for a few days, and he fed them with melons instead of meat. This entirely changed the character of the surly brutes, and they became as tame as performing seals.

Was this love for wild beasts what tempted Jogin-Da to travel as a stowaway to Africa, the continent renowned for its ferocious fauna?

But, I wondered, why did he choose a trained seal as his companion?

~

There was not much time for wondering. The locomotive was spewing steam. The bells began to clang. Shrill shrieks rose all along the length of the platform. Jogin-Da made involuntary grimaces as he covered his ears with his hands. He hated noise and fuss, and detested the sight of passengers scurrying to their seats at the last moment. He was, I knew, a man of peace, who preferred quietness and efficiency.

'If a man wants to sell you a gold bangle,' Jogin-Da shouted above the general din, 'or a silver bracelet, don't buy it. Even if he wants to make you a present of it, ignore him. Pretend to be deaf.

And this is most important: remember, you are no longer a child. If a woman ...'

The whistle screeched lustily. The piercing noise made Jogin-Da shudder, and his words were drowned in the universal pandemonium associated with the departure of a mail train from Asansole Junction. He jumped away from the platform's edge as the train jerked forward.

'Jogin-Da,' I cried frantically. 'My ticket! It is with you. And my luggage receipt ...'

He cupped his hands to his ears while the train gathered speed as it slid along the platform.

'My ticket,' I shouted, leaning out of the window.

I saw Jogin-Da raise his right hand to make the sign of blessing. He indicated by gestures that my railway ticket was either in his pocket or in mine. I shouted again, but it was too late. By now the train was out of the platform.

I looked silly. I noticed some of the passengers were staring at me. They must have thought I was a fool. Not knowing what to do I began fumbling nervously in my pockets.

~

'Son!' A grave-looking man addressed me. He was a living replica of a bronze statue of Edward VII I had seen somewhere. To judge by his looks he must have been as sedate as the statue in his daily life. It was a marvel to hear him speak, and a still greater marvel to see him adjust his spectacles. 'Son! It is no use fussing over a ticket which you have not got. Getting nervous won't help you. By the way, who is the man who saw you off? His face seems familiar.'

'He is Dada.'

'*Dada*! I am surprised. You mean to say that he is your elder brother? Why, he is old enough to be your grandfather.'

'Everyone calls him Dada. I call him Jogin-Da.'

'Hum! Jogin Dada. Everybody's elder brother.' The grave-looking duplicate of Edward VII's image muttered half-audibly. He seemed to be distressed and more worried than myself, and murmured something about someone being done in and losing his luggage into the bargain.

I refused to pay any heed to his soliloquy. 'It is no use getting flustered,' I said to myself. 'Jogin-Da has registered my luggage. He knows what's best. He could, however, have given me the receipt and the ticket as well.'

'Son!' This time it was the traveller next to me who spoke. He stopped fanning himself with his palmyra-leaf hand-fan swirled on its handle like the rattles boys use for raising a din at football matches. Poor man! He was suffering from heat. This was not surprising because he was extremely bulky, triple-chinned; his enormous body sprawled over seats meant for three common mortals. He reminded one of the elephantine deity, Ganesa, the god of Good Luck, and like Ganesa he seemed to be full of good humour. There was a twinkle in his eye which made me smile. 'Son! Jogin has got your ticket all right. I can swear he is at this very minute collecting the refund at the Asansole booking office.'

It was impolite, but I pretended to be deaf.

'Do you understand,' Bronze image of Edward VII explained. 'He is selling your own ticket back. Jogin is a well-known figure in the lobbies of the Legislative Council. He is considered to be a crook.'

A man in the far corner of the coach cleared his throat and came to my rescue. He had on his head a *samla*—a brimmed turban—the distinctive head-gear of the special pleaders in the lower courts of law. 'You can't call anyone a crook with impunity,' he started. 'It is slander.'

The triple-chinned Ganesa regarded this as a huge joke, and roared with delight. His whole body wobbled. To enjoy his mirth better he closed his eyes and swirled his hand-fan vigorously. Bronze Edward VII did not deign to take any notice of the special pleader's intervention; he pulled his spectacles down to the tip of his nose, and fixed his eyes on me.

'To call a man a crook is slander,' the special pleader repeated. 'Defamation by word of mouth is slander. It is punishable in criminal suits and in civil suits, for damages.'

'Slander be blowed.' The god Ganesa's human incarnation suddenly passed from hilarity to solemnity. 'Jogin would be the last man in the world to deny that he has been living on his wits ever since the day he started talking.'

'Does he know Jogin-Da at all?' I asked myself. 'Perhaps he is one of those who have listened to Jogin-Da's backbiters.'

'Jogin is not only a crook, but a clown as well.' Ganesa went on. 'He knows the publicity value of eccentricity. He recognized me at once. That's why he did not get into the coach to lecture to our young man.'

This was annoying. I stared out through the window, and regretted being dragged into the general discussion about Jogin-Da.

'In his younger days,' Bronze Edward VII at long last condescended to explain to the lawyer, 'Jogin used to wear a beard, and was then known as the Babaji. Now he is clean-shaven, and is everybody's Dada—the universal elder brother! The more one lives the more one learns.'

Through the corner of an eye I noticed Edward VII whispering something to Ganesa, and Ganesa started to scrutinize me from head to foot; they nodded at each other, and more whispered confidences were exchanged. The special pleader too was interested in their secret, and bobbed his head to stare at me: he was no longer concerned in giving me an exposition of the laws concerning slander.

What made them take stock of my features?

~

I reminded myself of Jogin-Da's injunctions.

Did I look like a prospective buyer of a non-existent gold mine? Or of a pair of gilded bangles of brass, filled with lead? Which one of the three was going to begin the patter—the sales talk? 'It generally starts,' Jogin-Da held, 'with a got-up disputation among the members of the same gang, and then they will invite you to give your opinion on the matter. Sometimes it opens with a simple catchphrase "The train is likely to be punctual for a change" or "Have you heard the latest news? The King of Greece has been bitten by a mad monkey" or some such nonsense—and the conversation next shifts to the main issue: How you can make a fortune out of nothing—for a mere song—or a simple bagatelle of a thousand rupees. First, he will collect packets of a thousand rupees from his partners, and immediately turn to you for your packet. If you can't give him a thousand, he will reduce his price to a hundred. He will swear by his mother that he is doing you a favour by offering a fortune for a hundred rupees, and if you are still firm, he will automatically descend to ten, and then to one. If you persist in refusing his offer, he will finally beg you on his knees to accept his bargain for a farthing! You would be doing him a favour by pocketing what he offers. But don't be a fool. Only a fool is moved by a crook's patter, and throws good money away. In the days of Lord Coorjohn I bought a platform ticket at Howrah to no purpose. I wasted a copper coin…'

The more I thought of Jogin-Da the more I felt like laughing. He was in many respects rather odd. Though reputed to be an extremely well-to-do broker he was frightfully stingy. Once he dived into a cesspool to retrieve an accidentally dropped penny and nearly drowned himself.

The special pleader gave me a nudge, and my reminiscing came to an end.

~

'Do you know you are liable to pay double fare at the end of the journey?'

'I beg your pardon.' I was surprised at the pleader's persistent interest in my welfare. How was I to shake him off? I repeated mechanically, 'I beg your pardon.'

'Legally speaking,' he expounded with due solemnity, 'the railway authorities are entitled to collect a fine as well. What will you do if they ask you to pay the double fare from Bombay? You can't get out of the difficulty without the help of witnesses. What proof is there that you got in at Asansole? It looks as though your trip to Howrah will cost you a couple of hundred rupees.'

At this the triple-chinned Ganesa began laughing again. And I joined in: that was the best I could do. For I had not a single cent with me. Jogin-Da took my purse to buy me my ticket and to pay for my registered luggage, and now the purse, the ticket, and the luggage-receipt were all with him. It was the sight of my long tubular purse which disgusted him.

'It is not a man's purse!' Jogin-Da exclaimed with horror as soon as he saw it. 'It looks like an obscene thing. Where did you pick it up?'

I explained to him that it was a parting gift of the village watchman's family: Ramdas's wife and daughter had specially knitted it for me. They knew that Calcutta was full of pickpockets, and the safest means of carrying money in the metropolis was to keep it in one's waist-band.

'Never mind their knitting it for you. It looks positively repulsive. Only women wear such ridiculous snake-shaped contraptions at their girdle.'

I was most unwilling to part with my present from the Ramdas family. But my protests were of no avail.

'You are not a woman,' Jogin-Da expostulated. 'If you produce this purse in Calcutta you will be arrested for being queer. Give it to me, and take my wallet in exchange. But let me first get your ticket and register your luggage. Meanwhile you jump into the train and make yourself comfortable.'

I did not get Jogin-Da's wallet in exchange for my purse. I was—literally and metaphorically—penniless, and travelling without a ticket. I thought, however, of my grandmother's saying: 'Providence protects the helpless.'

II

The train was moving fast. As I watched the continuously shifting landscape through the square frame of the window nearest to me, I thought of a cinema-screen. Then, I do not know how, without any conscious effort on my part, my memory began projecting on to an imaginary screen scenes of my younger days: of railway journeys in the company of Jogin-Da.

I thought of my grandmother—my mother's mother—whom I called Didi-Ma, and of my mother's sister-in-law, Mummi-Ma, who lived with my grandmother in the Palit Mansion at Chandernagore. When did I first hear Didi-Ma say 'Providence protects the helpless?' How old was I then? My memory did not give me any clue to my exact age. I must have been very young: somewhere between infancy and boyhood; at that intermediate period when children cease to care for paper boats and yet are not old enough to crave for real ones; at that age they are readily diverted with gaily coloured toy vessels.

My most treasured possession at that time was such a toy sailing ship painted in bright vermilion; it was a gift from Jogin-Da. I brought it proudly with me to Didi-Ma's house at Chandernagore where I was to spend my holidays.

'You are not going to amuse yourself with that plaything,' Mummi-Ma—my Second Aunt—exploded even before giving me a welcome kiss. 'You must not cross the threshold with your Vermilion Boat.'

I was dumbfounded. For weeks I had been looking forward to my stay at Chandernagore mainly for the fun of floating my toy vessel in the river Hooghly: it was so close to the Palit Mansion. Why was I to be denied that pleasure? I stood still as a stake on the doorstep, hugging the boat tightly to my heart. What was the good of holidaying at Chandernagore if it meant the sacrifice of my treasure?

'A boy playing with such a thing,' Mummi-Ma went on, 'got drowned this very morning near the jetty. If mother sees your boat you will be sent back at once to where you came from.'

I stood where I was. I did not know what to say. There was a lump in my throat. My lips twitched involuntarily. But I did not utter a word: I was doing my best to swallow my tears.

'Give it back to me.' Jogin-Da snatched away the boat but he gave me a friendly pat on my head and an understanding wink.

I knew the meaning of that twinkle, though I did not acknowledge it in the usual way. How could I? Mummi-Ma's eyes were fixed on me as she made the further announcement that I was to stay within the compound of the house: the quays and the jetties were out of bounds for me, unless I was escorted by an adult.

'Oh!' I sighed. But my dejection was gone the moment I heard Jogin-Da's clear cough: it implied that I could count upon him. I smiled as Mummi-Ma embraced me, and took me up in her arms; she was now all tenderness, and covered me with kisses as she called me 'a very good boy' and her 'treasure'.

Though there was no going out that afternoon to paddle in the mud shoals of the river I did not feel unhappy any more. I knew I would get my Vermilion Boat back and there would be opportunity enough for me to sail it in one of the large ornamental cisterns and fish-ponds of the house. There were plenty of convenient pools within the walled enclosure of the Palit Mansion. In fact, every courtyard, or almost every courtyard, had a tiny pond of its own: a peculiarity of my grandmother's house, which I prized highly.

~

This house—the ancestral seat of the Palits of Chandernagore—was a ramshackle affair; a huge, towered edifice in a ruinous state with only a few inmates: the permanent ones were just two: Didi-Ma, my grandmother, and Mummi-Ma, the Second Aunt. Its very appearance was forbidding. The neighbours never referred to it by its real name—the Palit Mansion; to them it was the Haunted House, because it was very old and steadily disintegrating.

To tell the truth, it was not so much a house as a collection of detached buildings, of all ages, connected with one another by covered galleries or colonnaded cloisters, which enclosed square courtyards or quadrangles, bearing strange names: such as the Elephant Yard, the Horsemen's Court, the Dupleix's Durbar, the Dancing Girls' Repose, the Perfume Garden, the Silk Mart, and so on.

Though all the separate buildings and the connecting galleries were falling to pieces, the central structure with its pinnacled tower was in an excellent state of preservation. This was the most ancient part of the Palit Mansion, dating from the epoch when the French acquired Chandernagore—by purchase and treaty rights—from the Great Mogul. Fully fifteen years, I understood, were spent in building it, from 1673 to 1688. Its architect was a military engineer called Le Prestre, a first cousin of the Marquis de Vauban. 'Monsieur Le Prestre,' the patriarch of the Palits was said to have complained, 'you have taken a long while to finish this. I know it is not easy to put up a solid structure on a mud bank. Yet fifteen years may mean an aeon to an old man. I wonder if the building will prove to be really enduring.' 'It will last as long as the French flag flies over the fort of Chandernagore,' replied Monsieur Le Prestre. 'You mean to say that this house is as well built as Fort Orleans!' 'Much better, I should say,' replied the master mason on behalf of the architect. 'Fort Orleans has been erected on Vauban's plans whereas in raising the Palit Mansion Monsieur Le Prestre has introduced improvements unknown to his cousin.' 'Well,' the satisfied patriarch caressed his chin and smiled; he wanted to know if the architect and the master mason had any counsel for him; what should be done to preserve the Palit Mansion after Fort Orleans had crumbled to dust? 'To keep an old house intact,' advised the architect and the master mason, 'one must renovate it every year.'

And that was what the Palits did with the towered portion of their building. This part was not only solidly constructed and encased with stone facings, it was also well looked after, regularly repaired; hence it presented a different aspect from the other buildings.

~

There are not many really old buildings in Bengal.

It may sound strange, nevertheless it is true that the attractive green pigeons—the *hariyals*—and their rivals in beauty, the grey and lilac turtle-doves, have been singularly inimical to the preservation of such buildings in my country. These birds have as their allies the climate of the Gangetic delta and the monsoon rains, which encourage rapid growth of such fig trees as the Pippala, the Sirisa, the Udambara, the Nigrodha—trees capable of throwing out aerial roots to secure nurture from Bengal's moisture-laden air: these are the favourite fruit trees of the pigeons and the doves; they thrive on their berries.

Unfortunately, the birds have always loved to build their nests, not in the trees, as do others of their kind, but on the roofs and in the eaves of human habitations. The old houses seem to attract their special attention, and the more inaccessible eaves and cornices are their favourite shelters. They gorge themselves with berries in the orchards, gardens, forests and jungles and leave their droppings in the nooks and crannies of houses, temples and towers. With the droppings, seeds are transported to the crevices of buildings, and there they readily take root. The monsoon rains feed them and the mosses prevent their easy detection.

Let the smallest sprout of a Pippala tree remain undisturbed for one year, and it will spread out its roots like an octopus extending its tentacles to capture its prey; and like an octopus the plant will destroy the building on which it lodges, not immediately, but slowly and—alas—surely. For by the time the monsoon rains are over and the sprout of the Pippala has emerged from the sheltering cover of mosses, it is too late to evict it. Its career of destruction has not only begun, but has already gone far.

Fight it if you will, but it is the tender shoot of the fig tree—no bigger than a baby's little finger—which will win in the long run. One may take a ladder to reach the high cornice the moment one notices the sprout, and one may pluck it off. But its roots will remain embedded in the wall, and these will produce in due course a dozen sturdier shoots for every one pulled off. One may cut off these dozen shoots, and there will sprout forth a score. Let the score be removed, and a hundred will be found in their stead.

Meanwhile the roots will be boring their way through the wall, cautiously feeling their passage to the earth, avoiding the light like thieves in the night. They will steadily weave their network of cord-like claws. Gradually faint fissures hardly visible to the naked eye, fine as patterns on crackled china, resembling gossamer cobwebs—will cover the walls from roof to basement. These will, by and by, extend and expand. The fissures will broaden into cracks allowing infiltration of rainwater. A new monsoon will come and these will be transformed into ugly slits and dangerous seams.

A musty smell will then fill the house: the stench of death and decay: the warning that the building is no longer fit for human habitation, and it will soon be taken over by the creatures that flourish in darkness.

'It is now my house,' arrogantly proclaims the voiceless fig tree to the householder. 'I hold you now in my vice-like grip. If you try to uproot me you will destroy your home immediately. If you delay you will get no mercy either. I have now spread the network of my suckers from the roof-tree to the corner-stone. The walls of the house have been eaten through and through. They are now mere coverings for my roots.'

'It took my forbears years of labour,' the householder laments, 'to build this family seat. And now this wretched fig tree has destroyed it in one generation!'

He curses the attractive *hariyals* and turtle-doves, but that does not help him. Unless he is quick in evacuating his house he may find the exit barred by the new roots put forth by the intruding tree, and what was once his home will become his sepulchre.

'What have I done to merit this fate?' asks the householder.

'Done?' The triumphant fig tree is eloquent. 'You have done everything to merit your fate. You slept when you should have kept vigil. The unwary merits destruction.'

A seed no bigger than a grain of mustard, nurtured by the wind and the rains, brings down a huge edifice in the space of thirty years.

~

'Thirty years!' I told my grandmother, 'That's a long time, Didi-Ma.'

'Long for a man,' grandmother replied. 'But not long for a family nor for a people. If a seed of poison is allowed to grow it will destroy a people in the same way as a house. It takes only a generation to destroy the heritage of the past.'

Unable to grasp fully what grandmother had in her mind, I repeated the old saying: 'To keep an old house intact, repair it every year, and look into every crack and cranny.'

'That's what I have been trying to do, my jewel,' grandmother sighed. 'But I am old and infirm. It is not easy ...'

To keep well repaired a house of many courtyards and some fifty living-rooms meant a lot of money, and my grandmother had very little. Those of her family who used to bring money were all dead: they died long ago. Not only they but also all the others: relations and friends capable of offering succour. 'Didi-Ma hasn't many whom she can call her own,' Gomosta Moshay told me. 'You are her daughter's son. She can count you as her own. And no one else.' 'But what about Mummi-Ma?' I asked, vexed at the thought that the old Estate Manager was overlooking my Second Aunt, who though always draped in white—widow's weeds—looked pretty in my eyes. Did she not allow me the privilege of brushing her raven-black hair which fell in cascades to her ankles when undone? 'Does not Mummi-Ma count?' I repeated indignantly. 'Yes, and no. She is only a widowed daughter-in-law. She is sick. She will die on the same day as Didi-Ma. What can she do to save this house?' 'And Jogin-Da?' I asked with equal warmth. Gomosta Moshay simply shrugged his shoulders; he was not particularly fond of Jogin-Da, whom he considered a hanger-on, anxious to buy at a cut-throat price some of the treasures that still remained in Didi-Ma's coffers. I was not old enough to comprehend all that the Estate Manager said; this much only I understood: Mummi-Ma was too sick to be of any service to Didi-Ma, though she did her best to hide the fact that she was suffering from a slow fever that sapped her strength.

Thus the main burden of running the house—in the traditional way—fell upon grandmother. Though she was old and infirm she persisted in keeping up all the time-honoured customs and usages. In this respect she was inflexible: no remonstrance had the slightest effect in inducing her to lighten her self-imposed routine drudgery.

Every living-room, the tradition demanded, should have a light from dusk till bedtime. As there was no money to keep so many lamps alight, each evening when it grew dark and the conch-shell was blown with prayers at the foot of the sacred basil plant, grandmother would totter from one room to another to make her round of the whole house with a light: a heart-shaped earthenware lamp filled with vegetable oil in which floated the burning wick. In every room the lamp was put on a pedestal while the windows, or rather, the Venetian shutters, were carefully closed—as people do only when they retire at bedtime—and curtains were drawn over the mirrors, if there were any in the room; grandmother would then say a benedictory prayer for a peaceful night, and withdraw with her lamp to repeat the same ritual in the next room. In those apartments, known as Guests' Chambers, where imposing four-posters were ready for unexpected visitors (who never came) she lingered longer: she scrutinized the beds to see if they were well made; the pillows and bolsters were readjusted, the sheets carefully smoothed, fresh water poured into the earthenware carafes, the tumblers wiped, a candlestick placed near the bed and a hand-fan, as well as a bowl containing spices; a second containing a rose or two floating in rose-water was placed in the Guest Room exclusively reserved for the newly married.

'Mother overdoes everything.' Mummi-Ma complained. It was she who had to throw open all the windows and shutters every morning, and make and unmake the beds in the Guest Chambers, and a hundred other tasks: some of which could have been readily omitted had grandmother been more amenable to reason.

The domestic help was kept busy looking after the sitting-room and the library. It was the library that took up all her time. She had to take out each book separately, dust it, and then put it back in its original place. This was toil enough for a single human being, and how she managed to do her work thoroughly—beginning it again in every three weeks—remained a mystery. Mummi-Ma had her doubts: she suspected that the domestic aid skipped her work; the number of volumes in the library was something like one hundred thousand.

'What can one do with so many books?' I once asked Mummi-Ma.

'Sell them, or burn them,' she replied bitterly. 'Mother says these can't be sold because they are in languages which no one reads nowadays. The books take up more time than the whole house put together.'

'Why can no one read them?'

'Because they are old.'

'Can grandmother read them?'

'She can. But her eyesight is failing. And when will she find time for reading?'

'Are there pictures in them?'

'Now, don't bother me just now.' Mummi-Ma flustered with her duster.

I was told that though there were thousands of books in the library and grandmother's eyes were bad, each volume had its allotted place, and the slightest disarrangement was bound to be detected by her. 'That would make her unhappy,' Mummi-Ma explained. 'Those with Mogul and Rajput paintings have been sold. The remainder will not find a buyer. Now, now. These books are not meant for children.'

'Are there none with pictures?' I persisted. Mummi-Ma's answer did not satisfy me, and I went straight to grandmother to complain to her.

'Aren't you too young to understand them, my jewel?'

'Understand!' I was indignant. 'Didi-Ma, do you think I am still a child? If I don't understand you may explain them to me. Anyway, you may show me the books with pictures.'

Perhaps my aunt was right, I concluded, when I was allowed to handle those massive tomes and leather-bound volumes of all countries and all ages. They were not meant for a boy of my age. I could not make much of Botticelli's illustrations to Dante's *Divine Comedy* nor of Holbein's woodcuts for Erasmus's *Encomium Moriae*. Other volumes were not much better: even those kept in an iron chest, incunabula printed by Pierre Le Rouge, Imprimeur du roi, and by Robert Estienne (also Imprimeur du roi), and others of their line.

Some of the books were definitely disappointing: those with illustrations of imaginary Indian scenes, for example, *Alexandre le Grand* by Quinte Curce and translated by M. de Vaugelas: Edition nouvelle, enrichie de figures. One volume made me laugh because grandmother handled it very carefully as though it were brittle.

'It has a picture in it,' grandmother said. 'Just one. Have a look.'

'Who is this funny man with a goatee?' I asked contemptuously.

'He is Ronsard.'

'Why has he put a chaplet of laurels round his head?'

'Because he is the Prince of Poets.'

'That's funny. Do you like him?'

'Yes, I do. Let me read something for you.'

Grandmother valued that first edition of Ronsard for two reasons: first, because she liked his poetry, and then, because it bore the autograph of Dupleix. Dupleix, I was told, used to visit the Palit Mansion when he was the Administrateur of Chandernagore. That was about 1720. It was he who had suggested that one of the big rooms in the house should be called the King's Chamber. Though no king, or prince ever honoured that apartment with his visit it retained its name from Dupleix's time. Dupleix was one of grandmother's heroes, and was always referred to by her as 'Our Governor'.

I presume someone must have told me at that time—whether rightly or wrongly, I do not know—that Dupleix was also responsible for the suggestion that led to the addition of a flag-mast to the top of the hundred-foot-high pinnacled tower of the house: the *Cheel Kuti*—the Falcon's Rest. This was a sufficient reason for me to share grandmother's admiration for 'Our Governor.' I readily agreed with her when she said that Dupleix was a remarkable man.

That flag-post was a marvellous embellishment to the tower.

The top of the Falcon's Rest was an ideal vantage point to survey the surrounding countryside. And that tall flag-mast was a perpetual temptation and a challenge to me: I wanted to climb it without touching the cords and ropes attached to it: it was rigged up like the mast of a sailing ship, and had even a crow's nest.

The Falcon's Rest was my conning tower, and the whole house was a ship, and the countryside round about me was the sea: an emerald-green sea. Though my ship never moved I was not disappointed: the view from my tower was extensive and bewitching. It made me feel as though I were a falcon myself, watching the earth from a niche in the clouds: enjoying a privilege denied to common mortals.

A stranger once made disparaging remarks about the land I gazed upon; he called it dull and monotonous. 'It is green like a card-table,' he complained, 'and flat as a prairie.' The poor man! He must have been colour-blind, boorish and hard of hearing as well.

Green certainly the landscape was, and flat too. But it was not dull, nor was it monotonous in my estimation. It was resonant with the songs of many singing birds and redolent with the fragrance of many flowers: to the eye it was a revelry of colours; it was full of life and light, of shades and half-shades; it was enlivened by its infinite varieties.

Did not the easily obtained wide view compensate for the flatness of the land? Did not the multi-coloured flowering trees, higher than manors and mansions, add to its gaiety? Trees so covered with blossoms that their foliage and branches could be barely discerned: the enchanting flame-of-the-forest, the incomparable Gloriosa Superba, the purple pomegranates, the scarlet jacarandas, the golden showers, the moonflower magnolias: the trees that blossom all the twelvemonth round. And what about the bushes and shrubs changing their gorgeous garbs of efflorescence in every season? The red and white oleanders, the carmine and vermilion hibiscus, the saffron champaks, the cream and orange nyctanthes, and others of their kind; and the sacred plants, at whose feet our people love to spread exquisite prayer-rugs, the amaryllis, irises, nasturtiums, sword-lilies and tulips; and the lambent canna, the odoriferous tuberoses, and the scented belas. These are only a few of the flowering trees, plants and shrubs seen from the Falcon's Rest: I need not mention our roses, nor the lotuses, nor the hedges of hasnuhana, nor scores of other aromatic plants, known, no doubt, in other parts of the world where they flourish perhaps in greater profusion.

Almost beneath my feet flowed the sacred Hooghly river in all its majesty: the thousand-mile-long waterway for our boats and barges and ships: rivercraft carrying sails of orange and red and blue and umber. The river made a crescent sweep beyond the Koné Bouér Mandir—the Temple of the Newest Bride—to hide itself behind the colonnade of the serried saals and a forest of gold-mohur trees. I could just see on my extreme right the reed-covered island sanctuary at the bend of the river: the favourite resort of scores of lovely night herons.

Before me, like an unrolled carpet of stupendous dimensions, the landscape stretched out right to the horizon's brim. On its bosom reposed scores of villages with their thatched cottages of whitewashed cob, and flat-roofed houses of sienna-coloured burnt brick: every little hamlet surrounded by hedge-milk bush of emerald green, and shaded by glorious banyan and peepul trees, or topes of giant figs; there were the regular rectangular fields of ripening paddy, golden as the girdle of the goddess Lakshmi, our deity of bounty; square patches of gamboge-yellow mustard seed, and of the dense blue flowering gram-pulse, the amber-coloured sugar-cane, and the dark red seemuls; and the long stretches of grazing grounds, the irregular areas of fallow land, everglades and heaths—all of varying, contrasting tints and tones. Through these ran our raised roads of cinnabar-and-red hue, bordered with citron bushes, henna hedges, fruit-bearing trees, and the fantastically fronded palmyras. The footpaths were like black pencil lines playfully drawn on a schoolboy's map.

It looked like a chequered floor-cloth of many colours and varied patterns. Or rather, as I loved to imagine at certain moments, a pleasant draughts-board for the gods. When did the gods play their game? Who were their opponents? What was the stake? Where were their pawns and pieces?

Dwarfed by the distance, pygmies' beehives were the conical haystacks and circular corn-barns. No bigger appeared the remote groves of mango, orchards of jambolonas and lichis, clumps of bamboo, and clusters of palms. Scattered among them in that immense area, half-hidden in luxuriant vegetation were the ancient landmarks: the domes and temples, the towers and shrines, the palm-fringed sacred pools, and the stone-encased flights of steps—the sanctified ghats—leading to lotus-adorned expanses of water.

These were the pieces, I thought, the gods used in their game. Of course, I had my doubts: I was never quite sure. Did the gods play only in the dark? When no one could watch them? And did they replace their pieces in their usual sites, at the first glimmer of dawn, so that no mortal wayfarer should miss them during the day?

I asked grandmother if the landmarks ever shifted their sites.

'Alas!' Grandmother sighed. 'They do. The landmarks do disappear from their sites. Not of their own will, nor on account of the gods. But because of the demons.'

'The demons?' I wanted to know more about them.

'The demons are waging a perpetual war against mankind. They are the tempters. They ask man to forget God.' Grandmother pointed in the direction of Calcutta: there was a blue haze of smoke from the factories.

It was not easy for grandmother to climb the tower. Yet she did mount the spiral staircase right to its very top: once every twelvemonth. 'To keep an old house intact,' I recalled, 'one must look into every nook and cranny.' Grandmother was mindful of her responsibility. Though infirm, half-blind and bent with age, as long as she lived she made it a point to climb to the roof of the Falcon's Rest on the twenty-third of March every year, and carry out as thorough an inspection as was possible for her. She examined not only the flat of the roof, but also the landscape to see if the blue haze of the factories had advanced more than in the preceding year, and if all the familiar landmarks were intact. She also tested the flag-mast, its cords and rigging.

I had too much respect for her to do any damage to the ropes. That was why I never managed to examine the general view from the crow's nest. It was impossible for me to climb a fairly smooth pole some twenty feet in height without touching the cords. It was a dizzy affair. 'After all,' I reasoned, 'this rigging is not meant to bear my weight. It is best to leave it alone.' Its main function was to help grandmother hoist a flag—a white flag—for a few minutes on every twenty-third of March.

'How do the demons remove the landmarks?' I asked grandmother. I was getting past the age of fables and fairy tales. She was at the foot of the flag-mast with her white flag. 'Can temples and towers be easily lifted?'

'The demons do not lift them,' grandmother replied. 'They simply demolish them. Can't you see the smoke screens in the distance? The demons are breathing smoke, and each year they are advancing. They will probably overrun the whole landscape in ten or in twenty years' time.'

I was incredulous. I did not, however, interrupt her.

'Factories are being put up,' she continued. 'More and more factories every year. More and still more men are being huddled together in the towns to lead a joyless anonymous existence. Such men behave like demented demons. They pull down temples and shrines, and show as little respect for the dead as for the living. They give no thought to the future. Joyless men are godless. They behave like demons.'

I did not explore the subject any further. The demons then concerned me less than did the sundial at the foot of the flag-mast: it was a bronze sundial covered with strange inscriptions, and curious designs: dragons and willow trees and pagodas like the Burmese monument in the Lady Bagan—the Eden Gardens—of Calcutta. It was made, I was told by Mummi-Ma, from patterns sent from Pekin by the Jesuit Fathers. In fact, the dial was made for them; it was destined for the modern observatory they had put up in Pekin. But on account of an unofficial war that was then raging between the English and the French in the Far East, it could not be shipped to China. Finally, it was bought by one of grandmother's forbears and installed on the top of the Falcon's Rest.

Though it bore the device 'I record all sunlit hours' the dial was absolutely useless as a timekeeper even in our cloudless summer: its gnomon was missing. This most essential adjunct to the sundial was knocked off by a shell from an English man-of-war and never replaced.

'That happened on the twenty-third of March,' grandmother explained. 'In the year following the Battle of Plassey. It was a day of great humiliation for all of us. Our misfortune was due to that traitor.'

If it were good to remember the famous, according to grandmother, it was equally important to recall the infamous: one must profit from the lessons of the past.

'Didi-Ma,' I asked, 'who was that traitor? What did he do?'

'He was the man who sold the plans of our Fort Orleans to the English General Clive.'

At a time when France and England were officially at peace, General Clive wanted to occupy Chandernagore. He thought a mere show of force would induce the garrison of Chandernagore to surrender. In this he was mistaken. So he decided to wage war in earnest. Chandernagore was invested both by land and sea. But the hundred guns of its citadel, Fort Orleans, held the enemy at bay, while fast frigates were dispatched to Pondicherry to inform the Governor-General of the treacherous assault launched by General Clive. 'A long drawn out siege of Chandernagore means grave risks,' Admiral Watson told his friend General Clive. 'The French vessels from Pondicherry may come up the river Hooghly any day. My fleet will then be caught between two fires: the fire of Fort Orleans and the fire of the vessels from Pondicherry. Can't you advance by land and silence the guns of Fort Orleans?' 'Dear Watson,' Clive replied, 'the guns of that very Fort Orleans are preventing my further advance. Have you any other suggestion?' 'Can't you find a Judas or a Mir Kassim in Chandernagore? You are excellent in contacting traitors.' 'That's an idea. Thanks for the suggestion. But there are no Jews in Chandernagore. And the Moslems and Hindus of Chandernagore are more French than the Parisians. They will not accept any bribe from me. Anyway, I shall think the matter over.'

Clive was, according to grandmother, as expert a forger as he was a clever soldier. He hit upon an original way of reducing Chandernagore. He forged a few letters and these were allowed to be 'smuggled' into the besieged town, and an impecunious French officer was misled by one of these. He was completely taken in: he was led to believe that his father in Paris was in dire distress and could be saved through Clive's generosity if he gave a copy of the plan of Fort Orleans to the English General and a sketch of the emplacement of the sunken barges in the Hooghly river to Admiral Watson: these barges prevented the passage of the English men-of-war up the river.

'In less than three hours after Clive had received the plans,' grandmother recounted, 'the hundred guns of our citadel were silenced, and its flag-mast shot away. We had no option but to surrender. And the white flag was hoisted on the twenty-third of March from this tower.'

I expressed my indignation at the behaviour of 'that traitor' and declared had I been there at that time I would have prevented the hoisting of the white flag. It was a relief to hear that the ships from Pondicherry did eventually come to Chandernagore's succour and the French flag flew once more from the Falcon's Rest and from the ruins of Fort Orleans.

'Didi-Ma, what happened to that traitor when the ships came from Pondicherry?'

My resentment vanished when I heard that the betrayer of Chandernagore met with a sad end: he killed himself with a pistol shot at the very foot of the flag-mast of the Falcon's Rest.

'It was for the sake of his father,' grandmother recounted, 'he accepted Clive's bribe.' So, his action was not incomprehensible. His salary was in arrears. 'Paris often forgets those who serve France abroad. The way they treated Our Governor was a disgrace.'

'Our Governor' was, of course, Dupleix. Though young I came to know some of the personalities often mentioned by grandmother. They were of all times and ages: Madame Grand who married Prince de Talleyrand; Mr Hottenberg, Chief of His Danish Majesty's Settlement of Frederiksnagar, who wore the decoration of the Order of Elephants; Marquis de Bussy, Comte de Lally, Monsieur François Martin of Pondicherry; Admiral de la Bourdonnais also of Pondicherry, and many others.

Grandmother lived in the past, but it was the future that worried her most: not her future, that did not concern her very much; all that she wanted for her own sake was to live long enough to see me finish my matriculation. It was the future of others which tormented her: ugliness was gaining ground, and that was a calamity. Once the neighbouring town Frederiksnagar was as clean and as pretty as Chandernagore: it had a small garrison of twenty-five gendarmes, dressed in red and white Danish uniforms, and that was enough to maintain law and order. Now Frederiksnagar was as dirty and as squalid as Calcutta. It no longer bore the name of its foundation, but had a new name: Serampore. The same was the case with the town of Chinsurah. Hooghly's case was no better. People were flocking to the towns and the land was being bled white.

'This fertile land of Bengal,' grandmother feared, 'will in this way be changed into a second Rajputana. Once Rajputana was as green as Bengal. It is now a barren land. Too many people came to Rajputana and used up her soil. And there are already too many people in Calcutta. Too many joyless men and women. They increase like weeds and behave like demons. What took generations to build up they will perhaps pull down in a day.'

'In a day!' The thought troubled me. 'It takes a fig tree some thirty years to destroy a house.'

'But joyless people can do the same in less than thirty hours.'

My zeal, or rather my determination, to protect the Falcon's Rest from all possible destroyers found expression in chasing away the birds from the pinnacles of the tower. The orchard behind the house was the best place for them. What business had they to hop about my tower and leave their droppings behind? I was jealous of my tower, and I felt very proud and important on the days when Muhuri, who did the bookkeeping for Gomosta Moshay, came up the spiral staircase to inspect the flag-mast.

Muhuri's visit indicated that a marriage was to be celebrated, and the flag-mast decorated with bright pennants and strings of candles fitted inside brightly coloured glass tumblers. I welcomed those visits and wished they were more frequent. Unfortunately, the auspicious days for celebrating marriages were few, not nearly as many as I would have wished: it was sheer joy to see the rows of fairy lights decorating the Falcon's Rest.

When any wedding took place in the neighbourhood, grandmother's house was generally used for the celebration. The strings of light on the flag-mast were lit as soon as the sun went down. Similar rows of fairy lights—heart-shaped earthen lamps whose cotton wicks floated in vegetable oil—looking like dolls' lanterns, were laid along the cornices, balconies, and arches of the building surrounding the Dancing Girls' Repose. This courtyard was scoured, swept, washed and wiped, and then covered with brightly coloured rattan and raffia mats and also with such pieces of carpet as could be found in the house and collected from among the neighbours. A marriage meant rejoicing for the whole locality—particularly among the women. They would come in their scores to help: to put everything right—orderly, trim and tidy—in honour of the bride and the groom. Each one of them brought her contribution, as far as her circumstances permitted, towards the expenses, entertainment, and general gaiety. They cooked meals—for at least a hundred mouths. They filled the Haunted House with their buzzing. 'This is exactly what the house was like,' recalled Gomosta Moshay, 'when I first came. In those days a hundred people used to live here. It was known as the house of liberal hospitality and generous largess.'

Who were those hundred people about whom Gomosta Moshay talked? Anyone claiming ties of friendship or relationship—however remote—with a Palit was welcome to stay in the house as long as he wished; he and his dependents were treated as members of the family. What happened to them? I did not get any information on this matter. Perhaps I was not interested in Gomosta Moshay's reminiscences. What concerned me more was the general appearance of the courtyard known as the Dancing Girls' Repose during a wedding ceremony; that was the meeting-place of the guests of the bridegroom's party and those of the bride's household. Each guest as he came into the courtyard was greeted with folded palms and garlanded with wreaths of flowers. It was the task of the children of the locality to see that every guest received his chaplet of white blossoms. I had a vague suspicion that the youngsters were allocated this uninteresting job simply to get them out of the way. However that may be, I did enjoy the ceremony of formally welcoming the members of the groom's party: they were treated on a different footing from those coming from the bride's side. The latter were the local people—so they were as good or as bad as we were —while the others were strangers: people who did not live in Chandernagore nor had any connection whatsoever with Chandernagore. Therefore, we had to be careful. 'Most strangers are savages!' The picture-framer whose shop was just behind the two cafes patronized by the tourists from Calcutta had little respect for them. 'The way they behave in Cafe Rigolade as soon as they get in there is unbelievable. And the others who patronize the bar of Un Petit Rigaudon are no better. Once off the steamer they want to get tight quickly. Then they want to buy a bale of silk for a rupee. Mind you, for a rupee! "Aren't we in French territory?" they ask each other, and then moan: "Silk ought to be cheap here. What's the good of coming to Chandernagore if we can't have silk and women for a song?" I tell you, most strangers are savages. Be careful when you come across them.' As I had great respect for the picture-framer I took his counsel to heart, and did my best never to reveal to any member of the bridegroom's party that one of the courtyards of the house was called the Silk Mart. Grandmother had no silk to sell, and if a guest got into his head the idea of securing a bale of silk for nothing it would have been a calamity: the tradition demanded that whatever a guest asked for he was to receive—even if he wanted an elephant it had to be produced no matter what price the bride's father had to pay for it!

On wedding nights the King's Chamber was lit up with huge chandeliers. The newly married were shown all the deference due to royalty. They wore crowns on their heads and sat cross-legged on improvised thrones: gilded seats, covered with cloth of gold. Like a royal couple granting an audience they received the blessings of their elders before others were admitted to their presence. Their durbar lasted all night through, and they never got a wink of sleep. Nor did those who crowded round them—mostly women—telling them all sorts of stories young people were not meant to hear. While to keep everyone awake, I presumed, the musicians kept up an uninterrupted din from sunset to sunrise with oboes, trumpets, clarinets, and horns.

Grandmother's house on such nights looked like a dream palace. The window-sills of every habitable room carried rows of fairy lights, and everywhere inside the building there were bright Roman candles. Every corner was filled with sound and gaiety. No one went to bed—neither the guests of the bride's party nor the strangers who came with the bridegroom.

I had, of course, to be careful and keep out of Mummi-Ma's way: otherwise I ran the risk of being caught and dragged away into my room and forcibly undressed and put into bed. 'I have enough bother with mother,' was her usual formula. 'She is so tired, but she refuses to retire. And now you! What business have you to romp about at midnight? This is not your wedding. You had better come along with me.'

Though I liked my Second Aunt, I regarded her as a spoilsport. There were, however, ways and means of avoiding her and enjoying fun in my own fashion. The easiest method was to run about on the pretence of some urgent business, and disappear in that part of the house condemned as derelict: the portion which never saw any light even on wedding nights. It was virtually cut off from the central structure and its adjoining wings. I knew my way well through the labyrinth of broken columns and fallen plinths. For my purpose the cloisters and the court of the Elephant Yard were no good. The Dupleix's Durbar was equally useless. They were very much like the quadrangle called the Dancing Girls' Repose—entirely covered with flagstones. The best place to hide was the flight of stone steps running into the pool of the Perfume Garden. The Perfume Garden was the courtyard that had the biggest reservoir of water in its midst, the Sandalwood Tank; it was not only bigger but also deeper than the similar ponds in the Silk Mart or in the Pilgrims' Rest. Moreover, the flights of steps on the four sides of the Sandalwood Tank ran right down from the ground level to the very bottom of the pool.

At one time blocks of sandalwood used to be kept dipped in this reservoir; it was then fed with running water, which worked a number of fountains in different parts of the house and filled the whole atmosphere with the heavy fragrance of sandalwood. That was, however, long ago: perhaps even before grandmother was born. In my time the Sandalwood Tank exuded a foetid stench of water-weeds. Its water was stagnant and looked green. It was my aunt's eyesore: she hated its sight so much that only to please her grandmother had put up a huge screen of trellises for silvery pink roses giving out a heavy musk-like scent; this barrier of thornless Bourbon Zephyrine Drouhin roses cut off all view of the Sandalwood Tank from Mummi-Ma's room. But such was her detestation of this Tank that she often complained that the cause of her slow fever and perpetual headache was the smell of asafoetida exuded by the water-weeds of my favourite hiding-place. Whenever she had attacks of hay fever she murmured about the pollen of weeds growing in the courtyard of the Perfume Garden. She never came near it, and I knew even if there were a general conflagration and her safety lay in running across the Perfume Garden she would have gladly allowed herself to be roasted alive rather than save her life by crossing the weed-covered courtyard which had the Sandalwood Tank in its midst.

Was not such a place ideal for hiding?

On that memorable day when I was ordered to stay indoors because some silly boy had drowned himself in the Hooghly river, I decided to try out my Vermilion Boat in the Sandalwood Tank. I did not breathe a word to anyone, except to Jogin-Da. Perhaps that was a mistake. But it was impossible for me to foresee everything.

Anyway, while sailing my boat I noticed a water-weed behaving in a queer way: it was trying to interfere with the boat as though it were a living thing. Then it began following my brightly painted vessel, nibbling at it from time to time. Had the boat not been newly decorated I would not have minded a water-weed meddling with it. But I did value my boat's fresh coat of beautiful vermilion, and it was not at all to my liking that a water-weed should behave like an ill-bred puppy trying out its teeth on anything that attracted its attention. Of course I knew that a water-weed had no teeth. Still it was none of its business to rub itself continually against my boat.

I got hold of my perch and gave it a push. The greenish water and the floating scum on its surface did not permit scrutiny of the troublesome weed, but it seemed to be trying to push back my perch. That made me think it might not be quite an ordinary water-weed, but something living: some sort of a funny fish like the *Bahin* fish or *Kunchay*—a lamprey or an eel. Both of these varieties of fish were sold at Hogg Sahib's Bazaar in Calcutta; they were said to be very tasty and therefore in great demand. People paid a higher price for lampreys and eels than for the well-known rohu fish. I had, of course, never tasted them. I had not even had the opportunity of examining any of them at close quarters.

My curiosity was roused.

I forgot all about my Vermilion Boat, and busied myself with this living water-weed, resembling an eel. I tickled it with my perch. It responded by nibbling at it. I wished I had my fishing rod and tackle with me. As I had not, I tickled it once again and noticed that when it opened its mouth the inside was all white, like a blob of milk-white cottonwool.

'Hey! Cottonmouth!' I called out. 'What are you doing here? How have you come into this Sandalwood Tank?'

The cottonmouth became pugnacious. It bit hard at my perch.

By now, I was sure that it was neither a lamprey nor an eel: nor any variety of fish known to me, it rose to the surface of the water for a moment and then dived again under my Vermilion Boat. That was enough for me to note that my cottonmouth was brightly coloured: its back was olive green and its sides bore dark bands, while its belly was saffron yellow. A fairly attractive thing. I thought it would look quite original to put it in one of those empty goldfish bowls in the corridor leading to the library. Perhaps I could also put my Vermilion Boat in the same bowl and examine how my cottonmouth would behave.

No sooner did this thought strike me than I began undressing. I decided to take a plunge into the Sandalwood Tank to secure the cottonmouth. Of course, I was not as sensitive to dirty water and reeking weeds as Mummi-Ma. There was no one about, and I got into the water without making a big splash.

'Look before you leap,' Gomosta Moshay always murmured whenever Jogin-Da talked to him about buying him shares in the Stock Exchange. 'If there is easy money, why don't you go in for it? I believe in the old saying: "Look before you leap."' I overlooked Gomosta Moshay's counsel and then suddenly, I believe, I made a noisy whoop: because the feel of the miry water was something unexpected: it was disgustingly filthy. Whether it was due to my cry of disgust or the noise of my splash or some other reason, I do not know, but the moment I got into the water I heard Gomosta Moshay crying at the top of his cracked voice as though he were being murdered.

His plaintive signal of distress brought on the spot at least a score of men, women and children—the fruit-gatherers to whom the orchard of the house had been farmed out—all wailing as though they too were going to be hanged. They were all screaming—begging me to come out of the Sandalwood Tank immediately.

It was easy for them to advise me to leave the Vermilion Boat alone and get out of the water. But I was as naked as an eel, and there were at least a dozen women and girls round about the Tank. How could I come out? The more I shouted at them to go away the more they howled and more women came rushing in. Meanwhile, I was struggling hard with the cottonmouth.

My situation became still more awkward when I found Mummi-Ma on her knees at the edge of the water sobbing like a foolish child: she had evidently forgotten all about her attacks of hay fever and headaches, and what was still worse she was no more dressed than I; she had rushed out of her bath with only a bath-glove in her hand.

'Come out, my darling,' she entreated. 'If anything happens to you mother won't live a moment longer. You are her only hope.'

It was all too easy for her to wail and to call me her darling and her treasure, but she was kneeling on my tiny heap of clothes. Had she had any common sense she would have thrown them at me, and I could have wrapped something round my loins to come out of the water.

Moreover, my situation was not quite as simple as Mummi-Ma thought. I was in a precarious plight: just then I was engaged in fighting for my life, battling hard with a couple of extremely pugnacious water-animals. There was no time to bother about shrieks and entreaties. Cottonmouth was a very much bigger creature than I had calculated, and it was joined by a second one about six feet long. Both of them were bent on attacking me, and I was manoeuvring to avoid being caught between the two: I had not foreseen the presence of the second cottonmouth in the Tank, and then to make the situation still worse another one of the same nasty water-beasts rose from the bottom to join force with the other two. This third one was the biggest of the lot. It was dark grey and must have been seven feet long. Its body was like a cobra's, and that made me think it must be venomous.

'Catch a fox by its tail,' they say in the Penhari Parganas, 'and a wolf by its ears.' 'But,' the village Punditji advised, 'when it is a viper you don't catch it, you trap it, for its touch is poison. If you are forced to fight a viper, fight it with a stick and keep it at arm's length. Hit it on the head and hit hard. You must not expect any mercy. It is either/or. Either you kill the reptile or the reptile kills you. Only a bold man can throttle a snake by grabbing the brute by its neck.'

I recalled all this. What I was fighting was neither a lamprey nor an eel, but a brace of poisonous water-snakes, called moccasins. Jogin-Da was then experimenting with a mother moccasin and its young ones. Without my knowing it he had released a whole family of these cottonmouths in the Sandalwood Tank. He had warned Gomosta Moshay, Muhuri, the fruit-gatherers, and the neighbours about these snakes, but somehow he had overlooked me and Mummi-Ma: grandmother did not, of course, count; no one ever bothered to tell her anything, and Jogin-Da too had not taken the trouble to impart the secret of his experiments with snakes to her.

'Providence protects the helpless,' grandmother murmured as tears trickled down her cheeks. By then all was over, and there was no reason for her to weep; yet big drops welled forth from her eyes. 'They are tears of relief,' she said, but that did not make much sense to me.

'This child,' declared the Padre Sahib of Dupleix College, 'has been the object of divine mercy.' He nearly knocked over a bottle of delicious Dijon cassis as well as Profulla Babu's glass as he stretched out his arm to give me his blessing.

Gomosta Moshay stood in a corner shivering as though he had an attack of dengue fever. His teeth chattered. Profulla Babu had called on Jogin-Da to have a look at the moccasins: he looked extremely grave and said very little. Neither Jogin-Da nor Mummi-Ma were there. As far as my Second Aunt was concerned, I was almost sure she was having a second bath to cleanse herself of the stench of the Sandalwood Tank.

I was being caressed and petted and blessed, though I merited a good whacking. I had no business, I knew, to meddle with Jogin-Da's experiment: he was then trying to breed non-venomous moccasins from the venomous ones. He believed that if no one showed any hostility to a family of ferocious creatures they were bound to become tame.

Poor Jogin-Da! As soon as I had been fished out of the water Mummi-Ma rushed at him—naked as she was—and gave him a thorough drubbing. And he took it lying down: all on account of the Vermilion Boat.

I smiled when I thought of this, and forgot about my worry: the loss of my luggage receipt, my travelling without a ticket, and my not having a single penny in my possession. I murmured to myself Didi-Ma's saying: 'Providence helps the helpless.'

III

The train was slowing down. It was now nearing Burdwan. Two of my neighbours were evidently getting off there: Bronze Edward VII and the triple-chinned Ganesa. This was a relief. I did not relish the way they had stared at me all the way from Asansole.

'Son!' Edward VII prodded my ribs with his spectacle case before opening the door of the coach. 'Don't pretend to be a deaf buffalo. You must be Bipin's son.'

I was simply amazed.

'You have Bipin's face and his smile as well,' Ganesa added. 'Both Abul Kassem and I have been watching you for some time. You have your father's mannerisms too.'

I grinned to hide my embarrassment. I gathered that both of them had known my father well, and if I needed any service from them they were at my disposal. All that I had to do was to call on them at the Legislative Council Building in Calcutta. Ganesa was called Kabir Ahmed.

I thanked them and felt greatly relieved when they got off the train. As classmates of my long-deceased father they knew more about him and his physiognomy than I did: though I had half a mind to ask them whether I did not resemble my mother to some extent, for in Chandernagore everyone told me that I was my mother's very image.

After they had left the coach I started wondering if I had done the right thing by giving them the parting salutation in the Penhari way. Both of them were Mohammedans and perhaps I ought to have salaamed them. Of course this sort of worry would have made a Penhari villager laugh: in my village every elder was greeted in the same fashion irrespective of his religion; it mattered little if he was a Hindu or a Mohammedan or a Santal. But I was no longer in the backwoods, to use the term of Kolej Huzoor, and Burdwan was not a hamlet of the Penhari Parganas. At the platform of the Burdwan station there were water-carriers with distinctive arm-bands bearing the words: 'Hindu water' and 'Mohammedan water'. Men who sold tea had also similar arm-bands: 'Hindu tea' and 'Mohammedan tea'. I realized that the backwoods had been left behind and it was time for me to shake myself up to greet modern civilization, electricity, gas and what not, along with the distinctive signs, 'Hindus only' and 'Mohammedans only'.

There were knots of people on the platform to greet Abul Kassem and Kabir Ahmed. I noticed the special pleader with the brimmed turban buying a sheaf of newspapers and talking to Kabir Ahmed. Then he held a further hurried consultation with Abul Kassem and showed him the headlines of an illustrated paper. Was his destination Burdwan too? No, I was mistaken: his conversations with the two legislators were soon over; he was back in the coach murmuring with immense satisfaction: 'Bipin's son!'

'Now,' I groaned inwardly, 'I shall have more bother.'

The special pleader decided to install himself on the seat vacated by Abul Kassem and began cross-examining me. What interested him most was the name of my solicitor.

'I haven't one,' I told him truthfully.

'But you must have someone.' He shook his head thoughtfully, and tried to force one of his illustrated papers into my hands. I refused to be tempted: I was no longer in the Penhari Parganas. 'With lawyers one never knows,' was a common saying among my villagers. 'It is better to keep oneself out of the clutches of legal experts. They offer you help and they then fleece you.' Jogin-Da once consulted a muktear over a very simple affair and had to fork out fifty rupees for the advice he received. I was not innocent enough to be led into a trap by a special pleader whose consultation fee was bound to be far higher than that of a muktear—the lowliest in the hierarchy of legal practitioners.

The special pleader looked puzzled. He gave a push to his brimmed turban and wiped his forehead to clear his thoughts. Meanwhile his illustrated paper circulated from one hand to another. Many heads were turned in my direction. I lowered my eyes and regretted the departure of Abul Kassem and Kabir Ahmed: they did not try to foist a newspaper on me.

'But you can't conduct your own case,' the special pleader persisted. 'The matter is serious. It will be fought, I assure you, right up to the Supreme Court. Even the Law Lords in Westminster are bound to be interested in it.'

I listened to him stupidly.

'He pretends to be a deaf buffalo,' someone remarked, acidly. I did not bother to turn my eyes in the direction of the voice. 'Didn't Abul Kassem say that Bipin Bihari was stiff-necked? Bipin Bihari's son is just pig-headed.'

'Perhaps he does not want to tell anything,' another voice commented. 'He has worries enough. There is no reason why he should divulge family secrets.'

'But I mean him well,' the special pleader argued. 'I wish him well. An inexperienced youth like him does not know what contempt of Court is. He should not give interviews to journalists and prejudice the judges against him.' Turning towards me he asked me again for the name of my solicitors.

Ignoring Jogin-Da's excellent injunctions, I got embroiled in the general discussion. The more I affirmed that my journey to Calcutta had nothing to do with a lawsuit the more the special pleader protested, and the more my immediate neighbours became vociferous.

'He is no baby, I tell you,' bawled from a distant corner the man who had accused me of being pig-headed. 'He is certainly in touch with the members of the Legislature.'

The special pleader mopped his forehead again.

The ticket collectors got in. But they did not bother me for my ticket. Nor did they ask me any questions. They simply gaped at me with their mouths open as though I were a wild animal. By now, everyone was convinced that on account of an impending lawsuit in which I was involved I had become somewhat queer. The special pleader did most of the talking with the ticket collectors, and they—two of them —in their turn raised such legal quibbles that I thought they were muktears in disguise. Anyway, I thanked them inwardly for their failure to ask me for my ticket. Soon they became so absorbed in my imaginary lawsuit that they did not bother to collect tickets from anyone in the coach.

'His case,' the special pleader repeated for the fourth time, 'is bound to be long drawn out. It may last longer than the Dumraon or the Bhawal case.'

'But what have I to do with the Dumraons and the Bhawals?' I was getting exasperated. Were they not perhaps making a mistake about my identity? My family name was neither Dumraon nor Bhawal.

'Precisely!' The special pleader threw up his arms in the air as though he was acting on the stage. 'Precisely, I repeat. Now do you want to deny your parentage? If not, please tell me are you or are you not the son of Justice Bipin Bihari?'

'But what has that to do with a lawsuit?'

'There you are,' proclaimed the special pleader triumphantly. The ticket collectors nodded their approbation. The whole coach was satisfied with the pleader's forensic ability and his gift of cross-examination. Everyone was delighted at my admission of the fact that I was my father's son and that my father had died long ago and that I was not present at his deathbed.

The special pleader felt, I thought, like patting himself on his own back: he was so elated. He thumped me on the back; the ticket collectors shook hands with me; my neighbours prodded me in the ribs; someone passed on a box of sticky dates to me; and an elderly lady who had been sitting quietly in a corner all through the journey could contain herself no longer: she suddenly burst into tears, on my account.

'To cheat a boy of his paternal heritage,' the poor lady sobbed, 'I call that wicked. Little Son! Remember God and God will remember you. He will not deny you justice.'

The special pleader, the ticket collectors, and several others rushed to the other side of the coach to console the weeping lady. I was left in peace. I was ready to laugh, but decided to maintain a grave face: I had no intention of hurting the feelings of some fifty passengers in the coach. I listened with interest to snatches of the special pleader's words of consolation to the elderly lady: he was lecturing to her about the laws of succession among the Hindus, the Mohammedans, the Jains, the Jews and the followers of the Aga Khan.

Suddenly my attention was caught by the banner headlines

of the paper the special pleader had left on his seat: 'Dead Judge's son seeks justice!' 'Cheated of his inheritance by a forged will. The original testament discovered after an age. Intricate points of law raised,' I picked up the paper and hardly believed my eyes when I read: 'Our Special Correspondent's Special Contribution.' It recounted a cock-and-bull story of my impending visit to Calcutta for the sole purpose of suing a number of well-known personalities—all of them my first cousins!

I rubbed my eyes: there was no mistake that the person referred to was no other than myself. I re-examined the list of men supposed to have forged my father's will: they were all my near relations—the very people I intended to see immediately after my arrival at Howrah. As a matter of fact, they had written to me some time ago that instead of staying in the Masters' Mess—Hostel of the Teachers' Training College—I should live with them. Jogin-Da did not, however, approve of that idea, and as he was my legal guardian I had to bow to his decision. Nevertheless, in my own mind I had entertained the plan of eventually moving over to a relative's house after a few weeks of hostel existence.

What led the Special Correspondent of that trashy rag to write such a malicious yarn? What would my cousins think of me if they came to know about that mischievous article? Never had I seen so many false allegations condensed in so few lines.

Only now I understood the implication of the special pleader's queries. Who could have written that disgusting article accusing honest people of conspiring to rob an infant? For I was no more than an infant when I lost my parents. What was the motive behind those strings of spiteful lies?

My perplexed mind made a number of guesses and counter-guesses: my conjectures then cancelled each other out. At the end of a prolonged period of hard thinking I was no wiser than at the beginning when I had picked up that wretched paper. I barely noticed the passage of time and the fact that the train had been moving at a snail's pace soon after passing Memari Junction.

The Bombay Mail was several hours late owing to a partial strike of railway workers in the Calcutta area. At one point near Lillooah it looked as though the passengers would have to walk the rest of their way to Howrah. Anyway, the train did eventually steam into the Howrah terminus to everybody's satisfaction—except mine: I wished I were back in the backwoods—in my own Penhari Parganas. What evil spirit goaded me on to seek enlightenment and culture in Calcutta? How was I to show my face to my relations? They were bound to suspect that I was responsible for that scurrilous article in the rag *Aj-Kal*?

The first thing that attracted my attention at the Howrah Terminus was a huge poster: 'What Calcutta thinks to-day India thinks to-morrow. Read the Illustrated Weekly *Aj-Kal* and keep abreast of the news.' I felt like defacing the poster. Next to it was another of equally striking dimensions and containing two spelling mistakes: it exhorted one and all to use Rati-Bilash Oil to beget healthy children. A third one, no less imposing, proclaimed the virtues of a brand of pills capable of increasing one's brain power. Had I not been in a depressed mood I would have enjoyed reading all the advertisements that decorated the walls of the railway station. But laughter was at that time out of the question, and my gloom became deeper when I gathered that Calcutta was in the throes of a general strike.

There were no buses, no trams, no cabs, no taxis, no rickshaws—no transport of any kind.

'What has happened?' I asked a man who was touting for a hotel nearby.

'A hartal,' he replied gleefully. 'A general strike. The Pontoon Bridge is likely to be disconnected soon.'

The workers of Calcutta, I understood, were manifesting their solidarity with their ill-paid brothers of the East India Railway Company, and therefore the passengers of the Bombay Mail were expected to shift as best as they could. When grave issues were at stake the inconvenience of a few hundred travellers did not matter.

The tout lost all interest in me when he gathered that I was without luggage. His establishment did not cater for suspicious characters!

IV

The dirt and squalor that greeted my eyes as soon as I emerged from the Howrah Station was almost indescribable. Calcutta's reputation for cleanliness was never great. The general state of affairs was made much worse, I assumed, by a strike of the dustmen and the street-sweepers. India's premier city presented the appearance of a vast cow byre. What a contrast with Chandernagore! The trim and spotlessly clean French town with its neat rows of shady acacias and whitewashed houses with red, blue and green shutters and bright, gaily striped awnings was an Eden compared with the grey megalopolis before me.

I gazed round about me for fully five minutes, and my heart sank at the appalling sight of grim buildings, chimney-stacks, factories, go-downs, garages, dwelling-houses, and shacks, all huddled together. The only redeeming feature was the broad Hooghly river and the immense flights of stone steps encasing the river banks. All the same, had I had any money with me, I would have immediately returned to the railway station and bought a ticket to take me back to my Penhari Parganas.

The look of the largest city of India frightened me. 'First impressions are always misleading,' I said to myself to chase away my depression. There was not much time to lose. It was getting dark, and I had to think of my night's lodging. The Masters' Mess—the Hostel of the Teachers' Training College—was right at the other end of Calcutta, miles away from Howrah. 'It would be impossible for me to reach it before nightfall,' I reflected. How was I to find my way in the general blackout? The Gas and Electricity workers were on strike like other workers. 'A charming situation,' I murmured.

Being an optimist I thought it would be quite easy for me to find an inexpensive room near the Howrah terminus. I was mistaken. My disillusionment came very soon.

Such hotels as were in the neighbourhood of the railway station proved to be mean, soot-smeared, insanitary, flea-ridden hovels, though their names were high sounding: the Palm Beach Palace, the Golden Gate, Super-Parisian Plazza, the Imperial Residence, the New Plaza-Athenée, the Vegetarians' Paradise, the Wishing Cow. They were not merely filthy, but frightfully expensive. As I was without even a suitcase, they asked me everywhere to settle my bill in advance. That was, of course, impossible; my purse was with Jogin-Da.

~

So I decided to try my luck in the Dharma-sala near the Neemtolla Ghat: the free serai destined for pilgrims. It was just beyond the Pontoon Bridge over the Hooghly river. I called myself an ass for not having thought of the place before. It would have spared me the insulting words they hurled at me at the Wishing Cow Hotel.

'The Dharma-salas are admirable institutions,' I heard more than once in my village from people back from their pilgrimages.

'They are unique: monuments of abiding piety.' 'Anyone who has journeyed to a sacred resort,' they told me, 'learns as a matter of course what a Dharma-sala is like. It is a collection of four huge blocks of balconied buildings enclosing a large, well-shaded, square courtyard. All that is necessary to be lodged in such a serai—endowed by pious people for the benefit of pilgrims—is to ask the caretaker for a room. He will immediately do what is necessary for you. You will not only get your room free but your meals as well: all for nothing. Of course, a Dharma-sala is neither an almshouse nor a hospice, and you cannot stay there indefinitely. For the first night, you are welcome; for the second night, you are tolerated; and after the third night, you are asked to go. However that may be, for a single night's stay no place is as convenient as a Dharma-sala.' The meals in such endowments were said to be extremely simple. That did not, however, frighten me. I was accustomed to Spartan diet and was no gourmet. 'The Dharma-sala is the place for me,' I decided. 'There are no tips and no extras of any sort.' I blessed the soul of the pious founder of the Neemtolla Ghat Dharma-sala.

'How much can you spare?' asked the caretaker at my request for a night's lodging.

'Is this not a free institution?'

'A free institution!' The man suddenly became insolent and started raving. 'My brother-in-law! Are you an imbecile? Or what? A buffoon? I had to pay a thousand rupees to get into this caretaker's lodge, and even then I do not know for how long. You expect me to give you a free room. You are a fine one! Go and sleep in the Maidan or in the house of a merry widow. That's the place for jesters like you.'

~

Near the Dharma-sala in a narrow side street stood a quaint building. Its walls were covered over with the letters M and H. It had a projecting porch bearing signboards in various scripts, Urdu, Devanagari, Bengali, and Roman. 'A polyglot place,' I concluded, 'for a polycephalic establishment.' Its entrance evidently gave admittance to at least three habitations: 'Model Hotel for Modern Hindus', 'Mohammedan Hammam', and 'Massage House'. In spite of its grotesque letterings this place looked outwardly clean and decent. Near its entrance sat a plump woman counting her beads. She had a white cat on her lap. Her extraordinarily pink appearance attracted my attention. She was, evidently, suffering from albinism. As I stared in her direction my gaze caught hers, and she smiled.

'That's a good augury,' I murmured. 'She seems to be friendly. Maybe, she will help me to get an inexpensive room.' So I spoke to her.

'Haven't you begun rather early?' she asked mysteriously, and laughed at her own joke.

I felt confused and looked puzzled. At this she giggled all the more and stretched out her hand to tickle me under the chin in a familiar way. Her friendliness made me smile. 'She may suffer from albinism,' I reflected, 'but she is at least human. Not heartless like the dozen people I have accosted since my arrival at Howrah.' I repeated my request for a room for one night only.

'Of course, I have a room for you. I always have rooms for young people. You are a college student, aren't you?'

I nodded.

'I simply adore them, and tell them, it is better to begin early than to repent late. Come in, and choose your room.'

I thanked her profusely, and told her that I had no luggage with me. Did she want to be paid in advance? If so…

'No, no,' she interrupted. 'You pay when you vacate the room.'

That was, of course, extremely kind of her. 'When do you want to come? Now? But where's your girl? I should like to talk things over with her. We don't want to get into trouble with the police. This is a decent house, you know, and we charge by the hour.'

I mumbled something about my having only male acquaintances in Calcutta. At this she suddenly flared up and began screeching: she became an altogether different being. A minute ago she was so friendly, but now she looked like a Fury. Hers was a decent house, she repeated. She never allowed a male tart to cross her threshold. She had her sense of propriety. So long as she lived she would not allow her house to be polluted. I deserved to be flogged: I was so young and yet so brazen.

I shrugged my shoulders and left her screeching to herself. I wondered if albinism was by any chance contagious, and decided to wash my hands and face at the first water-tap.

One cannot always count upon providential succour. Not a drop of water came from the taps I tried. 'The men at the waterworks are on strike,' I concluded, not knowing that it was customary in Calcutta to cut off all water supply at certain hours of the day and during the night as a measure of economy.

Where was I to go? I could, of course, retrace my steps to the banks of the Hooghly and wash myself in the river. But what about my night's lodging? It was most important that I should find something before it became totally dark. The problem was for the first night only. For, I knew, my financial worries would end the moment I presented myself in the office of the Registrar of the University in the Senate House: I was entitled to receive the first instalment of the scholarship due to me. It then occurred to me that I might try to find my friend Tu Fan's Chop Suey Restaurant in China Bazaar.

Tu Fan the Chinese boy was an old-time acquaintance. I had not seen him for ages, but had, thank God, kept up a desultory correspondence with him. Was his Chop Suey shop likely to remain open in spite of the general strike? I asked someone for the way. A dozen men proffered me their services. Each one gave a different suggestion for reaching China Bazaar. All of them, moreover, wanted to know the nature of my business in that part of the town, my name, my address, my family tree, my source of income, my personal failings, my purpose in roaming about the streets of Calcutta and troubling honest citizens with useless queries. My failure to satisfy their curiosity made them angry and they started a heated argument among themselves.

~

I walked on till I came across two Chinese children looking like a pair of almost identical India-rubber dolls: the one being a mirror image of the other, only differently dressed and of a different height. The younger one, a mere toddler, wore a red satin jacket and black shantung pyjamas, while the big brother—not much older—was in blue jeans and a sleeveless *tussore* shirt. Their hair was closely shaven from the neck halfway up the back of the head, giving the top the appearance of a jet black velvet cap. The baby boy had a torn paper kite in his hand and a sadly woebegone expression. The elder brother was executing somersaults, Catherine wheels, and other gymnastic feats to entertain him. I stopped to smile at them.

The baby smiled back, and presently drew my attention very gravely to his tiny bangles and earrings. 'They are sweet,' I commented. 'The loveliest I have ever seen.' Soon the elder brother asked me, rather diffidently, if I could make a plaything out of the torn kite. Of course I could, and a toy boat was made in no time; it was even given a name: the Vermilion Boat. That proved a success. The boys clapped their hands with delight, and we became friends. I hummed for them a song, my grandmother's favourite lullaby:

The ship that on the river rides
Is built about with pine,
The cords are woven all of silk,
The sail of satin fine.

The helm, it is of bright, bright gold,
The mast of ivorie,
And sailors twain come sailing it
Out of a far countrie ...

Guided by the India-rubber dolls I came to the China Bazaar: a most colourful quarter, hidden in a maze of winding and intersecting lanes, scarcely known to many of Calcutta's indigenous inhabitants. What a contrast to the rest of the city, I thought. Its residents were friendly, and so was its general atmosphere. Its main street wore an air of festivity, thanks to its open-air market. 'An everyday affair,' I was told, though it looked like a rare country fair: complete with its boisterous musicians, picturesque acrobats, pole dancers, jugglers, puppets and performing animals. 'Here is joy!' Calcutta's China Town seemed to call out. 'Here is entertainment on every hand for the mere trouble of keeping your eyes open. Here is life! Here is colour!'

There were rows of booths lining the sides of the principal thoroughfare. The place was crowded with a multi-coloured throng of men and women of the humbler sort: Indian and

Eurasian buyers, and Chinese sellers, all chattering and laughing, as merry as magpies. They had an infinite variety of alluring goods on sale: goldfish in glass bowls; lacquered clogs, canvas sandals, and leather shoes; Chinese lanterns, and oil-paper sunshades; joss sticks, and incense-burners; yards of jasmine garlands, bunches of roses, golden champak flowers—pinned with thorns in plantain-leaf cornucopias; singing birds, fattened geese, and chow-chow puppies; iridescent air balloons which floated overhead like immense soap bubbles; wooden toys, storks and herons made of buffalo horns; sprays of paper flowers and strange plants, with vividly coloured eggs nestling among them like exotic fruits; conch-shell bangles, and jade ornaments; sandalwood boxes, and camphor-wood chests; luscious fruits piled up in fantastically high pyramids; roasted ducks, steaming hot rice, and fried fish still sizzling from the pan in which they were cooked; ...and pink sugar mice, shredded coconut cigarettes, aniseed peas, liquorice hats, caramel horses, chocolate soldiers, and other sweet delicacies to ravish every young heart.

I regretted I had no money to buy anything for either the children or for myself.

Were they born stoics—those two Chinese children who showed me the way to Tu Fan's Chop Suey Shop? Instead of asking for any present or reward they insisted on my accepting a parting gift from them: a tiny reed flute; it was a 'silent' dog-whistle. Their gesture moved me.

'I will treasure it all my life,' I assured them.

V

I was lucky. The Chop Suey Shop was open.

Tu Fan gave me a hearty welcome in his own fashion: he

sniffed as though he had a bad cold and did not want to use his handkerchief. His cordiality made me think of the days when we went to the same kindergarten on Rani Nilmani's Estate.

'Just watch me wag my ears in your honour,' he said. He did wag his ears: a trick he had learned from Mohan, the pygmy elephant, my favourite pet when I was a child.

Though I had not written him a line he had some vague premonitions about the exact date of my coming to Calcutta. 'There is no smoke without fire,' he said as he produced a copy of the paper *Aj-Kal*: the very issue I had read in the train. 'You are a celebrity now.'

'Or perhaps a notoriety,' I murmured.

'*Aj-Kal*—To-day and To-morrow—is widely read,' Tu Fan assured me.

This wretched *Aj-Kal* was one of the many mushroom periodicals which cropped up annually in Calcutta to flourish for a few seasons, and then to disappear as suddenly as it had attained its wide notoriety by publishing a series of fantastical 'true stories'. Before ceasing their publication, the editors of such periodicals generally transferred their offices to Chandernagore to escape their creditors. They were a curious lot: professional blackmailers.

In Chandernagore they were known as 'Hickey's bastards' and were little loved. In fact, they were more detested than the tourists who visited the French territory to get drunk and buy silk at bargain prices.

No one in Chandernagore objected to the presence of political refugees from Calcutta or of the undischarged bankrupts and forgers from all over India. Even professional smugglers busy with sending silk out of the French territory without going through the customs formalities were tolerated. But the editors of mushroom periodicals were detested: 'They are Hickey's bastards,' they used to say. 'And we can do without them.'

When Tu Fan finished this account of the many libel suits pending against the editor of *Aj-Kal,* I muttered the Chandernagore curse: 'Blast this newest bastard of William Hickey.'

~

For those not acquainted with William Hickey's many exploits I may mention here that according to the men of Chandernagore he was the first man to start mushroom periodicals in Bengal when John Company ruled the country.

Hickey, a man of ebullient nature, was Irish by descent. His original profession was law and his perennial interests were gay ladies and mellow claret. His hobbies were many, and as his parental purse was meagre how was he to indulge freely in his follies? Fine dogs, gay ladies, good wines, racehorses, and high stakes cost money. Hickey's appetite for articles of luxury was enormous and he needed a lot of money; in fact, lots and lots. Card tables and loaded dice did not bring him enough. Practising law meant labour. Hickey did not believe in labour. All that he needed was plenty of money without toil. To acquire this he planned to become a Nabob.

As most of the contemporary Nabobs were connected with India, he concluded that India was his predestined country, and to India he came—in quest of Golconda's gems, golden guineas, frail females, languorous odalisques, harems full of houris, and such other delights associated with the eighteenth-century conception of India. Then came one sad disenchantment after another. Misfortune dogged Hickey's steps. At one time the choice before him was reduced to matrimony or murder. At another time he was saved by his knowledge of law from the claws of an adventuress who nearly shoved him into a lunatic asylum. He did not relish hairbreadth escapes. The tropical sun made his orgies painful and upset his digestion. He detested disgorging what he had swallowed. His card tables ceased to attract his victims. The men of John Company he came across refused to be fleeced. This was the last straw. William Hickey resolved to turn over a new leaf: he became a journalist. The press was a power even in those days; Hickey set up a printing press of his own make in a stable which once sheltered his horses, and from that vantage point he started bombarding his enemies—in other words, those who did not relish losing their money at his gaming house—with scurrilous pamphlets, his paper-shells. This brought him some money: he was an excellent blackmailer who suffered from occasional fits; outbursts of good humour, outbursts of bile, outbursts of self-punishment, outbursts of persecution, outbursts of world-bettering, and—the most interesting of all—outbursts of patriotism.

When suffering from one such fit he visited Chandernagore and wanted to nail the Irish Harp on the flag-mast of Fort Orleans, the town's main bastion.

From the days of Dupleix the men of Chandernagore preferred the French flag to any other, and they did not find a profligate card-sharper and blackmailer's humour quite to their taste. When he talked about his hailing from an island which was a large piece of emerald they became suspicious, and when he referred to a mountain of diamond near his ancestral home they had fits of laughter. Hickey's eloquence was wasted on the men of Chandernagore. Neither did they care for the pamphlet he distributed among them: 'Thoughts on the times, but chiefly on the profligacy of women and its cures.'

Since then the men of Chandernagore have persisted in doubting the honesty of all cheap orators, professional world-betterers, and embittered women-haters. These three are generally bracketed together—because Hickey claimed that it was for the benefit of mankind that he was indulging in his scurrilities and idiotic outbursts.

~

Being Didi-Ma's grandson I referred to the editor of *Aj-Kal* as one of Hickey's many illegitimate progenies.

'You are lucky in a way,' Tu Fan tried to console me. 'Had there not been a general strike you would have been mobbed at the Howrah Station. Haven't you noticed that the paper gave the details of your time of arrival?'

'I am not a national figure. Why should the people of Calcutta bother about me?'

'Ah! my dear friend, Calcutta is not Rani Nilmani's Estate,' Tu Fan began. 'Different people pray differently.'

'What has prayer to do with this affair?' I interrupted.

'The nightly prayer,' he continued, without heeding my interruption, 'of those on the banks of the Yellow River is against floods and famine. Of those in Pekin for a less corrupt regime. Of those in Paris for less taxation. Of those in Calcutta for a bigger dose of sensational news.'

As Tu Fan had offered me hospitality and the loan of some money I did not think it polite to interrupt him too often: I let him do his talking; he was so happy to tell me about the peculiarities of the people of Calcutta.

'Believe me,' he went on, 'an opium addict will die if his daily dose of opium is suddenly stopped. The same tragedy would overtake Calcutta if you robbed the city of its daily quota of sensationalism.' He then explained that there was for some time past a marked dearth of exciting news in the cheap press of Calcutta: people could not be eternally fed with legends about the Sea Serpent. 'Therefore the story of your alleged grievance came in at an opportune moment...

'Calcutta is not like any other city in the world. You must bear that in mind. It is unique.'

The citizens of this unique city, I understood, were keenly conscious of their responsibilities and duties to their less fortunate brethren in other places. They believed in their God-given task of redressing injustice—injustice in any form, and in any part of the country, and in fact of the world. That being the case, it was only natural that the readers of *Aj-Kal* and through them a large section of Calcutta's population should be perturbed to learn that a forged document—prepared by some unscrupulous people—some ten or twenty years ago had robbed a poor young man of his ancestral estate!

'But this is not true.'

'Don't get excited,' Tu Fan laughed. 'Just listen and learn. The citizens of Calcutta are lovers of justice. They have little time to bother about the truth of a matter. Only the other day there was a twenty-four-hour general strike in sympathy with the overworked shirt-makers of Paris. A big crowd nearly burned the French Consulate down and there were talks of an organized general invasion of Chandernagore. Then it turned out that there are no shirt-making factories in Paris. On Monday last, Calcutta celebrated a partial hartal in sympathy with the underpaid Canadian dockers. Now we have heard that the scale of payment to the dockworkers in Canada is the highest in the world. The day before yesterday there was a lightning strike to protest against the rising standard of university examinations.'

'I am not concerned with these strikes,' I said. 'What concerns me most is my position vis-à-vis my relations. What will they think of me? Would it be worthwhile to write to the editor of *Aj-Kal*?'

Tu Fan thought for a minute. He did not know what would be the best procedure. According to him it would be wise to leave the matter as it was. The people of Calcutta had short memories, they would soon forget all about me. 'To meddle with the journalists,' he concluded, 'would be meddling with vipers. You may, however, consult Profulla Babu. He knows you and your guardian as well.'

It was a blessing that *Aj-Kal* had not put down Profulla Babu among those whom I was supposed to be suing. Profulla Babu was no relation of mine. But he was one of the few people who knew me from my childhood. He was for many years lecturer in geography at Dupleix College in Chandernagore.

VI

'Our friend Tu Fan is an optimist,' Profulla Babu remarked as he poured out a glass of cassis for me.

Did he think of my visits to Chandernagore as a boy when I used to manifest a craving for syrupy drinks? Evidently I was to him still the child who nearly drowned himself in the poisonous waters of the Sandalwood Tank in Didi-Ma's house. 'How annoying,' I said to myself as I sipped at the tumbler only out of politeness. Each time I called on him I had to empty a pint of cassis of Dijon to please him. His stock of this sugary concoction seemed to be inexhaustible. It was replenished, I understood, every three months through the generosity of a Jesuit Father who taught in St Xavier's College—Profulla Babu's alma mater.

'The Chinese of Calcutta are given to facile optimism,' Profulla Babu continued. 'People who rejoice in shadow-pictures and in paper-lanterns possess a persevering quality unknown to the rest of the world.'

Geography was said to be Profulla Babu's speciality. But there was hardly any subject in the world which he did not discuss. 'He does not discuss,' my hostel mates complained. 'He dissects! Everything comes within the orbit of his inspection and sweeping generalizations.' All the same, I knew they had a high regard for him. He was an old man, over seventy. The students cared little for the opinion of those labelled to be on 'the wrong side of forty,' but Profulla Babu was an exception. He was, nevertheless, somewhat long-winded in his conversations.

'Whenever there is a change of regime in China,' Profulla Babu expounded, 'you will hear all the Chinese all over the world hailing it as a welcome change: "The corrupt old order is dead," they will tell each other, "Long live the new order!" They are like that because of their inherent wistfulness for a stable future. This I call optimism. Tu Fan might not have lived in China, but he is a Chinese all the same. A Latin American is not necessarily a Spaniard, but he has the Spanish traits in him. He swerves from anarchical liberty to militaristic dictatorship.'

This was not of much help to me. All I wanted to know was the best suggestion he had for rectifying the evil done by the false report in the paper *Aj-Kal*. According to Profulla Babu nothing could be done to change the state of affairs.

'Your alleged intention of suing your relations will not be forgotten till Doomsday. And you ought not to be surprised to find many doors closed to you permanently. Without your knowing it you have made a multitude of enemies in Calcutta long before you crossed the Pontoon Bridge over the Hooghly river.'

He dusted carefully two old-fashioned globes that stood on a low table before me. They were attractive things: the only objects worth admiring in his extremely disorderly sitting-room. The walls were lined with almirahs—bookshelves—of varying sizes and heights. The few pieces of furniture he had were shabby—picked up one would say from a junk shop. I looked out through the window: the view was uninviting. Beyond the verandah was the lawn: it was ill-kept, apparently seldom mown; wooden palings and bamboo fences separated it from the neighbour's grounds. There was, however, at one end a noble tamarind tree clad in thick, viriscent foliage: its unusual tint reminded me, strange to say, of our legendary Raja Vikram's throne of justice, carved out of a single block of precious chrysoberyl, emitting both green and red hues.

Apart from the article in *Aj-Kal,* I had another, and more important, problem in mind. I did not, however, know how to shift my conversation to it. It was about my Latin coach, Roma.

I had more or less reconciled myself to the idea that to my cousins in Calcutta I was a black sheep, and they would have nothing to do with me; and if I had at all referred to their coolness towards me it was not so much to complain about them as to open up a conversation which would permit me to bring Roma's case to Profulla Babu's notice: for it was he who had introduced me to her.

At one time Roma used to teach at St Mary's in Elgin Road. Then, I do not know why, she changed her school and went to Diamond Harbour, and took to coaching candidates for the Oxford and Cambridge Senior Examination and for the University B.A.

I knew I was one of those who readily pick up a language and forget it as readily. Once my Persian was not too bad, and then one fine day I found out that I was no longer capable of writing the Persian script. The sad discovery was made in a curious way. Shortly after my meeting Roma it struck me that I ought to show myself off and scribble a few lines of Persian in her autograph book, when it was presented to me for my signature. The lines I had in mind were of the poet Mir who lived in fifteenth-century Delhi:

> Of the lustre of your eyes I shall
> tell the gazelles of Hindustan;
> Of the fire of your lips I shall
> tell the rubies of Badakshan.

My pen, however, refused to move, and not a single word in Persian script came from it. It automatically produced a scrawl in Bengali writing!

I did not want the same thing to happen to my Latin. My weekly lessons were, therefore, a necessity, and they were going on all right till an unforeseen bother occurred one afternoon in the common room of Masters' Mess where I was staying.

'Aren't you ashamed of taking lessons from a woman?' Bijan Mandel, one of my hostel mates, asked gravely. 'Be careful!' counselled some others in a paternal tone. 'Otherwise you may run the risk of being a co-respondent in a divorce suit.'

'Roma is not married,' I replied.

'You seem to know her family history well,' Bijan Mandel commented sarcastically. 'Maybe, she will threaten you with a breach of promise action. With Eurasians you never can tell.' 'She must be at least ten years older than you,' added the cross-eyed fellow who came from Madaripur. 'You will be a sorry sight tied to her apron-strings.'

'She does not wear an apron,' I retorted. 'She is always in slacks.'

'Show some common sense, my man,' advised Yehudi Daud Benisraeli: he was reputed to be well versed in worldly affairs. 'If I were you I should stop taking lessons from her. Eurasian women are renowned husband-hunters.' 'Just tell her,' the cross-eyed student from Madaripur piped, 'you do not want any more lessons from her.'

Of course, I could not do that without consulting Profulla Babu.

He seemed, however, to be too much engrossed in expounding his views to divine my real worries.

~

'You may well say,' Profulla Babu began again, 'that you are not responsible for the newspaper reports. But that will not help you.'

His eyes moved from the celestial globe in his room to the terrestrial one. As I have said before, these were attractive things: among the best the eighteenth-century Netherlands ever produced. They came originally from Antwerp. Like the sundial on the Falcon's Rest these too were destined for China, and then they came to Goa, from Goa to Satgaon, and then to Dupleix College of Chandernagore. They were offered to Profulla Babu when he retired from the staff.

'So far as the terrestrial globe is concerned,' Profulla Babu explained as he made his globe rotate, 'there is neither East nor West. Any dividing line between the conventional East and the conventional West is purely arbitrary. However, North and South do exist. They are realities. The equator separates them. The seasons proclaim their existence. The belt of the equator is a very real thing. Much more real than the International Date Line in the Pacific.'

I listened in silence and gave a polite nod.

'You will do well to bear that fact in mind. Please also note that Calcutta is similarly divided into two distinct halves; in theory at least you are expected to belong to one of these two. For an inexperienced person it is well-nigh impossible to have his feet in both camps.'

I made a non-committal murmur. What was he driving at?

'Let me make my point clear. Suppose you are present at a street accident, and before you lies the victim. Your first duty would be to find out if the wounded man believes in homoeopathy or in allopathy. You would be committing a grave sin if you offered any non-homoeopathic nostrum to a believer in homoeopathy. Such an inconsiderate action on your part would set automatically one half of Calcutta's inhabitants against you. While the other half will eye you with suspicion till they have a public confessional of your medical leanings. The homoeopathic half of Calcutta shuns the non-homoeopathic counter-half.'

The northern and southern halves of the city, I learned, are not areas in the geographical sense but in the spiritual sense. One half of Calcutta speaks Bengali, the other half does not. One half considers the Parsnath Temple to be beautiful, the other half regards it as an abomination; one half believes that Calcutta was founded by Job Charnock, the other does not: to this half Job Charnock is simply a myth.

He also referred to *Gulliver's Travels* and to the feud between the Big-endians and the Small-endians—the never-ending dispute between those who broke their eggs at the big end and the others who did the contrary.

'There are further complications. A believer in homoeopathy and a doubter of the sacredness of the goddess Kali is no friend of a brother believer in homoeopathy who does worship Kali.'

'So,' I finally blurted out to help him to shorten his monologue, 'there are an indefinite number of clans and sub-clans in Calcutta.'

'Exactly. You will have to be a clever tight-rope walker if you want to avoid displeasing any of the clans and sub-clans of the two major tribes of this city. This is not Chandernagore, nor your Penhari village. I would advise you to lie low, and to expect no friendliness from any true-born citizen of Calcutta. As for Calcutta's filth you will get accustomed to it and learn to repeat the usual formula: "Calcutta is too poor to be clean." Do not forget to keep this cant in mind, and never ask a City Father anything about Calcutta's budget. It is bigger than that of Paris...'

I left him without discussing anything about Roma, my Eurasian coach.

VII

Perhaps that was just as well. What advice could he have given me? Moreover, I knew I had the habit of accepting only such counsels as conformed with my own decision. 'God knows,' the men of Penhari say among themselves, 'we are stubborn, and He will never let His will clash with ours.' Though I was only half-Penhari, in most matters I behaved like a full Penhari: that was the view of my fellow students.

'You are as stiff-necked as a Santal buffalo,' taunted my fellow student Satyen Guha, because I would not join the political party of the *topiwallahs*, to which he belonged, nor buy a *topiwallah* buttonhole—'100 per cent Patriotism.' 'You are a buffalo,' he repeated.

'That's better than being a weathervane,' I retorted, but I knew in my heart of hearts that there was ample justification for his calling me obstinate.

In less than a month after my arrival at the Howrah Terminus my pigheadedness had made me thoroughly unpopular among my fellow students. In due course I found myself classified as a bore, and finally I became the minority of one in a hostel lodging about one hundred young students. 'A luckless lion!' Roma defined my situation. 'Penned in the same penitentiary as a drove of dreadful Daniels.'

'It is some achievement.' Roma remarked ironically one day when catcalls were heard outside the room of the hostel, where we met for our lessons. 'What have you done to drive all of them mad?'

It was impossible to do any work with that noise going on intermittently all through the morning. For a moment I felt like telling her the whole truth. Then somehow a sense of shame prevented my divulging the cause of those catcalls. I was thoroughly disgusted with my rowdy companions. She was the main cause of their latest quarrel with me.

~

It started, as I have already mentioned, in a plain fashion: as a bad joke. I was hooted for keeping up my interest in Latin. They thought it simply funny that I should follow scrupulously this particular injunction of Padre Johan of Jamtara. 'You don't care a straw for your crazy priest,' they argued. 'If you did you would stick to his other suggestions as well.'

I had no desire to get into an argument over this. So I did not reveal to any one that I had various ambitious projects in the back of my mind. One day I hoped to ransack old archives and translate into Bengali the accounts of Bengal by the early Christian missionaries: for this purpose Latin was essential.

'Why bother about Latin?' they persisted. Satyen Guha propounded the view that it was unpatriotic to waste time over Latin.

'Anything,' I retorted, 'that does not please you is either unpatriotic or unrevolutionary.' I knew they thought it degrading to master well any foreign language. An attempt to acquire a nodding acquaintance with English was tolerated, but to aspire to its complete mastery was tantamount to sin! It was thought good form to write English in the style of *Amrita Bazar Patrika*—with deliberate quaintness, conscious grammatical and spelling mistakes—and to take pride in that achievement; otherwise one ran the risk of being dubbed a hireling of the Imperialists, a boot-licker of the British, a paid agent of the English reactionaries, and what not. 'We must learn enough English,' Bijan Mandel made it clear, 'to make sense of the contents of English publications. And no more.' 'To go beyond that,' Satyen Guha added, 'is plain boot-licking. We have done this sort of boot-licking far too long. It is time to give it up. Look at the Japanese. Do they care two hoots about faultless English?' 'And the Russians?' asked a fellow who was a great admirer of Chumchicke Adhikari, better known among the students as Comrade Chum, 'and the Chinese? Pidgin English is good enough for them. Our Babu English ought to be more than enough.' 'In other words,' I spoke deliberately, 'what suits your convenience ought to suit the convenience of the world! Well, I am different from you and from the rest of the world. That's that. I want to keep up my Latin.'

'Well,' they talked in chorus, 'if study Latin you must, there is no reason for your having a woman teacher.'

'Fancy taking lessons from a Eurasian woman!' Satyen Guha raised his eyes heavenwards to make his expression of horror more theatrical. 'She calls herself Roma. It is simply disgusting that a decent Indian name should be soiled.'

'Her name,' I interrupted, 'may be derived from a city which happens to be a bit older than Calcutta.'

They stared at me, and I continued: 'Rome may be an insignificant town compared with Job Charnock's foundation. It happens, however, to bear some greater significance in world history. It was the seat of the Caesars. It is even now the seat of the mother church of that insignificant organization known as the Roman Catholic Church. As Roma happens to be a Catholic I presume her name is derived not from the Sanskrit source but from the Roman.'

'My God!' They pretended to be shocked. 'You dare take up the defence of a Eurasian woman. You are the limit. The Eurasians are the scum of the earth. No sane Indian ought to have any truck with them. All of them are in the pay of the Imperialists. Roma is certainly a spy. How can a decent human being speak up for her?'

That settled it. My mind was made up there and then.

'Put me in the category of indecent men,' I said, 'if that gives you any satisfaction. I am not a *topiwallah*. I lay no claim to professional patriotism. That's the exclusive monopoly of those who prefer Babu English.'

This was only the beginning.

The matter cropped up from time to time. The line of our arguments was always the same. The more they proffered their advice the more I became obdurate: they had no business to run Roma down, especially as they knew nothing about her. 'She must be living somewhere in Garya Road in Ballygunge,' one day the lanky fellow called Pulin Dindaw sniggered, and I felt like hitting him. 'Does your fieldwork force you to go there very often?' I asked, and my retort silenced him. Most of the houses in the Garya Road area were of the type where rooms were rented by the hour: like the M.H. House where I had looked for a night's lodging on the afternoon of my arrival at Calcutta. Pulin Dindaw claimed to be a social reformer and a world-betterer; he felt shocked at my rejoinder.

However, he gave vent to his feelings by calling Roma a Nagini—a serpent-woman, and quoted moral verses from Bhartihari for my edification:

> Avoid the poison-glances, my friends,
> The serpent-woman flee;
> Her crooked path has crooked ends,
> Her hood is coquetry.
>
> If you are stung by common snakes
> Perhaps you will not die;
> If poison from a woman takes,
> The doctors say good-bye.

Gradually I began losing my temper whenever any of them made the least mention of Roma. Finally, from sheer mischievousness I started my counter-attacks. I propounded the view that as good professional patriots—future glory of the party of *topiwallahs*—it was their duty to take greater interest in Eurasia. Was it not an obligation on all genuine patriots to explore every possible way of making the country great? If so, my friends ought to contact Eurasians—or at least children of mixed marriages. 'Why?' 'Because,' I propounded, 'everything great and good in Indian history has come out of mixed marriages, or contacts with the non-Indian world.' 'For example!' The list, I asserted, was pretty long: Buddha headed it because his family name was Sakya, then came Asoka Maurya, Kanishka Yueh-Chi, Akbar Badsha, Sanskrit Drama, Kushan pottery, Gupta sculpture, Mogul miniatures, Islamic domes, modern Bengali literature, the Indian Penal Code...and the greatest glory of all, Calcutta.

I talked often in this vein, and found great satisfaction in irritating my adversaries. Then I gave a lantern-slide lecture on pre-Mohammedan Indian Monuments. It was well attended, especially as my poster—the reproduction of a female nude from Sigiriya—was prominently displayed at College Square. Profulla Babu was very helpful in securing me loans of slides from the Indian Museum and the Asiatic Society, and I too did my best to contact the relations of a Javanese boy I knew—Soetomo of Svenska-Bibi's Kindergarten, and got a few more on my own. The talk was, I thought, a roaring success—owing to my slides of Bamiyan, Boro-Bodur, Angkor Vat, the Cave of the Thousand Buddhas in the Gobi Desert, and of Khmer works of art.

My hostel mates became green with envy, and then purple with rage.

Few, if any, of the other listeners understood or suspected the implication of the devilish trickery I played in the selection of my slides. I do not think that even Roma and her friend Anita, the violinist, guessed what was in my mind. My true motive became, nevertheless, obvious to my hostel mates within a few minutes.

Most of the slides were of Indian monuments *outside* India.

I extolled Angkor Vat. I waxed eloquent over Brambanam. I made dogmatic assertions: a glorious achievement like Boro-Bodur—in dimensions no whit less than the Great Pyramid of

Cheops, and in magnificence far superior to the plain but much publicized pile of Egyptian stones—Boro-Bodur, with its miles of exquisite bas-reliefs and hundreds of statues of surpassing beauty, was possible because the Indian artists and artisans of ancient days did not suffer from xenophobia and willingly sought inspiration from the nymphs of Greater India, of the outer world. I rubbed in as best I could that the Indian arts, crafts and letters flourished best only when stimulated by foreign contacts.

'The mysterious quality of Indian art—its emotional appeal—is due, no doubt, to the greatest paradox connected with India's history: in spite of the country's geographical isolation from the rest of the world, her story is inextricably interwoven with universal history. No man can fully appreciate India unless he has a feeling for Greater India and a general interest in the mainsprings of human civilization.

'It would be calamitous,' I concluded in a pompous tone, 'if at any time we sought total isolation or aspired to narrow nationalism. Robbed of foreign contacts and the stimulus of challenge, our culture would languish and wilt.... A stream feeding into itself and fed by itself ceases to be living water. It becomes a stagnant pool; a foetid marsh; a source of pestilence; a fit dwelling-place for croaking frogs.'

I thoroughly enjoyed my mixed metaphors and my mood of triumph for about an hour. However, by the time I got back to the hostel the 'croaking frogs' all banded together and they did beat everything out of my system. I was de-bagged and pummelled. 'Roma must have egged you on to give this lecture,' they all shouted. 'She has hypnotized you. She is a witch. You ought to be ashamed of her.'

'Why should I? She is not like the blue stockings you know. Is she not pretty?'

'Good-looker she may be,' they admitted. 'All Eurasian women are good-lookers. But she is old.' 'She has slanting eyes and no waist to speak of,' Bijan commented. 'She must be at least twenty-five,' grunted Daud, the Social Anthropologist. 'Don't insult your youth by associating with an old woman. She is a hag.'

'She was a harridan the other day,' I retorted. 'Now she is a hag. Let her be anything. How she concerns you I do not know. You have finished your ragging, I believe. If you have, leave me in peace.'

~

Being a stiff-necked buffalo I did my best to go on provoking my fellow students in various ways. At an inter-college debate I propounded an unpopular thesis and was loudly booed for my pains.

The subject was 'Parliamentary Democracy,' and the House was divided into two almost equal halves: one supporting the idea and the other advocating the Soviet System. The Soviet System block had introduced a clever amendment for the alleged purpose of safeguarding the interest of the silent millions of the backwoods. As one of the backwoods men I was cheered when I got up to speak, and then I heard them shuffling their feet, because I moved the rejection of the Soviet System as well as Parliamentary Democracy. I was for the traditional Village Councils, Nominated Councils, Open Ballots, and totally opposed to universal franchise. 'Universal adult suffrage,' I declared, 'will put the country at the mercy of the bazaar demagogues, xenophobic mob-leaders and irresponsible *topiwallahs*.'

'Such a speech,' Bijan Mandel sounded the warning, 'merits your expulsion from the hostel. Ragging seems to have no effect on your thick hide.'

I was, however, saved by the skin of my teeth: I had won a heat in the hundred-yard race, and my record in the inter-college swimming contest was not too bad; there were a few other minor victories to my credit. Lovers of shining objects did not want to empty out of the hostel showcase my silver trophies. So I was saved.

There was no further suggestion about my expulsion. They however, decided to ostracize me. I was totally boycotted. No one bothered to speak to me any more.

'To be alone,' I bragged to Roma, 'is not the same thing as being lonely. I can do without them.'

What made me behave so differently from the rest? Perhaps it was owing to my native soil: the land of the Penhari Parganas. The tract where I was born is peculiar. 'Na!' 'No!' is the first word a child in the Penhari Parganas utters. Whereas in the rest of the world a baby's first cry is 'Ma!' 'Mamma!' A son of the Penharis deems it a sin to acquiesce to what he believes to be wrong or unjust. He is not unwilling to change his mind, but he must be convinced that his suppositions are wrong before he accepts a new thesis.

~

And the catcalls and clods of earth failed to convince me that they were right and I was wrong. They, however, brought my Latin lessons in the common-room to an end. It happened in an abrupt fashion.

'We should do well to ignore them,' I counselled Roma on the day they kept up their hootings and whoopings without any break from the moment she came in.

She shook her head and suggested that it would be better if we discontinued our lessons. I felt hurt when I saw her quietly start packing up her things. She did not appreciate my peculiar situation.

'If she leaves me in that way,' I said to myself, 'it would be bowing to their unjust decree.' So I decided to go out in the verandah and see what I could do. Just then a well-aimed lump of earth struck me full in the face.

'Can't you continue our lessons elsewhere?' I asked Roma as I did my best to remove the mud from my face.

'No,' she repeated. 'I think it would be better if we do not meet any more.'

'But,' I blurted out, 'my quarrel with them has been on your account. And you want to let me down.'

More missiles flew in and I rolled up my sleeves for a good fight. Roma took hold of my hand to restrain me and whispered that we might perhaps meet at the Church of Reis Magos near the Ghulam Muhammad Mosque on Friday morning and then talk things over.

In a way those clods of earth were a blessing. But for them Roma would not have given me a rendezvous. My previous invitations to her to go to a cinema had been rejected. That evening my hostel mates stared at each other when they heard me whistle to myself all the while. They did not know that I was feeling superior to all of them lumped together. Not one of them had ever been to a rendezvous. The only women they had been out with were their mothers and sisters.

I felt extremely proud, and looked forward to the coming Friday: the day of my first rendezvous in Calcutta; in fact, the very first one in my life.

VIII

It took, it seemed to me, an unusually long time for that Friday to come. When it came I made the discovery that it was a general holiday: one of those rare occasions deemed sacred both by the Hindus and the Mohammedans.

Anniversaries calculated by the solar year seldom coincide with those measured by the lunar twelvemonth. The Hindus reckon by the sun, and the Mohammedans by the moon, and their dates do not tally. But once in a blue moon the almanac-makers find out that the Hindu Holi festivity and the Mohammedan Muharram are on the same day. This happens, if I am not mistaken, once in every thirty-sixth year. Therefore the day of my rendezvous with Roma was particularly auspicious.

I whistled as I made my shoes shine. I did my best to make myself as tidy as my footgear. The operation was carried out in the early hours of the morning in a corner of the balcony of my dormitory, I did not want any of my hostel mates to comment on my general appearance, and evaded them by taking refuge in an outer shed which was used as the green room when we had our dramatic performances in the courtyard.

It was pretty early when I left the hostel. So I decided to have a stroll round College Square, and was elated to find five little finches hopping about near the statue of Vidyasagar. Seeing five of them together means good luck. It was good to begin with a favourable augury and I wished there were seven of them. That would have been the acme of all the best auguries.

College Square was deserted. Peace and quiet reigned everywhere. 'It's a general holiday,' I reflected. 'That is why the streets are empty, and all the doors are shut.' There were no trams or buses, nor any cars or cabs. Calcutta wore the air of a sleeping city. Its very atmosphere seemed hushed. 'How wonderful,' I murmured half audibly. 'Even the crows have stopped cawing. A real miracle!' Crows, as every visitor to Calcutta knows, figure high in the city's list of nuisances; they blacken the air in their millions and outrival the street hawkers with their incessant croakings.

'It is a marvellous day for an outing,' I repeated to myself, and called the hostel porter a fool though he was not by my side, but he had muttered something about my taking undue risks in going out of the hostel compound. 'Durwan!' I addressed the empty air, 'you are a blockhead.'

I used sidestreets as short cuts to reach the corner of Dhuramtollah as quickly as possible: the site of the Big Mosque. I was a full hour ahead of my time, and I did not mind walking. The Church of Reis Magos stood not far from the Big Mosque. As I had plenty of time at my disposal I wanted to have a look across the Maidan from the gallery of the Big Mosque: a sight worth seeing. 'Like examining Paris,' in Profulla Babu's language, 'Paris from the top of the Eiffel Tower. You don't see the Tower and feel happy.'

It would be, of course, invidious to compare Calcutta with Paris, which I knew only from photographs. But if photographs were to guide my judgment I would say the Big Mosque beats the Eiffel Tower hollow. It is a much uglier structure.

The Big Mosque with its tulip-shaped domes built in imitation of Tipu Sultan's Mausoleum at Seringapatam may rightfully claim to be the biggest horror in the whole of Calcutta: though some think that the Jain temple of Parsnath and the Hindu shrine at Kalighat deserve to be placed on the same footing. But both of these edifices are tucked away in labyrinths of sideways and crooked lanes. One has to hunt for them. What is hidden is as good as non-existent. Therefore, these two do not deserve to be included in the list of notable landmarks.

But the Big Mosque! It occupies one of the best sites in the city. It stands at the corner of the Chowringhee and Dhuramtollah, and overlooks the only open space worth mentioning, the Maidan of Manohar Dass.

An inscription at its entrance states that Prince Ghulam Muhammad, son of Tipu Sultan, put it up in gratitude to God, and in commemoration of the Honourable Court of Directors of the East India Company granting him the arrears of his stipend in 1840.

'That Ghulam Muhammad Mosque is an eyesore,' I muttered. In fact, I rarely passed it by without hurling a few anathemas. That day too as it suddenly swung into view, I showered my choice imprecations on the long defunct East India Company, its Court of Directors, Prince Ghulam Muhammad, and the nameless architect responsible for that vile monument. 'Why on earth,' I growled audibly, 'did John Company offer any stipend to a fellow devoid of all aesthetic sense? This awful building disgraces the site it occupies. It is a horror seen at close quarters and a nightmare when seen from the Maidan. I wish something could be done about it.'

That was, of course, a vain hope. No Mohammedan shrine, however ugly, could, I knew, ever be demolished by hand of man in any part of India. That would, I gathered, be violating the established law of the land: equity and tolerance for all religious creeds. This consideration did not, however, prevent my wishing its destruction.

'Failing that,' I prayed, 'may God in his goodness roast in hell-fire everyone responsible for that horrid shrine. May Calcutta's many millions of pigeons drop tens of millions of fig seeds in its every nook and cranny.'

This, too, was a foolish expectation. The denizens of the air manifested, as far as I could make out, a peculiar predilection for everything historic and beautiful.

I thought of the charming little structure known as the Church of Reis Magos—my meeting-place with Roma—which was built by the Portuguese long before Job Charnock hoisted the English flag near Neemtollah Ghat and laid modern Calcutta's foundation. Compared with the garish Big Mosque of Prince Ghulam Muhammad, it was a microscopic affair: its seating capacity was barely a hundred. But it was attractive, a real gem from the architectural point of view. Though within a stone's throw of the Big Mosque, yet somehow it was this ancient Portuguese place of worship which attracted the birds with destructive propensities and not the other structure! Several fig trees were flourishing on the walls of Reis Magos, and its foundations were already undermined. The church was doomed. It was likely to collapse any day. And with its disappearance another old landmark was destined to become a vague memory. 'The only church,' I reflected, 'where a service in Latin is conducted every day in memory of a donor will soon perhaps become completely forgotten.'

In many respects Reis Magos was of exceptional interest. First, as I have said, architecturally, it was a beauty. Secondly, it was the only church in Calcutta where a daily prayer was offered in memory of an Iraqi woman who left an endowment for this purpose. Thirdly, because of its historic associations, which would readily fill a volume.

I knew this church well. It was one of my own discoveries. No guide-book mentioned it and no crowd of curious tourists ever crossed its threshold. Few worshippers bothered to pray in it. It was almost abandoned but for the short daily prayers conducted for the peace of the Iraqi woman's soul. Its walls were cracking; its ceiling was bulging, and its floor caving in. Nevertheless, it told a stirring tale. It was full of history. Its inscriptions were of primary importance to all concerned with Calcutta's past—of old Calcutta which existed long before Job Charnock came to Bengal to found new Calcutta. Its architect was one João Gomez de Soto, who must have been a proud man judging from the epitaph on his tombstone: 'He raised this Church of the Magi as a challenge to the Taj Mahal and its builder.'

The verses which run along the edges of his tombstone read:

Pois com esforços e leaës
Serviços foram ganados
Com estes e outros taës
Devem ser conservados.

'Since these high honours were gained by strong and loyal deeds, they must needs be retained by the same and similar virtues.'

In size, let me repeat, the Church of Reis Magos was insignificant. Those who judge beauty by mere bulk would, no doubt, laugh at João Gomez de Soto's assertion. But those who believe that a thing of captivating grace need not necessarily be voluminous or colossal would do well to examine the church near the Big Mosque of Prince Muhammad and see for themselves whether or not it is a perfect gem of its kind: a *chef-d'œuvre* of Indo-Portuguese architecture—a moving expression of faith of a small group of refugees who had escaped general massacre at the hands of the Great Mogul when he demolished all places of Christian worship in Hooghly and Satgaon. With consummate skill, de Soto translated this spirit of rededication into stucco and stone and constructed a peerless masterpiece. Alas! The last of its kind, just as the Taj Mahal is the last of the Great Mogul architecture.

'One day,' I said to myself, 'I shall show Roma how I have taken some brass rubbings in the Church of Reis Magos, and the inscription on João Gomez de Soto's tomb.'

A week earlier when I had spread before Roma some of my choicest brass rubbings she expressed genuine surprise. 'How do you take them?' she asked, and I felt proud as a peacock: she seemed to be as ignorant of the monumental brasses as my fellow students. Here then was something which she could learn from me!

My rubbings, I ought to admit straight away, were not of art, but they were all interesting: true copies of inscriptions and designs on brass or copper; epitaphs, ex-votos, or memorials of fearless seafarers, restless adventurers, or saintly souls: all of them were exceptional beings—people who had been goaded by diverse motives to wander halfway round the world to seek their last resting-place in the delta of the Ganges.

I have often wondered who were the designers of the brasses in Chandernagore, Chinsurah, Serampore, Satgaon, Fulda, and of course Calcutta. Why did these plaques go out of fashion after a certain date? Why were some of them in dog Latin while the rest were in the mother tongue of the person commemorated? Why were some of the texts deliberately frivolous? One epitaph read:

Here I, Jock Scott frae Peterheid
At saxty year lie dour and deid,
A bachelor—for wed I wadna:
And och! I wish my father hadna!

Some were definitely mysterious, and made me wonder whether the obscurity of the text was intentional or involuntary. For example:

Erected to the memory of

Hephzibah Gardy

Known as Hepsie

ACCIDENTALLY SHOT

As a mark of affection by her brother

In the certain hope of a

BLESSED IMMORTALITY

Reader, go and do thou likewise

A. D.

17 50.

In my conversations with Roma I pretended to be a great authority on monumental brasses all on account of a short article of mine which had appeared in the Sunday edition of *The Statesman* and *Friend of India*! 'To take brass rubbings,' I explained to her, 'you need a large ball of cobbler's wax and a roll of thin white paper. The rest is simple. You stretch your paper over the brass tablet, and fix it down by weights round the edge. Then start rubbing your wax ball all over the paper.'

The wind swept a discarded newspaper from a corner to the pillar box I was passing by. The scattered leaves began swirling about me as though endowed with life. They wanted to harass me and dog my steps: one would have thought they were determined to obstruct my way. A dirty sheet got entangled between my feet. I cursed as I trod on it.

This reminded me that I had forgotten to tell Roma that she should carefully remove the dirt and grime of the ages covering a brass tablet before superimposing a clean sheet of paper on it.

'The cobbler's wax should also be melted on the fire,' I murmured to myself, 'and allowed to resettle before rolling it into a ball.'

~

Just then I heard a shout. It was like a cry of alarm, and sounded all the more ominous on account of the absolute emptiness of the street and general silence of the atmosphere.

'*Khabardar*!' someone yelled, 'Look out! Halt!'

Was I challenged by a military sentinel? Where was the sentry-box? I looked around me. The summons to stop came from a corner. In fact, from a narrow side lane, one of those winding passages barely a few feet wide, in which thriller-writers revel; it debouched into Chandni Bazaar Crescent which I was then traversing. Where was the man who challenged me? I did not see anyone. What did he want of me? I shuffled on a few steps forward.

'Halt! Halt immediately!' It was the same voice that shouted. The air was filled almost immediately with a droning noise: its volume rapidly increased; it sounded like the buzzing of many angry wasps; the subdued mutterings of a multitude of enraged men. 'Stop where you are. Don't advance a step more.'

'Pass on!' Almost simultaneously came this contradictory cry from the other side of the street, and a hundred other throats bawled the same command: 'Pass on! Don't stop! If you linger you are a dead man.'

This took place so unexpectedly that I had hardly had time to realize what all these yellings were about. Who were my challengers? What did they really want? Not knowing what to do, I stood hesitatingly where I was.

A death-like trance descended at once on the scene: a muffled stillness; something sinister.

~

It did not take me long to realize that I was caught between two fires: flanked by two hostile crowds, one of which wanted me to stop and the other to move on. My situation, as far as I could judge, was desperate. It was many times more hopeless than my plight in the Sandalwood Tank when the mother moccasin came to attack me.

Less than a hundred yards away shone the flaunting cupolas of the Big Mosque. Within a hailing distance—though hidden from the view by the curve of the Chandni Bazaar Crescent with its huddled houses—was the main artery of Calcutta's traffic: Dhuramtollah Street. And there I stood all alone in the middle of the road: at the crossroad, where the tortuous Purana Spiral Lane intersected the Chandni Bazaar Crescent.

I looked towards my right and then towards my left. And my throat became dry. The two narrow passages debouching into the Crescent were crammed with people: serried ranks of men; they were so tightly huddled together that they reminded me of the packed trucks conveying animals to the slaughterhouse.

On my right was a mass of turbaned heads with a sprinkling of red fezes and black astrakhan caps. Evidently they were Mohammedans. They had butcher's knives and choppers in their hands. Some of them brandished soda-water bottles: these were, I guessed, filled with petrol or kerosene.

Facing them, on my left, separated by the narrow width of the Crescent was a surging throng of men in white caps or saffron and yellow headgear, wearing garlands of red hibiscus round their necks, and carrying brass-bound bamboo staves in their hands. A number of them bore ostentatiously flaming torches though it was broad daylight.

Before me all was empty: as empty as the litter-covered thoroughfares I had traversed to reach the spot where I stood: my tryst with destiny. The deserted street showed no sign of life. The balconies were equally lifeless. The closed doors and shuttered windows transformed the houses of the living into the abodes of the dead.

Something, however, suddenly stirred in the distance. I gasped as I strained my eyes. It was only a black kitten playing with an empty paper bag, and I gave a sigh of relief: 'Thank God, it is not Roma.'

~

Wolves when hunting in packs, I have been told, know no fear. None can frighten them nor curb their ferocity till they have slaughtered their quarry and assuaged their thirst in its warm blood. Only when they have gorged themselves to surfeit and drunk their fill, they break away from the pack; each wolf slinks back to its lair cowering lest it should come across the sheepdogs.

The men on both my flanks looked like such wolf packs. What was their quarry? What did they want of me? They appeared to me more frenzied than fierce wolves: they had the ferocity of the beasts that hunt and the cunning of the creatures that crawl. The howlings of wild animals give warning to their victims, but these men were mute. To reach the spot where they confronted each other, they had moved in silence for miles, using dark alleys, crooked by-ways and narrow passages. Like serpents on the trek they wanted to fall upon their prey undetected and without any forewarning save their hissings at the very last moment.

Each gang, I guessed, had followed the tactics of the rival gang. Their cunning was met with equal cunning, and that was how they had met halfway. Each now held the other at bay. They were now facing each other: ready for the leap, ready to claw and draw—for disembowelling and dismembering.

Only the width of the street separated the two throngs of fanatics bent on murder and destruction. And there, in the midst of that not-too-wide thoroughfare, was I, ordered by one horde to stop and told by the other to go away. In silence they deliberated my fate, while I remained shuffling my feet.

On what carcasses did they want to gorge themselves?

Then it dawned upon me in a sudden flash that all these men were out for no immediate personal gain. Their objective was to set the world aright, and to establish the brotherhood of man. For that high ideal they were eager to bash faces in, to crush bodies into pulp, to batter heads till brains oozed out, to gouge eyes out with their own fingers, to dig their hands in bowels ripped open, to set houses and shrines on fire, and to spread destruction and devastation everywhere.

For that purpose they had chosen a day that was sacred both to the Hindus and to the Mohammedans.

IX

Only now I realized why the porter of my hostel had protested against my going out. He, like many others, had a vague inkling of a possible St Bartholomew's massacre in the city of Calcutta.

Had I kept my ears open and paid some attention to the newspaper reports of the latest debates in the Legislature, I too would have drawn the same conclusion as the illiterate porter and stayed behind barred doors and shuttered windows.

Only then it came to my mind, the memory of some of the stormy meetings among students several weeks ago.

Those wild gatherings had their origin in a visit of a musician who called himself Chumchicke Adhikari. He was said to be an anarcho-communist, a Post Graduate scholar and exceptionally brilliant in pure mathematics. But when he called at our hostel he was introduced as a simple guitarist who had travelled extensively. His face was not unfamiliar to me, for I had seen him with Comrade Dynamiter and Ramoni in the Asansole area. I do not know whether Chumchicke Adhikari, known as Comrade Chum to his friends, immediately recognized me or not. However, as he did not give any sign I did not take the trouble to thrust myself upon him. I had little liking for him when I had first met him in Ranigunj, and my distaste increased considerably when I found that our musical soirées were transformed into purely political meetings, thanks to his clever manoeuvres.

He was invited to give a series of talks on Music Appreciation: Music in the Byzantine World, Music in the West, Modern Trends in Western Music, and so on. He succeeded, however, in twisting the themes into 'A Survey of Music in the Bourgeois World and in the non-Bourgeois World'. After each talk his listeners were invited to his house for further discussions and to listen to illustrative gramophone records and to see short educational films.

Students were given endless cups of tea as they listened to the exposition of his thesis: True music—and in fact, every form of art—can flourish only in a free society like the USSR.

What prevented India's attaining the same degree of cultural height as Russia? The answer, according to him, was simple: India lacked the concept of true freedom. How then was this idea of true freedom to be inculcated? Here again, the solution was fairly simple: India's future teachers, schoolmasters, lecturers, and professors must accept the principle of a Permanent Revolution, and then transmit it to their students and pupils. Why was a Revolution necessary? 'Because,' Chumchicke Adhikari asserted, 'chaos is necessary for the birth of a star.'

The country, we were assured, was almost ripe for a revolution—a revolution with a small 'r'—provided there were a few determined young *realists* ready to risk their lives for the Great Cause. Idealists—whom he counted as starry-eyed fools—were not needed; they were no good, being as bad as the misguided reformists who backed the Government in the Legislature. The era of idealists and reformists was over. Hard-headed—but clear-thinking—realists were needed. Not many: just a few; a mere handful would do; only a score of those ready to do whatever was expected of them. 'The present revolutionary situation must be exploited,' the speaker emphasized.

'Why?' someone asked.

I craned my head to see the face of the interrupter. I saw only his profile, but that was enough for me to identify him. He was the tiny fellow whose people came from Satgaon; his maternal grandmother lived at Jater Dol on the Ganga Sagar. They called him Mug, but his family name was Furtado. I was friendly with him and was fond of his violin-playing. Incidentally, he was an amateur chef, almost unbeatable in preparing different varieties of curry. Like myself, he considered himself a stranger in the midst of all true-born sons of Calcutta. Another reason for my getting along well with him was his assertion that the country yokels of

Bengal would do well to remain as they were—without Calcutta's civilizing influence. Other students made fun of him because he went regularly to the Sunday communion service at the Portuguese Church in Armenia Bazaar where he lived with a Goanese family.

'In what way?' Mug repeated. 'How can the present situation be exploited?'

'In every possible way,' came the immediate answer. 'In order to establish a classless society every contradiction in the present bourgeois order should be seized upon and utilized to the maximum for our purpose. Every available lever should be used to widen the cracks in the social structure.'

Chumchicke Adhikari paused for a moment to scan the expression of those sitting just in front of him. Mug, I noticed, bent his head to avoid the scrutinizer's gaze.

'Where there is no peace,' Chumchicke Adhikari went on, 'we shall speak of peace. And where there is peace, we shall wage war: relentless civil war. We have on our side all the young poets of England, the best scientists of France, the most remarkable dramatists of America, the entire youth of China. All realists are with us.'

'Who are we?' I felt like asking. But I missed my chance. How was Mug taking all that in? As I was in the back rows and Mug sat facing the speaker it was impossible for me to watch his expression. I suspect he looked blank. Whenever he failed to follow an argument, his vacant looks gave him away. Evidently that was the case, for suddenly Chumchicke Adhikari stopped in the midst of a sentence and whispered something to the student who chaired the meeting. He then nodded to Mug.

'What does the speaker mean by a realist?' Mug stammered. 'Does he mean those who write in a realistic style? I mean authors like Zola.'

'A realist,' Chumchicke Adhikari began without giving Mug the time to finish his sentence, 'is a man who knows his objective. A man who has mastered the art of running with the hare and hunting with the hounds, and does not dream of planting a stake in the sky. Is that clear?'

No one gave any answer.

However, to make his clarification yet clearer, he told us, 'off the record', how some students of dramatic art had rendered considerable service in the organized—but publicized as spontaneous—demonstrations against the increasing price of cloth. A lot of professional beggars from Kalighat were hired for this purpose, but the dramatic students in their make-up considerably heightened the gruesome effect of long files of almost naked men and women covered with alleged festering wounds inflicted upon them by the police. Another batch of students were equally helpful in bringing in a large number of squatters from the mofussil to Calcutta's public squares. 'Such students were certainly "realists"', declared our speaker.

'But,' Mug raised his hand to ask more questions. 'What's the object of these demonstrations? The people of Calcutta are sufficiently aware of the shortage of cloth, houses, rice, and of a hundred other things.'

'We are not concerned with public opinion.' The speaker chuckled. 'We want to see how many outsiders voluntarily take part in our demonstrations. We also want to undermine the prestige of the Government.'

'What good will that do to promote culture?'

'Indirectly it will help us a lot. It will hasten the day of India's liberation. Her attainment of *true* freedom. And with true freedom the ground will be prepared for the growth of the people's culture—the only culture that matters.'

There was a break for serving out some *rasogoollahs*, *jalebis*, and other varieties of sweetmeat. I saw Chumchicke Adhikari empty a large tumbler of tea—in the Russian fashion. 'In Russia,' my neighbour told me, 'they drink tea out of tumblers.' Chumchicke Adhikari did not, however, drink his tea out of the tumbler. He poured it into a high-brimmed saucer and lapped it up. He did not care for any milk; in its stead he dropped in an entire unpeeled lemon and a few heaped spoonfuls of sugar. During the rest of the evening he dipped his spoon from time to time into his tumbler to take out the undissolved sugar and to lick his spoon clean. 'Sugar,' whispered again my neighbour from Bangabashi College, 'is an article of luxury in Russia.' From the same student I gathered that Chumchicke Adhikari had many names, such as the Great Chum, and Comrade Chum, while some of his friends referred to him as The Wrangler. 'He is always willing to be helpful to everyone,' another student confided to me. 'If you have at any time any worry, just call on him.'

By now the distribution of sweetmeats was over. Chumchicke Adhikari cleared his throat. That was the signal for us to be quiet.

'What is the object of the Revolution?' he began. 'I mean the Revolution with a big "R".'

No one answered, as before.

He stared in front of him for one full minute. The silence was disconcerting. Finally, he decided to answer his own question.

'The object of the Revolution is to bring in the New Order: People's Democracy. Call it Socialism, if you will. Or Communism, if you prefer it. Our main objective is the creation of a classless society: a society in which everyone will have an equal chance; a fair chance and a decent standard of living and a reasonable share in the country's cultural life. We cannot promise much at this stage. But this much we do guarantee: there shall be no more rich and no more poor. There shall be equality. Equality is the watchword of all anarcho-communists, of all who want people's democracy. That alone is the touchstone for us. What do you say to that?'

'Of course,' several voices murmured, 'we are all for democracy.'

He immediately raised his forefinger in the air, as a sign of warning. There was a general hush. He then explained that very often people failed to understand the real implication of the word democracy.

'Hear! Hear!' I bawled.

Chumchicke Adhikari beamed. His grin spread from ear to ear. He smiled, I thought, not for one person but several: Chumchicke Adhikari, the Great Chum, Comrade Chum, the Wrangler, and a few others. He gave an approving glance in my direction and nodded: the first sign of recognition I had received from him.

To the hushed audience he expounded the meaning of true democracy: bourgeois democracy was not the same as free peoples' democracy; in bourgeois countries like England and America, the workers—the intellectual workers as well as manual labourers—were exploited, whereas in a true democracy like Russia there were no exploiters and no exploited. 'The exploiting bourgeois blood-suckers,' he emphasized his statement by thumping his fist on the table, 'reactionaries with bestial propensities have no place in a free democracy.'

A short film on the Russian Ballet was shown next.

As I was sitting in the back rows I had the opportunity of examining the ciné-projector. It was a real beauty: a portable projector, no bigger than an ordinary microscope case, and I presume no heavier. It was greatly coveted by me. I thought of the man to whom Jogin-Da had sold a mastiff; he was said to be an amateur 'bioscopist'. I was willing to become one to handle such a neat thing. The pictures this attractive projector threw on the screen were perfect. 'Does it come from Russia?' I asked the man who operated it. It did not: it came from America. 'But,' he added, 'in Russia there are much better things. The bourgeois countries are jealous of Russia's progress. That's why they have boycotted all Russian products. Have a private talk with Comrade Chum after the show. He will tell you a lot more about Russia.'

There was some sort of a hitch with the sound track. 'Due to some confusion in doubling,' the cinematograph-operator explained. Instead of ballet music we heard a series of twangs, sharp and short, similar to the noise we make on our *ektaras*—cheap mandolins—when some breezy tourist wants to hear our music and expects us to give *megha-mallar* in the midst of hot summer, or the *durbari* tune in broad daylight; we palm off such noises as our musical masterpieces, and goggle our eyes with feigned amazement and profound admiration when records of such musical achievements as 'Chu-Chin-Chow' or 'The Trumpet-Major's Daughter' are given for our benefit. We shake our heads and give some more noises with bamboo flutes with one hole in them, and declare them to be our highest achievement. The Russians, I was almost sure, had done something similar with their newly introduced system of sound recording. Perhaps they were experimenting to find out to what extent students in India were capable of distinguishing between music and noise. My view was not, however, shared by the cinematograph-operator. He announced that owing to some misunderstanding a Chinese sound track had been given with the ballet film.

I regretted very much that Tu Fan was not there to tell me what this alleged Chinese discourse was about. As he was not a university student there was no possibility of my smuggling him in.

To come back to the film, it was certainly interesting. I was prepared to accept the cinematograph-operator's statement, namely, 'It was more than interesting, it was really illuminating.' There were, however, moments when concerted giggles and half-smothered outbursts of laughter were distinctly heard. As there were no Russian ballerinas present in flesh and blood, those manifestations of rudeness did not really matter.

At one stage some ill-bred fellows from City College made no attempt to moderate their untimely hilarity, and their lead was taken up by the majority of all present. This happened when some of the Russian ballerinas in tights and extremely short stick-out tulle skirts were exhibiting their bottoms and making jerking movements in a peculiar fashion to imitate 'Les Biches'—pronounced in the Russian fashion by Chumchicke Adhikari—'Less Bitches.'

To make up for the irreverent chuckles some of the students from Presidency College applauded lustily when the film show was over.

'Such dances,' the cinematograph-operator began reading out from a sheaf of mimeographed sheets, 'such ballets form an integral part of Russian life. In no bourgeois country has the art of dancing reached such a high degree of perfection as in Revolutionary Russia.'

There were a few murmurs. Mild protests? Or marks of approval? I was not sure. I regretted having taken a back seat. The operator was now reading out his text standing next to Chumchicke Adhikari and it was not easy to follow all that he was mumbling like a nervous schoolboy.

I was all ears by now: I wanted to catch every syllable of what the Russians had to say on dancing and dances. Did I not come from that part of the country where every phase of life finds its expression in symbolic dances?—in graceful gestures and in rhythmic movements? In the Penhari Parganas there are dances to celebrate marriage, dances to welcome the seasons, dances to bid them farewell, dances for every occasion. 'Our dances,' the village Punditji never failed to remind his callers, 'give dignity to labour, and transform our travails into manifestations of joy.'

'Can any country,' the cinematograph-operator continued reading, 'can any civilization give anything remotely comparable with these Russian dances in their grace and their beauty? All over the world, even in the reactionary bourgeois countries like America and England, all informed critics and connoisseurs are of one opinion about the Russian ballet: the Russian ballet—the product of the Russian Revolution—is the finest manifestation of the callisthenic art.'

It was impossible to contain myself any longer. I noticed Mug too was fretting. Being in the first row he was feeling somewhat diffident about attracting too much attention upon himself. He was under the stern gaze of Chumchicke Adhikari, and evidently too frightened to put any further questions. So I decided to speak up for him as well as for myself: we were the only two backwoodsmen in that gathering.

'Come to my village in the Penhari Parganas,' I bawled. 'And see for yourself how we dance. Our dances too form an integral part of our life.'

'I beg your pardon,' the cinematograph-operator stammered. He seemed to be too shocked to realize that I was contesting his statement about the superiority of the Russians—'Les Biches'—over our dancers. He looked at Chumchicke Adhikari and received an assenting nod, which he interpreted as a sign that he should ignore me. 'The dances you have just seen,' he continued with his text, 'are the spontaneous expressions of the new cultural manifestations of Revolutionary Russia. Their spontaneity...'

'The Russian ballets are danced on the stage,' I interrupted. 'Whereas our dances take place in the open air. Which ones would you call more spontaneous? These artistes—"Les Biches"—they move like automata compared with our dancers. Certainly they lack grace...'

'Who is that?' Chumchicke Adhikari, though he was not chairing the meeting, started making a racket with his teaspoon. He made signs to the cinematograph-operator to fold up his sheaf of papers.

I shot out my hand.

'Oh! You!' Chumchicke Adhikari made a puffing sound and breathed out like a deflated balloon. 'You seem to be everywhere. One day in Asansole. Another day in Chandernagore. And now you are here. You ought to be in a lunatic asylum.'

The way he spoke made some of the students laugh. They interpreted Chumchicke Adhikari's remarks in their own fashion; in other words, I was a regular trouble-maker, and that was the epithet they used for me.

'That's no answer to my question,' I shouted back.

The cinematograph-operator pretended not to hear me. Chumchicke Adhikari busied himself with a superficial hair in his ear which suddenly began to trouble him, and he wanted to pluck it out. He did not believe in bourgeois conventions. As he was a Post-Graduate scholar and we were mere undergraduates, I presume his behaviour was nothing extraordinary in our company.

'Have you or have you not seen the dances in the Penhari Parganas?' I bellowed.

'Hush! Hush!' hissed several voices. The hissing came from the corner where the most noisy students from Presidency

College sat together, forming a block of their own. They did not like me because of my introducing a resolution in the University Union deploring the conduct of one of their favourites: a first-year student who had imitated Subhas Chandra Bose's gesture and pummelled a professor.

~

The professor in question was accused of *lèse-majesté*! He had dared tell an unpleasant truth, namely, the dearth of Hindu historians: 'Though rich and varied, Sanskrit literature has no great historical works to its credit. Hindus have no authors like Thucydides, Polybius, and Procopius. Nor anyone like Ibn-Khaldun, Abul Fazl and Ferishta.'

This, every student knew to be God's truth.

Years ago, when Subhas Chandra Bose was an undergraduate, such a statement had created a general stir in Calcutta. 'Mother India has been insulted,' wrote Hickey's bastards in their yellow journals, and Subhas Bose avenged Mother India's honour by thrashing his professor! 'Well done!' commented the illegitimate progeny of the professional card-sharper who introduced the art of journalistic blackmailing into India.

As Subhas Chandra Bose was in great vogue just then, what could be more natural than to imitate him? The first-year undergraduate's action received the wholehearted commendation of the students of Presidency College. The Subhas Bose cult was not restricted to Presidency College alone. It was widespread. 'He is so manly,' the women students used to chant, particularly those who were ugly and had not a ghost's chance of finding husbands, even if they had decided to maintain and mother them all their days. There was a rumour that Subhas Bose was going to be married to a German widow called Frau Mon von Putz. Without ascertaining if there was any truth in this gossip scores of women students decided to change their first name into Mon. There were debates and discussions over this charming first name, Mon. No one knew if it was an abbreviation of Mona or Monica or Monday or Montaga or even Montague. That was of little importance to the women students of Calcutta. Those belonging to Beeton College (pronounced Beeton, but written Bethune)—originally an institution for *purdah* ladies—where they taught women students all sorts of subjects, excepting the only two appreciated by men—the art of cooking, and the art of looking pretty—these women decided to have a holiday of their own in honour of Subhas Bose's alleged sweetheart Frau Mon von Putz. At the end of the twenty-four hours joy strike the ladies returned to their College bereft of their long locks. Their plaits, tresses, and curls were sacrificed on the altar of hero-worship. Frau Mon von Putz's hairstyle was, I think, called a *fringe*—the Chinese hair arrangement which reached New York via Hollywood thanks to a cinema star, Anna May Wong, and which went from New York to Berlin where it was taken up by ladies with wrinkled foreheads—and it was the *fringe* of Frau Mon von Putz which the Beeton College women wore when they rejoined their classes. All of them smelled formidably of gum arabic!

Women all over the country—even the most doltish ones — generally took every trouble to enhance their beauty and their charm. But the wonderfully intellectual women students of Calcutta, especially those known as the Beeton Babies, did the contrary. They tortured themselves to look as ugly as possible—to resemble a widow, Frau Mon von Putz—all on account of a photograph showing Subhas Bose shaking hands with her—a

German matron. Mother Nature has—most inconsiderately—bestowed more or less permanent waves and curls in our women's hair; even when cropped, such hair cannot take the Chinese pattern automatically. Therefore the Beeton Babies had to plaster their *fringes* on their foreheads with thick daubs of atrociously smelling pure gum of Arabia Felix. They all looked hideous; and they behaved as they looked—like wild-cats. They were as uncontrollable and as noisy when I spoke on my resolution at the University Union condemning the scion of Presidency College, whose spirit of hero-worship had constrained him to knock down a professor. As the debate over the resolution progressed, the women admirers of Subhas Bose fretted and fumed. Finally they became possessed. They wanted to scratch my eyes out—there and then—for my alleged unpatriotism. Mug Furtado who seconded me was howled down. 'Go back to Portugal,' shrieked the women. 'Go back to Goa, you Goanese macaw,' shouted in unison the students of Presidency College: they had as their leader a bearded second-year student with a husky voice, bearing the sonorous name of Dionysos Papaconstantinodouros, who in spite of his name, was a true-born son of Calcutta: an ignoramus who did not know the Greek alphabet and had not even heard of the existence of Greek historians.

I looked at Mug, and Mug looked at the rows of plastered *fringes,* and we both shook our heads. We feared lest the spells cast by the bearded Dionysos and his worshippers should transform the wild-cats into demented Thracian women. We trembled for ourselves. It looked as though they were bent on outraging us for our failure to be as patriotic as they.

Then the unexpected happened. The wild-cats went out of the Union premises hysterically weeping and loudly wailing, bitterly clamouring for their lost locks and shorn tresses. For no other than Subhas Bose himself turned up at the meeting and did something unforeseen, unsuspected even by his intimates: he congratulated me for my having tabled the motion!

He spoke for a few minutes only. But that was enough to make a world of difference. He deplored his own action as student—when in a moment of excitement—he had done something wrong: something indefensible; he had hit Professor Oaten. He was very sorry that his admirers should think of condoning this unjust action of his. In brief, he did not care for such admirers. He advised them to seek other heroes—men who committed 'Himalayan blunders' and 'tolerated no criticism from their followers'.

'Let them follow,' he declared, 'if they so desired, hyper-sensitive, dogmatic, irritable fanatics—men like Gandhi...' (Terrific booing drowned the names of Subhas Bose's rivals.) 'Men who talk of love and whose eyes always glow with hate. Men who want their followers to sacrifice their individuality and personality. Men who are surrounded by automata, by packs of Pavlov's dogs' (Wild cheering.)

He went out, as he had come, quite suddenly. But even before he had stepped inside the hall, he had made it clear that he was not engaged to Frau Mon von Putz, nor to anyone. During his goodwill tour in Germany he had shaken hands with many—men as well as women—and Frau Mon von Putz might have been one of them.

The Beeton Babies before walking out of the Union hall gave for a few minutes what seemed to me a highly entertaining demonstration of throwing fits. I relished the sight. It was a real pleasure to watch the writhings of repentance of one woman student of Jadavpur Medical School, called Moyna Vansa-Varmana, or rather, ex-Moyna Vansa-Varmana. She was not a bad-looking girl and knew how to dress attractively. Instead of rejoicing in her distress, I ought to have shown, in theory, at least, some compassion. But I was not Padre Johan of Jamtara nor the Punditji of my village nor Didi-Ma of Chandernagore, and I did delight in watching the wicked suffer. Ex-Moyna Vansa-Varmana was the chief instigator of more than one ragging to which I had been subjected. In spite of this—as she was not graceless in her looks as were most of the women intellectuals of Calcutta—I had begged her (when we were working together in the Experimental Psychology Laboratory) not to put on a *fringe* nor change her name to Mon. 'If change your name you must,' I exhorted her, 'change it for something attractive. Why not call yourself Monna Vanna? That would not be so very different from your present name.' 'None of your French India nonsense,' she replied as though all women in Chandernagore were called Monna Vanna. 'I won't have any of your French names.' 'But,' I explained to her, 'Monna Vanna has nothing to do with Chandernagore or with France. It is an Italian name. Listen how it sounds. The Italian is almost as beautiful as Bengali.' I then repeated to her one of Didi-Ma's favourite sonnets:

> *Io vidi Monna Vanna e Monna Bice*
> *Venire invêr lo loco là ov' i'era,*
> *L'una oppresso dell' altra meraviglia...*
>
> (I beheld Monna Vanna and Monna Bice
> coming towards the place where I stood
> one marvel following the other...)

As Bice in Italian is pronounced somewhat like Bitch-éh, she misunderstood my motive, and called me a grinning gibbon, an ill-bred country goat, a French poodle, a toad, a Santal head-hunter, and various other names. She then turned up her nose in the air to proclaim that I was unpatriotic for not admiring a name approved by Subhas Chandra Bose the Netaji. My suggestion had a disastrous effect on her head: she got herself shingled to procure a gum arabic *fringe*, and then adopted a double-barrelled first name, Mon-Von.

Had she any common sense she should have covered her head and veiled her countenance instead of giving an exhibition of herself with a blubbering face. Her lamentations were the loudest because she saw how Subhas Bose patted me on the back and asked me to meet him at Sarat Bose's house. 'I want to see more of you,' he told me. 'Ring up this number any time and ask for extension Asia.' (Had she known that later on I was going to have long discussions with her hero, Subhas Bose, in the Mad Ox Park she would have, I am sure, wailed still louder.)

Deserted by his women votaries the bearded Dionysos ceased declaiming, and finally slunk away. No one stepped into his shoes to be the cheerleader of the Presidency College undergraduates.

In the circumstances, Mug thought I would do well to withdraw my resolution. But I was obdurate. 'It is not Subhas Bose's past,' I made it clear, 'that concerns us here. We have had no Polybius among our Sanskrit writers, and this must be rubbed in. I cannot let that idiot from Presidency College escape unscathed.' My obstinacy was partly due to Padre Johan's counsel: Unless we acknowledge on our knees our shortcomings—with due humility and contrition—we shall not be redeemed.

I need not go into any further details about that affair. My resolution was lost at the Union, but I had the satisfaction of knowing that the university authorities—in spite of a threat of strike by the students of Presidency College—did eventually reprimand the object of my anathema. I became, therefore, all the more the target of attacks from the students of Presidency College.

~

They wanted to be even with me, and kept on hissing, 'Hush! Hush!'

Their intervention helped Chumchicke Adhikari to hold a confabulation with his cinematograph-operator and a couple of others; his object, I discovered in a minute, was to sidetrack my question.

True appreciation of art, he pontificated, depended much on general education, and persons suffering from bourgeois nationalistic predilections were not qualified to pronounce any judgment on matters concerning aesthetics. Nevertheless, he thought it desirable to remind everyone present—not excluding the students suffering from xenophobia like the two interrupters—namely, Mug and myself—that all art critics in England and America were in agreement about the supreme and unrivalled excellence of the Russian ballet. 'It is incomparably superior,' he reiterated, 'to every form of dancing in any part of the world.'

'Why quote the English and the American critics?' I persisted with my questioning. 'You don't accept their views on other matters. Who tells you that they are right in their assessment of the aesthetic quality of the Russian ballet? How can they compare it with Indian dancing? Our Penhari dancers have not toured in America nor in England. Anyhow, let me hear what you think of our *Kajri* dance?'

I was expecting too much. I was foolish enough to hope that Chumchicke Adhikari would admit the obvious. Only much later it occurred to me that a man who had trimmed his beard to look like Lenin was not the one to give an unbiased opinion on the traditional Indian *Kajri* as compared with *Les Biches* of Russia.

As a result of my pig-headed intervention in defence of the dancers of Penhari Parganas, I failed to receive the notices of subsequent addresses given by Chumchicke Adhikari. This led to my missing a number of cultural and educational films sent from Russia.

For some time Mug kept me informed of all that he saw in the cultural soirées: how tons of tomatoes were grown in the Arctic regions, how Russian teachers and writers were accorded palaces to live in, how parachutists were trained for the preservation of world peace, how Russian children were trained to throw hand-grenades for the same purpose, how wheat could be cultivated on sand trays inside a laboratory, and heaps of such 'shorts' on an infinite variety of interesting subjects.

Somehow, I felt that I did not miss much by my absence from these gatherings, and therefore did not bother to raise the issue of my not receiving the notices at the University Union.

Mug's reports were sufficient for my purpose. I wanted to know something about Byzantine music, mosaics, architecture, and, of course, dances from all parts of the world. These 'shorts' never came to Mug's notice as long as he was going to these soirées.

Later on, Mug committed a grave blunder, or rather, a series of blunders, practically all on the same day. He saw a Russian film on the benefits of mixed sunbathing—whether on the shores of the Black Sea or of the Caspian, Mug was not quite sure, and this was of no great importance. However, Mug felt greatly disgusted at the hairiness of the Slav sunbathing beauties.

Being a fool he talked about it to the Goanese family with whom he was living. They in their turn were horrified, and talked about their horripilation to the priest of the Portuguese Church in Armenia Bazaar—the one who conducted the communion service attended by Mug. The padre was shocked and Mug was counselled to keep away from the film soirées arranged by Chumchicke Adhikari.

Thus Mug failed to hear Chumchicke Adhikari's exposition of the thesis: 'On the need of exploiting the religious differences in the bourgeois city of Calcutta for the promotion of the Great Cause.'

Vague rumours did, however, reach his ears as well as mine. But I had no definite information about the date and the place—precisely when and where—two groups of workers of different sects were to be set by their ears to fight, to widen the cracks in the fissiparous bourgeoisie structure, and thus hasten the oncoming of the Great Day—the Revolution with a capital 'R'.

~

Taking all things into account, it must be conceded that the poor toiling masses of Calcutta were no more bloodthirsty than any other section of the community. Their lot was hard and their future insecure. But in this respect they were no worse off than the overwhelming majority of the non-manual workers—the intellectuals, and the semi-intellectuals, the teachers, the clerks, the typists and others of this category. The only difference was this: whereas the latter knew that there was no shortcut to prosperity, the ill-informed factory hands were too willing to believe that their misery was due exclusively to the wickedness of a few: 'The bourgeois gangsters,' according to Chumchicke

Adhikari, 'and their associates.' If only these associates could be eliminated, Adhikari asserted, there would be an immediate improvement in the general situation.

But who were the associates of the bourgeois gangsters?

Chumchicke Adhikari was not too willing to name them. He restricted his oratory solely to the denunciation in more vehement terms of the allies of the bourgeoisie: these auxiliaries were worse than their masters. Then at an opportune moment it was revealed: 'To destroy the power of the bourgeoisie, one must rob it of its hirelings—the Lumpen-Proletariat.'

Who were the Lumpen-Proletariat?

Chumchicke Adhikari's answer varied. It depended on the person who raised the question. To those who believed in the sanctity of the cow, it was the wicked beef-eater; to those who had no objection to beef-eating, it was the vegetarian cow-worshipper. 'To weaken the bourgeoisie,' Adhikari counselled, 'every contradiction in the social structure should be exploited to the full. A realist must not be too squeamish about bloodshed.'

Rumours spread with alarming rapidity in the working-class areas of Beliaghata and Entalley. Hearsays changed their forms and contents as they passed from one quarter to another. There were whispers about the Mohammedan threat to burn down the Temple of the Daughter of the Mountains on the day of *Muharram* and the counter-threat of the Hindus to desecrate the Big Mosque on the same day.

'The bigger the lie,' the advocates of People's Democracy expounded, 'the greater its success. The hungry sheep will swallow anything and follow you everywhere, provided you show some interest in the welfare of the flock.'

X

All this came to my mind, and I bit my lips.

I was caught between two factions who wanted human sacrifice: they breathed hate; they propagated fear. Hate and fear are infectious. They contaminated the air.

I felt contaminated. But it was no longer hate that was uppermost in me. How could I hate the experimental guinea pigs of the anarcho-communist Chumchicke Adhikari? Once my hate was gone, there was nothing left to sustain me. Fear turned my blood into water. My knees became wobbly. I realized, however, that the moment my knees bent, a hundred blows would fall on me, and over my dead body the mob-fight would rage.

'As long as I manage to keep myself erect,' I murmured to gain courage, 'I am comparatively safe. But what will happen if Roma turns up now?'

'*Are-are-are-are-are*,' growled the mob on my right.

'*Maro-maro-maro-maro*,' snarled back those on my left.

The fearful gnashings of defiance ceased for a moment when a brass-bound bamboo staff came hurtling through the air to fall at my feet. Was it destined for breaking my skull? If so, how could one have missed the target at that short range? It came from the side that had asked me to pass on, and later urged me to run away from the scene. Did they then intend to help me? Was the stick thrown at me so that I might use it as a weapon against those who carried butcher's knives?

I looked at the bamboo staff lying by my feet. At its one end was a long razor blade; it was neatly fixed, almost flush with the body of the stick. It was as good as a butcher's knife. No, it was more than that: it was far more formidable.

'If you are to sell your life,' a voice cried, 'sell it dearly.'

I did not say anything, and did not even bother to turn my head in the direction of the voice. I stood as I was: perfectly immobile. Perhaps my limbs were paralysed with fear. So was my tongue. Maybe that was why I did not move nor say anything. Anyway, I made no attempt to shift my position.

'Pick up that stick,' shouted the same voice.

'No, I won't touch that stick.' This was what I wanted to say, but my lips uttered no sound. Though frightened I still had, as I have said earlier, some wits about me, and this much was plain: that the moment I made the slightest gesture to get hold of that brass-bound bamboo staff a hundred knives would fly at me, and that would not have done me any good.

'Go your way,' shouted the ringleader of the Mohammedan crowd when he noticed my refusal to seek protection from the Hindu quarter. 'Pass on! Leave the field free!'

'*Maro-maro-maro-maro*,' fulminated the Hindu faction.

'*Dharo-dharo-dharo-dharo*,' howled back the Mohammedans.

By now I was out of my temporary state of coma caused by fright. 'Let them growl,' I muttered, and was surprised to discover that my lips did move once again and words did come out of them. 'I will stay where I am. The wolf packs howling defiance are less ferocious than those prowling in silence.'

Gradually the silence broke, and with the rising of shouts and shrieks—threats and counter-threats—my spirits rose too. There were cries of abuse and screams of defiance; there were challenges and counter-challenges. The din they finally raised could be heard from afar. All that was extremely heartening to me. For I knew Roma was now safe: there was no likelihood of her strolling in the direction of a howling mob to look for me. A heavy weight was off my chest. If anything happened to her the sin would have been on my conscience.

Long ago she had proposed the discontinuance of our lessons—long before I was pelted with mud—but being pig-headed I had insisted on keeping them up. It was I who had implored her for a rendezvous. Therefore, the least I could do was to prevent any calamity befalling her. Now, however, it was all right. My unburdened heart turned me into a pugilist: I was ready to face the wolf packs with a bold face, and began rolling up my shirt-sleeves.

'Look straight into the eyes of your enemy,' they say in my village. 'Look straight, and it will give you courage.' It was, however, impossible for me to look straight on my right and on my left at the same time. So I kept turning my head from one side to the other.

'If you don't want to go away,' shouted the spokesman of the Hindus, 'pick up that *lathi*. Join us.'

'Young man!' cried the Mohammedan gangleader. 'Go your way. Our fight doesn't concern you.'

'No,' I said as loudly as I could. 'I am not moving from this spot.' I did not know if in that clamour any of my words could be heard. But the fact that I was trying to say something induced the ringleaders to hush their respective followers. I profited from this silence, and shouted at the top of my voice: 'I will not move an inch.'

'Don't be a mule,' cried someone, whether from my right or left I was not sure.

'Who dares call a scholar names?' I shrieked back. 'Let him step forward and get his ears boxed.'

And there was a general hush.

~

For good or for evil, the scholar is respected everywhere in the country. A monarch, so runs our saying, deserves deference in his own domains, but a scholar commands it everywhere. In the Penhari Parganas a scholarship-holder is as good as a scholar, and I was addressed as such. My Penhari blood was up. And Penhari sayings came flooding to my mind.

'No,' say the men of Penhari even when the rest of the world shouts with one voice: 'Yes.'

'There is an antidote to everything,' they say in my Penhari regions. 'There is an antidote to fear. It is pride.'

It was the Penhari pride that sustained me in Calcutta when the rest of the students were against me. And it was the same pride that made me now face without flinching the throngs on my right and on my left. It was also the pride of Fort Orleans of my Chandernagore that forced me not to capitulate. No white flag for me when I knew the justice of my cause: I was determined to frustrate the project of the world-betterer Chumchicke Adhikari.

The ugly Big Mosque of Prince Ghulam Muhammad meant nothing to me; and the Temple of the Daughter of the Mountains meant no more: in fact, I did not even know its whereabouts. But I did not want these places to be destroyed by the dupes of the man who thought that the Russian muscular women—'Les Biches'—were more graceful than the least of our Penhari dancers. A man who in spite of his being a clever mathematician could be such an ass was likely to be an ass in other matters as well.

I assumed, rightly or wrongly, that as long as I stood between the rival factions they were not likely to start fighting. And then perhaps the police too would turn up—eventually—to disperse the gangs. All that was, therefore, necessary for me was to hold the fort as long as possible, and not to hoist the white flag. The more I thought of Chumchicke Adhikari the more my blood boiled.

'A shrine,' I repeated to myself, 'be it Hindu, Mohammedan or Christian is sacred. I will not let any place of worship be desecrated by Adhikari's cat's-paws.'

~

I glared towards my right and then towards my left, and shrieked again: 'Who is the ass that has brayed insults to a scholar?'

No one answered. I gave a kick at the bamboo staff near my foot and threw it in the direction of the Hindu crowd, the side from which it had been cast at me.

'Take it back,' I cried. 'A scholar has no need of a bludgeon. He needs no help from fools. He wants to box the ears of the ass who has called him names.'

The tension then broke as though by magic. There was some twittering, and this soon turned into loud guffaws, followed by wild cheerings. Instead of my boxing the ears of the man who had called me a mule, I found myself being dragged about the street by my hair: Roma was chastising me before that highly amused crowd. They yelled with delight and clapped their hands.

'Ho! Ho! Ho!' they roared. 'The scholar has met his match! Ho! Ho! Ho! The *Kristani*—the Christian girl—knows how to handle her scholar!'

Though completely taken by surprise, I was grateful for Roma's intervention. The situation was saved, and I blessed the gods. For laughter, I recalled the Penhari saying, is the gift of the gods to man, and not to the wolves: a crowd that laughs is a crowd of brothers, a band of God's children.

Roma must have come up the Chandni Bazaar Crescent while my attention was focused on one side of the street, or rather the lane known as the Purana Spiral Lane.

She was a sight!—with a purring kitten perched on her shoulders; the same one which I had perceived some time ago in the distance, playing with a paper bag. She wore a pair of bell-bottomed sailors' slacks of brilliant brick red; her sleeveless silk shirt of vivid orange was most shockingly unbuttoned: it was so tightly tugged under her broad belt that her very nipples were distinctly outlined against the clinging silk, not to say anything about the contours of her half-exposed bosom. Her tousled hair fell in wild ringlets over her shoulders.

'Why have you kept me waiting?' she screamed. 'For hours I have been looking for you in the church. Did you want to give me the slip? You are no man.'

I was dumbfounded. Was she mad? This was not the Roma I knew. She seemed a different being.

'Good people!' She screamed her complaint to the laughing crowd: 'Look at my man! He buries his nose in books, and takes every pretext to leave me to myself. Am I so bad-looking? Am I ugly?'

Many throats proclaimed that she was as pretty as a flower. Some made ribald jokes.

Roma retorted with alacrity, bandying similar remarks. She wagged her finger at the ringleaders, accusing them of being no better than impotent seniles: she had her grave doubts about finding a single 'he-man' in the whole throng capable of satisfying a reasonable woman's amorous demands.

More ribald comments came from all sides.

The bird in hand, Roma retorted shamelessly, was worth more than two in the bush! What was the use of exhibiting her charms before such men as had slunk away from their conjugal beds early in the morning to indulge in an orgy of street fighting. 'A fine excuse,' she jeered, 'for being brave and running away from your wives!'

The men guffawed, and Roma laughed too. She had hysterical fits of laughter. I was simply petrified to see her behave in that way.

'Which woman would care to have men like you in bed?' She held up the kitten high in the air. 'This male kitten is better than my man. At least he does not want to run away from a woman. Look at that big, blue-turbaned fellow over there. He looks pretty fierce, but I tell you he is no good in bed. Once he made a date with me, and then failed to turn up. He must be useless. If he has a wife, she ought to give him a beating.'

Several blue-turbaned fellows protested. Their neighbours bantered them. Roma had another fit of hysterical laughter. The men laughed as they dispersed. Some declared that they commiserated me. 'Life is like that,' one gigantically tall fellow murmured next to me: 'With women one never knows.'

The street emptied. We two were left alone.

It is curious how I overlooked at that time the practical demonstration of the Penhari saying: In times of grave danger it is the cleverest hind—and not the king-stag—that commands the herd. I forgot all about the risk I had run only few a minutes ago. And instead of thanking Roma, I reproached her:

'Your vocabulary of obscene words seems to be pretty rich.'

'It has spared Calcutta a holocaust.'

PART TWO

Of Sensuous Fires

I

'It was just touch and go,' Roma murmured as she readjusted her dress and rearranged her hair. 'I had to change myself quickly into a mad woman to humour the crowd.'

She tried to smile, but she was trembling all over. I said nothing, because I was seething. If she could adjust her dress in a provocative way for hooligans why was she trying to be so prudish with me? She never allowed me to touch her arm: she never took mine in hers and there were scores of Eurasian women walking about in the Lady Bagan interlaced with their gallants. Did she think I was no good?

'I wonder how long it will take you to get over the shock?' she asked.

'Shock!' I gave a hollow laugh, and bragged about my immunity to all shocks. I told her that if I were to recall the aches and pains I had gone through in life it would fill a volume. 'There are certain luxuries I can't afford. And suffering from shocks is one of them. I am congenitally immune to such flutters.'

~

Little did I know then that the aftereffect of that Friday's narrow escape was to endure for a long time. This discovery was made only by and by—certainly not immediately, I do not even know precisely when I found out that it had transformed me into a different being.

Outwardly, I remained as I always was, or at least my physical appearance remained so. But inwardly, I went through a series of adventures. I was gnawed with nightmares and sudden attacks of panic. Strange dreams began haunting my nights. Even in daytime occasional visions of terrifying scenes floated unasked before my eyes.

Why did an incident from Mila Repa's life prey upon me? On one like myself who knew so little of Mila Repa's country, Tibet? Had it something to do with the degrading influence of fear?

In Mila Repa's biography one reads: Once when a feast was in progress, and the horses of the guests were stabled on the ground floor, according to the custom of Tibet where dwelling-houses repose on wooden piles or piers, a maid-servant came down on some errand. Confounded by eerie chimeras, this woman imagined she saw a scorpion as big as the biggest Tangut yak pulling and gnawing at the central pier of her master's house. Terrified by the vision she immediately rushed away crying for help. But her alarm communicated by itself to the horses, and the frightened animals began fighting furiously among themselves: the stallions breaking their tethers hurled themselves madly upon the mares, and the colts upon the fillies. In the wild stampede that ensued the supporting piers were so badly shaken that the whole building came down with a tremendous crash, burying under its ruins the entire company of the invited people as well as the horses. Why did I think of the terror-stricken horses? Why did not these animals run away? If saving their own lives was the primary cause of the stampede why did the stallions choose to throw themselves upon the mares, and the colts upon the fillies? Why did they seek their own destruction in this fashion?

Insignificant events of long, long ago came crowding to my memory to assume exaggerated dimensions. For no reason in particular the image of Gomosta Moshay of Chandernagore drifted back to my mind. (He died shortly after I had lost both my grandmother and second aunt.) He reappeared in my visions not as I had known him usually to be, but as he had looked on the afternoon when I was fished out of the Sandalwood Tank: standing in a corner of Didi-Ma's library, and at his feet crouched a half-naked woman with disordered locks which covered her face. This woman bore some traits of my Mummi-Ma, of Roma, and of the woman suffering from albinism I had come across on the day of my arrival at Calcutta as well as of the female acolytes I had seen going to the Golden Pagoda of the Lord of Love in the Chitpur district.

Once in my nightmares I found myself swimming in the sea, somewhere near the Sagar Island, and the billows were coils of venomous serpents: not moccasins, but gigantic reptiles, scaly and slimy creatures, many feet long, somewhat like enormously elongated huge lizards and basset-hounds. They wanted to entangle me in the convolutions of their sinuous tails, and I made desperate efforts to swim out of their reach, only to drift towards a strange whirlpool, which sucked me in. I woke up with a start and found that I was covered with sweat and panting for breath.

I had also dreams of a strange, wave-tossed ocean of saffron oil, whose foam-crested breakers dragged me about as though I were an inert piece of log. The only way of reaching the shore was, I calculated, to let myself be carried by the rushing breakers, and this was what I did. But the moment I clutched at the cliffs to lift myself out of the waters I discovered that I was trying to attach myself to a sandbank. However, the sandbank gave way under my weight, and I found myself once again at the mercy of the waves which were fast receding and taking me away as they withdrew from the shore. The ocean was now a viscous mass of abandoned tails of huge lizards and monstrous basset-hounds. A feeling of infinite disgust and of intense fascination overcame me as I handled those slimy objects. At my touch, they burst into flames. Their dazzling brilliance made me shout, and the shout roused me from my slumbers.

On one occasion when aroused from sleep by such a nightmare, I got up from my bed to wash my temples in cold water. Outside the verandah there was a concert of cats. I threw some water in their direction to silence them and slunk back to my bed again, after having remade it. I verified the time: it was nearly two o'clock in the morning. As I lay awake with my eyes closed, I imagined menacing figures surrounding me and counselling me: 'You must remain pure—in word, thought and deed.' There were other voices which whispered: 'But you are impure. You have soiled your bed and your body. You are a monster.' I buried my head in my pillows: I did not want to listen to those eerie admonitors. As my eyes closed in sleep, my ears vaguely heard the chime; my hearing caught only the first stroke; I must have fallen asleep when the clocks sounded the second stroke.

My nightmare started again. This time the scene was set in a volcanic island whose rose-coloured sand beaches were strewn with beautiful harp-shells, conches and cowries. The spectacle thrilled me with a strange delight. I wanted to gather as many of these shells as I could in the cup of my folded hands. But somehow they proved to be elusive and slipped like quicksilver through my fingers. In trying to collect the shells I had overlooked the volcanoes. They were in eruption, and thus demanded my attention. As I watched them I became more engrossed in trying to recollect where I had seen them first: they seemed so lovable; those shapely mountains of gold grew out of a land at once familiar and unknown and I was not in the least surprised to find myself there. What attracted my scrutiny later was the form of the craters: they were like the bell-shaped structures ending in shining single pinnacles, which crown most Buddhist shrines—not unlike the Shwe Dagon Pagoda of Rangoon, or a Tibetan *Chorten*—the symbol of Nirvana; they were surmounted by glowing clusters of rubies. From these issued streams of quicksilver of dazzling brilliance. I knew it was burning lava and my safety lay in flight. But my legs refused to move. I was incapable of making the slightest movement. My whole body was paralysed—not from fear, but through fascination. While my conscious mind counselled me to run away, my unconscious inner self urged me to rush into the middle of the valley which separated the two mountains. Meanwhile, the air thickened, breathing became gradually and more difficult, and the flow of the silvery lava augmented; steadily it inundated the land, and its level rose. It flooded the spot where I stood transfixed. It came up to my knees, and then to my neck and finally to my lips. The lava tasted of brine and it burnt my mouth. I was drowning, yet my limbs were unwilling to move. When all of a sudden I discovered that I was no longer a human being, but a wriggling worm floating precariously in a sea of shining mercury.

It was a horrible feeling, and I yelled. I cried for succour. I shouted for my mother—for the mother I never knew and who had never known me—the fruit of a dead woman's womb. In response to my cry I found my phantom mother by my side, and she was trying to smother me by stuffing my mouth with handfuls of horsehair. I was nearly killed when the sound of a gong broke my nightmare and brought me back to life.

I sat up in my bed, and remained for a while in a huddled position, with my knees drawn to my chin. I was panting, as I usually did when awakened by nightmares and horrid dreams, and my whole frame was bathed in perspiration. My heart was pounding against my breast as though it would burst. I heard the same voices which accused me of impiety and impurity just before I had lost consciousness in sleep. They were breathing distinctly into my ears: 'Now you know you are impure. You are polluted. Your clothes are polluted. Your bed is polluted. Your bedstead is polluted. Your room is polluted. The air you breathe is polluted. You are pollution itself...'

The voices would, no doubt, have gone on in this way had not the clocks started chiming once again. All of them sounded one: just one stroke and no more. I shuddered at that sound—because the stroke of one amazed me. I got up to examine not only my watch but the clock in the passage as well as the timepiece on my writing desk. It was just two o'clock!

Between the two strokes of two—in the brief lapse of the time intervening between the first stroke and the second of the clocks, timekeepers, timepieces and watches, as well as of radium-dialled wrist-watch of mine—I had lived through an age-long adventure! Within a second I had fallen asleep and woken up, and in between I had journeyed to strange dreamlands and witnessed extraordinary scenes! 'That's unbelievable,' I said to myself.

'How do you measure the speed of thought?' I recall the village Punditji asking a fresh graduate of Experimental Psychology. I was then of tender years, and the subject of the discussion was certainly beyond my grasp. But I do remember that this graduate intensely disliked the Punditji's cross-examination, and paid little attention to what he had to say about Mila Repa, Asita, Asva Ghosha, Buddha Ghosha, and others who had written on the psychology of religious conversions.

'The speed of thought!' the graduate of Experimental Psychology muttered when the Punditji had left him. 'That's just a figure of speech. Even before I had opened my mouth he pretended that he knew what I had to say. Your old Punditji must be extremely ignorant. He thinks that Mila Repa and his crowd knew about Freudism long before Freud. Pavlov's discoveries do not seem to impress him very much. He is a crusted old bigot. How could Mila Repa know anything of Experimental Psychology when there were no laboratories?'

As I have just said, I was then too young to understand anything of the discussion between the Punditji and the young graduate of the University of Calcutta. But my mind did retain a few snatches of the Punditji's remarks, and these came back to my memory on that night.

'During the duration of a split second,' according to the Punditji, 'a man can live through an aeon.' He gave several instances from Sanskrit and Pali works, whose titles unfortunately evade my memory now. On another occasion I heard him tell the same student of Experimental Psychology: 'When confronted with a terrible crisis demanding an immediate decision, one man may within a fraction of a moment make a general survey of a lifetime's experiences for the appraisal of the situation. And another man may simply fall into a state of coma. Much depends on the man and his general upbringing.'

I wondered if my story would have interested the Punditji. Had I not known it for a fact that I had fallen asleep some time after the first stroke of two—at two o'clock in the morning—and wakened up in time to listen to the second stroke, I would not have believed that my nightmare about the bronze mountains emitting lava had lasted for less than a second.

The rest of the night I spent sitting on my bed, afraid of falling asleep lest more nightmares came to torture me. I thought of my past dreams, and of the curious interpretations different people gave to them, of the Dream Book of Artemidorus, and of many queer stories current in the Penhari Parganas.

~

A sleepwalker called Jadav was known for his habit of getting out of his bed in the middle of the night and roaming about fruit orchards in his sleep. A grove of jambolona trees had apparently a special attraction for him, and though fast asleep he would gather as many fallen fruits from the grounds as he could. Every morning he had to scrape his tongue: it was all blue with the juice of jambolona fruits he had swallowed during the night.

Some thought that Jadav's nocturnal outings were just dreams, while others realized they were true. 'Only too true,' reported the village watchman, Ramdas. 'One night Jadav may inadvertently pick up some poisonous fruit or root, one bite of which would kill him.'

'That would be a calamity,' remarked somewhat ironically those who thought that Jadav's sleepwalking was just a got-up story.

'It would be still worse,' said Ojha, a professional exorcist, 'if he tastes some of the magical herbs that change a man into a tiger. He would then be converted into a man-eater on the spot. Jadav would do well to get himself exorcized.'

Everyone except the watchman, Ramdas, laughed at the

exorcist. Some said: 'It is a fine story.' Jadav too thought the same. He accused Ojha of trying to make money out of him, and quarrelled over this affair. As Ojha did not belong to our village no one sided with him.

Not long afterwards the villagers discovered that Jadav's cottage was empty. He was to be found nowhere. He had simply vanished. As his disappearance coincided with the arrival of a man-eater in the neighbourhood some thought Ojha the exorcist was perhaps right; the man-eating tiger was Jadav transformed into an animal on account of his having inadvertently swallowed some magical herbs in his sleep, and he was getting even with some people he hated when he was a man.

Ojha the exorcist, too, became frightened. His village was not far from ours, and the distance of a few miles was nothing to a tiger. So he sought the aid of a *shikari,* and the man-eater was finally killed. It was found to be a *bora*—a tailless tiger.

'That proves,' declared Ojha the exorcist, 'this beast was a man. An ordinary tiger—a natural one—has a tail, and a very long one too. But a *bora*—a tiger without a tail—is a man transformed into an animal.'

Of course, no one knew if the man-eater was Jadav transformed into a tiger or if it was a natural animal which had devoured Jadav. In those circumstances it was decided to cremate the carcass as though it was a human corpse. The general consensus of opinion was that Jadav suffered from nightmares, and was led by his nocturnal visions to roam about in the dark till he killed himself either by falling inside a water-hole or by becoming the prey to a wild animal.

I thought of Jadav, and wondered if I too was destined to become a night-prowler. Were my nightmares just the beginning of my gradually becoming queer like Jadav and ending life in a horrible way? What made me think of Jadav, of tigers, and of tailless *boras*?

~

'A cataclysm,' they say in my village, 'may occur in the twinkling of an eye. A man sees a vision and ceases to be the same as before.' This saying reminded me of the incident which occurred some time ago in the palm grove of the village.

While on his way to a shrine an acolyte—a newcomer in our midst—accidentally got hit by a falling coconut. The blow felled him to the ground, but he managed to get to his feet almost immediately. Perhaps he was dazed for a second, and no more. But that second was long enough to bring about a profound change in him.

When the villagers ran to give him succour, he begged them to keep away from him.

'Why?' asked the surprised men and women.

'I have become polluted,' sobbed the young acolyte.

'Don't be silly,' they all laughed. 'We all saw you knocked down by a falling coconut. A coconut is not a lump of beef.'

'No,' the acolyte moaned. 'You do not know the truth. I have sinned and defiled myself.'

'With whom have you sinned? And when?'

'Even now,' replied the young man. 'With a tigress. Not a real one. But a woman who changed herself into an animal for my sake.'

'Now, now,' they murmured. 'What are you talking about? Where's the woman?'

'I don't know where she is just now. But it was she who hit me with that coconut.'

'Talk sense, young man. Do you think we are all crazy?'

'Let me then confess my sins,' began the acolyte and recounted how one year ago while passing through the very palm grove of the village he was accosted by a stranger who asked him if he knew what it felt like to be under a tiger's skin. On receiving a negative answer the stranger declared that he was a magician by profession, one well versed in the art of changing a man into a tiger and of restoring him into his human form. 'Though you are a priest's acolyte,' the magician added, 'it would do you no harm to see for yourself how I change myself every night into a tiger.'

'Goaded by curiosity,' the acolyte went on, 'I followed the magician and accepted his offer to be in his service for one year. My daily work in his house was simple: every evening when it became dark I had to tie round his neck a charmed necklace, which immediately changed him into a huge Bengal tiger, and in the morning when the tiger came back home I had to remove the string of beads to retransform him into a man.'

What the magician did during the night in the shape of a tiger, the acolyte did not know: the question did not interest him; but it did intrigue the magician's wife. One evening after the magician had left the house, the acolyte asked his master's wife: 'Why does not the master ask you to put the charm round his neck? That would be much simpler than keeping me here for that purpose.' 'He is afraid of me,' replied the woman. 'He fears I may make a knot in the string of magic beads and prevent him from becoming a man again.' 'But why should he suspect you of having such intentions?' 'You are too young to understand,' the woman smiled and gave him a curious look. 'But you will learn in due course.' Some days later they heard that a woman in the neighbouring village had given birth to a tiger cub. At this the magician's wife whispered to the acolyte: 'From to-morrow I shall be a merry widow. I am ready to lay a wager that as soon as it becomes day they will bring to this house a pair of dead tigers. Perhaps you will help me to skin them.'

The novice failed to understand why the arrival of two dead tigers in the morning made the magician's wife sing light-heartedly. Anyway, he heard the *shikaris* profusely thank her for having informed them that the fruit garden of the woman who had borne a tiger cub was the mating-place of a pair of man-eaters after dusk. The riddle, however, came to be solved the moment the acolyte noticed both the carcasses were garlanded with charmed beads, one necklace was the very same he had tied round the magician's neck on the previous evening. 'What are you waiting for?' the magician's wife snapped at him as soon as the *shikaris* were gone. 'Shut the door, and skin the tigers before we remove the charms. Can't you see they have brought me the bodies of my husband and his lady-love—the woman who bore him a tiger cub?'

The amazed young man was then told by the magician's widow that she was determined to make up for her lost days, or rather, nights: she wanted to have a good time with him. 'But,' the novice protested, 'I have taken the vow of chastity. I cannot break it.' 'In that case,' the woman counselled, 'let us change ourselves into tigers. It would be no sin if you make love to me in the shape of an animal. Moreover it would be fun to see what it feels like to be under a tiger's skin.' All remonstrance was of no avail. The magician's wife made him tie a charmed necklace round her neck at the same time as she did likewise with him. And they were both transformed into tigers.

'Since that day,' the sobbing acolyte told the villagers, 'I have been sinning with her regularly. To tell you the truth only a few minutes ago I was embracing her in this very palm grove.'

'Then how have you become a man again?' they asked.

'As soon as our embrace was over,' the young man continued, 'she complained of thirst and wanted to drink some coconut milk. I was asked to climb a tree and get her a few coconuts. This I refused to do, which made her very angry. She then scaled a coconut tree herself like an agile monkey. It made me dizzy to watch her go up and up. "Look out," I heard her growl all of a sudden. "Take this coconut on your head. You are a lazy brute." And down came the coconut on my neck and smashed the charmed necklace. So I have become a man once more.'

'Never have we seen a tigress climb a coconut tree!' the villagers declared. They shook their heads. They would certainly have believed his story had he not referred to the very last incident about the tigress's scaling a coconut palm. 'Young acolyte,' they said, 'you have simply been dreaming. You lost your consciousness for a second, and that was enough to cloud your mind with nightmares and dreams. Your talk about your sinning is all rubbish. It is no use telling us fabulous stories in broad daylight. At least wait till it is dark.'

The poor acolyte, however, refused to be consoled. He kept on sobbing and asking for the purification ceremony: he wanted expiation of his sins. The villagers did not know what to do with him. There was not the slightest trace of any tiger's footprints in the palm grove nor anywhere in the neighbourhood of the village. It was perfectly clear that he was suffering from hallucinations. Finally they decided to consult the Punditji.

'If the acolyte believes he has sinned,' the Punditji gave his opinion, 'the sin lies on him. And he should go through the expiation ceremony.'

'But,' protested the villagers, 'we saw him with our own eyes walking alone through the palm grove and getting knocked down by a coconut. This account of mating with a tigress is just a yarn. He must have been dreaming when he lost his senses.'

'Dreams or no dreams,' the Punditji propounded, 'his sin lies not in the deed, but in the very thought of an action he deems to be sinful.'

II

'If a man believes he has sinned,' I repeated to myself the Punditji's saying, 'the sin is on his conscience. The belief makes him a transgressor. The thought has robbed him of purity. And he shall find no peace till he has expiated.'

It was a melancholy reflection. It tormented me. My mind became agitated. For no logical reason as far as I could make out my resentment rose against Roma. I imagined her to be the tigress responsible for the fall of the poor acolyte.

She was held accountable by my irrational inner ego for my nightly trials and daily repentance.

Rarely did my elusive hidden self allow my conscious mind to have the final say. I knew its decrees were illogical. But those decrees swayed me, and made my existence a torture. Why was I so emotional and so easily affected by the comments and events of little importance to others? Was it due to the soil where I first saw the light of day?

I recalled vividly the obstinate, and logically untenable attitude of a Penhari peasant on the occasion when he was wholeheartedly supported by my villagers. This man's horse had been requisitioned—I forget for what purpose. Maybe, at a time when the dykes were on the point of breaking and every available beast of burden was commandeered for carrying rubble to strengthen their walls. Whatever that might have been, owing to some confusion our peasant did not get his own horse back, but a substitute—a better one. He refused it point blank. 'I want my own animal,' he insisted. 'It was an old nag, blind of one eye. It had a limp. I don't want a fine horse in its exchange. Neither do I want any money. For it was not worth anything in hard cash. If I take a better horse or any money it would be sin.'

Those born in the Penhari Parganas are not logical in their ways. They lack common sense. 'And,' I said to myself, 'I am one of them. Moreover, I have in my vein some Chandernagore blood too. Men of Chandernagore are said to be crazy about pretty women.'

What kind of queer amalgam was I? A bundle of contradictions: dogmatic, biased and warped.

~

What good did it do me to quarrel with Chumchicke Adhikari and to keep up a perpetual feud with him? He was the only man genuinely interested in the undergraduates of the University and particularly in those going in for the Teacher's Diploma. He was always at their service. The so-called Welfare Officers were mere nincompoops compared with him: not one of them ever bothered to find out the problems that worried the young students, nor were they much concerned about their interests. Yet, most foolishly, I argued and debated with Chumchicke Adhikari on more than one occasion.

My first dispute with him was, as I have already said, ever a purely theoretical issue: the relative aesthetic values of the Russian ballet *Les Biches* and our traditional village dance called the *Kajri*. The second—a more serious disagreement—was also connected with dancing: the advantages of appreciating European ballroom deportment.

Chumchicke Adhikari wanted the future teachers to learn Western dancing. 'One day,' he told us, 'some of you will certainly be going to Germany and then to Russia with Mexican passports, and perhaps to other parts of the world as well.' 'But we have no money for travelling,' we all deplored. 'There are so few travelling fellowships.' 'You need not bother about money.' Chumchicke Adhikari gave us his assurance. 'I will see to it that you receive invitations from abroad. But when you are in Rome, remember, you will have to do as the Romans do. Therefore, you must learn ballroom dancing. In all international gatherings—in Europe and in America—the participants are expected to be sociable, and it is an essential feature of sociability in the West to take part in ballroom dancing.'

It was, of course, out of the question for Chumchicke Adhikari to arrange for dancing lessons in the College Square area. (The real reason for his failure to secure a floor might have been something other than the explanation he then furnished. Perhaps it was due to the ridiculous names of the steps he wanted us to learn: 'Camel Walk', 'Goin' Doggo', 'Yussur! That's My Baby', 'Yes! We have no bananas', 'I miss my Swiss Miss' and others similarly titled.) 'The Indian Penal Code,' we were told, 'is a strange weapon. It can be twisted in any way by the authorities to suit their purpose. A man's house can be raided on the flimsiest of pretexts: it may be searched by the police on the mere suspicion of harbouring a criminal, or perhaps, because they think there is a gambling party in the inner courtyard. And the Indian Penal Code will uphold this arbitrary violation of privacy by the police. Any irresponsible person can walk into a police station and accuse his neighbour of living immorally with his housekeeper, and such is the beauty of our Penal Code that the police will be expected to render every aid to such a blackmailer and raid the neighbour's house to suppress immorality.'

Not knowing anything about law I ought to have remained quiet. But being troublesome I started fretting: 'What is he driving at?'

Finally, came the answer why lessons in ballroom dancing could not be arranged in the College Square area: the Indian Penal Code demanded a licence, and such a licence entitled the police to walk in at any time to our soirées without being invited. 'We don't want the police to sneak in at our meetings. Do you all agree?' asked Chumchicke Adhikari.

'Agreed,' we all shouted.

'That being the case,' he continued, 'it would be well to go to a place which already has a licence to have a band. Your Students' Union card will give you free admittance to the premises I have in mind. There you will have the additional advantage of fraternizing with the seamen of all countries.'

'It would be of special interest to those learning foreign languages,' added a woman who accompanied Chumchicke Adhikari. She was said to be the mathematics teacher in the Burra Bazaar Polytechnic. 'There you will meet seafaring people from all parts of the world. You may, if you want to, speak to them in their own language. You will also learn there another great lesson: how to acclimatize yourself to an international crowd. There are other significant points as well. The days when the university students belonged to the so-called middle classes are over. You belong to the proletariat as much as the seamen do. You do not know anything about your future. You may or may not be hired to do a teacher's job when you have finished your studies. The seamen too do not know their future. They are hired for a trip and when the trip is over they may or may not be hired for a second time in their life. Their future is one of uncertainty. So is yours. You are mariners on the sea of uncertainty. You are the brethren of all seamen of the world.'

The mathematics teacher at Burra Bazaar Polytechnic went on in this vein for a full hour. Had I been shrewd I should have drawn my conclusions from such a speech, and left the matter of ballroom dancing at that. But shrewdness was not one of my virtues, and the temptation of learning something new overcame me: I stayed on, and I heard that our lessons would be given in the Ultra-Modern Sailors' Lido and Water-front Cabaret in Kidderpore.

Apart from mastering the art of ballroom dancing, I thought of learning on the sly some seamen's steps: solo dances. Even in the Penhari Parganas—to say nothing of Chandernagore—sailors were reputed to be eternally jolly. 'It would be such fun to spring a surprise on my villagers by giving some sailor's solo dances in the main square,' I rubbed my hands and applauded my wonderful foresight.

And then—who could tell?—I might, I thought, come across some remote descendants of such wonderful seadogs as Bourdonnais and Bougainville, Vasco da Gama and Magellan, Drake, Cook and Nelson. 'If I come across a fellow called Watson,' I said to myself, 'I shall give him a piece of my mind and tell him that Admiral Watson used ruse to silence the guns of Fort Orleans at Chandernagore. On the twenty-third of March, 1758, a cannon ball from Admiral Watson's man-of-war knocked off the gnomon of the sundial in my Grandmother's house.'

An atrocious oleograph entitled 'The Boyhood of Raleigh' haunted my mind. It was one of those excruciatingly painful things with which a well-intentioned lunatic had garnished an exhibition of 'British Art in Reproduction'. (This exhibition was said to be a counter-blast to Chumchicke Adhikari's infinitely more interesting rival show, 'Anti-bourgeois Art of Renoir, Matisse, Chagall and Picasso.') But as Chumchicke Adhikari went on exposing the benefits of going to the dock area to learn ballroom dancing, my heart softened, and gradually I became charitable about the bogus piece of art known as 'The Boyhood of Raleigh' or 'The Childhood of Raleigh' or whatever else it might be. 'As a painting,' I reflected, 'it is pure junk compared with contemporary French canvases, but as a pictorial anecdote it is interesting.' It told of Raleigh, a great sailor and a great writer. In a way, Millais's picture fulfilled its function. Was that not enough?

'You must not,' Profulla Babu often told me, 'expect the impossible from an English artist. England's weather and England's religion make it unlikely for English painters to reach a high standard. Certainly they are far below the average level of the French. But when it comes to their seamen, England's superiority is absolutely unchallenged.' 'Every sailor,' I reached the conclusion, 'in the Kidderpore Cabaret will tell me a lot about Raleigh—just as our peasants in the Penhari Parganas will readily recount yarns about our famous wrestlers.'

Moreover, I had promised myself, long before coming to Calcutta, not to miss anything that interested other students. To back up my decision to spend every Saturday evening in the Kidderpore district, I thought of the Punditji's saying: 'To be wise one must explore many things—both pleasant and unpleasant.'

With high hopes I went to the Ultra-Modern Sailors' Lido and Water-front Cabaret accompanied by a jaundiced student from City College. This poor fellow was congenitally jaundiced and at the same time he suffered, I gathered, from *hæmalopia*. He seemed to be pretty proud of his diseases, and explained to me that hæmalopia was a defect of vision, which turned everything seen into red. 'Seeing red,' I said, to cut short his account of innumerable ills to which he and other human beings were liable to be subjected. Perhaps it was imprudent of me to have had such a companion, and maybe his hæmalopia was temporarily transferred to me. Whatever might have been the cause, I began seeing red as soon as I stepped inside the Sailors' Lido and Waterfront Cabaret, and had to come back home—to my hostel—soon afterwards, with my tail between my legs like a severely whipped dog. A chucker-out aided by a dozen sailors—descendants of Raleigh, Drake, Nelson and Cook—threw me out of the place.

The trouble started on account of my sarcastic remarks to Chumchicke Adhikari on what he called modern ballroom dancing.

'You call that dancing!' I taunted. 'Why, that's the same as the hopping of monkeys. It is ugly. It is painfully vulgar.'

'This is a foul place,' loudly wailed the jaundiced student from City College. 'This is an immoral place.' He began blubbering that he had promised his mother to remain pure till he had finished his studies. 'The place is full of decoy women. The atmosphere is revolting.'

A few other students too murmured that it was not what they had expected. The victim of jaundice and hæmalopia broke down and began sobbing about his mother: he was a perfect ass. On account of that donkey's hee-hawing I got into deeper waters than I had anticipated.

Chumchicke Adhikari lost his patience, and accused me of being the ringleader of all trouble-makers. Someone shouted that I was 'a stooge' and this cry was taken up by a number of Presidency College fellows. One of the 'hostesses' who had just begun a floor-show stopped her performance to come up to me and accuse me of being the result of an abortion.

'Not of abortion,' I corrected her. 'But of Caesarean section.' This she misunderstood to be some sort of abuse or criticism hurled at her.

'Take that,' she said as she slapped my face. 'And take that for calling me a decoy woman.' By now a dozen people were pummelling me.

~

In the dark, huddled up in my bed I tried to analyse what was wrong with me. 'To know the real cause of a disease,' they say in my village, 'is half-cure.' I wanted to cure my shortcomings which made me so difficult in the company of Chumchicke Adhikari's favourites.

The atmosphere of the dancing hall in the Sailors' Lido and Water-front Cabaret was undoubtedly revolting. But there was something more that made me quarrel with everyone in the place: it was frustrated hope. I had looked forward to an evening of romance—something of surpassing beauty, of such exquisiteness that its very memory would thrill my inner being, and bring that peace which is associated with visions of glory.

It was asinine to expect too much—particularly in a district of Calcutta where no sane man would search for things lovely. Yet, strange as it may sound, I had hoped for such a discovery. I had looked forward to discern—in a quarter known to be grim—sights that would remind me of the Rajput illuminations of 'Lovers' Tryst at Night,' Whistler's 'Cremona Gardens,' 'The Showman' of Seurat,' and Uccello's 'Stag-hunt by Night.'

What led me to search for beauty in such a sordid haunt?

Calcutta's squalor was overpowering, and I was unhappy. But in spite of my misery and loneliness and general dissatisfaction, I did notice Beauty at times furtively unveil her face in the midst of the grim city's quagmire. She crossed my path when I least expected to encounter her.

'She is a shy goddess,' they say. 'She shuns the throngs. Nevertheless, she never wholly forsakes them nor any realm, however wretched. For without her men would be changed into beasts.'

How true this saying is I realized the day I saw Beauty bless a group of half-naked street urchins: she made her appearance only for a moment; the instant these children suddenly rushed forward to retrieve a stray paper-kite; the pattern the boys and girls formed just for one brief second was an adornment for Urvashi's garment. On another occasion, she appeared in a different form: I was then watching indifferently a motley collection of idle spectators, troublesome busybodies, curious loafers and exasperated tram-drivers cajoling an obstinate Brahmany bull lying sedately across the rails of a tramway; there was nothing interesting in that—stray cattle are as big a nuisance as the crows in Calcutta—but the scene changed unexpectedly; suddenly the bull got to its feet, espying an intruding rival zebu, and the people ran helter-skelter, endowing the spectacle before my eyes with a liveliness that had Beauty's grace; thus I saw a tableau worthy of a master craftsman's undivided attention. 'Now you are here,' I breathed my prayer to Urvashi, 'Beauty incarnate! Glorious Coryphasa of the incomparable Apsaras. Blessed be thou!'

In an unfrequented, narrow, labyrinthe and sunless passage—called Cut-throats' Lane—I often passed and repassed a blind wall, bulging with age and overhung with chaotic tangles of grime-laden foliage; it evoked no emotion in me save that of sheer boredom. Rarely did I bestow on it more than a cursory glance as I threaded my way along its side. But the hour I perceived an unexpected shaft of bright sunbeam striking it to reveal the intricate artistry of its cracks and to paint the silhouetted shadows of the suddenly illuminated leaves into palpable patterns of intense blue, I held my breath in amazement, and stood transfixed to the spot: I contemplated and marvelled; at the touch of Urvashi's magic fingers the monotonous excrescence of a wall flanking the drab and dark and crooked Cut-throats' Lane took on an unfamiliar air of enthralling enchantment; it was a picture of hypnotic fascination. It was a benediction to gaze on it.

Such scenes as well as other gifts that Beauty bestows everywhere were not unperceived by me. I rejoiced in them: the glimpse of a haunting face, at once familiar and strange in the midst of a moving crowd; the charm of a graceful gesture—maybe, in the deliberate swing of the bare limbs of a burdened body; the sight of a pair of dancing birds that loved to be fed by me; the magic in the harmony of well-chosen words ...

All these, I knew, could be found in such areas of Calcutta as came within my usual orbit. My heart, however, yearned for visions yet unseen. 'I don't want to miss anything,' I repeated to myself a hundred times. 'There must be some corners in this city of many millions where everything is beautiful. It is impossible that Calcutta should have received its original epithet without any justification whatsoever. A hundred years ago it was called the City of Palaces and Pleasure Gardens. Palaces have undoubtedly vanished, but what of the Pleasure Gardens? There ought to be some vestiges of them. Perhaps I shall find some remnants of them in the water-front district. Maybe, the Ultra-Modern

Sailors' Lido and Water-front Cabaret will bring home to me the beauty of Venice at carnival.'

~

Chumchicke Adhikari's soirée dansante was very different from what I had longed for. My disappointment was indeed great. But behind that disappointment lay, I suspected, my irrational inner self.

Looking back, my dissatisfaction with Roma was equally unjustifiable. At that time, however, I did not take it in this way. All that I did was to repeat to myself as I lay sleepless in my bed: 'Roma's stock of filthy words is beyond my comprehension. She behaved like a common tart before that vast crowd in the Chandni Bazaar Crescent.... She is shameless. She behaved like a common tart...'

III

During the day my mood was different: I was repentant, for having harboured harsh thoughts against Roma. My changing frame of mind led to my excessive shyness before her, or to equally unjustifiable bumptiousness: I tried to be what I was not, and that led to my confusion.

I do not know what made me tell her about my misadventure in the Modern Lido and Water-front Cabaret and Chumchicke Adhikari's newest undertakings for promoting international cultural contacts. She just laughed, and joked. 'It might have done you some good,' she said, 'if you had explored further your contact with Adhikari's decoy women.'

I was really shocked. But she did not take me seriously.

Though she listened to me patiently with a face of assumed gravity her eyes brimmed with sly mirth.

'What do you say to all that?' I asked as I ended my recital of the agonies of the student from City College—the one whose mother expected him to remain chaste till he had finished his studies.

'He, too, should have tried out one of the decoy girls,' she twittered.

I did not say a word more, but asked myself: 'Is that not the language of a common tart?'

~

'But what is a common tart? What is she like?' I interrogated myself, and discovered that my information was nil or as good as nil.

Long before coming to Calcutta I had put that question to Kolej Huzoor who was then studying at Burdwan Raj College. During a holiday he had come to my village to spend some time with a relative. He often talked to me about his knowledge of the world and about *smart women* in Burdwan and other big towns. Such women, according to him, were divided into many categories: 'Hostesses', 'ex-Coriphées', 'Would-be Coriphées', 'Nautch Girls', 'Bayadères', 'Sports', 'Peaches', 'Bombay Ducks', 'Lucknow Ladies', 'Pagoda Trees' and so on. The list he gave was more impressive than the Latin terminology of different cloud-formations. He ended up with advice: 'If you don't want trouble, avoid a common tart. An uncommon one is a different story. But a plain tart must be avoided at all costs.'

'How am I to know who is common and who is uncommon?' I asked innocently.

'That's difficult to explain to an oaf,' he mumbled. He thought for a moment, knitted his eyebrows, and wanted to know my exact age. When I gave him my age, he puffed his cheeks and whistled; he then proposed my accompanying him straight away to Burdwan. This, of course, was out of the question for the time being as he wanted something like fifteen rupees for the lesson, how to distinguish between a common tart and an uncommon one. And I had not that sum in my post-office account.

Later on, I came across a lot of money quite unexpectedly—somewhere near fifty rupees for acting as a guide to Jogin-Da, and Kolej Huzoor willingly undertook to look after what he called my 'initiation ceremony' in the Mahajantooli district of Burdwan.

'Remember,' he counselled, 'for a common tart there is no need for a go-between. Neither do you leave any tips for her maid. If you do, you are a sucker. First, because she hasn't one; secondly, you will be then fleeced to the skin. She will ask for an additional rupee, and then for your purse to keep it as a souvenir. She is a gold-digger and a brazen one at that. Therefore, it is dangerous to go to a common tart for fun.'

'And with an uncommon one? What must I do?'

'Tip her maid generously,' Kolej Huzoor advised. 'Remember, her maid is not an ordinary maid, but an apprentice. One day she may become an artiste. You should bear that in mind. Sometimes the maid is prettier than the mistress. In fact, a well-known artiste will have a dozen maids: all her apprentices. You may tip them either individually or collectively.'

'And how do I tip the mistress? I mean the artiste.'

'You don't tip her at all. Only an ass would think of tipping an artiste. You offer her your gift and the fee is slipped in with it,' He then explained how it was imperative to give all such women some present whenever one called on them—except to the common tarts, because, I understood, one never called on them. 'You just pick them up, and later curse yourself for your folly.'

I also gathered from him that all *smart women* bedecked themselves with expensive jewellery, and it was owing to them that the artisans and goldsmiths of Calcutta, Benares, Burdwan, and other cities were flourishing. They were also the most faithful patronesses of merchants in precious stones, like diamonds, emeralds, rubies, sapphires and *neelas*. And no *smart woman* worth speaking of would dream of beginning her trade without owning at least five thousand rupees' worth of necklaces, bracelets, bangles, anklets, rings and other ornaments.

'I thought women took to this profession because they had no money.'

'You may think anything you like.' Kolej Huzoor looked at me with profound scorn. 'A lot of novelists also think in that way and write a lot of nonsense, and a lot of fools waste time and money reading such novels.'

I felt ashamed of my ignorance, and let him have his say without any further interruption.

'An artiste,' he began again, 'a real artiste takes to her profession because she is born to it: she is born for it and she lives for it; it is her vocation. She is like a man of genius. Kabir was born to be a poet though his ancestral profession was weaving. Tulsi Das was born to write epics though for generations his people were ploughmen. The same is the case with the true artistes in the Mahajantooli district of Burdwan and in the Pagoda Tree quarter of Calcutta, and in other places. From the day of her birth, the inner daemon prepares an artiste for the exercise of her gifts.'

'I see,' I mumbled in admiration of Kolej Huzoor's ability to explain complicated matters to an ignorant youth like myself. I wished, nevertheless, that he were less verbose.

'But,' he went on, 'that is not the case with common tarts. A tart is a woman who has talents for nothing and a hatred for work, and along with it a weak mind. She takes to whoring as a monkey takes to pilfering without going through any apprenticeship or training. She may maintain a pimp, who takes away her earnings, but that has nothing to do with her character in general. Though idiotic novelists have written a lot of junk about a common tart's desire for affection and love and such sentiments, you can take it from me, a common tart is incapable of loving, just as a colour-blind person is incapable of distinguishing colours.'

I nodded to indicate that I was listening to him carefully.

'I shall take you to the home of an artiste,' he declared. 'You will see for yourself how she lives in the residential part of Mahajantooli. But tell me first, how much would you like to spend for a really good time? Remember, for an initiation ceremony there are *smart women* who would gladly pay you money instead of your spending a cent. But I would not advise that for you. Come with me to the Mahajantooli district of Burdwan. I shall fix up something worthwhile for you.'

I did go with Kolej Huzoor to Burdwan one afternoon, and made an ass of myself.

Evidently Kolej Huzoor had made a date—not with one, but with a houseful of artistes, and had forgotten to tell me about that. Furthermore, he had not given me the least hint about the hierarchy of the artistes. I got confused even before entering the house of the accomplished ladies of the Mahajantooli district. It suddenly struck me that it was perhaps sinful to enter that area, and I wanted to back out of the whole affair at the last moment. 'You can't do that,' Kolej Huzoor said firmly. 'You can't let them down. Where is your sense of honour? A man's word is his bond. You are expected and if you don't come with me I shall lose face. It is not friendly of you to let me down. It was you who started the conversation about tarts.' Like a sacrificial goat brought to the altar of the goddess Kali I was literally dragged up the Mahajantooli Road. To avoid a scene in the street I had no choice but to do what he wanted, and then all of a sudden he told me he was suffering from bellyache and wanted to get to a friend's house. The friend's house proved to be the residence of the artistes. In the circumstances one may well imagine my perplexity.

In my confusion I began making a fool of myself by tipping the wrong person. The one I thought to be the maid was the mistress!

A mistress of a house, in my reckoning, was to be an elderly person, or at least, semi-elderly: someone resembling one of my aunts like Mashi-Ma of the Penhari Parganas or Mummi-Ma of Chandernagore. But my assumption was totally wrong. In that place it was impossible to distinguish the ladies by their looks, dresses and ornaments. How was I to know who were the apprentices and who were the friends and who were the women visitors and the musicians? As ill-luck would have it the person who took charge of my shoes was the mistress herself and I tipped her.

The floor was covered with a thick carpet and there were cushions and bolsters neatly arranged round the walls. There were a number of traditional low tables—ottomans—all brightly lacquered furniture. As soon as I was pushed into the entrance hall by Kolej Huzoor I knew I was lost. Anyway, I had enough sense to realize that the inmates of the place lived in what we call the old-fashioned way, and it was best for me to kick off my shoes once I was beyond the threshold. The person who rushed to help me remove my footgear was, as I have said, the artiste herself, or to be more correct, the mistress-artiste, who had at least a dozen young women as her pupils, and she looked the youngest!

Had I not been confused I would not have shoved a folded five-rupee note at her, for I did perceive that the palms of her hands were dyed red with henna and her nails were gilded and her gold-hemmed sari was excessively transparent. Her toenails too were gilded. My common sense ought to have told me that no maid on God's earth could gad about running errands and doing shopping for her mistress dressed in such finery. What misled me was the large number of heavy bangles on her arms: in the Penhari Parganas peasant women load themselves with such armlets of bronze or brass, and in the semi-obscurity of the passage the gold ornaments of the mistress looked very much the same as the cheap jewellery of our country women.

My gaffe was overlooked by the kind lady. In fact I would not have realized my mistake had not Kolej Huzoor made a whoop like a langur monkey; he began bellowing in a way that made the whole house shake. 'Old boy!' he bawled, 'you make me laugh. Show her rather the present you have brought with you. She is the artiste who will look after your initiation.'

I did not hear the end of his sentence because I became extremely upset, though I am sure the rest of the house heard it. The whole locality must have been disturbed by his bellowing and roarings and idiotic outbursts of laughter. I blushed at his bad manners and became tongue-tied.

My silence was interpreted by Kolej Huzoor—on what authority I do not know—as my disapproval of the looks of the artiste, or perhaps of her talents: I had no knowledge either of the one or of the other: I sat with my gaze fixed on the patterns of the carpet and did not dare look anywhere else.

There was little chance of my doing any clear thinking, for Kolej Huzoor was jabbering all the time about me: how he had undertaken the painful task of letting me know something about the facts of life.

I felt like telling him to shut up: every country child knows from the day he starts toddling all about the mysteries of animal breeding, and he puts two and two together to draw his own conclusions. Kolej Huzoor, being an ass, wanted to show himself off and started talking about my desire to back out of the engagement with the artiste at the last moment. This made my situation still more awkward.

'Bibi-Jan,' Kolej Huzoor addressed the artiste, 'I hope you will not mind if my friend shows a liking for one of your sisters.'

What warranted that shameless donkey to speak on my behalf in that fashion?

'I tell you,' he went on as though speaking through a megaphone to inform the whole district, 'my friend lives in the land of the Santals. There the girls wear nothing. *Mairi*! I swear on my mother's head! They wear absolutely nothing. Just a fig leaf. Grown-up girls and women as well. They go about stark naked. Some do at times put on a fringe of grass—just here. What do you say to that? And that oaf has never thought of having a good time with any of them.'

'Perhaps he is shy,' one of the many ladies ventured to remark in my defence. But Kolej Huzoor brushed that argument aside. He was determined to give a cock-and-bull version of his holidays in my village and how he came to know me; then followed a spate of lies the like of which I have never heard in my life: how he ran the risk of being assaulted by every woman he came across in the Penhari Parganas, how they all wept when his holidays came to an end, how he had to tear himself away from their embraces.

'They are all very hot, you know,' he repeated a dozen times. 'In spite of that my oaf of a friend knows nothing about the facts of life. So I decided to look after his education.'

I said nothing. Even if my tongue had moved I would not have spoken a word: anyone with a grain of sense would not, I am sure, believe a word of Kolej Huzoor's nonsensical rubbish.

Instead of leaving me in peace, he suddenly decided to regale me with his monkeyish suggestions: 'Old boy! Does not Bibi-Jan please you at all? What about Durga? She is the one in the saffron sari. Give her the glad eye, old boy. Can't you see she is smiling. Are you for outsizes? If so, just tell me. You are in a flower garden, my friend, and you have every choice.'

'Would you care for some music?' Bibi-Jan asked me as she offered me some *pan* and spices.

I wanted to thank her, but my tongue remained glued in my mouth. Kolej Huzoor found my embarrassment highly entertaining and began guffawing once again.

'Can't you see he is shy?' remarked one of the ladies. 'Perhaps he would like some dancing. Or does he prefer music?'

'Music! Ho!' Kolej Huzoor shouted as he slapped me on the back. 'Where's your flute, old boy? Show the ladies what you are capable of.'

The idiot knew perfectly well that I had not brought my flute with me, and even if I had had it with me it would not have been possible in the state I was in to produce a single note.

'*Music has charms*!' he began again. To show off his knowledge of the outer world he repeated his ejaculation in English: for whose benefit I could not make out. 'Old boy! Let us have *Kamod Ragini*. Or would you care for *Ragini Todi*? Even the wild hart is tamed by *Ragini Todi*. Well, this is your show. You make up your mind.'

The ladies got busy with their musical instruments. Bibi-Jan, noticing that I had not tasted her *pan*, offered me once again the silver platter on which folded leaves of piper betel covered with decorative gold foils were neatly arranged. I shook my head and refused her offer: Jogin-Da's advice came to my mind: 'Never accept anything from a total stranger. It may contain drugs.'

I thought of Jogin-Da, and became hot and dizzy. What would he have said if he suddenly came into the room and found me sitting cross-legged on the floor and Kolej Huzoor stretched at full length with his head on the lap of Durga and his hands pawing two of Durga's companions. Though all the windows were wide open and the room adjoined a long verandah—there was as much fresh air as one could ask for—it seemed to me that the whole place was stuffy. Perhaps that was owing to the smoke of the hookah which was produced for Kolej Huzoor's benefit. Or was the atmosphere drugged? Unwittingly my thoughts roamed, and I recalled an account I had read somewhere of a police officer decoyed into a cellar filled with chloroform vapour: his death was a foregone conclusion, but he defeated Fate by making a superhuman effort before it was too late.

I jumped up and made a dash for the door without bothering to collect my shoes.

How I came out of the house without stumbling on the steps remains even now a mystery to me. Once out in the open air I felt better. Before me was a fountain. As I bathed my temples in its sparkling water I felt my usual self again, or perhaps even better—a bit of a swell. I looked around me hoping to see at least some 'smart' Raj College students about. Unfortunately there were none. I was anxious to create the impression that I too was as 'smart' as any of them. Was I not coming out of a house full of artistes? In theory at least, I was no longer a complete oaf.

Under the trees on the opposite side of the Square of the Fountain stood a girl of about my height. She was whistling from time to time. She must have seen me dashing out of the 'sporting house'. Was she making fun of me? I examined her through the corner of my eyes without turning my head, and felt a bit more assured: she seemed not to be concerned with me. I took out my handkerchief to wipe my forehead. Something fell to the ground: it was the present intended for the artiste who was to initiate me into the mysteries of love-making.

What was I to do with it? It was an otto-container—tastefully hidden in a rose of gold and silver—a lovely piece of filigree work. I could not take it back home. If it came to be detected it would cause an infinity of bother—explanations and counter-explanations with my aunt Mashi-Ma with whom I was then living: she was not quite as accommodating as Mummi-Ma of Chandernagore. And there was the risk of Jogin-Da being summoned to lecture me on the need of leading a virtuous life. I might have been an oaf, but was sufficiently alert to know that any sign of my ever having stepped inside a 'sporting house' would have caused an earthquake in the household. The best thing was therefore to get rid of my rose.

I heard the girl whistle again. Was she whistling for me? I admired her boldness. It was clever of her to attract my attention in that way.

The Mahajantooli district of Burdwan, I assumed, was exclusively inhabited by 'smart women' as well as some common street-walkers, and only 'the cheapest' of them solicited openly during the night. Apart from the women of this last category, all the others met their 'guests' by appointment—rendezvous, arranged through an intermediary. As it was getting dark, I drew my own conclusions about the girl who was whistling: she was certainly one of the cheapest the cheap; otherwise she would not have started soliciting at dusk.

I looked around again to make sure that there was no one else about. The place was absolutely deserted but for us two: myself and the girl. There had been a dog swimming in the basin of the fountain a few minutes ago, but it was no longer there. It was therefore perfectly clear that she was whistling for me. I felt suddenly bold and highly flattered. No one had ever thought of soliciting me in that way, and here was a nice girl who considered me old enough to be openly invited.

I swaggered up to her, scrutinizing her from head to foot and from foot to head as I approached her. The expression of her face pleased me immensely. The way she pouted her lips as she whistled made her more attractive. Her eyes were large, somewhat almond-shaped. She wore a simple blue sari and no jewellery save a pair of thin bangles of crystal, or maybe plain glass. 'Poor thing,' I said to myself, 'she must be the poorest of the poor. For even the most destitute woman in my village or in Chandernagore would have a few more expensive trinkets on her. She cannot be a widow, otherwise she would not have a blue sari on.' The more I examined her the more I found her charming.

How was I to open my conversation with her?

'In countries where it rains in all seasons,' Kolej Huzoor asserted, 'the opening move is easy: one starts with some indifferent remarks about the weather. For example, "It looks like rain" or "It's going to be fine". In Germany you click your heels and bend the upper part of your body stiffly and murmur, "Fräulein! Haven't we met somewhere before?" Remember, in Germany it is important that you should click your heels.' That jackass of a talking machine whose brain worked like a mechanical calculator had told me nothing whatsoever about the opening gambit in a place like Burdwan, especially when it was fine.

In Burdwan as in the rest of Lower Bengal the weather rarely varies from day to day during a season; if it is fine it is bound to remain so for nine months, and when it rains it pours, and keeps on pouring night and day for three months. 'Only a prize lunatic,' I debated within me, 'would refer to weather in a place like Burdwan.' As for clicking my heels, it was out of the question: my shoes were in the entrance hall of the 'sporting house'. If I had been in Paris I could, of course, have profited from Kolej Huzoor's instructions. 'Allow me, Madame,' I would have declared, 'the honour to *trinquer* with you. Grant this favour to a stranger who wants to drink to the health of a most sympathetic person, to your health, Madame.' However, I was not in Manchester, nor in Berlin, nor in Paris, but in Burdwan—in the heart of the Mahajantooli district by the Square of the Dolphin Fountain, and the girl before me was neither English nor German nor French, but Bengali—a most pretty Bengali girl—with exotic almond-shaped eyes and an oval face with a pointed chin.

Not knowing what to do I gave a nervous cough. At this she turned her face towards me, and smiled. 'Judge a woman by her smile,' they say, 'and a man by his cough.' Hers was a friendly smile. 'Evidently,' I concluded, 'she has judged me by my cough,' and I was immediately at my ease. The preliminary move was successful. I congratulated myself on my boldness: I was as good as any adult in opening a conversation with a strange woman.

'How do you like this rose?' I asked, holding my gold-and-silver filigree thing delicately between the tips of my forefinger and thumb.

'Isn't it pretty?' she responded most naturally. Her eyes

sparkled, and she became prettier as her smile spread over her face. I noticed a tempting dimple on her left cheek.

'For a mole on my lover's face,' I murmured in Persian, 'I shall give all the wealth of Samarkhand,' Evidently she did not understand any Persian, and that made it perfectly clear that she was not an artiste. 'An artiste worth anything,' Kolej Huzoor was absolutely sure, 'must know at least a couple of languages, and Persian is one of them. Whenever business people give dinners for their visitors from abroad they hire artistes to sit next to the foreigners and entertain them. They never take their wives with them lest they discover the amount the husbands make from their business deals. You know what our women are like. Once they find out that their husbands are making an extra rupee they will immediately start nagging them for more jewellery.' 'Well,' I said to myself, 'the pretty almond-eyed girl is not an artiste. So much the better. Her house will not be full of maids, apprentices, friends and what not.'

'Your filigree rose is really lovely.' Her voice sounded like the tinkling of silver bells. It had just a touch of quaintness which enhanced the charm of its melody.

'Would you like to keep it? Let me offer it as a present to you.'

'Oh, no!' she protested. 'How can I accept such a thing? It must be frightfully expensive.'

I thrust the rose in her hand. She turned it round nervously. It was a pleasure to watch her face brighten as she carefully examined the workmanship while I admired the way she had arranged her hair: long plaits coiled round and round her head created the impression of a crown. She praised my piece of filigree work, but would not accept it. However, I refused to take it back.

'This is yours,' I repeated insistently. 'Please keep it, and make me happy.' I made use of the formula Kolej Huzoor taught me for handing a present to an artiste. The girl did not say anything, but kept on turning the rose in her hand: the mechanism for storing perfume inside it interested her enormously. She had never seen such a thing in her life. So I came closer to her to show how the otto-container worked, and whispered: 'Why did you whistle at me?'

'Heavens! I am not as ill-bred as that. I was whistling for my dog.'

'That,' I argued within me, 'is just a face-saving formula.' And my admiration for her steadily rose: she was bold, but not brazen. It was good to come across a street-walker who was not devoid of delicacy. I came still closer to her. 'Listen,' I murmured. 'It is getting late for me. I do not live in Burdwan. Tell me how much do you usually charge for entertaining your visitors?'

She suddenly turned ashen, and slowly stepped back from me with her eyes fixed on mine: her pupils dilated as if she were frightened by the sudden vision of a spectre. Her lips twitched but no words escaped from them. She dropped my rose as she raised her hands to cover her face as though to avert a blow. She then burst into a flood of tears.

'My God!' she sobbed. 'What have I done to you to merit this insult? Do I look like a common tart?'

I scampered away as fast as my legs could carry me. I did not look back. Though I was an oaf, I knew the greatest insult a man could hurl against a woman was to call her a tart.

~

And that was the epithet I gave now to Roma in my soliloquies!

What made me do that? Why did I think of her in that malicious way? I, who was particular about chivalrous behaviour towards all women—not excluding the common street-walker: I, who gave the promise to my grandfather that I would always bear in mind his injunction: whatever a pretty woman might do to a man should be regarded as a grace and a favour.

Who could explain to me my irrational thoughts and my unjust accusations? Why was I restless? Why was I a victim of constant nightmares? Why did I hear the wild music of scudding hooves of spectral stallions combating phantom mares? The neighing of ghoulish horses snorting fire and dashing down rose-tinted shores to drown themselves in a scarlet sea whose billows were myriads of harp-shells and whelks emitting streams of flame; the thunder of the fierce stampede of the invisible coursers rushing to their doom began plaguing even my wakeful hours: they brought me days of anxiety and nights of anguish.

IV

Reluctantly—after a long struggle with my better judgment—I reached the conclusion that it would perhaps do me some good to secure Profulla Babu's counsel.

He was certainly a most well-informed person. But there was, however, one grave shortcoming in him: he preferred the general to the particular. Broad generalizations—to stimulate thinking—were his speciality. Individual cases interested him only in so far as they helped to make his expositions most explicit. Then again, he never gave any direct answer, except on very rare occasions.

The best way of tackling him was to put an indirect question and then make one's own deductions from his inevitably long discourse. Shortly after arriving in Calcutta, when I had called on him to discuss my affairs, the first thing he did was to explain to me how I should behave during the period of my stay in

India's premier city. Instead of telling me his views straight off, he dragged me to see a football match in the neighbourhood.

The game was not an exciting one; the two contending teams were Gant-kuttahs and Hari-Ballavs. 'Rather funny names,' I told him. (*Gant-kuttahs* mean *Cut-purses* and the *Hari-Ballavs* are *Lovers of God*!) 'That's Calcutta, my son,' he remarked. 'Now watch when a goal is scored.' I did watch him and was surprised to notice that whenever a goal was made he produced a parti-coloured handkerchief—the colours of the successful team—and waved it most enthusiastically. He had two such handkerchiefs, and with equal enthusiasm he cheered for the *Cut-purses* and the *Lovers of God* as the circumstances demanded. 'This is the best you can do in Calcutta,' he advised me. 'Caution is the word for wisdom here. Now let us clear out before the game ends. Otherwise we may get involved in the free-for-all.'

A second match, or rather a free fight, I understood, was usually fought among the partisans of the contesting teams as soon as the official game was over.

Profulla Babu being very elderly rarely ventured far from his house, but for my benefit he undertook the trouble of going to a football match. His sole objective was to impress upon me the importance of maintaining perfect imperturbability in Calcutta!

~

My plan of approach was well thought out: I was going to talk to him about an address given in the University Union by Prem Swami, and then ask him his views about the Swami, and what should a young man do to keep himself chaste in words, thoughts and deeds. What led a man to have frightful nightmares and obscene dreams and unkind thoughts?

Prem Swami, whose disciples—avowed or nominal—counted by the thousands in Calcutta, was at that time a favourite with the University students. Jogin-Da's conversion to vegetarianism and love for venomous creatures was brought about by the Swami, and my legal guardian was not the only one to take the Swami's doctrines seriously. In fact, the Swami's followers were then more numerous than those of Mohandas Karamchand Gandhi or Annie Besant.

Previously I had heard that austere living and chastity were the twin themes on which Prem Swami generally talked. 'If marry you must,' one of his pamphlets especially intended for students announced, 'I am not the person to dissuade you from such a course—especially if your parents arrange it for you. But I do exhort you to remain chaste even after your wedding.' In that particular leaflet a number of different authorities were quoted to justify this thesis: the majority of them were Indians, but there were some strangers as well, a number of early Christian Fathers, about whom I knew nothing, as also Carlyle, Ruskin and Tolstoy. It was from Prem Swami's writings I learned that Carlyle's relationship with his wife was purely fraternal, Ruskin's love was platonic, and Tolstoy repented of his sensual attraction for his spouse.

At the meeting in the Union building Prem Swami gave a general exposition of what he called the Way to Nirvana. Nirvana, according to him, was absolute bliss, which was readily attainable if one abstained from killing, marrying and handling gold and silver.

The Swami, it was rumoured, was a widower. His marriage was arranged by his parents: as a dutiful son he had obeyed all parental injunctions. But as long as his wife lived he had treated her as his sister. This had not, however, prevented his bringing at one time a lawsuit against her for her refusal to produce the household accounts for his scrutiny: the wife was suspected of saving money from what she received for running her house. However, the Indian Penal Code did not permit a husband to prosecute his wife on such grounds and Prem Swami lost his case.

This took place long ago. The *Kusum-pur Sangbad* of the Penhari Parganas had an editorial on it, and it was discussed even among our villagers. Our people's conception of conjugal relationship was different from that of Prem Swami. The mistress of a Penhari household was accountable to none but herself for the money she spent or saved, and it was her birthright to collect the entire earnings of her husband. It was she who doled out the pocket-money to her lord and master.

Yet in the same Penhari Parganas there were some people—men as well as women—who regarded Prem Swami as the oracle of God.

Apart from his avowed followers—who sent him voluntarily one-tenth of their earnings—Prem Swami's admirers included all those afraid of the atheists, agnostics, free-thinkers, and socialists, anarchists and communists. In other words, many industrialists, financiers, moneylenders, landowners, and others of this category gladly contributed to the Swami's propaganda fund.

~

These and various other things about the Swami I came to learn by and by. On the day I called on Profulla Babu to talk about my troubles I used the theme of the Swami's visit to the Union as my opening gambit for a conversation.

'Did he ask or did he not ask for money?' Profulla Babu interrupted, even before I had begun. 'He did. And did he or did he not declare that the collection was a poor one? He did. Did he not also talk on austerity and chastity? He did. Well, he has not changed a bit. The same old gramophone record is being played over and over again.'

'What do you think about his views concerning chaste living?' I summoned, I do not know how, enough courage to put the question which was uppermost in my mind.

'Chastity, my son, is a most marvellous virtue!' Profulla Babu laughed sarcastically, and then without giving his personal opinion on my question he brought in the general theme about Calcutta's attitude towards this issue. 'Calcutta is simply wallowing in chastity. Prem Swami's followers are talking chastity. Ramakrishna's disciples are lecturing on chastity. Aswini Kumar Dutt's admirers are spewing out chastity. What more do you want? At the same time Calcutta is maintaining a larger number of whores than all the cities of the world put together. It is carrying on the biggest commerce in aphrodisiacs of any port on God's earth. Officially there is not a single licensed house in Calcutta nor a single store for narcotics. Prem Swami is deadly opposed to such things. And would you believe it, the Swami's followers are reaping a fine harvest from Calcutta's brothels and dope shops. That's the long and the short of it.'

Profulla Babu went off at a tangent, and I heard from him that though Prem Swami was opposed to normal conjugal relationship he was not opposed to non-platonic love among people of the same sex: that was the Swami's remedy for India's ever-increasing population.

Evidently the Swami was a bundle of contradictions; he was opposed to the destruction of any life, and at the same time he and his followers maintained hired thugs to commit murder.

'His religion does not permit him to partake of anything grown in a ploughed field,' Profulla Babu continued. 'You may well wonder why? The answer is simple: ploughing involves cutting into two poor earthworms caught by the ploughshare. According to him, all living creatures are sacred—except man: because man is conceived in sin. The more obnoxious a creature the greater is man's responsibility towards it! This is arrant nonsense. He maintains from the money he receives from his admirers a hospital in Belgaum for sick scorpions.'

'What does he then eat?' I asked timidly. 'He advised the students to abstain from all animal food to start with. And then to practice from time to time abstention from all solid food. Does he live on milk only?'

'He lives mainly on nuts. His followers are expected to do the same. He is opposed to ploughing the fields, and wants his admirers to put up factories. What about our food? Prem Swami's answer is simple: "We shall buy what we want from Siam, Burma, Indonesia, Argentina, Canada and USA. Let the sin of destroying earthworms be on their heads." With what will you buy your food? Why, the Swami explains it with equal clarity: "Our labour is cheap; we will undercut Great Britain, America, Germany and Japan. Let us go ahead with industrialization." It would be a fine sight to see the whole of Bengal changed into an industrial slum!'

'But cannot slums be avoided?' I asked. I regretted this wandering from my original subject, but that could not be helped.

Profulla Babu shook his head: Prem Swami was for corrugated iron sheds. Austerity was his watchword. Ferro-concrete was only for factories and shrines and banks.

I gathered a few more odd titbits about the Swami's hopes and fears. The only country he dreaded was Soviet Russia: because Russia could produce inexpensive manufactured goods with prison labour; she was capable of undercutting India.

~

On my way back to my hostel I pondered over Profulla Babu's comments on Prem Swami, and strangely enough my thoughts wandered back to the Sandalwood Tank in my grandmother's house. There I had heard the name of Prem Swami pronounced for the first time on the afternoon of my escape from the moccasins.

Didi-Ma held the Swami responsible for the risk I had run in the Sandalwood Tank with my Vermilion Boat, because Jogin-Da's experiments with the venomous water-snakes were undertaken at his guru's behest. Man's dislike for reptiles was, according to the Swami, responsible for their poison fangs, and if only someone exercised sufficient patience and manifested enough love, they would within a year's time give birth to non-venomous young ones. Jogin-Da, an ardent admirer of the Swami, was then engaged in this breeding experiment which I spoiled by poking at a baby moccasin with my perch.

'The fellow reeks of cant,' was Profulla Babu's final judgment on Prem Swami. 'In the name of religion he wants to have a horse foaled with a horn-tip.'

V

A few days later a further attempt to secure Profulla Babu's advice was frustrated on account of a flock of crows.

It was nearing sunset, and I was alone with him on the flat roof-terrace of his house, watching one of Calcutta's prettiest sights: innumerable little flags of all colours and patterns were being waved by hundreds of joyous boys and girls from their level house-tops; the youngsters were all signalling to their pet pigeons.

'Pigeon-flying,' I was told in my village, 'is the favourite game of all young folks in Calcutta.' My informant was not wrong, and I wrote back home: 'There must be millions of pigeons in Calcutta. Perhaps ten pigeons to every inhabitant.' I discovered that not only children but adults as well were pigeon-minded. Hawkers often stopped me in the streets to extol the virtues of their tumblers, turbits, tambourines, trumpeters, turtle-doves, pouters, peacock-necks, fantails, blue rock birds, homers and other varieties of pigeons. At times they produced long rolls resembling horoscope scrolls to justify their demand for fantastically high prices for some miserable-looking fledglings: pedigree carrier-pigeons. Pedigree carriers and good fliers fetched, I understood, as much as a thousand rupees or more. 'The art of training pigeon fledglings,' I wrote in another letter, 'is said to be highly interesting and extremely complicated.'

As I had neither the time nor the money for indulging in the luxury of pigeon-flying, I contented myself by simply watching others enjoy it. And the roof-terrace of Profulla Babu's house in the crowded residential area of Shyam Bazaar was ideal for this purpose.

I am sure Profulla Babu, too, in spite of his apparent indifference, was relishing the spectacle. I was gradually preparing myself to question him when the bother over the crows upset my plan.

'Have you ever assisted at a parliament of crows?' he asked all of a sudden as he pointed in the direction of the tamarind tree—Raja Vikram's Throne—at the far end of his ill-kept lawn. He added: 'Here is your chance.'

'When crows cry bad luck is nearby,' I murmured. 'The crows over there are cawing ominously.' I was no lover of those wretched birds. The common crow all over the world looks the same. But those of Calcutta have special characteristics: they are the noisiest in the world, and—to make up for it—they bear, instead of sooty feathers, graphite-black plumes, highly glossed with deep purple, intense blue, and dark green. Moreover, they have a peculiar ashy-brown collar round the neck.

'Either it is their parliament in session,' Profulla Babu remarked, 'or, it may be, they have gathered as a court summoned to deal with some serious offence in crow-country. Let us see what they do. The accused is perhaps the one over there: in the midst of the lawn, near the onion-domed shrine of the basil plant. It is all by itself.'

True enough: there was a large, solitary crow hopping about the grass-plot with its head cocked sideways; its feathers were awry, and it was cawing uneasily. Scores of its compeers—some jostling on the lower branches of the tamarind tree and some crowding the fences opposite—watched its movements in silence and listened to its raucous plaints.

'The House seems to be equally divided,' I remarked. The scene reminded me of the sittings of the inter-college debates addressed by me: two groups eyeing each other, separated by the gangway, and in their midst an isolated but obstinate croaker.

'Caw! Caw!' called out a crow from the tamarind tree, and the cry was taken up by the rest of the company.

'Caw-awe! Caw-awe!' responded with zest those sitting on the bamboo fences.

The lone one on the lawn immediately stood still, its comical mood was gone. It looked as though it were surprised at the unexpected clamour coming from both quarters at the same time. It turned its head from one side to another as it deliberately preened its feathers to look neat. Finally it decided to address only those nestled in the branches of the tamarind tree.

Its compeers, however, seemed to be no longer prepared to give it a hearing. The whole congregation raised a throaty clamour to drown its piteous cawings. Then as though at a given signal they all rose in the air, making an infernal Babel of croakings and squawkings. They flew up in a spiral of widening circles.

The solitary crow twisted its neck skywards to watch the flight of its brethren. It reflected for a few moments and decided to follow their suit. As a preliminary it flapped its wings. However, the instant it took to the air, the whole flock fell upon it as one bird to prevent its leaving the lawn. It was savagely attacked: it was to stay, they decreed, where it was—near the shrine of the basil plant—between the tamarind tree and the bamboo fences.

After administering a thorough chastisement the crows flew back to their original perches; the flock separated into two, some returning to the tamarind tree, and others to the fences. They then watched as before in silence every movement of the condemned culprit on the lawn.

The badly battered crow got to its feet with difficulty. Its movements were awkward, and its gait unsteady. Evidently it was maimed and crippled, incapacitated from hopping any more. It now presented a sorry sight: its feathers were ruffled, its body covered with gashes, and one of its eyes missing. It was no longer uttering any plaints. It shook its wings as it tottered: it was unable to keep its balance.

'Caw-awe! Caw-awe!' boisterously croaked one of the carrion-eaters possessing a greater vocal strength than the rest. It was a call to the whole flock—to those sitting on the branches of the tamarind tree as well as to those on the fences—and the entire congregation responded lustily. From the tree and from the fences they flew down with alacrity and fell in full force upon their solitary brother. They began pecking and tearing at it mercilessly.

The condemned bird made frantic attempts to escape. But every time it made the slightest endeavour to fly it was knocked down by a dozen of its brethren, all ardently bent on the job: they worked in relays in order to give every member of the flock a fair share in the communal chastisement.

'They have decreed the supreme punishment,' Profulla Babu said. 'The sentence is being carried out.'

There was not the slightest mistake about that. They pierced the condemned one with their claws, stabbed it with their beaks, battered it with their wings, and smothered it under their weight. It was a helpless crow they made away with: it looked very much like any other of its clan—no better and no worse.

Why was it so ill-treated by its brethren? Why did they go on striking it long after it was lying lifeless on its back? A most bedraggled corpse, devoid of all feathers and plumes; a pitiful lump of shredded flesh: a sickening sight. The crow was judged and executed within a few minutes. Could I have done anything to save it?

'Yes,' replied Profulla Babu, 'if only you had tied it round your neck from the moment its trial began till the day of its death! And you would have been cursed by that crow into the bargain.'

'Why?'

'A crow does not make a flock! A mateless existence is no existence at all.'

Were it endowed with human tongue, according to Profulla Babu, the crow would doubtlessly have thanked me at first for saving it from its executioners, but with the passage of time it would have fretted and started blaming me for its companionless cycle of days and nights. 'My fate is hard,' it would have complained. 'Because I have associated with you none of my tribe would have anything more to do with me. I have lost my caste and my face. My mateless life is unbearable. Why did you intervene on my behalf? Who tells you that my brethren were bent on executing me? Perhaps all that they desired was to chastise me and then take me back in the flock. You wanted to have the satisfaction of doing a piece of so-called good work. You wished to satisfy your own vanity, and I am the victim of your alleged generous impulse. May you be cursed: for my life is joyless; my existence of forced chastity is galling.'

I did not look at the problem in the same way as Profulla Babu, and asked him: 'Is it not a man's duty to do good wherever he can?'

'Be a man first before you can talk about a man's duty,' was his enigmatic reply. Then as a teaser he asked if I could figure out the nature of the crime the crow had committed which brought upon its head the death sentence.

'There may be many reasons,' I murmured. 'I believe my guess would be as good as anyone else's.'

'I don't want a hasty answer. Take your time. Sleep on it and find a reply that will give satisfaction to yourself as well as to others who are free from Prem Swami's cant.'

He gave a few hints about answers which were no answers. The crow could not possibly have been sentenced for cowardice, for the laws of the crow-country never demanded, according to him, courage from its members; all crows are notorious cowards. Was it then the stigma of theft? That too should be ruled out: because all crows are thieves, and thieving among themselves is customary. Was it then the enormity of treachery? This also was unlikely, loyalty being no virtue among crows. Was it the offence of associating with a bird of a different feather? Here again, the response should be in the negative: crows, though sly, often rear cuckoos and gladly associate with vultures to gorge on carrion.

'In a jig-saw puzzle,' Profulla Babu concluded, 'there is a key-piece. Just as in an arch there is a headpiece, the most important item in the whole structure. Once you find it the rest will be easy to reconstruct. Solve my puzzle and you will see how most of the besetting problems of Calcutta will take a different aspect.'

'How long do you give me to find the answer?'

'Take as long as you will. Perhaps you will consult Roma. Two heads are better than one.'

VI

Instead of consulting Roma I decided to have a talk with Tu Fan.

As luck would have it I came across him on my way to the Science College near the Vandar Bhavan: that huge pile, in Sitaram Lane, off Upper Circular Road. Tu Fan called on the Vandars once a week on business.

'What sort of business?' I asked. The Vandars were orthodox vegetarians, and were not likely to patronize the Chop Suey Shop of Tu Fan.

'Come with me,' he said, 'and see for yourself. You will have some fun.'

I was only too glad to join him. There was no great harm in missing a lecture. Whereas getting inside a multimillionaire's abode was a piece of rare luck.

The owner of the Vandar Bhavan was Hanuman Vandar, the banker. He was reputed to be the wealthiest follower of Prem Swami and a formidable rival of the Birlas, equally renowned for their opulence. Though a multi-millionaire the way he had his residence constructed gave one the impression that he must have been born in a prison and wanted to perpetuate the memory of his happy childhood days by living the rest of his life in a grim pile resembling the gloomiest penitentiary. At least this was the impression one obtained from its outer appearance.

The Vandar Bhavan was built like a cheerless mediaeval fortress and was surrounded by a massive ferro-concrete wall of some twenty feet in height. The only bright touch of colour in the whole structure was the coat of arms above the main portals of heavy iron grilles: it was devised by Hanuman Vandar, without any reference to a College of Arms, and consisted of two massive polychromatic statues of leopards—about the size of the Gurkha guards protecting the entrance—upholding a bejewelled turban, big as the legendary Auk's egg, bearing the inscription: 'He who loves God, fears Nought.' The text was in English, and originally the word 'Nought' had been written as 'Knot'; the traces of this correction were distinctly visible.

'What does a multi-millionaire look like?' I was curious.

Tu Fan laughed. 'Next time you pass by the Vandar Bhavan,' he advised, 'keep your eyes open. If you find a dozen Gurkha guards watching someone gathering cairns of cow-dung from the street, you will know that the dung-gatherer is either Hanuman Vandar or a member of his family.'

'How is that? Is it because Prem Swami regards cows as the holiest creatures on earth?'

'Maybe. But there are other reasons too. For example, "Waste not, want not", "Blessed are the humble" and dried cow-dung cakes make good fuel. "Save the penny and the pound will look after itself." Before meeting Hanuman Vandar I thought that the Chinese of Calcutta were the most close-fisted people in the world. Now I think differently.'

~

Tu Fan disappeared in the guard-room of the Vandar Bhavan to collect some fish, and I was left by myself to admire a huge, stone-lined lotus pool in the middle of the quadrangle of the house.

The circular pool was divided into two dozen segments, each cut off from its adjacent ones and fed by jets of water gushing from a curious collection of stone beasts. 'A house containing such a lotus pool cannot be called an ordinary prison,' I said to myself.

The more I looked the more I marvelled and the more was I overcome by a feeling of dizziness. The uniqueness of the bestiary was striking: the alabaster creatures which fed the pool consisted of a bull, an elephant, a horse, a monkey, a sheldrake, a crocodile, a rhinoceros, a buffalo, a bear, an antelope, a goat, a fish, a snake, a lion, and a number of legendary animals whose names were unknown to me. As the stone elephant was more than life-size and the rest of the statues were, for the sake of aesthetic unity, made as big as the alabaster pachyderm, one may well guess the dimensions of that horror of a fountain.

Suddenly my dizziness increased and I rushed towards the water's edge to wet my temples. Cold water had a steadying effect: it made me feel somewhat better.

Tu Fan called out for me. As I was going to leave the fountain I had a fleeting vision of a tiny fish as gorgeous as a kingfisher. My sickness disappeared as though by magic.

'Come here, Tu Fan,' I cried. 'Come and see a marvel. What sort of fish is that?'

'Siamese fish. I am taking a dozen of them with me. You will see them better in my glass bowls. Come along with me.'

I was literally dragged away from the lotus pool otherwise I would have spent hours watching those gorgeous specimens of Siamese fish. They were torpedo-shaped, and furnished with voluminous, silky fins which they trailed behind them. In size they were not much larger than the ordinary goldfish: perhaps three inches long. But they were much more attractive. They were of various tints. The one which first attracted my attention had a light-blue body and lapis lazuli fins which spread out like veils of transparent Benares silk. There were others no less beautiful: with ruby red body and scarlet fins or with iridescent green body and dark emerald fins. It was a feast to the eye to watch their glorious colours and graceful movements as they sported in the water.

'Why are there so few?' I asked. 'Only one Siamese fish in each one of these gigantic segments.'

'Come home with me and you will learn why.'

~

'Their scientific name is Betta splendens,' Tu Fan explained. 'Certainly they are the loveliest fish in the world. The finest of their kind. Hanuman Vandar has spent a fortune in securing the very best that Siam can supply. But they have caused him nervous dyspepsia. And I am profiting from it.'

'How?'

'It is the bad habits of the Siamese fish that have upset him.' Tu Fan laughed heartily. 'I have been asked to find out if your Jogin-Da's diets would wean them out of their wicked propensities.'

I stared vacantly. Were they poisonous? No. What was then wrong with them? Each fish had to be kept away from its brethren otherwise there was every likelihood of their killing each other in a fratricidal fight.

'You are joking, Tu Fan.' I thought he was trying to pull my leg.

'No,' he shook his head. 'I am serious. Hanuman Vandar once went through an expiation ceremony—a month without any solid food—on account of an accident in his lotus pool.' Once the tank was overfilled and the fighting fish swam out of their separate enclosures and fought each other to death. This was considered to be a grave sin and Hanuman Vandar inflicted a penance upon himself! 'If a pair of these magnificent Betta splendens got together they would go on sparring and attacking each other till one is killed. "Fight to death" is their principle. "No quarter asked and none given"—that's their law. Some varieties of fish do fight at mating times but with the beautiful Siamese fish any time is a good fighting time.'

I was really surprised.

'They are like the brothers in a Bengali household. No love is ever lost between them.'

~

As a devoted follower of Prem Swami, Hanuman Vandar was greatly distressed at the bellicose propensities of the Siamese fish, and was determined to change their nature. They were being fed on a special diet prepared by Jogin-Da, and Tu Fan was entrusted with the task of verifying the progress they were making in their acquisition of Prem Swami's principle of *ahimsa*: Love one another.

Like other disciples of Prem Swami, Hanuman Vandar believed that a creature's nature was primarily a matter of food, and secondly, of training. 'Forced chastity and vegetarian dieting,' he told Tu Fan, 'will certainly work miracles. I am more concerned in the welfare of the fish than in anything else. There are people who bother me for donations for hospitals, orphanages, and similar institutions for men. But I tell them that man can look after himself, and let him do so. It is the poor lowly creatures, perverted by human contact, who are my main concern.'

~

The reason why he interested himself in fish was easy to understand for those versed in the Jain legends about the prophet called Aranath. No one knows when Aranath lived, but tradition says he was the eighteenth prophet of the Jains and had a fish as his distinguishing symbol—or *vehicle* in technical terminology. Hanuman Vandar happened to be born on the anniversary of Aranath's alleged birthday. This fact was interpreted by Prem Swami as a divine injunction for Hanuman Vandar to concern himself with the welfare of fish.

As fish propagate without mating, Hanuman Vandar fell in love with them the moment he heard the Swami's interpretation of the significance of his birthday. 'They are chaste,' he reminded himself very often. 'They are innocent. They are not like men rejoicing in lust and in cruelty.'

'Look at the fish,' Hanuman Vandar sermonized one day to a group of American tourists from Santa Barbara, California, 'and let us improve our ways.'

These Americans were no ordinary tourists: their clothes were devoid of buttons; they were admirers of Prem Swami and like the Swami they subsisted mainly on nuts and buttermilk. The motive of their visit to Calcutta was to interview the prime object of their reverence, Guru Prem Swami; but the guru happened to be at Belgaum, in his *ashram*—the retreat—attached to his Scorpion Hospital. They telegraphed to him as their scheduled journey did not permit their going to the other end of India, would he therefore condescend to return to Calcutta to give them his benediction. The guru's secretary wired back the blessings of the holy man and informed the party that the Swami was undergoing one of his periodical fasting penances: therefore the tourists would do well to meet his favourite disciple, Hanuman Vandar, in his stead.

They were cordially received in the Vandar Bhavan and lectured on the virtues of the fish. Not only the eighteenth prophet of the Jains, Aranath, but also the early Christians had fish as their symbol. This information as well as other historical data about the denizens of the deep produced a profound impression on the visitors.

'Look at the fish,' Hanuman Vandar spoke with genuine emotion. 'They live chastely. They do not indulge in lust. They plough not, reap not, neither do they sow. Nor do they care for wheat or rice. They thrive on God's gifts—simple weeds growing under water. They are the most peace-loving creatures in God's creation. It is a pleasure to watch their deportment in a lotus pool.

As I gaze at my goldfish in that stone-lined tank before you I feel the blessing of divine peace filling my heart. Oh, that man would live in peace with his brother and practise chastity like the fish.'

Unfortunately in the band of American visitors there was a bright boy who had bought a dozen Siamese fish in Hogg Sahib's Bazaar. Being ignorant of the ways of the charming Betta splendens he had put all of them in the same jar and discovered in a trice their terrible fighting capacity. His male specimens contended with one another in their usual way till they had killed themselves off. The boy returned to Hogg Sahib's Bazaar to complain about the unexpected end of his newly-acquired possession and was told by the dealer about the bellicose habits of these glorious fishes.

Since boys will be boys, even when dressed in buttonless clothes, the Californian youngster asked Hanuman Vandar at the end of his sermon *On brotherly love through chaste fish-like existence*: 'Mister! Why do Siamese fish suffer from lust?'

The question was disturbing. Hanuman Vandar was at that time ignorant of the existence of Betta splendens. Did the boy want information on the facts of life? If so, it was outside Hanuman Vandar's scope. According to Indian tradition no one is supposed to know the facts of life—not even adults. Hanuman Vandar hesitated.

'Why do the Siamese fish fight?' The American boy did not suffer from squeamishness. 'They must suffer from lust,' he asserted. 'They kill each other.'

~

That was the beginning of Hanuman Vandar's troubles: his insomnia and nervous dyspepsia, his search for Jogin-Da and for

Tu Fan, his bidding good-bye to his goldfish in the lotus pool and replacing them with Siamese fish.

He experimented with a few pairs of Siamese fish and found out for himself that the American boy was right.

'Their fighting habit has been acquired through man's evil influence.' Hanuman Vandar conjectured. 'Everyone knows that the dealers in goldfish and Betta splendens in Hogg Sahib's Bazaar are fish-eaters. It is their touch that has affected the character of these fish. Naturally, some fish are more sensitive than others: Betta splendens are like racehorses; they are easily upset. I shall get a few from Siam and see what happens,'

The especially imported specimens of Betta splendens from the Land of the White Elephant and the proverbial twins behaved no differently from their brethren purchased at Hogg Sahib's Bazaar: Hanuman Vandar became alarmed. 'Man's nefarious influence is gaining the upper hand in the universe,' he wrote to Jogin-Da. All varieties of fish were, his reasoning told him, extremely peace-loving since the day of creation; otherwise Aranath the eighteenth prophet of the Jains would not have chosen the fish for his symbol. 'Therefore,' he concluded, 'the fighting habits of the Siamese fish must have been recently acquired. Something must be done to wean them from their unnatural traits.'

Jogin-Da's reputation among the followers of Prem Swami was spreading steadily. Occasional newspaper articles commended his alleged success in breeding non-venomous moccasins. If serpents could be trained to shed their poison fangs it was natural to conclude that the Siamese fish could also be taught to give up their bellicosity. Jogin-Da never lacked self-confidence. He proposed dieting for Hanuman Vandar's Siamese fish and their solitary confinement: they were to be denied access to their harems till they had learned better manners. ('Though,'

Tu Fan commented, 'it must be said to the credit of the fighting fish that they rarely ill-treat their females. In this respect they are better than most men.')

As Jogin-Da believed that the Chinese were responsible for cultivating the sedate goldfish, he further suggested that Tu Fan should be employed to verify the progress in the acquisition of peaceful habits by Hanuman Vandar's new pets.

This was, of course, a great boon to Tu Fan: he knew all about the fighting Betta splendens. As a matter of fact long before Hanuman Vandar had seen the first Siamese fish he was running a gambling party once a week in the upper floor of his Chop Suey Shop on the results of fish combats. Jogin-Da's recommendation spared him the bother of buying his own Siamese fighters. Moreover, it brought him some additional money: the fee he charged for the trouble of collecting fish from Hanuman Vandar's lotus pool and returning them there and also for keeping records.

There was some haggling over the amount Tu Fan demanded: the multi-millionaire bargained like a Kabuli garlic-seller, but finally he accepted Tu Fan's terms: he had no choice. His religion prevented his carrying out any combat within the precincts of his mansion, and he had no confidence in the other Chinese of China Bazaar. However, he enjoined Tu Fan that in no circumstances should any of his fish be allowed to fight for more than ten minutes, and if any of them showed signs of exhaustion before that time limit the fight must be stopped at once.

~

'The day I succeed,' Tu Fan confided to me, 'in spotting a couple of non-fighting Betta splendens I shall get a Rolls Royce as a present from Hanuman Vandar. But what shall I do with a big car? It is greater fun to watch the fish fights. I shall explain to you how the gambling is done.'

A contest between a male specimen of Betta splendens and another of the same size and weight can last for hours; and it can be as exciting as a match between two master-wrestlers, the ultimate issue remaining in doubt right to the very last second. A fish is judged victor whose opponent—after a reasonable interval—remains 'floored'. These and various other details about the rules and regulations in fish-fights were carefully explained to me by Tu Fan.

For those who wonder what a Siamese fish-fight looks like, I may mention here that Tu Fan usually puts two males of different colours in a water-filled glass bowl hanging from the ceiling. The bottom as well as the sides of this bowl must have been of magnifying glass because the three-inch fish looked like baby crocodiles when seen from the floor. The contrasting colours of the fish made their identification simple, and the spectators squatting on the floor or sitting on the benches which lined the walls of the gambling-room had no difficulty in following every movement of the fish on which they had staked their money.

When released in the bowl, at first each fish swam about gracefully displaying its trailing diaphanous fins: it hardly bothered about its opponent. 'It is just showing itself off,' Tu Fan whispered. 'Backers are now making their choice.' The combatants later started eyeing each other seriously as they moved in circles, each giving the other a wide berth. 'The circling movement,' Tu Fan continued, 'is evidently sparring for an opening. Or rather, a sham opening for the first part of the fight. The second and the more important part comes towards the end of the time limit.'

The timing started only from the moment when a fish made a sudden dash to tear off a bit of its rival's transparent fins. It quickly retreated with its spoil in its mouth, and made gobbling gestures as though it wanted to swallow what it had snatched from its adversary's body. However, a second later it spat out contemptuously before its rival's face everything it had swallowed or had intended to swallow.

'This is to provoke the other one. "You are repulsive!" The fish is no doubt abusing its brother. "Your fine frills are impossible to the taste!" It wants its rival to lose its temper.'

The other one was not slow to retaliate. It too did its best to denude its opponent of its fins. This tearing and biting and spewing went on till both the combatants were stripped bare, totally divested of their veil-like fins. They then looked like two tiny torpedoes.

'Like torpedoes they will now move at a lightning speed. The phase of insults and counter-insults has ended. Now the second part of the battle has started.'

'Some of your spectators are getting excited,' I murmured.

'They are the veteran gamblers,' Tu Fan whispered back. 'They do not know what to think of the red one. It has never been matched against the green fish—their favourite.'

Both the fish began once again manoeuvring and sparring for position; they made swift moves and sudden halts—circling and darting, diving and flitting, gliding and sliding, sweeping and swooping, and dashing and splashing. The water was churned. It was a pretty sight: the streaks of red and of green whirling inside the bowl, illumined by a powerful arc lamp.

All of a sudden the red Siamese fish grabbed its green rival by the jaw, and the two became locked together. In this position they rolled about the bowl, moving from one end to the other—turning and twisting on their sides—each trying to drag the other down to the bottom and there smother it to death.

After a while they separated.

'In order to regain breath,' Tu Fan said. 'They will restart soon enough. One seems to be aimlessly cruising about, and the other is almost touching the bottom. These are just manoeuvres. Now they have begun again.'

Had the red one touched the bottom of the bowl 'the counting' would have started immediately, and perhaps it would have been counted out. But it was a clever devil and won in the long run by forcing the green one to admit defeat.

'Did you notice,' Tu Fan asked, 'how the red one got hold of the upper jaw of its rival to choke it to death?'

The Siamese fish, I was told, have their code of fighting: no fish will ever attack its opponent until it has of its own accord abandoned the bottom of the bowl for a fresh encounter.

Tu Fan never allowed any of the fish to fight till death: that would have been violating too flagrantly Hanuman Vandar's injunction; moreover, it would have demanded hours of waiting.

'To tell the truth,' Tu Fan remarked after the game was over, 'ever since the males have been kept away from their harems they have been extraordinarily ferocious. But tell me, isn't it a pleasure to watch their flashing colours as they roll about gripping each other?'

'Certainly,' I agreed with him. 'But without their trailing fins they look less attractive.'

Tu Fan smiled. 'They will grow again,' he assured me. 'God created them for fighting each other, and he will give them back their fins. I shall tell you when I put the red and the green ones again in the same bowl. You will see for yourself that they will look exactly the same as they did at the beginning of to-day's fight.'

~

It was perfectly ridiculous, Tu Fan held, to make attempt to breed peace-loving Siamese fish. He was equally contemptuous of my Didi-Ma's thornless blackberries in Chandernagore.

'What has happened to her blackberries?' He shook his head. 'She spent months and years in producing thornless brambles and roses. Now that she is dead tell me what has happened to them? They are being nibbled away by goats and cows.'

Tu Fan shook his head again and sighed. It was good of him to remember Didi-Ma. He had been to Chandernagore only a couple of times. Yet he recalled all the details of Didi-Ma's house, her likes and dislikes, her favourites and her aversions.

'Her blackberry and bramble jams,' he, however, admitted, 'were better than the best guava jelly. That's why I often remind Hanuman Vandar of your Didi-Ma's saying, "If you want to improve anything, try to improve what gives man pleasure." Your Didi-Ma was a sensible woman.'

I agreed: she produced thornless roses and non-prickly brambles; she read a lot; though she did not write much she valued other people's writings; she had a chestful of manuscripts—Abbé Coeurdoux on *Comparative Philology*, Victor Jacquemont on his *Indian Travels*, a rough draft of *Colomba* in Mérimée's own hand and of various other manuscripts by personalities not so well known as these three. She was indeed a wonderful woman.

'Whatever she did,' Tu Fan agreed, 'brought delight to everyone. And she never talked of religion like Hanuman Vandar or your Jogin-Da. I am not a scholar and do not pretend to know much. But can you tell me what good will it do to breed tame Siamese fish?'

Of course, I did not know. All that I knew was Prem Swami's doctrine: 'Man is the most pernicious creature on earth, and man's redemption lies in imitating the ways of lowly creatures and in improving their lot.' As both Hanuman Vandar and Jogin-Da were Prem Swami's disciples they were doing everything to please their spiritual master.

Tu Fan told me that at one time Prem Swami addressed gatherings of the Chinese residents in Calcutta and exhorted them to take to vegetarianism as the first step to their spiritual rebirth. These meetings, however, came to an end soon because of uncomfortable questions put to the Swami. Someone asked whether it was sinful to commit suicide: 'Since human life is considered to be an evil by the Swami would it be correct to deduct that it is permissible for a man to shorten this evil?'

'What answer did the Swami give?' I asked. The question interested me.

'He talked a lot about karma and reincarnation. Finally he expounded that only sinful creatures are reborn as men to expiate the crimes committed in a previous existence. Therefore no man has any right to shorten his period of ordeal on earth. It would, however, be all right if he killed himself by an expiatory fasting, or by offering his body as food to lower creatures.'

'Did you ask him what would happen to a pious man after his death?'

'He may be reborn as a cow. That's why he is particularly opposed to slaughter cattle that have gone dry. "Killing a cow," Prem Swami assured his Chinese listeners, "is as good as murdering a pious man." It is simply extraordinary how some millions of people consider Prem Swami to be the reincarnation of Aranath the Jain prophet.'

~

I did not raise any specific questions about Roma with Tu Fan. However, I told him casually that I was suffering from nightmares and wondered if he had any cure for me.

'Have you ever tried opium?' he asked. 'But before I give you any of this drug I must consult Father.'

VII

'There must be some hidden meaning in your dreams,' Tu Fan passed on to me what he had heard from his father. 'Once you know the meaning everything will be quite clear.'

It was, of course, repeating the obvious to a student of Psychology. One of my hostel mates had actually succeeded in curing himself of his nightmares by daubing a canvas with a horrible pattern of lurid colours and masked faces: some time before his appendix had been removed, and as he had a tendency to attacks of pneumonia he had only been given a local anaesthetic; his eyes had happened to be badly bandaged and he had seen at least part of the operation done on him. That was the beginning of his nightmares. His cure came, as has just been said, with his painting a picture.

'Perhaps,' Mug Furtado told me, 'Chagall too is getting rid of his nightmares in this way.' As I was no good with the brush it was out of the question for me to paint my dreams. However, I listened carefully to Tu Fan.

'You must give form to your dreams. That's what my father advises.'

How was I to give form to impossible snakes and fiery maned horses?

'Maybe,' Tu Fan continued, 'there are certain things you like and dislike at the same time. If you dream of snakes, why do you not visit the snake-pit in Behala?'

'That's an idea.'

~

I did some thinking and reached the conclusion that part of my worries might have been due to my changing attitude towards Jogin-Da. My admiration for him was diminishing steadily. It was he who was responsible for the reports in the periodical *Aj-Kal* about my alleged desire to institute a suit against all my relatives in Calcutta. The reason he gave for his strange action was unbelievable: he wanted me to keep away from them and concentrate wholeheartedly on my studies!

At one time I was genuinely fond of him and regarded him as a good sport. Moving about with him meant good money as well.

As Prem Swami's disciple, Jogin-Da was debarred from touching gold and silver. He was thus constrained to take with him an intermediary whenever he made a cash deal; and I acted as his secretary and intermediary for some time. It was great fun to go out with him to Burdwan, Hooghly, Memari and other places. I was then too young to understand the nature of his business. 'He is a broker,' they told me. 'He deals in everything. From bricks and mortar to rice and wheat.' Jogin-Da's clients did not always offer him *hoondies* or cheques, and therefore it was imperative for him to have someone with him to collect his cash payments; he did not mind handling paper money and cheques, but it was gold and silver which his religion forbade him to touch.

The only occasions when he had no scruples in handling the precious metals were when he was constrained by his conscience to prevent another from indulging in luxury. Even then his religion demanded his putting away the confiscated gold and silver in safe deposit as soon as possible.

'It is sinful for you,' Prem Swami exhorted his disciples, 'to handle a dagger. But if you see someone carrying one it would then be your duty to snatch it away from him. It would be a grave sin if you forget this injunction.'

This command of his guru caused an unforeseen complication in Jogin-Da's life—all on account of a number of Sikhs. And in a way it was they who were responsible for my many trips to Burdwan in Jogin-Da's company. His regular clients had gradually discovered that payment by promissory notes and cheques were preferred by him and my services were, therefore, becoming less necessary. This, of course, meant my losing tips; I became somewhat uncomfortable. However, the arrival of the Sikhs in Burdwan proved to be a godsend.

'A Sikh's religion obliges him,' Jogin-Da lamented, 'to carry a sword with him at all times.' To disarm a Sikh would have meant bloodshed. And at the same time Jogin-Da could not possibly ignore his guru's injunction. He was terribly upset till he consulted a *muktear*—a special pleader of the lower hierarchy—who practised in the Sub-Judge's Court at Asansole.

'That which is hidden does not exist,' proclaimed the *muktear*. 'That which is not seen does not exist either. Such things do not exist, so far as you are concerned. Do you agree?'

Jogin-Da hesitated to give an answer.

'The mere hearsay that Fort William lodges several thousand soldiers who possess loaded guns does not force your co-religionists in Calcutta to carry out the quixotic project of rushing the gates of the fort to spike the guns.'

'That's true,' murmured Jogin-Da.

'Who tells you that the Sikhs in Burdwan walk about carrying drawn swords?'

'Not drawn swords,' Jogin-Da admitted. 'But daggers. They

carry their daggers very visibly, dangling from an iron bracelet of the right hand.'

'All right,' interrupted the *muktear*. 'In that case the solution is simply this. Just hire a *chobedar*—a staff-bearer or a mace-carrier—to accompany you. He will walk before you and shout his warnings the moment he espies a Sikh. You will then either close your eyes or turn your head in a way that would prevent your casting your glance on a Sikh. What is not seen by you does not exist for you. Is that clear?'

Jogin-Da agreed. He did not, however, hire a bearer with a silver-mounted stick; he hired me instead; I became his *chobedar*—without a silver stick—during my holidays.

I took to my job seriously and my admiration for Jogin-Da increased. For I heard everywhere he went that in business matters he was scrupulously fair. 'He never cheats any one of his dues,' they said, and I am sure they told me the truth. Of his own accord he decided to give me a percentage of his earnings or rather profits made in Burdwan: it was one *pie*—a copper cent—for every gold mohur (or its equivalent) he made. That led to my earning as much as fifteen rupees a month, while he made a few thousands.

Comrade Dynamiter of Asansole often used to taunt: 'A profitable religion never lacks proselytes. Prem Swami's disciples are like the Quakers in England: they are pacifists because they can make more money in peace-time than in times of war. Their religion is money-making.' I did not know much about the Quakers except that they did not appreciate Padre Johan's worshipping the beautiful statue of the Virgin Mother which Kumar had sculptured for him. So I had nothing to say about them. But the day I received my commission—in paper money—from Jogin-Da, I ran straight to Comrade Dynamiter and showed him my five rupee notes. What do you say to these?' I asked him, and told him to his face that Jogin-Da gave me fifteen rupees for accompanying him to Burdwan, and his religion was certainly not a paying concern to him.

Dynamiter simply shrugged his shoulders, and said that my views would change as I grew up and one day I would find out that Jogin-Da was a humbug and Guru Prem Swami was a rogue.

I thought of Comrade Dynamiter and began wondering if that day was already upon me.

~

'You must face facts,' the village Punditji usually counselled. 'Face that which frightens you. That is the best means of overcoming your fear.'

What were the facts before me? And how was I to face them? Tu Fan suggested my visiting two places to rid myself the nightmares about reptiles. One was the snake-pit in Behala and the other was the shrine of the Snake Goddess, Manasa Devi, in the Golden Pagoda district. In both these places, if I were to believe the pamphlets issued by Prem Swami's followers, experiments were being carried out to breed non-venomous snakes—on Jogin-Da's principles.

VIII

I succeeded in dragging Roma to see the Snake-Pit in the Palace of the Talukdar of Pagulpur. It was thought to be one of the sights of Calcutta. One guide-book referred to it as the biggest reptile house in the world. That it was of considerable size there was not the slightest doubt; this might be judged from the fact that the present-day Dog Racing Stadium of Behala occupies what was once the main oval of the Talukdar's Snake-Pit.

My visit to the snake-pit started rather inauspiciously and would have ended disastrously but for an insignificant accident. Instead of meeting Roma at the Esplanade Tram Terminus I proposed her coming to Behala Bridge by herself. And that was a mistake.

~

At the Esplanade there were a lot of touts, as usual. These shamefaced fellows rarely accost men accompanied by their womenfolk. Somehow, they preferred to direct their barrage of patter upon young men, and one of these rogues nearly spoilt my outing.

But before I come to him I ought to mention something else: about the present I bought for Roma, I wanted to make up for my unkind thoughts towards her. It was, of course, impossible for me to make a full confession and therefore I decided to show my contrition by offering her something really nice. Nice presents, however, cost a lot of money, and I had not much to spare; moreover, I did not know her taste. So I bought a set of attractive semi-precious stones for her: opals, moonstones, grenades, lapis lazuli, tourmalines and topazes. It was an odd collection, I must admit, but I hoped that she would like at least some of these, and if any happened to be her birthstone I could perhaps get them mounted for her. My packet was wrapped up in an ordinary piece of paper. This was done on purpose to give her a surprise, and also to avoid any reproaches for buying my gift from an expensive shop like Lalchand Hirachand's Jewel House.

To go to Behala I had to change my tram at the Esplanade Terminus. As I was somewhat early, I decided to have a look at the wares displayed in the covered shelter in the middle of the Esplanade Gardens. And that was foolish of me. I ought to have taken the first available tram for Behala. But I didn't, and thus nearly brought about my own undoing.

A lot of vendors were selling periodicals—mostly pseudo-scientific—imported from America and England: dealing with gynaecology, sexology, crime and punishment, wireless, sunbathing, hypnotism, telepathy and occult sciences in general—a strange medley of subjects. There was, however, a small knot of people surrounding a man draped in a saffron *namabali*—a priest's counterpane—embroidered with sacred formulas, and he was not hawking any periodicals. Naturally he attracted my attention. 'An unusual sort of a hawker,' I murmured to myself. Unwittingly I must have thought aloud, for I was immediately accosted by a fellow who had been watching me for some time.

'Do you know what he is selling?' he wanted to know.

I did not.

'Well,' the man addressed me in a friendly way, 'I shall tell you: he is selling nothing, but giving things away—for a small consideration. Had he opened a shop he would have made a fortune in no time.'

I listened and did not say anything.

'He is a pious man,' the other went on. 'He is a real sadhu. Compassion has moved him to show charity towards Calcutta's unbelieving millions.'

'What exactly is he giving away?' I asked, being a fool: I ought to have left alone the admirer of a pious man exercising charity.

'You may easily get from him a free booklet on Madan Annand Modak.'

'What's that?'

The man came very close to me and whispered: 'It increases virility. It will make you bold as a tiger.'

I turned away from him. But perhaps my blushing made him impudent. He followed me about like a dog—no longer whispering, but barking the virtues of the nostrum—and thrust a packet into my pocket. He was a disciple of the man in *namabali* and was anxious to be of service to me 'for a mere bagatelle of a gold mohur'. It was imperative for him, he declared, to raise some money before sunset: his house was mortgaged and his wife was contemplating suicide, and he himself was starving. I threw back his packet at him as I ran after a tramcar going in the direction of the Old Kidderpore Bridge. The importunate pest flew after me like a monkey and took his seat by my side, loudly calling Heaven to witness my ill-treatment of a poor, starving man. I was accused of letting him down: he had come to the Esplanade Tram Shelter especially for me, and I was unwilling to part with a few paltry rupees for a medicament prepared exclusively for my benefit. Other passengers stared at me, and a walrus-moustached man sitting opposite to me began grumbling about the ways students misbehaved in Calcutta. 'They are a lawless crowd,' he muttered. I became red in the face, and did not know what to do.

Meanwhile, the tout had reduced the price of the medicament I did not want, from one gold mohur to ten rupees; and then suddenly he dropped it to one rupee. Just to get rid of him I gave him half a rupee and asked him to leave me in peace. It looked as though it were more than he had expected: his mood changed immediately as he thrust into my pocket, almost forcibly, a packet of Madan Annand Modak wrapped in brown paper as well as a sheaf of pamphlets. He was a shameless fellow: before jumping out of the moving tramcar he bawled at the top of his voice that for students his guru was always ready to make concessions. Even after he had got off he kept on shouting: 'No packet is genuine without that red sheet I gave you. Please read it and talk about it to your friends. The Modak will make you bold like a tiger, full of vigour. You will be able to face any woman in the world without trembling.'

I thought I was lucky to get rid of that tout with a half rupee. Had he accompanied me right to the terminus where Roma was waiting for me it would have been a real calamity. I took out a leaflet to see what it said about the famous Madan pills. The name of this product seemed familiar to me, for Calcutta's walls were once plastered with posters extolling its capacity of curing beriberi and other diseases prevalent in the rainy season.

Those pamphlets proved to be of absorbing interest. They consisted mainly of testimonials from satisfied clients: their number was legion and included almost everyone worth knowing in the universe. Each page bore a crude, smudgy woodcut portrait of an eminent personality as well as a few lines extracted from some famous speech or a saying. 'These excerpts alone,' I said to myself, 'are worth more than a gold mohur. One can easily compile a good "Ask-me-another" from them.' Abraham Lincoln's Second Inaugural Address followed a quotation from the Duke of Wellington's comment on Lord Combermere: 'He is a fool, and a damned fool; but he can take Rangoon.' There was the full text of Bernard Shaw's 'Letter to *The Times* on behalf of the monkeys of the world' and of Gandhi's appeal against the use of rat-traps by the peasants in the Khaira district. ... A marvellous collection of authors, poets, politicians, saints, freaks, highwaymen, seamen, and many others—of all countries and of all ages. It surpassed in its variety of languages and scripts the leaflets accompanying Kutnow's Powerful Powders, which I considered up till then a record-breaker with its thirty-two different scripts of the world.

I had not finished examining the pamphlets when I found the tram already at my journey's end, I hurriedly got up as I emptied my pockets of those pamphlets and that wretched packet of Madan Annand Modak.

A minute later I was cursing myself and all the touts of Calcutta. I was ready to kick myself, but it was too late. It was the packet of the nostrum which I had pushed into Roma's hands and her collection of semi-precious stones was in the tramcar's waste-paper container along with the pamphlets. Roma smiled and looked prettier than ever but I felt like crying. I knew the moment she opened the packet our friendship would come to an end. I begged her to give it back to me because it was unworthy of her.

'Then why did you get it for me?' she twittered.

'It is not what I intended to get,' I mumbled, not knowing what to say.

'That doesn't matter,' she murmured, and thanked me once again for the gift. The maximum concession I got from her was the promise that she would not open it till she had reached home.

What was I to do? 'The Madan pills cannot be poison,' I argued within me. But that was just whistling in the dark. 'What about the red sheet?' I asked myself. 'No packet genuine without this red sheet!' That sheet was, I knew, worse than poison. I recalled what it stated: 'Madan Annand Modak is good for Males as well as for Females. It is a sure and infallible remedy for all Diseases, particularly for the following: Baldness, Debility, Lack of Brain Power, Loss of Memory, Giddiness, Hysteria, Chronic Venereal Diseases, Sterility, Adultery, Impotency, Nymphomania, Still Birth, Pregnancy. Reduced price for bona fide students.'

I might have been an ass, but not quite so big an ass as not to realize the gravity of offering such a thing to a Woman. For the life of me I do not know how I dared to look Roma in the face that afternoon. I had then only one thought in my mind: 'Let the earth swallow me.' 'Lord!' I prayed fervently as I walked by her side, 'Let me vanish into thin air. Let me disappear from the earth without leaving the slightest trace of myself.'

Naturally, in those circumstances I scarcely paid any attention to what Roma said or what I saw. I moved about with her like an automaton and viewed everything through a haze. I hardly bothered to examine the outward appearance of the Palace of the Talukdar of Pagulpur. The Snake-Pit was in the innermost quadrangle of that vast pile built in imitation of the Atala Mosque of Jaunpur on the Gumti river. I gave only a cursory glance at the entrance, which was through a covered passage resembling the nave of an immense church supported by pointed arches.

Thousands of pigeons lodged in this passage. They numbered, if I were to believe the red-turbaned guide who took charge of us, fifty thousand: the favourite ones of the owner were called the Rishmis. I was not interested in what the man was saying, though Roma seemed to be impressed by his fantastical account of the silken-tailed pigeons. 'Each one of them,' the guide bragged, 'costs fifteen hundred rupees. You may buy a pair for three thousand rupees. And if you want more than a pair you will not get them from us even if you paid fifty thousand rupees. They are the favourites of the Master.'

Beyond the arched entrance was the first quadrangle. Its sides were lined with large cages containing all varieties of monkeys. The savage pigtailed monkeys—as big as mastiffs—seemed to be the ones which the Talukdar loved. Roma made some remarks about these ferocious beasts which in their jungle haunts will readily attack and kill men. This elicited a new piece of information from our guide: before becoming a disciple of Prem Swami the Talukdar amused himself by breeding prize pigtails and watching the fights of these monkeys with mastiffs. 'Now, however,' he added, 'the Master is interested in reptiles. He wants to breed a non-venomous species of snakes.'

Before being taken to the Snake-Pit we were allowed to have a peep into the Talukdar's private suite. The man who was spending a fortune every day in maintaining his menagerie of literally thousands of beasts slept on the bare floor: a piece of frayed rug was his bed and bedstead. He led, we were told, a life of austerity like the other disciples of Prem Swami.

The guide took me apart to tell me that his Master's religious conversion forced him to give up his harem. He was no longer a slave to his concubines, officially known as the Supernumerary Begums, nor to his four legal wives, the real Begums.

I was not interested in that sort of gossip.

'His tastes have changed,' the guide persisted in whispering. He cast a glance in the direction of Roma who was then engrossed in examining a cuckoo clock. 'But,' he continued, 'he prefers the company of young men. He likes good-looking students.'

I could have slapped his face. But the thought of the packet of the Madan pills in Roma's handbag made me take everything in a different light. I was too depressed to feel angry with anyone but myself.

Cuckoo clocks filled the Talukdar's private suite. His reception room was as bare of furniture as his sleeping quarters. The walls looked barer than those of an abandoned barn. The emptiness was enhanced by the torn rugs on the floor and brackets crowded with cuckoo clocks, musical boxes, and toy chalets. He was a connoisseur of mechanical songsters.

'My Master is a saintly man.' The guide turned his eyes heavenwards to impress Roma. 'Like Prem Swami he loves plain living and pious thinking.'

'I presume so,' murmured Roma as she winked at me. I was too worried to pay any heed to her frivolity.

The quadrangle which was known as the Snake Yard was a most impressive affair. It was not surprising that the upkeep of his snakes, as well as the menageries in the different quadrangles was ruining the Talukdar. It was common knowledge that he was right up to his neck in debts. Wicked tongues insinuated that his financial embarrassments led to his religious conversion in the hope that Prem Swami's disciples would help him to overcome them, and a makeshift arrangement was made at Prem Swami's behest for this Moslem convert: the Talukdar's estate was mortgaged to Hanuman Vandar in exchange for a big loan.

The Snake-Pit itself was an immense oval, fenced all round, and dug into the earth—some twelve feet below the ground level. It looked like a gigantic swimming pool without any water. Its sides were lined with the smoothest tiles of porcelain, whose almost oily surface made it impossible for the snakes to scale it. The utmost the reptiles could climb up without immediately slipping down was perhaps a yard. No snake, however, bothered to give a demonstration of its scaling capacity while I was watching them.

They seemed to be more interested in going in and out of the beehive compartments of the huge rockery which formed a sort of island in the midst of the oval. Inside this rock garden there lived, I was told, several thousands of reptiles. Some of these showed only half of their bodies—the ends of their tails or their heads—and manifested complete indifference to the ceaseless movements of the rest of their company, which evidently found considerable pleasure in continuously wriggling up and down the rough surface of the stones.

There were a few isolated iron cages with heavy crossbars: prisons of the larger serpents like the boa constrictors, pythons and others of their kind.

The sight of the pit would certainly have disgusted me had not my thoughts been elsewhere: all the while I was turning over in mind the stupid adventure with the tout at the Esplanade Tram Terminus. I barely saw what was passing before my eyes. Even the gruesome spectacle of the bigger snakes making sudden darts to the barriers of their cages to catch some of the smaller reptiles that inadvertently came too near them did not affect me. I watched unperturbed several of the larger ones trying to poke their heads through the crossbars of their cages with the bodies of their victims hanging down from their mouths.

There was not much of Prem Swami's *ahimsa*—'Love one another'—in that place. The snakes seemed to be as unaffected by Jogin-Da's diets as the Siamese fighting fish.

What sort of dieting were these snakes subjected to?

Apart from the fact that the snake venom was collected regularly by the Agrawallah Vaccine Institute for medicinal purposes, I got nothing worth mentioning from the guide.

Was it true that Jogin-Da advised the Talukdar on the nature of food suitable for serpents?

The guide pretended to be deaf and talked about the professional snake-charmers in charge of feeding and cleaning the cages of the bigger reptiles and of the oval as well. 'They move about this place among these creatures,' he declaimed for the benefit of a number of other spectators apart from Roma and myself, 'just as you or I would move about a goldfish pond.

They do not pay any heed to where they plant their feet. They are amazing the way they handle snakes.'

'Are they also Prem Swami's disciples?'

'No. They are Santals. They call themselves Sapuriahs.'

'Santals?' Roma gave a sidelong glance at me. She then murmured that I ought to know more about the Sapuriahs than our guide as I belonged to the Santal country.

'What sort of snake-pits have you in your country?' asked the guide, turning towards me.

I mumbled something about our snake-pits in the Penhari Parganas being very old and empty at present of reptiles. All that remained of them were broken piles and the inscription: 'You must face what frightens you.'

My recital came to an unexpected end, because of a sudden cry of alarm from Roma.

'Ah! Ah!' she wailed. While taking out her handkerchief she had dropped my present into the pit! 'It is gone. Ah! Ah!'

'What a blessing,' I said to myself and felt like falling down on my knees to express my gratitude to providence. A pleasant assurance immediately lightened my movements. I became a different being.

The guide tried to fetch a Sapuriah to retrieve the brown packet, but I restrained him. It was a relief to see the pills and the brown-paper wrapping gobbled up by a number of charmingly-striped snakes. My spirits rose. I felt like whistling.

I became bolder than I had ever been in Roma's company, and took her by the arm to drag her away from the Snake-Pit. She who never permitted me to touch her little finger allowed me to pet her in public. 'Roma, you must not worry,' I spoke in a paternal tone. 'That present was nothing. I told you before it was not worthy of you. I shall get something better.'

'Certainly it contained a long letter,' she murmured. 'What did you write? Did it contain a rosary? Or a string of beads?'

'Tell me, what is your birth-stone? Let us now go and see the statue of Rishmi.'

~

The stucco statue of a semi-nude lady—probably Rishmi—in the act of feeding a number of pigeons, hens and mice, could hardly be considered a work of art. It was weather-worn and overgrown with moss. Few visitors bothered to look at it. In fact, I myself would not have spent a minute over it had not the guide drawn my attention to a bronze plaque with Latin words. 'An old brass,' I murmured to Roma half in earnest and half in fun. 'It bears two exotic names, Padre Anton Pfeffer and Padre Gregor Mendel.'

'You can't call it really old,' the guide commented. 'It may be only sixty or seventy years old.'

That was true. The plaque informed us that it was put up in 1866 in recognition of the help received from the tables of Rishmi by the aforementioned priests.

'Who was Rishmi?'—'She was born towards the middle of the eighteenth century.'

'What did she do to deserve this monument?'—'Rishmi bred different sorts of animals,' the guide explained. She was the wife of the gardener of a former Talukdar of Pagulpur. 'It was for the pleasure of her Master she discovered the art of breeding the silken-tailed pigeons. The birds are therefore named after her.'

Rishmi devised a simple plan for explaining her method of breeding exotic pigeons. She was illiterate, but knew how to handle the brush. She drew on a scroll two birds—the father and the mother—of two different varieties and underneath them she showed the results of her crossings: the descendants of the original parents. Her scrolls were like genealogical charts.

'Looks like a forecast of Mendelian laws,' I remarked.

'I presume I am one of Rishmi's exotic birds.' Roma smiled.

It was from her I heard for the first time the limerick on mixed marriages.

> There was a young lady called Starky
> Who had an affair with a darky:
> The result of her sins
> Was quadruplets, not twins:
> One black, and one white, and two khaki.

All that the guide said about Rishmi was interesting, and it was nice to have felt Roma's arms interlocked in mine! But the visit to the Snake-Pit was no solution to my worries.

The vision of the Daughters of Mara—the phantom temptresses—continued to torment me.

PART THREE

And Many Waters

I

Information about *old* Calcutta and the ancient temple of the Snake Goddess Manasa was not easy for me to secure.

Even about *new* Calcutta reliable data are meagre: all that one knows is that it came into existence when Job Charnock discarded his usual oriental dress to put on an impossible theatrical costume: heavy English broadcloth, and an ill-fitting, full-bottomed wig, a broad-leafed Flemish beaver hat to crown his head and a buff belt with a massive gold buckle to girdle his ample paunch.

It happened on a Sunday in the broiling month of August, sixteen hundred and ninety years after the Nativity, when the almost Indianized Charnock, garbed as an English gentleman at the request of the Viceroy of the Great Mogul—Prince Azim Khan the Æsthete—hoisted the flag of St George on the mud banks of the river Hooghly.

A small crowd sheltered under the shade of a nearby *neem* tree watched him. They believed that the flag-post was planted at a point equidistant from the three villages—Sutanati, Govindapur and Kalighat—acquired on behalf of Charnock's employers known as John Company. They cheered. It was fun to see a new flag go up: the standard of St George with the cross and a drawn dagger in the top corner next the staff.

There was no chaplain present for blessing this foundation ceremony, and Job Charnock did the Bible reading.

The Great Book had been fetched from the house of the Palits of Chandernagore. It was the Douai Version that had originally been sent; but Charnock was not a Papist. Though that very morning he had sacrificed in the Barrackpore cemetery a cock in the pagan fashion to the memory of his first wife, he insisted, as a good Anglican, on the other version: King James's text. The Authorized Version reached the landing ghat by the *neem* tree not a minute too soon. The Great Book was thrown open quite haphazardly—in the fashion in which Virgil was consulted in the Middle Ages—for some sort of a prophetic clue about the new acquisition of John Company. Though he had the run of the whole Bible a curious fatality led him to choose a most tactless text.

'Many waters cannot quench love,' Job Charnock read out. 'Neither can the floods drown it.'

'That's true,' loudly exclaimed one of the listeners: he was a *do-bhasi*—an interpreter—who also served as a scribe to the pilgrims visiting the temple of Kali at Kalighat and the shrine of Manasa at Sutanati. 'That's very true,' repeated the crowd: they followed the interpreter's lead.

Job Charnock looked in the direction of interrupters. Near the *do-bhasi* stood a buxom Hindu ex-widow—Job Charnock's new love—and his gaze caught hers. The lady blushed, and Job Charnock smiled. It was for her sake the flag-post was planted near the *neem* tree: the exact emplacement of the funeral pyre from which she had been rescued some weeks earlier by the gallant and faithful servant of John Company, Job Charnock—one of the most remarkable (and least known) sons of Albion.

'We have a little sister,' Job Charnock began reading again, 'and she hath no breasts.'

'That is not true,' vigorously protested the interpreter as he turned towards Job Charnock's lady-love. 'She has breasts and well-formed breasts too. Like sweet melons.'

The Hindu ex-widow drew her veil over her face. Job Charnock muttered that the interpreter was a fool, but was not altogether displeased at the reference to the charms of his object of affection.

Did the Biblical text forecast his destiny, or that of his new foundation? Who could tell? He skipped, inadvertently, a couple of lines, and concluded his reading with the ninth verse of the last chapter of the Song of Songs:

'If she be a wall, we will build upon her a palace of silver: and if she be a door, we will inclose her with boards of cedar.'

'She will be neither the one nor the other,' commented an Indo-Portuguese priest from Satgaon. 'Calcutta will behave like a queer woman: a barren trollop, mother to none.'

At this some storks—hitherto watching quietly the business of flag-hoisting—burst into fits of laughter. As people had never before heard storks cackle, they too joined the birds in expressing their mirth in an appropriate way to end the ceremony of founding modern Calcutta.

The visitor from Chandernagore who had brought by boat the Bible from which Job Charnock read his text took due note of all these happenings. He did not laugh. He wondered if the new foundation would one day rival Chandernagore's attractiveness.

'Modern Calcutta must have a modern coat of arms,' the citizens began arguing among themselves. 'We must have a crest. What shall it be?'

'A stork,' suggested ironically the visitor from Chandernagore. 'It will bring babies to Calcutta's childless lap.'

This received general approval. 'Let our device be a stork,' they all repeated.

'Why a stork?' asked the surprised Viceroy of the Great Mogul when they sought his formal approval. Viceroy Azim Khan the Æsthete was renowned for his fastidious taste. He was a lover of things beautiful; he usually dressed in exquisite yellow and rose-coloured garments. He had no liking for storks. 'Why not a heron?' he inquired. 'There are herons on the banks of the Hooghly. These lovely birds are far more auspicious than the ordinary storks.'

'Maybe,' they replied. 'But a stork is reputed to be pious. It pretends to be a vegetarian and will not steal a fish when someone is nearby. It thrives on toads and frogs. It flaps its wings like a robed doctor arguing a point. It wears the air of an English sabbath all the week round.'

'In that case,' proposed the man from Chandernagore, 'you would do well to have as your device a stork with a fish in its beak.'

'That's an idea.' They were delighted with the suggestion.

In due course the men of Calcutta had the satisfaction of admiring the new foundation's coat of arms; it was embellished with a Latin tag furnished by the College of Heralds in London. As they knew no Latin the motto had to be interpreted. Two pundits gave two different versions: 'I gobble as much as I can,' declared one translator, while the other proclaimed: 'Progress before everything.'

'This double meaning does not really matter.' The happy citizens rejoiced. 'We can afford two mottoes. We have scored a victory over Chandernagore.' Chandernagore's arms bore a French text—*Ni vous sans moi, ni moi sans vous*—comprehensible to every schoolboy in Chandernagore, but Calcutta's Latin motto was unintelligible even to the pundits of London. 'Is this not a real triumph? Who cares for the French nonsense about clarity? Our flag is the same as London's flag—the cross and the dagger—and our motto is as obscure as London's fog.'

'Calcutta's motto is double,' the men of Chandernagore remarked. 'Calcutta will hobble and gobble.'

~

Since that memorable Sunday in August Calcutta has been gobbling and hobbling. It has steadily expanded—*progressed*—at the expense of the neighbouring villages and attractive hamlets, beautiful gardens and fruit-yielding orchards. Sacred fanes and sanctified groves, sanctuaries of ricebirds and sheldrakes, ornamental grounds and no less delightful lotus pools, clumps of bamboo and topes of peepuls, and paddy fields and open heaths have disappeared and are disappearing in Calcutta's maw.

'We must progress faster,' said some of the City Fathers. 'We must gobble more,' responded their admirers. 'Let us build over the only open space in the heart of the city. The Maidan is an eyesore.' This led to a stormy debate: because the Maidan was endowed as grazing fields for cattle by Manohar Dass in the days of John Company. Prem Swami's followers renowned for their love for cows opposed the motion. There was a tie in the voting and this led to a wilder storm in the Corporation Hall. At this juncture one City Father rose to ask, 'What about that stork?' 'Which stork?' 'The one which decorates the city's coat of arms. Let us forget about the Maidan for the time being. The stork is more important.' Prem Swami's followers nodded their assent. The debate took a different turn.

It was proposed that Calcutta being the Premier City of India it behoved that it should have a more imposing coat of arms than a solitary stork swallowing a single fish. Immediately there was a general agreement on principle, and later started arguments and counter-arguments; whether two storks holding two fish in their beaks would be preferable to a dozen gobbling away all the fish in the river Hooghly. This new turn in the discussion greatly grieved the followers of Prem Swami: they were vegetarians, and their preference was for a pair of nutcrackers.

'Why nutcrackers?' some innocent souls inquired.

'An intelligent person is expected to find the answer for himself.' That was the blunt reply of the spokesmen of the Swami's disciples. 'A trace of obscurity enhances the general charm. Take the Latin tag attached to the present coat of arms. Who knows its real meaning? Why is the University of Calcutta changing the inscription of its official seal? From *Advancement of Learning* it will become *Shri.* And what is the real meaning of *Shri?* Is it just *Mister?* Or is it *Let us make money?* Or does it imply *We have beaten Bacon hollow and have no concern for Advancement of Learning?* Anyway, the University has discarded the Lion and the Unicorn and opted for the Lotus bearing the mystic word *Shri.* Let us too have something mysterious. I propose nutcrackers.'

Some applauded, while others shook their heads disapprovingly.

'In any case,' the orator continued, 'we do not want a stork on our coat of arms. It evokes slavish memories of the olden days when we were not progressive. The hypocritical stork is the symbol of an English Sunday. Who cares for such a thing on our coat of arms?'

The rest of the speech was drowned in thunderous uproar. They all declared that they did not care for storks: storks were not vegetarians and incapable of cracking hard nuts. The problem of hard nuts was in the mind of the City Fathers.

There were some odd bits of old Calcutta—of Calcutta dating from the days long before Job Charnock was born—which the Corporation wanted to crack.

'Our external device,' Prem Swami's followers assured all journalists, more particularly William Hickey's numerous descendants, 'will give us inner strength. Under the standard of Nutcrackers we shall break the resistance of the odd bits of old Calcutta and force progress on them. A modern city must not have scruples in sweeping away old corners. We don't care for the wailings of old cronies. We will rebuild old temples in modern style, in ferro-concrete.'

~

'Let Prem Swami and his gang be hanged,' muttered a student from Bajra-Jogini. He was a hot-headed fellow, who shaved his head once a week to keep his brain cool, and I had rarely spoken to him: speaking to him meant quarrelling—a weakness from which all sons of Bajra-Jogini seem to suffer ever since their native place gave birth to a great peace-lover called Asita. 'They think of rebuilding the Temple of Manasa the Snake Goddess in ferro-concrete'—the son of Bajra-Jogini growled with indignation as he read out this piece of news.

All of a sudden I discovered that I had some affinity with him, and that his quarrelsomeness might have been due to his nostalgia for the green fields and ancient monuments.

That night a few students scaled the walls of the hostel compound—it was strictly forbidden to leave the precincts after ten o'clock, but we did not care—and went straight to the Old

Cathedral of Calcutta. Our climbing over the railings was not approved by the night-watchman, but our blood was up; had he tried to intervene the fellow from Bajra-Jogini would have murdered him in the name of his mother: she was called after the goddess Manasa. We lit a bonfire in the ill-kept compound of the church, and painted on the walls of the octagonal mausoleum of Job Charnock—Calcutta's first Governor—excerpts from his 'Foundation Speech':

'If she be a wall, we will build upon her a palace of silver. And if she be a door, we will inclose her with boards of cedar.'

'What is Calcutta?' we wrote underneath. 'Is she a wall? If so, why put up sheds of corrugated iron instead of palaces of silver? Is she a door? If so, why enclose her in plywood shacks instead of boards of cedar?

'Why replace the old temple of Manasa with a modern ferro-concrete horror? When *new* Calcutta was founded a solemn promise was given that *old* Calcutta's shrines should remain inviolate till Doomsday.'

We wrote a few letters and telegrams in the nearby General Post Office or General Telegraph Office, I am not quite sure—the one that was open both night and day, requesting editors of various newspapers to remind modern Calcutta of the oath given to old Calcutta on Sunday, August 24th, 1690. Our messages were addressed even to William Hickey's descendants and, of course, to Prem Swami.

Old Calcutta, we pointed out, was referred to in the letters of the Fuggers of Augsburg, in the journals of Dürer of Nuremberg, in the notebooks of Rembrandt of Amsterdam. We left out the names of merchants and missionaries of England and France on purpose, but we did rub in that Bengal's master-poet Kavi Kankan Chandi wrote about old Calcutta's Manasa Mandir whose preservation was a matter of concern to all who cared for old Bengal.

The newspapers ignored us, or rather our messages: for they did publish photographs of our writings on the wall of Job Charnock's Mausoleum—the oldest specimen of English masonry in Calcutta; and we were referred to as a band of lawless hooligans from the *mofussil*! Prem Swami, however, condescended to give an interview to the hot-headed fellow from Bajra-Jogini.

'When a thing is old and broken,' the Swami expostulated, 'we declare it to be useless and throw it away. And I find no reason why some up-country young people should make so much fuss about that old and broken-down temple. My disciples will replace it by a new one. Something in ferro-concrete lined with alabaster slabs. It will be made as modern and as attractive as the shrines in Hollywood. I am for progress.'

My heart felt heavy the day I read in the papers that the 'Storks' had been defeated by the 'Nutcrackers' in the Calcutta Corporation, and the work of modernizing the Temple of the Snake Goddess Manasa had already begun.

One more landmark was being pulled down: the Manasa Temple was destined to become a memory like Rani Nilmani's Estate! I decided not to tarry any longer in exploring the shrine.

II

A narrow, winding lane, flanked by unbalconied three-storied brick houses closely huddled together, led to a flight of moss-covered steps and a masonry platform on which grew a number of peepul trees screening from view the entrance to the Temple of the Goddess Manasa and the Shrine of the Warrior God.

The approach was uninviting. It was not yet dusk but the passage appeared sombre as a tunnel—standing in its middle one could almost touch the walls on both sides. It needed street lights in daytime. It was not surprising that the City Fathers wanted to demolish the whole quarter. I felt some sympathy for them as I approached the steps.

The staircase leading to the platform and the screen of peepul trees brought me to the high wall surrounding the temple: entrance to it was obtained through an arched doorway. Beyond it were further flights of steps resembling the ghats on the banks of the river Hooghly: only instead of going down these went up to the main structure.

Once inside I began wondering whether I should remove my sandals immediately or wait till I reached the holy grounds where a *pujari* usually repeated the formula current in our temples: 'Take thy shoes from off thy feet, for the place whereon thou standest is holy.' There was no one about to tell me what was customary in the Manasa Mandir. So I hesitatingly stood where I was and stared vacantly in the direction of a free archway beyond which rose further flights of steps.

That archway was fascinating. It was not exactly what one would usually call an archway, but a series of six freestanding columns in a row: hexagonal columns bearing a horizontal beam, and each column linked with its adjacent ones, in addition to the straight top shaft, by arches coming from the entraves. Its function seemed to be purely decorative. It had, no doubt, symbolical implications as well: for there is hardly anything in a Hindu temple that has not a mystical significance. As might be guessed, even the structure of a column has its own value: a six-sided pillar is called *Skandakanta,* in other words, Beloved by the Warrior God, who, as our legends say, is the God of the Five

Senses, Eros, reincarnated as the Master of Six Senses to fight the demons of darkness. Anyway, as I had no one to consult there at that time I was not quite sure of the full implication of the free standing six-sided shafts.

Someone hailed me from a distance. Had I any leather goods with me? Any leather purse or belt? Or leather spectacle case? Or camera?

And I knew it was time for me to kick off my sandals and roll off my socks. The touch of the cold granite to the naked sole of the feet was like stepping into icy water. Involuntarily I squirmed. It took, however, only a few seconds to get adjusted to walking on bare feet. Out of the corner of my eye I noticed the clean-shaven *pujari*—the acolyte—smile. I took a long while in ranging my footwear along the bottom step: I wanted to be left alone; I had no need of a guide to show me round a temple and to cross-examine me. In some of the places of pilgrimage—particularly at Puri and Madura—they make a visitor repeat the names of his forbears right up to his seventh predecessors: two parents, four grandparents, eight great-grandparents, sixteen great-great-grandparents—up to one hundred and twenty-eight five-times-great-grandparents. All this in order to establish one's identity! I did not want to be bothered with such a roll-call.

'I shall wait till you are ready,' said the acolyte.

I had to look up and give a smile. I could not possibly say: 'Leave me in peace, and I shall find my own way.'

'Which shrine do you want to visit? The altar of the Warrior God, or that of Manasa-Devi?'

I thought of visiting both, but for a few moments my lips did not utter a word. The acolyte before me was a woman devotee—a *pujarini* and not a *pujari*. This was rather unexpected. Of course, I ought to have prepared myself for surprises of all sorts in that temple. First, its entrance was so mean; and secondly, immediately after crossing the sacred threshold, the flight of steps was such a staggering sight; and thirdly, the beautiful colonnade of six hexagonal pillars. From the days of Job Charnock the quarter of the professional gay ladies in Calcutta was the Golden Pagoda district, and the temple I was visiting bore the reputation of being primarily patronized by them. In these circumstances what right had I to be surprised to find a woman acolyte as my guide? After all, its presiding deity was the Warrior God—the Reincarnation of the Lord of Love. 'In such a place everything is possible.' I murmured, and barely heard the *pujarini* repeat for me the inscription beneath the tympanum of the bas-relief above the gateway of the main entrance. Though I heard indistinctly the verses stuck in my memory: they referred to the Warrior God in the phase of Eros, seated on a peacock and drawing his bow fixed with a flower-tipped arrow,

> I am the God of the sensuous fire
> That moulds all Nature in forms divine;
> The symbols of death and of man's desire,
> The springs of change in the world are mine;
> In many a legend and many a shape,
> In the solemn grove and the crowded street,
> I am the Slayer, whom none escape;
> I am Death trod under a fair girl's feet.

'I should like to visit only the Manasa shrine to-day,' I told my guide as I swung the cord of the huge bell which each supplicant usually pulls as he goes in or out of a temple. It was a thick cord, more like a ship's cable than anything. It had to be strong, I guessed, because the clapper was a bronze pestle of some six feet in length. The huge bell swung freely on its crossbeam supported by two gigantic leogryphs of red granite. I tugged at the cord and swung it hard, but the bell did not emit any sound. 'That's funny,' I mumbled and gave the clapper another hard pull. Yet not the slightest clang!

I felt ashamed of my failure to make that bell peal and jostled with the cord. The clapper did strike the sides of the bell, and did it vigorously. Nevertheless, I did not hear any sound worth mentioning: Why was it like that?

'The bell is deep toned,' the *pujarini* explained. 'Its sound is so full and deep that it can scarcely be heard by the human ear. The voice of Love sounds in the same way: it touches the heart even before it reaches the hearing.'

Jogin-Da, since the day I knew him, advised me to avoid all priests, priestesses, acolytes, and others connected with temples and places of pilgrimage. 'They are just frauds,' he told me. 'Dissolute creatures, that's what they are. If a temple pleases you as a building, visit it always on your own, and pretend to be deaf if anyone talks to you.' Maybe, that was why I was at the beginning prejudiced against the *pujarini*. It is also possible that I did not like her scanty costume and shaven crown and eyebrows. But the moment she had finished her comment on the inaudible sound of the bell, my attitude towards her changed. Her words reminded me of one of Padre Johan's sermons on the inaudible notes of the organ in his chapel.

~

Was I so very different from other students of my age? Why could I never find out the causes of my likes and dislikes? Unable to understand my own mind, how was I to uncover the meaning of other people's motives?

When I was at Chumchicke Adhikari's soirée dansante I made a scene over the semi-nudity of some of his 'decoy women' and yet in the land of the Santals—my own country—women were certainly not over-dressed by any standard. In theory at least, I ought not to have been shocked by the dress, or lack of dress, of the girl who gave the hula-hula dance. Nevertheless, I did protest and protest most vehemently when she gave a demonstration of a modern step.

As I was walking about the courtyards of the temple with the *pujarini* I asked myself if it was the costume of the hula-hula dancer which distressed me, or was it her dance? Wearing as her nether garment nothing but a slender belt from which hung a bunch of coloured straw which came halfway down—in between—her thighs and some strings of beads as her only upper garment, this 'decoy woman' stepped into the circle of limelight with her elbows stuck out. As the music started she laid her splayed-out hands on her hips and began slowly to move her stomach in a wide circle, her knees bending with the swing of the hips, and the stomach rolling out and round all the while. With the varying rhythm of the music she slackened or hastened her vulgar movements. While her hips swung wider and her stomach rolled quicker, she increasingly became a more and more disgusting sight: obscenity personified.

And the same I who had not hesitated to create a general row over the hula-hula dancer's scantiness of clothes was now at perfect ease in the company of a shaven-headed and shaven-browed woman acolyte whose costume was almost scantier! To tell the truth, at that moment I did not bother to entertain the least thought concerning her dress. I took her for granted as she was: a symbol like the other symbols which formed an integral part of the temple; she was like the deep-toned bell at the entrance of the temple or like the bas-reliefs of heroic and erotic figures on the walls—in perfect harmony with her environment.

~

She was certainly well informed about the different objects worth noticing in the temple: the lesser known deities in the niches, and the symbolic patterns on the pavement. These designs were, I was told, anamorphosed mosaics, which when viewed from a particular angle gave recognizable images. 'Otherwise,' I understood—and saw for myself—'they appear to be nothing but meaningless chaos.' These as well as many other things I should certainly have overlooked had I done my exploration of the Golden Pagoda—as the temple was popularly called—all on my own.

'All these things are done in parable,' she reminded me more than once, 'so that seeing they may see and yet not perceive, and hearing they may hear, and not understand.'

'But why cannot truth be told plainly and without beating about the bush?' I asked, and immediately remembered the saying of the Punditji: if truth were revealed abruptly, it would be rejected forthwith and the revealer of truth chastised with thongs of leather. On another occasion he remarked: 'Truth is like light. The greater its intensity the greater its blinding power. None but the worshipper of the Sun should gaze on his effulgence and derive benefit from his endowment.' Anyway, I wanted to know what the *pujarini* had to say to my question and repeated: 'What's the use of symbols?'

Perception of truth, according to her, depended much on a worshipper's spiritual state and his degree of initiation: an eagle may contemplate the day star, but not the wren. 'Most men are like the poor wren. They will be blinded if they are presented with the vision of truth without adequate teaching and preparation.'

~

Perhaps she was right.

Mysteries and symbols can rarely be explained rationally: that was the view of the lecturer from Vienna who gave an address on Freudism at the Senate House.

What was the reason that prevented Plutarch from writing about the mysteries he had witnessed I do not know. And I think it is best that the secret of the esoteric rites in the Golden Pagoda should not be revealed to those who are not mentally prepared to receive them. Once in the company of a *yogini*—a woman hermit—I rode through a forest fire on the back of a nilgai. Why did not the fire scorch me? 'One day you will know,' the *yogini* told me. 'But for the time being remember, "Fire burns and water quenches." Nevertheless, there are laws beyond the limitations of natural laws.' Perhaps she too was right in not unveiling to me the secret of her magic that enabled her to be a fire-walker and to save me from being burnt to ashes. Was I at that time in the proper mood to appreciate what she could teach me? I do remember I was then more concerned with her nilgai than with her superhuman gifts.

My mind was working all the time I was in the temple. As I watched the dance of the *devadasis*—the handmaidens of the gods—in the *nat mandir*—the pillared pavilion—attached to the shrine, I did my best to analyse what was going on in me. My mind, I thought, was like a living organism whose different limbs were at war with one another, or like a beam of white light whose components—the violet, indigo, blue, green, yellow, orange and red rays—were vying with one another to gain supremacy: it was like a house divided. That being the case, I concluded that my understanding of the mysteries of the shrine was inevitably prejudiced, and my interpretations equally confused and incorrect.

~

Nevertheless, I do believe that I was not unappreciative of the artistic treasures of that place. Though not as vast a structure as the more famous temples of Orissa, the Golden Pagoda was not an inconsiderable building. Its chief interests to me were its long flights of steps, which created an illusion of immensity that undoubtedly affected all worshippers in the same way as myself.

'Every step you take,' my guide explained, 'on the stairways or the winding newels is a riddle trodden upon: a riddle which the understanding cannot answer, yet which our innermost being recognizes.'

I must have trodden upon very many riddles on that occasion. For, as I have already stated, immediately after penetrating the porch of the entrance I was confronted with several long flights of steps which finally conducted me to the open vestibule of the *nat mandir*.

This vestibule was a charming structure—as graceful as the temple dancers whose presence in it was responsible for its name: *nat mandir*—the Pavilion of Coryphæas. It was supported by eight *Rudra-kanta*—sixteen-sided—columns, bearing a circular dome, the ceiling of which was sculptured all over with bas-reliefs representing the zodiac. The shape of the dome was unusual for Calcutta: it was of the type which the people of the Penhari Parganas associate—rightly or wrongly—with Rajputana. Some refer to it—more correctly—as the Hindu cupola, because its most ancient examples are met with in Hindu temples only: both its appearance and construction are different from the Byzantine, Persian, and other kinds of domes. Hindu arches are without voussoirs.

The canopy of the *nat mandir* consisted of concentric rings of such horizontal arches—the upper rim of each ring slightly overlapping the lower edge of the one immediately above it. The horizontal ones, being free of the lateral thrust—the chief bane of the buildings employing the radiating arch—permitted eight slender pillars to bear an immense hemispherical roof without any danger of its collapsing. This feat would have been impossible had the architect used a Byzantine dome which would have demanded massive walls for support and transformed the Hindu *nat mandir* into an Orthodox Greek chapel, giving it an entirely different character and robbing it of its peculiarities and of the purpose for which it was put up. I thought of Profulla Babu's rather blunt aphorism about architecture and art in general. 'Art,' he insisted, 'is essentially the expression of a people's faith.'

One could easily guess that the builder of the *nat mandir* bore in mind that the temple dances were to be given in daylight and at a vantage point which would permit the worshippers seated on the long flights of steps to watch the performances of the *devadasis*—the handmaidens of the gods—and to be mentally prepared for the greater mysteries in the inner sanctuaries. Perhaps he had also thought that the dancers should be under the dome of heaven and therefore the ceiling—the hemispherical roof of the pavilion—was given the sculptured figures of the zodiac and other celestial bodies, and thus transformed symbolically into the vault of the sky.

'Only those worshippers,' the *pujarini* said, 'who have covered the steps of the temple and are convinced that they have solved the riddles that trouble them are the privileged ones to sit where the *devadasis* offer their prayers with dances.'

While talking about steps, I may mention that on either side of the main entrance there were some more, which I did not climb: these were winding stairs or newels which led to an open gallery above the porch. Like circumambulation round an altar, which is done in a clockwise fashion—with the right-hand side turned towards the throne of the deity—the ascent and descent of the newels were regulated by symbolic conventions and were meant to be undertaken by the initiated only.

Beyond the *nat mandir*—the Pavilion of Coryphæas—an ascent of three further flights of steps brought me into a spacious rectangular hall with an apsidal end and a flat roof; its three sides were open colonnades, while the fourth one facing the entrance was a semi-circular wall. At the four corners of this large hall were four domed, circular chambers, all looking alike.

In the midst of the central assembly room, where I expected to find an altar, there was an opening in the floor—a sort of a trapdoor—through which I was helped down a long and narrow newel of dark steps and brought into the chapel of Manasa, the Snake Goddess.

It was a sombre place, lit only by the flicker of a few tiny lamps—deflagrating spoons—fed with sandalwood oil. I guessed it was many feet below the ground though I did not count the number of steps—or riddles—in going down or coming up. Its walls were covered with mural paintings which, unfortunately, could hardly be seen owing to the general gloom of the place. Neither was it possible for me to examine the bas-reliefs on the walls of the passages which brought me back to the open air.

The atmosphere of the chapel of Manasa was heavy with the perfume of sandalwood oil and of the flowers heaped round the altar. In a way, it was oppressive. It created in me a feeling of fright—or was it awe?—and I did not spend more than a minute in that underground sanctuary. The physical exertion of covering so many steps had made me perspire, but in the chapel I felt my brow was covered with cold sweat. In such circumstances I paid little heed to what the *pujarini* recounted to me about the foundation of the Manasa temple, about the combat between the gods and the titans and how the latter always regained their strength by re-entering their mother's womb and re-emerging as new—endowed with greater prowess; and how, in order to defeat them, the primal ocean was churned.

The story of the titans led her to make some general remarks, which had they been made elsewhere I should certainly have contested. For example, she said: 'Evil is good in another form, and wisdom lies in recognizing the truth that evil cannot be cured by palliatives.'

It is hardly necessary for me to recount the well-known story of Manasa. Nor how she became the most honoured deity of all seafarers and boatmen of Lower Bengal. What was more interesting for me was the parallelism that Profulla Babu had drawn on one occasion between the Book of Job and the Story of Chand Sadagar the Worshipper. In the Manasa chapel there were mural paintings showing the trials of Chand Sadagar, and therefore when I regained the airy Pavilion of the Coryphæas I asked the *pujarini* whether or not those wall decorations were based on the epic of the poet Kavi Kankan, who gave us the earliest account of Chand Sadagar.

'They were painted,' she replied, 'long before the Bengali epic was written.'

III

Chand Sadagar, so our storytellers say, was a merchant of great affluence and of equally great magnanimity.

He owned scores of ships—a regular fleet—which carried his merchandise to distant places—the Maldives, Ceylon, Madagascar, Macassar, Champa, Bali, Java, Sumatra, Malaya, and other places: to Egypt his vessels brought sugar-candies, called *Misri;* to China icing sugar, named *Chini.* His chief pride was his faith in the god Siva, whom he worshipped. He never bowed before any other deity, not even before Siva's daughter: Manasa.

'Siva sustains me,' Chand Sadagar declared whenever someone suggested that he should build a temple in honour of Manasa. 'Siva suffices me too. What need have I of any other god or goddess?'

Chand Sadagar made his habitual remark while on board a vessel bound for Malaya. This immediately led the captain to protest. The ship was then skirting the Sagar Island, the delta formed by the river Hooghly where it empties itself into the Ganga Sagar: the reputed birthplace and favourite haunt of the Apsaras, the semi-divine nymphs who emerged from the froth and foam of the primal ocean when the gods and titans churned it for ambrosia.

'Beware, Master!' The captain of the vessel whispered, 'Beware lest the Dread Sisters hear you.'

'The Dread Sisters!' Chand Sadagar laughed loudly. 'You mean the phantoms? Those known by the name of the Apsaras? I am not superstitious. Neither am I impious. What can the phantoms do to a servitor of the Great God? Am I not a worshipper of Siva? Do not the winds and the waves obey him? Is not Siva the

Lord of all things created, both visible and invisible? I am not afraid of phantoms.'

The captain pointed his forefinger in the direction of the Sagar Island, and then put it crosswise over his lips: he wished Chand Sadagar would not make disparaging remarks about the Apsaras and their heavenly sister, Manasa. As a regular seafarer he knew all about the phantoms and the disasters wrought by them.

'Captain!' Chand Sadagar continued, paying little heed to the warning gesture of his friend, 'Are you afraid of phantoms? Of those unreal visions whom people call Apsaras? Who are they, anyway?'

~

For the sake of the Apsaras, so they say, many a god abandoned his seat in paradise, and many a titan rose in revolt against the Great Creator. It was their beauty that allured the immortals as well as the mortals.

'Marvellously beauteous all of them are,' sing the poets. These sea-born nymphs wear heavenly vestures and resplendent adornments. They cover themselves with priceless gems and bewitching jewels—gifts of the sea which saw their birth. They are elusive, for they possess the faculty of changing their forms and of becoming invisible at will. Their voice is melodious, and their songs tell of unknown marvels; they scatter their music to the winds; they sing of the world beyond the horizon, of the treasures of hidden places, of the gifts of palpable darkness and of blinding light, of the joys of fierce embrace and sudden extinction. They dance when the lightning tears the cloud-laden sky, and the storm lashes the sea to frenzy, and the flame flickers from the snow-crested mountains. They are proficient in the art of sorcery, and they readily bewitch the visionary: for they are always longing for new lovers though they themselves are loveless. They are the friends of Manasa, the Mind-born.

'Whose children are we?' the Apsaras asked as soon as they emerged from the churning of the primal ocean. 'Where are our parents?'

The gods remained mute with wonder: they had never gazed on beings of such surpassing grace in paradise. And the titans durst not utter a word: they could not conceive such visions of consummate delight to be real. And the men deprived of the power of speech covered their eyes, for these nymphs emanated radiance which was blinding.

'Who are our parents?' asked again the Apsaras. 'Who are we? Where is our abode?'

'You are my children,' replied Siva. 'You are the fruits of my seed. The universe is your abode. You are the incarnation of my joy. You will be known as the Visions of Beauty.'

'And who is our mother?' asked Urvashi the first-born of the Apsaras. 'Where is she?'

Siva's consort gave no reply: the Apsaras were not the offspring of her womb. She gave a sidelong glance at Manasa, her stepdaughter, who came out of Siva's third eye: from the fiery orb in the midst of the god's forehead. Manasa the Mind-born was not her child.

'Have we then no goddess to present us in the court of heaven?' asked the Apsaras.

'You have me,' answered Manasa. 'I too have no mother, but I am Siva's daughter like you. Let me be a sister to you.'

'Let us be sisters,' they murmured with delight. 'Manasa, we shall be your handmaidens too. But abandon paradise for our sake and make—like us—the universe your abode.'

'So shall I,' responded Manasa as she rose to her feet to join the Apsaras.

The gods, however, restrained her. What would happen to paradise bereft of the Mind-born goddess Manasa, the deity of Wisdom? They persuaded her to stay in the heavenly world on her own terms: 'That none shall reach Siva's throne save through Manasa, and they that are befriended by the Apsaras shall be deemed to be her children.'

'Let Manasa's wish be fulfilled,' they all implored and the Great God Siva accorded the boon.

'Let us rejoice,' chanted Urvashi and the other Apsaras. 'Our sister Manasa is the greatest of all goddesses. She is greater than any. For none shall reach the throne of the Great God save through Manasa's grace.'

'May you be loveless,' cursed Siva's consort for the unseemly rejoicing of the Apsaras. 'May you all be spouseless. May you all remain barren. May you be as unreal as mirages.'

It is a way with the gods that whenever a permanent curse is laid by them an abiding boon is also granted at the same time. Thus the sea-born nymphs though bereft of palpable or tangible forms, obtained the benediction that they could always count Manasa as one of them.

~

Chand Sadagar was not ignorant of the stories and legends connected with Manasa and the Apsaras. Only a short time ago, before he left his mansion at Champak Nagar his head gardener, Mali, had begged him to bear Manasa and her sisters in mind during his sea voyage.

'Master!' Mali enjoined, 'it is time for you to pay homage to Manasa.'

'Why?' asked Chand Sadagar.

'For Manasa's absence has caused blight in your orchards and gardens. Your groves are now reduced to clusters of petrified trees, and your lotus pools are ponds for breeding pestilence. All this has happened since you commanded the demolition of the altar to Manasa. I beseech you to change your mind.'

Chand Sadagar shook his head and repeated, 'I worship Siva and he sustains me. What need have I of any other god or goddess?'

'May I then ask one favour?' asked Mali. 'Will you please drop this lotus flower in the Ganga Sagar as your boat passes the Sagar Island?'

Chand Sadagar took the lotus in his hand only to throw it away. For he recalled that one of the many names attributed to Manasa was *Padma*—the lotus. 'Certainly,' he said to himself, 'Mali wants to pay a tribute to Manasa in this way and appease the Apsaras. Otherwise he would not have proposed my dropping the lotus near the Sagar Island, the alleged birth-site of the companions of Manasa.'

Mali begged him again for the favour he had asked.

'I worship Siva,' the obdurate Chand Sadagar repeated. 'Never shall I offer any homage to any other deity. Manasa is a sorceress. She is not even a goddess. Only the other day she came to me in the shape of a lovely girl and asked me to repeat to her the secret *mantra*—the sacred formula—with which I worship Siva. "A *mantra* is inefficacious," she said, "unless it makes you think. Do you know what it means?" And when I told her that I did not, she vanished into thin air, taking away with her the occult source of my strength. She reappeared, however, a moment later in the sky to reveal to the world my *mantra* and to twit me with the reproach: "*This is not by chance, nor in the course of nature. But even now worship me, and I will restore you to power.*" What power do I need from a sorceress whose companions are mirages? I worship Siva, and he suffices me. I shall not do anything that might be construed as worshipping Manasa.'

~

When the vessel was sailing past the Sagar Island, Chand Sadagar thought of his head gardener and murmured to himself that none but a simpleton would dream of overcoming the perils of the sea by dropping a lotus flower into the Ganga Sagar. He began arguing with the captain and accused all seafaring men of being superstitious. 'Tell me,' he finally asked, 'is Siva powerless? Is he not the creator of the universe? When a man worships him what need has he to pay any homage to Manasa and her handmaidens?'

'Siva is indeed great,' replied the captain. 'Good and evil both emanate from him. There is nothing that does not come from him. But we are mortals, and without Manasa's guidance we flounder and perish.'

The ship groaned as the rudder creaked and the wind rose. The captain retired to his post.

'Chand Sadagar!' the wind whispered, 'why have you demolished the altar to the goddess Manasa? It was her altar that made your orchards fruitful, your lotus pools beautiful, and your gardens full of blossoms.'

'Never shall I bow to Manasa,' Chand Sadagar swore. 'I worship Siva.'

'But none shall see Siva's face save through Manasa's grace.'

'Go away from me. You are not the wind, but the voice of the phantoms. I know Siva will make an exception for me.'

'Why?'

'Because I am not like the others. I have raised altars to the glory of Siva. I have dug wells for the benefit of pilgrims who visit the Kailasa, Siva's Mountain of Precious Snow. I have denied myself every pleasure so that others may profit from my labours and turn their thoughts upon Siva.'

'Chand Sadagar!' the voice of the phantoms interrupted, 'Think again before you give foolish answers. Tell us why will Siva make an exception for you?'

'Go away, you phantoms!' Chand Sadagar cursed the Apsaras. 'Go away, you spouseless ones. A worshipper of Siva can do without you. Don't try to put the seed of doubt into my mind. Apsaras! You are barren. Yours breasts are bitter fruits. You are handmaidens to Manasa the Motherless. I hate her and I hate you, her companions. The Great God Siva is my sustainer. He is my strength and I fear nothing.'

Hardly had those words escaped from his lips than the ship split from the helm to the rudder: she had struck a hidden reef and disappeared into the bottom of the sea within the twinkling of an eye.

Chand Sadagar, as he began swimming for his life, heard someone whisper: '*This is not by chance, nor in the course of nature. But even now worship me and I will restore you to Power.*'

'That is Manasa,' Chand Sadagar muttered. 'I will never pay homage to that sorceress.'

A whorl dragged him down.

He down the gulf where the loud waves collapsed
Descending, saw with floating hair arise

The daughters of the sea in pale green light,
A million mystic breasts suddenly bare,
And came beneath the flood and stunned beheld
A mute and stupendous march of waters race
To reach some viewless pit beneath the world.

Unawed by the vision of these mysteries he made desperate efforts to save himself, and rose to the surface of the waters. The belief that his accident was due to the machinations of Manasa and the Apsaras decided his course of action. He was not going to succumb to the temptation of giving up his struggle against the waves.

Mysterious words in a strange language reached his ears. He did not grasp their real meaning; but they sounded bewitchingly harmonious and seemed to imply that his exertions were futile: he should come down to collect the treasures of Patala—the underwater realm—whose floor was strewn with rubies and garnets, whose very dust was powdered gold; these were riches enough to make any merchant happy.

'Who cares for easy money?' Chand Sadagar growled. 'Am I a *banya*, a Jain? A servitor of Siva never seeks shortcuts to success.'

The alluring calls became more and more persistent.

'These are the voices of the unborn children of the Apsaras,' Chand Sadagar reasoned. 'I will not listen to them. They shall not tempt me.'

Snatches of melodious songs floated to him from the froth and foam of the billows. They told him again and again of the wealth hidden in the bed of the sea, and begged him to explore the regions under the water, to wash away his sins in the torrents of the holy Mandakini—the secret fountain in the heart of the earth.

'Siva's name purifies me,' Chand Sadagar murmured. 'What need have I of an immersion in the Mandakini?'

Then the bare-breasted sea-maidens rose from the waters and chanted their sweet refrains as they disported round about him:

> In bowers of love men take their rest,
> In loveless bowers we sigh alone!
> With bosom friends are others blest,—
> But we have none! but we have none!

'Shameless jades!' cried Chand Sadagar. 'Stop your obscene singing! I don't want to hear you. I worship the Great God Siva, and to him alone shall I listen; him alone I obey. When he deigns to bless me then alone will my travails end, and not a moment before. Go away from me, you big-bosomed but barren-wombed whores. Look after your foolish beaux and your unborn babies. Leave me in peace.'

The sea nymphs merged with the waves to vanish for good, and Chand Sadagar gave a sigh of relief. He hated the sight of the Apsaras because they were Manasa's handmaidens.

A shark, piloted by a tiny fish, swooped towards him at a great speed. As yet he was a furlong away from the shore. He judged that in the race with the swift sea-monster his chances of winning were small. Nevertheless, he was determined not to yield. How was he to fight his formidable adversary? His eye caught sight of a large lotus leaf floating past him and that gave him an idea. He seized it and within its folds he trapped the slippery pilot fish that guided the shark.

Deprived of its scout, the shark became bewildered: it behaved like a blind man robbed of his stick. It circled round and round looking for its pygmy counsellor, while Chand Sadagar redoubled his efforts to reach the firm land. His limbs were, however, growing numb. It became more and more difficult for him to make his strokes. There were other sharks in his wake. Just then he espied a porpoise of a brilliant colour that had left the others of its school and was changing its hue every minute like a chameleon. It was, Chand Sadagar concluded, going to die soon. 'Perhaps,' he thought, 'it will help me before death overtakes it. Porpoises are known to be friendly towards men. I shall swim to it, and try to get on its back.' He was not mistaken in his conjecture about the porpoise, and thanks to the help it gave him, he succeeded in reaching the shore in safety.

He blessed the Great God Siva for his miraculous escape. He then unfolded the lotus leaf in which he had caught the pilot fish. What sort of a fish was it? He wanted to examine his catch carefully. Was it a remora, fabled to be able to stop ships in mid-ocean? The fish suddenly opened its mouth and uttered: '*It is not by chance, nor in the course of nature. But even now worship me and I will restore you to power.*'

Chand Sadagar cursed himself as he threw away the fish and the lotus leaf. For he recalled that Manasa was also called *Padma*—the lotus, and the Goddess bestriding the Porpoise. 'I ought to have faced the shark without any aid from Manasa,' he murmured, as he began his long trudge to his house in Champak Nagar.

This was only the beginning of his ordeals and these were very many. For he lost by and by his entire fleet, his estate, his wealth, and even his personal belongings: he was reduced to the state of a pauper.

~

The last and the most trying test was the loss of his only son Lakshmindar on his very wedding night. The son's death was due to snake-bite. But how could a snake get into the bridal chamber specially constructed of steel to prevent the intrusion of such noxious reptiles?

His daughter-in-law Behula—wedded and widowed on the same day—suspected that it was not an ordinary snake that had bitten her husband: it must have been an agent of Manasa, otherwise how could it penetrate through steel walls. She begged Chand Sadagar to evoke Manasa's help to restore Lakshmindar to life.

'No,' replied Chand Sadagar. 'I worship Siva alone and shall have nothing to do with any other god and goddess. Nor will I allow anyone in my house to call on Manasa.'

'My husband is not dead,' Behula sobbed. 'He is merely in a trance. He can yet be brought back to life if only Manasa would bless him. Please let us offer our prayers to her: the Goddess of Wisdom will not deny us benediction.'

'She may not,' muttered Chand Sadagar, 'But who cares for her intervention? A worshipper of Siva has no need of help from any other save him. He gives and he takes away: he is the great and he is the mighty. None can fathom the mysteries of his will. I take from him whatever he gives—both what seems good and what seems evil.'

Behula wept, but her tears were of no avail. The only concession Chand Sadagar made for her was to place the corpse of Lakshmindar on a raft and set it adrift on the river Hooghly. The tradition demanded that a person dying from snake-bite should not be cremated, and the obstinate merchant-prince—no longer a prince, but a pauper—acceded to this last demand of

Behula, who decided to accompany the body right to the Ganga Sagar where the river flowed into the sea.

'If by any chance,' Chand Sadagar enjoined Behula as the raft began moving with the current of the river, 'you come across floating lotus leaves, you must not touch them. Manasa is also known by the name of *Padma*—the lotus. And if anyone asks you to offer prayers to Manasa, remember you have promised me not to utter any words of prayer and praise. And if you see a porpoise, chase it away, for porpoises are Manasa's vehicles. Now go in peace and bury the body of Lakshmindar wherever you like.'

~

Near Jater Dol-on-Sea Behula's raft ran aground on an island formed by the shoals of the river. It was impossible to set it afloat again without helping hands. She looked around for succour. There was no one nearby save a washerwoman busy with her rinsing and washing. What help could such a woman offer to Behula? She was not much stronger. But she had a glory about her head, and that led Behula to call out to her.

'Please help me,' she beseeched. 'You must be a wise woman and, no doubt, know how to remove the trance caused by snake-bite. I have been widowed on my wedding-night even before my marriage was consummated.'

'Have you ever honoured Manasa?' asked the woman crowned with glory. 'I am Manasa's companion, handmaiden and half-sister. On earth I am called Neta, and in heaven they call me Urvashi.'

Behula bowed at her feet and confessed to her that though she was a worshipper of Manasa, on account of a vow she had given to Chand Sadagar, she was no longer allowed to pray to the Goddess of Wisdom, but she honoured her all the same.

'Why do you honour her?' asked Neta, whose other name was Urvashi.

'Because the blessing of the Mind-born deity Manasa makes man superior to the beast.'

'How did you worship Manasa before you crossed the threshold of Chand Sadagar's house? Did you adore her with fasting?'

Behula shook her head. That was not the way she had been taught to supplicate Manasa.

'Did you then supplicate her by torturing your mind?'

Behula shook her head again. That too was not her way of paying homage to the Goddess of Wisdom. To many such questions, she demurred in silence.

'Have you then worshipped her with your dance? Have you praised her with song? Have you honoured her with rejoicing? Or perhaps you have adored her by helping those that dance and sing? Or have you cherished her in any other way? Have you lived joyously and brought joyousness to others? All these are different forms of worshipping the Mind-born.'

Behula's face brightened. Her way of laudation was the same as Neta's. But the form of worship which appealed to her most was dance.

'If that be so,' Neta demanded, 'dance before me even now. Let me see if you have been a worthy worshipper of Manasa.'

But how could Behula dance? Was she not a widow? Was it ever meet for a newly widowed bride to dance?

'Those who worship Manasa have no need to mourn. And neither should you. Listen, if your dance brings back your husband to life will you then dance?'

'Yes, I will.' Behula replied. 'Most willingly.'

'Then dance, my child,' Neta commanded. 'And I will sing for you. With every rhythmic step that you take and every graceful gesture that you make one of the deities of heaven will come here to watch you and to give his blessing. Each blessing will bring back to Chand Sadagar one of his lost treasures. His sunken ships will rise again from the bed of the sea to cast anchor in the haven of Champak Nagar. His gardens and orchards will bloom again. His lost friends will be restored. And when you go back to Champak Nagar with your bridegroom Lakshmindar restored to life, you will teach him the great truth that Manasa has been his protectress since the day he was born. Tell him: when he toiled he supplicated her; when he dug wells and pools, he assuaged her thirst; when he fed the hungry, he gave her food; when he planted trees, he procured her shade; when he encouraged learning, he bought her books to read; when he built temples, he gave her shrines to pray; when he launched ships, he built vehicles for her to travel. Remind him: when he prayed to Siva, he blessed her. Now you know, my child, Chand Sadagar has always been a dutiful son of Manasa. Go back now to Champak Nagar with Lakshmindar and tell him all that you have heard and seen.'

Wonder-struck Chand Sadagar wept with joy as he embraced his son and daughter-in-law. He marvelled when he heard Behula's story: 'If that be so,' he murmured, as he gazed at the lotus flowers which bloomed once again—quite spontaneously—in the pools of his courtyard, 'Manasa! Why have you tortured me all these years?'

'Because your labour was travail,' replied one of the flowers. 'Because you refused to gaze on Visions,' whispered another. 'Without awareness there is no knowledge,' said a third one. 'And without knowledge there is no fullness of life. And without it, there is no wisdom, and devoid of wisdom, worship is only ritual. Though ritual is better than no worship, the gods desire Chand Sadagar to be a wise worshipper, leading a joyous existence.'

'All my days,' Chand Sadagar confessed, 'I believed that a true worshipper has no right to be happy in an unhappy world. Now I know the truth: Joylessness is unholiness.'

IV

'Porpoises are Manasa's vehicles,' said the *pujarini*. 'It is therefore natural that some of these animals should be kept in the sacred ponds of the temple of Manasa.'

These water-mammals symbolize such virtues as swiftness, affection, and fidelity. Their stylized representations decorate many fountains, lamp-posts, gateways, coats of arms, and a hundred other things in Calcutta and elsewhere. Poets and story-tellers have recounted their many qualities. However, in reality they are extraordinarily ugly.

'No wonder,' I said to myself, 'they are called swine-fish.'

The *pujarini* was just then patting one of these beasts. It was a friendly one, I must admit; it came to the edge of the pond as soon as it noticed us. I gathered it had a name of its own: Sisi-Magar.

Sisi-Magar behaved like a perfect pig. It ate without any ceremony the bunch of flowers given to me in the chapel of Manasa. I was horrified at its boldness.

'Sisi-Magar is not afraid of men.' The *pujarini*'s comment was superfluous.

I felt like telling her, 'No use pointing out the obvious to me,' though my knowledge of natural history was limited. According to the textbooks, porpoises are gregarious; they travel in companies—technically known as 'schools'—and love to dwell in the Mediterranean. Evidently each writer copies his predecessor, and I have yet to see a textbook in which I shall find some explanation about the presence of a large number of porpoises in the Hooghly river and their congregating at False Point at certain times of the year. I do know it for a fact that some of them travel in schools in the waters of the comparatively narrow Rup-Narayan (which is only half a mile broad near Kapila-Gram). In high seas our porpoises may frolic about the big steamers, but in our rivers they give the bigger boat a wide berth, and prefer to swim about the smaller craft. They seem to find some fun in ramming the frailer vessels with their bodies. 'Admiring a school of porpoises,' I remarked gravely, 'from a distance is one thing, and to have one at an arm's length is another.'

'Wouldn't you care to have a ride on its back?'

'No, thank you. I am not Chand Sadagar.' People have funny tastes. A Santal boatman of Burdwan had a couple of tame porpoises, and children on the banks of the Damodar river were often given joy rides on their back. The youngsters relished the fun. But the grown-ups became nervous. They wanted to try out the porpoises and when this was denied to them they gave vent to their irritation by keeping away their children from the kindly Santal. 'Sisi-Magar would do good business in Burdwan,' I said. 'Men of Burdwan simply love porpoises. They have a fountain made up of a number of bronze porpoises squirting water out of their mouths.'

I thought of the Mohajantooli quarter of Burdwan, and enquired if porpoises had anything to do with the gay ladies and artistes. The Golden Pagoda district of Calcutta was also decorated with a Fountain of Porpoises. Sisi-Magar too was cherished in the Pond of the Sacred Precincts of the temple whose principal worshippers were women trading in love.

I received no satisfactory answer to my query except that parrots, peacocks, pigeons and porpoises were the favourites of the God of Love who was also the Warrior God.

I did not bother my guide with too many questions, and the hidden meaning of one curious ceremony was totally lost to me: I saw a number of people raising a human image—a scarecrow—by a cord to a branch of a tree in the Sacred Precincts; they then began stoning it till it fell into fragments. There was a general scramble for these as soon as the head was smashed. The broken bits were carefully collected and ceremoniously wrapped up in a woman's sari, and finally propped up against a wall. The scarecrow of a man was now transformed into an effigy of a veiled woman. Its draping was printed all over with figures of porpoises.

The porpoise, I knew, is borne on the banner of the deity of Love. But what had that ceremony to do with Eros or Manasa?

Before leaving the temple I had another good look at Sisi-Magar: it looked not only ugly but stupid as well. But it was very friendly. So I was interested to know that it was destined to be released in the Ganga Sagar at the next Ganga Mela—the celebrations in honour of the river Ganges and the deities connected with the descent of the Ganges to the earth.

V

I debated for a long while within me; should I or should I not tell Profulla Babu about my visits to the temple of the Golden Pagoda district? It was Sisi-Magar that made me return to that place. Friendliness of the porpoise meant much to me, for I was rather lonely in Calcutta. I fed it regularly with bunches of radishes. What would Profulla Babu think of my childish exploits?

After pondering the reasons for and against this discussing with Profulla Babu I decided to take out a coin and spin it: the spin settled it; the answer was in the affirmative.

~

Profulla Babu was much older than Jogin-Da. In fact, he belonged to the generation which some of us considered to be 'the Age of Giants'—of men whose concern in politics was lukewarm, but whose interest in humanistic learning was profound, and their general reading extensive. There was hardly any subject on which Profulla Babu had nothing stimulating to say. In this respect he was the same as Hara Prasad Sastri, Iswan Chandra Ghosh, Guru Das Bannerji, Krishna Kumar Mitra, Ramendra Sundar Trivedi, and many others who are now mere names but whose conversation and advice meant a lot to the younger people of my time. Profulla Babu being the least famous of that illustrious group was readily accessible to me and others.

'Your Profulla Babu is a professional grumbler,' Daud Benisraeli—the student of Social Anthropology—complained.

'It would be better to call him a professional debunker,' Mug Furtado retorted on my behalf. 'If he is worth nothing, who asks you to call on him? You know perfectly well that he was right and you were wrong when he tore your essay to bits. What have you to say to his suggestion? "Before passing judgment on Polynesian social customs you would do well to interpret the origin of certain customs nearer home—right on your doorsteps." Was it a preposterous suggestion?'

'Nevertheless,' a few other students remarked, 'he is a born pessimist. Fancy telling us that the era of the uncommon man is over, and we are now heading for the age of the commonplace man. He does not believe in progress.'

'Because,' Mug replied, 'he is more concerned with the spiritual content of an age than with its material achievement.'

'He goes to absurd lengths,' Benisraeli murmured. 'Even architecture for him is a matter of faith. Your religion, he says, determines the style of the houses you build.'

I cleared my throat and delivered a neat speech on the architectural adornments of modern Calcutta. The High Court, built in imitation of the Gothic Cloth Hall at Ypres: a fitting place for haggling over legal matters; the Metcalfe Hall, a brick and mortar replica of the Athenian Temple of Winds, not unworthy of housing the highly cultivated gentlemen of the Inland Revenue Department; the Town Hall, a splendid Doric temple of stucco bearing Urdu inscriptions, built from the profits of a lottery organized by the Progress-at-any-Price partisans, and its plans approved by a democratic plebiscite: a suitable shelter for works of art by such renowned masters as Geflowski, Zoffany, Chinnery, Chantrey, Laszlo, Ramvarma, and others of their calibre; the University Senate House...

Benisraeli did not give me the chance of developing my thesis; otherwise I would have dragged in such modern structures as the flat-iron Temple Chambers, the stucco-statued Marble Palace of Jhoot-Malji, the Science College, and the Durbhanga House, and finished with the declaration: 'Calcutta's architecture reveals Calcutta's religion—Calcutta's faith in the doctrine of *Progress at any price*.'

'Tell me seriously,' Ben broke in, 'does any intelligent student bother about religion these days?' He emphasized the word intelligent.

Everyone stared at Mug, and Mug shrugged his shoulders. Religious certainly he was, but his record at the examinations was not brilliant. After withering Mug with his gaze, Ben continued triumphantly, 'Religion has been the greatest bar to India's progress.'

I knew the rest of his talk by heart: it was the same as Chumchicke Adhikari repeated time and again. Ben believed that the old had to be pulled down before anything could be done for the new. Though he had little love for Prem Swami he shared that religious fanatic's predilection for ferro-concrete structures. The Golden Pagoda meant nothing to him: a splendid, air-conditioned cinema would, according to him, serve a better social purpose in a progressive city like Calcutta.

'That's fine,' I interrupted. 'What you are saying is the expression of the religion of this age—religion of cheap entertainment.'

'Nonsense,' he snapped. 'I have not uttered one word about religion. I am only insisting that our objective must be plain. I am for social justice and equality. For my objective I am ready to do anything. If necessary I shall not shrink from hanging all reactionaries.'

'Your objective may be plain. Indeed, too plain. But do not forget Profulla Babu's saying: "I have lived through enough years of shift and change to realize that it is not the professed aims people strive to achieve that set the pattern for the future, but the habits of behaviour acquired in the process." Ends do not justify the means.'

'You are a downright reactionary. All country yokels are like you.'

'They make up 90 per cent of India's inhabitants.'

~

When I called on Profulla Babu I found him surrounded by a number of my acquaintances. Daoud Benisraeli was among them, and was their spokesman: he had presented Profulla Babu with a teaser.

Ben was complaining about the stupidity of the university authorities.

At an examination several scores of answer papers were found to have been written by one and the same hand! The examiners were upset: they consulted the Comptroller of Examinations and the Registrar, then the Principals, the members of the Senate and the Syndicate, the Deans and the Vice-Chancellor; they were all greatly perturbed. Physically it was impossible for one student to write out several hundred sheets of paper in the course of three hours. Moreover, the standard of answers in different sheets varied considerably. The feat was possible only for a prodigy. Some professional forgers who were serving their terms in the Presidency Jail and the Alipore Penitentiary were unofficially consulted by the authorities. According to them, reams of white sheets bearing the water-mark of the University must have been smuggled out and many weeks before the examination time a calligraphist must have sat down to the task of writing out varied answers to the questions set by the examiners. The candidates were naturally accused of bringing with them the answer sheets written by the remarkable penman.

The matter was serious. Much more serious than pummelling a professor. Far graver than the open sale of forged question-papers a fortnight before the examinations in College Square.

These question-papers were hawked right in front of our Senate House. 'Get ready for your finals and intermediates,' the pedlars barked. 'Question-papers for sale! The very questions you will be asked to answer! B.A. question-papers for ten rupees a set! B.Sc. papers for fifteen rupees! M.B. papers for twenty rupees! Money refunded if not satisfied.'

These hawkers were not ordinary hawkers who could be just told off by the hall porters of the Senate House. Chumchicke Adhikari was among them, and he was their protector. His protégés were all furnished with regular licence, number plates, accident insurance policies, and other paraphernalia.

The Comptroller of Examinations tore his hair and telephoned the police, and the police authorities rang back that they could do nothing about it. They themselves were helpless: a judge's writ had to be issued before those licensed hawkers could be dispersed. How could a police magistrate issue a writ without some adequate proof of law-breaking or the intention of law-breaking? What proof was there that the question-papers of the hawkers had been stolen from the office of the Comptroller of Examinations?

Chumchicke Adhikari had his laugh. 'Results of forthcoming horseraces are hawked about openly,' he chuckled. 'Old Moore's Almanacks and Gupta Press Panjika tell you what the stars foretell for the coming twelvemonth. What is wrong about making forecasts of coming examinations? Let all the sets be sold at the uniform rate of five rupees. We have the law on our side. Let us see what the university authorities do.'

The authorities did nothing—at least, nothing spectacular. They began printing an entirely new set of questions.

Activities outside the Senate House did not concern them. But the answer papers did: scores of them written by the same hand! They set up a commission.

'What do you say to all this?' asked Daoud Benisraeli with a grave face. 'We have been accused of cheating at the examination.'

'This means rustication,' Bijan Mandel theatrically groaned, 'if it can be proved.'

'Meanwhile,' murmured Gopal Sarma, wearing an equally serious expression, 'the results of our examinations are held up. No one knows when the commission will start its enquiry.'

'Much good will it do,' Profulla Babu growled, 'to collect the opinions of a confounded band of pettifogging bum bailiffs. If you want to spare them bother you should write to the Vice-Chancellor and tell him the truth.'

We looked at each other.

'You have been copying Tagore's handwriting,' Profulla Babu went on without bothering to scan our surprised faces. 'That's the long and short of it. He writes a bold hand. I commend your latest fad. Tagore is worth emulating.'

We were dumbfounded. For months we had been practising in secret the art of writing à la Tagore. Sayed Ali from Dibrughar and Jyotish Chandra Ray from Purulia wrote in a way that made it impossible for a bank clerk to distinguish their hand from Tagore's. The rest of us vowed not to be outdone by these two former students of Tagore's school at Santiniketan. It was a well-kept secret among us, and we were looking forward to mystifying the university authorities.

And Profulla Babu unveiled the mystery the moment he was confronted with it! His prestige among us rose immediately to unbelievable heights.

~

Tagore was not a popular hero in those days: in spite of his being honoured by the Swedish Academy and raised on the same high pedestal as those formidable German bores, Hauptmann and Heyse, the sale of his Bengali books only amounted to about a hundred copies a year. The distinguished, self-styled academicians of Calcutta hated him because he wrote in readable Bengali. Good Bengali, according to our bald pundits, should be something incomprehensible to human beings not deeply versed in Sanskrit. In this respect we were no better, for we held for a long time the same view as our learned elders and the mighty minds who ruled the University with a rod of iron.

Tagore, however, forced himself into our midst with a mighty bang. It happened on a dark night in this way:

It was about midnight when the corrugated-iron shed in the courtyard which served as the greenroom for the theatrical performances in the Masters' Mess came down with a terrible din. A well-oiled, clean-shaven and stark-naked thief known as Naga Gangoo the Lady-Killer was trying to tread on its roof, and he came down too, and with him fell a big sack filled with stolen books. The hot-headed fellow from Bajra-Jogini—our champion boxer—lost his temper at the row, and he gave the thief a thorough pounding. The shed was our pugilist's hiding-place for indulging in (correspondence course) yogic austerities and in *swadeshi*, or home-made cigarettes. Smoking, I need hardly say, was not permitted anywhere in our hostel nor in any building remotely connected with the University. A smoker caught *in flagrante delicto* ran the risk of rustication, and one may well imagine the anger of the son of Bajra-Jogini when he discovered the calamity wrought by the rascally Naga Gangoo: his favourite retreat was gone! Never in his life had that greasy thief received such a thrashing. This we decided was a sufficient punishment for the poor rogue: he was allowed to limp away after he had taken the oath never to revisit the Masters' Mess. We, of course, confiscated his bag with its contents. The books were brand new, and as they bore no indication of their ownership we decided to garnish with them the empty shelves of our sitting-room library.

Most of the volumes were time-tables of different railways—all quite useful for us—and the collected works of Tagore: several sets. No wonder Naga Gangoo's bag weighed heavily, for Tagore was a prolific writer.

From then onwards our interest in Tagore grew. This regard was considerably enhanced when we discovered that he wrote long autograph letters—his personal testimonials—to different hair-oil manufacturers, particularly to one firm which produced a concoction claiming to cure 'all affectations of the brain, the scalp and the hair,' and to contain the concentrated essence of the red hibiscus flower. Tagore's holographs beautifully reproduced and bountifully distributed by the hair-oil people became our models for improving our script. Reproductions of his photogenic head—also supplied gratis by the cosmetic producers—decorated our writing-desks. We proclaimed ourselves to be his disciples, and began scribbling in his style.

~

We were naturally disappointed when we heard that the university authorities had decided not to make any further enquiries about the unknown calligraphist alleged to have filled in several hundred pages with his writing within a few hours.

Profulla Babu's prestige rose, as has just been said, till one day it suffered a sudden eclipse on account of another apparently incomprehensible happening.

~

'The mystery of the Mussulmanpara Bomb Case solved,' claimed the posters of the paper *Aj-Kal* and a large number of people (including the Governor) were fooled. 'The student who threw that bomb,' the paper announced, 'has sent a written confession to the police, and wants to be hanged.'

Had that paper's 'Crime Reporter' been a little more clever he would have consulted me and I should have told him that there were at least a hundred others who had actually sent such written confessions or were contemplating doing so. This time there was no conspiracy, no oath of secrecy, each student acted on his own. Only after a letter had been sent did the self-confessed bomb-thrower tell his more intimate friends that he was sick of life: that he was a rogue and therefore he deserved to be hanged.

The contents of each confession were more or less the same, though not quite identical: 'I cannot tell you the whole truth,' was the usual burden. 'But I am the man who threw the bomb and killed a few innocent people some three years ago.' Some letters added: 'Please keep back the news from my parents till I am hanged.'

Profulla Babu was questioned as usual by Daoud Benisraeli, who did not suffer from any diffidence like the rest of us. Once he had entered the High Court by the Judges' Entrance. 'I have an urgent message for Asutosh Mukerji,' he told the policeman who wanted to stop him, and had actually burst into the eminent judge's chamber when he was having his lunch to present him with an autograph book. 'I like your cheek,' the judge was alleged to have said. 'You will go far in life unless you get clapped into jail.' To such an enterprising student of social anthropology Profulla Babu was small fry.

Ben grinned and cast a questioning glance in my direction.

'Has religion anything to do with these mass confessions?' he finally asked. He made a nice hit at me for he added that I referred to everything as a manifestation of Calcutta's religion.

'These letters have come from students of all religions and from some who have no religion at all. I cannot make out in what way religion is connected with an innocent man asserting that he is a murderer.'

'Religion, my boy, is something more than ritual. You may be a Jew, and Mug may be a Christian, and Kabir Chaudhuri may be a Mohammedan, and I may be a Hindu, but our fundamental religion is very much the same. Whether we profess it openly or not, secretly we all belong to the same creed.'

'How?'

'We are all terrorized and fascinated by Evil. It exerts a strange hypnotic power over all of us. Only some succumb to it more readily than the others; but we are all led to perform in the long run incredible acts of penance and self-abasement.'

'But,' Ben protested, 'we are more fond of fun than of self-abasement.'

'Fun!' Profulla Babu shook his head. 'Not those who dwell in cities. Mesmerized by the spectre of Evil we practise all forms of turbid pleasure. We do not know what fun is. Everything that we do is contaminated by the dual attributes of Evil—fear and fascination. Even such good deeds as we may do reek of nostalgia for Evil. That is why we seek joy in the art of debasing the body or by torturing it with discomfort. We maintain a façade of so-called simple living only to remind us of our spiritual vanity. We are outwardly ever-repentant, while in reality we are the most arrogant of all people. We have lost our gift of enjoying beauty. The beautiful and the repellent have gradually become one and the same to us.'

'Are not our public processions manifestations of our sense of beauty?'

'In the villages? There, they certainly are. But I am not referring to the villagers, but to the town-dwellers. Which public procession in Calcutta is considered beautiful by you? The display in honour of Parsnath? Or Subhas Bose's military parades? Such shows deserve to be spat upon by the simplest villagers. In our displays we have banished beauty and brought in vulgar ostentations. Therefore, I repeat, even in practising virtue we manifest a predilection for sordidness.'

'How?' Several voices protested. 'In what way?'

'Take for example,' Profulla Babu went on, 'our love of thrift. We consider it to be a virtue, and thrifty we certainly are. We never waste a rotten mango. When it has gone bad, we give it to a beggar to acquire merit! We generally let it go bad, because we are afraid of enjoying its taste. We keep an account of our pleasures, and make due note of our so-called anonymous gifts to give publicity to them in *Who's Who*.'

He took out the Indian *Who's Who* and asked Daoud to look up some of the most prominent names in it. A number of us murmured: we did not agree with him. What applied to the Dalmiahs, Birlas, and other millionaires did not hold good for the overwhelming section of the middle classes. But they all became silent the moment Profulla Babu raised the question: which one of us had a father who did not keep a special account book of his son's educational expenditure?

'Rearing children we deem to be a virtue,' he continued. 'But the day we have the slightest disagreement with our sons or daughters we produce the special ledgers. "My child!" we declare indignantly, "here is the account book which tells you how much you have cost me since the day you were conceived. So much for the midwife. So much for the milk you consumed. So much for your clothes. So much for your books, pens and ink. So much for your school fees. So much for your doctor's bills. If you do not wish to obey me implicitly, you are at liberty to leave my house.

But you must pay back the amount I have spent on you. You may pay a simple interest of 5 per cent. A bank would have asked for more." Is this a fact or not? If you are an obedient son you will see the account book produced at the time of your marriage. It is extremely helpful to a father when he fixes the amount of dowry for his progeny.'

'All young people are against the dowry system,' murmured someone: he was not quite sure if he was talking on his own behalf or for the whole company.

'You may be. But that does not disprove my thesis that even when we practise what we consider to be a virtue we tend to be sordid. Take another example: sanctity of life. In principle no one will quarrel with a man who is reluctant to destroy a living creature! But has such a man any moral right to live like a parasite and encourage vermin? And that's what Prem Swami preaches and practises. Once a week he strips himself naked and allows leeches to have their fill of his body's blood. And when his followers too busy in making money cannot find time for this weekly ceremony, they hire people to go through the disgusting process of self-abasement on their behalf. The Jains hire men to sit on ant heaps for the same reason.'

'We are not Jains,' Daoud Benisraeli interrupted.

'Whether we are Jains, or followers of Prem Swami, or disciples of Biswambar Misra our behaviour in the matter of self-abasement is very much the same. It is this spirit of self-punishment that helps us to glory in Calcutta's squalor; the same spirit that has led your friends to write to the police that they are responsible for a bomb thrown at Mussulmanpara long before they came to Calcutta. All of them want self-abasement. They are craving for expiation.'

'Expiation of what sins?'

Profulla Babu did not give an immediate answer. He looked at us and smiled, and finally declared that all of us knew the answer.

'But what is the answer?' asked Daoud impatiently.

'Unfulfilled sex life,' he replied slowly. 'Unfulfilled spiritual life. Dissatisfaction with everything in life.'

There was a pause, a death-like silence. I do not remember who broke it with the question: 'Is that our fault?'

'No, not yours. The sin lies with your mothers and with your fathers. You have been taught one set of values: values which may hold good for children, but not for young people. You are now questioning those values, and you have found out that instead of facts you were given cant—meaningless formulas—which your parents would love to believe, but cannot.'

He then elaborated the view that our aggressiveness was due to the fact that our mothers devoted little time to their own children, as their household duties kept them busy all the while, and the youngsters were continually thwarted and bullied by the older ones who took charge of them. 'That is why,' he concluded, 'you have all grown up with a feeling of inferiority, and you want to make it up by quarrelsomeness and periodic outbursts of self-punishment.'

We listened in silence. None dared say a word when he lashed Prem Swami, Aswini Kumar Dutt and others who proclaimed the virtue of keeping away from women in order to become spiritually advanced.

'They are a fine set of humbugs,' he murmured. 'What will happen to their young disciples is perfectly clear. They will preach chastity and practise profligacy. They will run from one woman to another, and then to a third and to a fourth, and insult all of them. Each woman who shows the least kindness to them will be accused of being a whore. And not one will be found as good and as noble and as virtuous as the mother who reared them.'

We dispersed quietly. We did not talk to each other about his final diagnosis of the cause that led the students to send letters accusing themselves of the murder they had never committed: they were, in his opinion, going through hell, because they had had some sex-experience with street-walkers; they were now haunted by two dominant fears: being infected with some disease and being polluted for life with sin; naturally, they wanted expiation by mounting the gallows.

Daoud Benisraeli knew that at least two of his intimate friends who had written to the police came within this category. But he did not say anything.

My thoughts shifted, I do not know why, to the Golden Pagoda. I wished I could tempt Roma to visit the place and see how Sisi-Magar loved to eat radishes. Could Roma be induced to put on a sari for a change? Draped in a sari she would easily pass for a Hindu woman. I thought also of the lovely silk *namabali*—a printed scarf—I had bought a few days earlier in a kiosk of the Sacred Precincts: it was meant to be a surprise for Roma.

This square silk scarf was a lovely thing. In its centre was the representation of Kama Deva, the Lord of Love, mounted on a peacock with his bent bow in one hand and the feathered arrow in the other. Its borders bore four lines of verses in his honour: a love philtre.

> With longing feathered, tipped with love,
> Its shaft is formed with fixed desire:
> With this arrow levelled well
> Shall Eros pierce thee to the heart.

VI

But Roma did not appreciate the lovely scarf. She flung it aside, and slapped my face. My suggestion that she should visit the Golden Pagoda one day with me made her furious. She abused Sisi-Magar and I received over and above a spate of harsh words.

'Haven't you thought of buying a gold and silver rose?' she asked sarcastically. 'The Golden Pagoda district is as reputable as the Mahajantooli quarter of Burdwan. You are old enough to know that. Do not pretend to be innocent. Now I see through you.'

I felt extremely small and cursed Kolej Huzoor in silence. That ass must have told Roma about my exploring the Mahajantooli quarter in his company. 'I shall be even with him,' I swore to myself as I left Roma to do some thinking on my own.

Was it the scarf? Or was it my account of the scantily clothed female acolyte that made Roma so angry? It could not have been either of these; because she had in the past accepted so many of my trifling presents, and as for the acolyte she was not like Chumchicke Adhikari's decoy woman. If Roma could at one time advise me to go out with the hula-hula dancer how could she possibly object to my having the acolyte as a guide within the precincts of the Golden Pagoda? No, I decided, there must be some other reason. But how did she know of my visit to a 'sporting house' in the Mahajantooli quarter of Burdwan? The only answer I could find was Kolej Huzoor: he must have bragged that at one time I used to hang round him like a dog.

That bumptious idiot was, as I have said before, several years my senior. After leaving the Burdwan Raj College he became a statistician to the Government of Bengal: a suitable occupation for a man who thought always in terms of charts and tables.

The very first time I saw him he gave me a catalogue of different cloud-formations; on the second occasion he furnished a list of the relative hardness of different stones; since then whenever I came across him I received similar informative lists of something or other. He was extremely well-informed, no doubt, but he suffered from a foolish desire to show off, and he lacked common sense. Once I thought I was the biggest fool in the world, but after hanging round Kolej Huzoor for some time I found out that there was someone still worse.

I ought not to have spoken to him about my visit to the Snake-Pit in Behala. My evil genius goaded me to see the effect of my bragging on a professional braggart. I told him how everyone stared at me because Roma was by my side and she looked extremely pretty in her Punjabi costume: jade-green muslin pantaloons and semi-transparent cerise blouse.

'Did you have her on your right or on your left?' Kolej Huzoor asked without letting me finish the sentence. He then began explaining different customs prevalent in different countries about escorting ladies. 'You protect her from the traffic side in the Anglo-Saxon world. You keep her always on your right in the European countries. In Prussia and in Calcutta you let her follow you like a dog. In Russia you order her to go before you carrying your luggage and fending the way for you.' The conclusion of all that lecture was simple: perhaps I behaved in an awkward way, and that was why the people stared at me!

'Nonsense,' I protested: I was no longer the schoolboy who was impressed by his list of clouds. 'She looked so attractive. It is not often they see a pretty face like hers. I had her on my left—the side nearest to the heart.'

'That's the old custom of Persia and of our countryside,' Kolej Huzoor grunted. 'You will find a note to this effect in Gibbon's

Decline and Fall. Bury's edition is the best.' He went on in this vein and never bothered to ask a word more about Roma. He was so filled with his own importance and knowledge of everything in the world.

But what led him to talk about me to Roma? Did he know Roma at all? Could he possibly have come across Roma when her father was working in the East India Railway Company's workshops in Burdwan? Even if he did, that was no reason for his raking up my past.

When could he possibly have met Roma in Calcutta? He, I concluded, must have met her some time between my first visit to the Golden Pagoda and my coming to the Ganga Sagar for the releasing of Sisi-Magar. What was the purpose of his telling her about my visit to the Mahajantooli quarter? Was it jealousy? Did he want Roma to be angry with me? If so, he must have met her shortly before she left her home to join me at Jater Dol on the Ganga Sagar?

Otherwise, I concluded, she would not have taken the trouble to come all the way to Jater Dol. Only a few days earlier when I had told her that I would love to have her along with Anita and Mug as my guests in my newly rented bungalow at Jater Dol she seemed to be delighted.

'What is your party for?' she wanted to know. 'Is it just to celebrate your coming of age? Or for something else?'

'You will see the illuminated boat-races at night.'

'Boat-races?'

I explained to her as best I could about the festivity in honour of Manasa and the ceremonies in connection with the river Ganges.

When the sun enters Capricorn a three-day religious fair is held near the estuary of the river Hooghly and all along the coast of the Ganga Sagar. Generally some two hundred thousand pilgrims gather there to visit different shrines, particularly the ancient temple of Kapila Muni, and to bathe in the Pagoda Creek. The sea—the Cradle of the Apsaras—receives offerings of coconuts, fruits and flowers, and also of five gems: pearl, diamond, emerald, topaz, and coral; after bathing in the sea the pilgrims circumambulate a huge stone altar resembling a lotus in honour of Manasa. Finally, after tame parrots, peacocks, pigeons, and porpoises have been released at dusk, the fishermen hold their illuminated boat-races in the night.

'That would be lovely,' Roma responded enthusiastically.

Of course, at that time I did not tell her anything about Sisi-Magar. I wanted to give her a surprise and releasing Sisi-Magar from the Vermilion Boat was the rabbit of my hat-trick.

All this had worked smoothly. And then at the end she slapped my face. What made her into a different being so suddenly?

~

To come back to Sisi-Magar, it gradually became so friendly with me that I forgot all about its ugliness. It made a funny gurgling sound whenever it saw me coming with bunches of radishes.

'You must have been a porpoise in your previous life,' once the *pujarini* told me jocularly. 'Or perhaps you are going to be one in your next existence. Never have I seen such friendship between a man and a porpoise.'

I told her that I had no knowledge of my past life nor about my future, but I was certain to miss Sisi-Magar when it was set free.

'You needn't. Setting free a tame porpoise doesn't mean losing it for good. Pet pigeons always come back to their cots. It is the same with porpoises. If you know someone living near a river bank Sisi-Magar will always revisit you there.' She told me of people at Chinsurah who had tame porpoises.

I did not quite believe her. But there was no harm in trying out her suggestion, and I had a talk with Mug Furtado, whose maternal grandmother lived at Jater Dol, a tiny village near the Pagoda Creek on the Ganga Sagar. Could I possibly go over there from time to time?

'But how will the porpoise know that you have come to Jater Dol?' asked Mug. 'Once it is set free it won't care for your radishes.'

'You needn't bother about that,' I replied grandly. 'Find me a cottage or some lodging at Jater Dol, and leave the rest to me.' I then explained to him that I had all the tips for informing Sisi-Magar about my presence. First, I was going to take it down to the Ganga Sagar in a sort of huge crate or rather a submerged raft which would be dragged by a bamboo barge. Secondly, this barge would be painted vermilion. 'Once a porpoise gets accustomed to a boat, it will by itself find means of revisiting it.' I repeated all that I had heard from the acolyte of the Golden Pagoda.

'So you need not only a cottage,' Mug replied reflectively, 'but a creek as well to anchor your boat. That's not difficult at Jater Dol. But you will get into trouble with our fishermen. They do not like dolphins.'

'Leave that matter to me. Find me a cottage, and the rest will be simple.' Of course, I did not need a creek for my boat. The vessel was meant to be sunk after the festivities, like the car of Juggernaut it could not be used twice.

~

Mug did find me a two-roomed cottage, surrounded on all four sides by a verandah—a bungalow belonging to the Archaeological Survey of India.

I felt my heart beat as I entered it. It was not much of a cottage, it was tiny, like a doll's house; but the fact that it had been rented in my own name made it as precious as a palace to me.

Only twenty-four hours earlier I had emerged from the state of tutelage: I was no longer a minor and my signature to a document was as valid as Jogin-Da's. I had, in fact, no further need of his authorization for signing anything.

'What does it feel like to be one's own master?' Jogin-Da asked me at the ceremony organized in my honour in the courtyard of Hanuman Vandar's mansion. Then, as though to disabuse me of my own feeling of importance, he added, 'Don't think I have come here for you. I have heaps of things to do. The day I saw you off at Asansole I said to myself: "From now on my ward will have to sink or swim on his own." In fact, I saw to your swimming. I took infinite trouble to get some of the papers to write about your coming to Calcutta. Do you realize that the article in the illustrated *Aj Kal* was written by me?'

It was no use giving him a piece of my mind. I just thanked him once again for all the trouble he had taken over me as my guardian. 'I hope I was not too troublesome a ward,' I added.

'Not at all, my boy,' he replied affably. 'Not at all. Even if you had been I should not have minded. I have been paid for my services. From this day onwards I shall receive nothing for giving you guidance, and I won't give any. I have come to Calcutta not for your sake, but to explain to a number of people my system of breeding peace-loving animals.'

There were quite a few journalists and photographers hanging round him. Jogin-Da gave them a neat address, the multigraphed copies of which were distributed lavishly. He described a pond of vegetarian alligators near Karachi: there the scaly saurians flourished on cucumbers and melons. He gave them also an account of peace-loving sharks which were being bred in a pool at Belasore. Porpoises, according to him, should be classified as dangerous beasts, but when subjected to proper dieting they too became as tame as the Siamese fish in Hanuman Vandar's lotus pool!

His listeners were all followers of Prem Swami and they gladly took in all he said. They considered him to be a superman endowed with occult powers. Jogin-Da, however, murmured modestly that his success was entirely due to the blessings of his guru Prem Swami. His concluding remarks stuck forcibly in my memory: 'We are now in a position to snap our fingers at all carnivorous atheists. We have succeeded in preventing the erection of a modern abattoir in Lahore. Public opinion has gradually been trained to see things in the same way as we do.'

I tried to recapitulate my views about Jogin-Da. Once I too thought a lot of him. And now I was losing the last vestiges of my regard for him. That very morning I had been at Jogin-Da's brother-in-law's house in Belgachia in response to an urgent summons.

What did his brother-in-law want of me?

Could I speak to Jogin-Da on a delicate matter? As I was said to be his favourite, Jogin-Da's brother-in-law thought that my personal entreaty would carry some weight. Could I say a few words on behalf of Jogin-Da's wife? It would be a great help if he would offer her some financial aid every month.

I did not know that Jogin-Da's wife was alive. He never spoke to me about her. What led to the separation?

'It was due to his sudden religious conversion. One day he went out for a walk and never came back.'

'What happened?'

'He wrote her a letter and advised her to serve God and look after the lowly creatures. That was the command of his guru

Prem Swami. Occasionally we do hear from him. But he has never sent any money to her. Can't you do something about it?'

'Heave a brick and receive a stone,' Didi-Ma used to say when she advised people to stay out of a domestic quarrel. 'When the dispute is between husband and wife, let them settle it between themselves. When a man has run away from home it is no use bringing him back tied hand and foot; he will run away again. You may, however, appeal to his sense of justice and charity.' The matter was indeed delicate. However, I promised to do what I could and did raise it in an indirect way at the party in Hanuman Vandar's quadrangle.

'My boy!' Jogin-Da drew himself up to his full height—he was one head shorter than I; he prodded me in the stomach as he began, 'History tells us that a prophet's wife must suffer. Prem Swami too abandoned his wife; he left her to look after herself shortly after he had discovered that her household account books were full of false entries. Anyway, my wife enjoys the privilege of being known as a religious man's spouse. Isn't that an honour?' Moreover, she deserved, in his reckoning, some physical hardship to expiate her past sins; her sins were many: she was responsible for his years of lustful existence in 'conjugal concubinage,' for his daily meals of abomination—fish and flesh, and for inducing him to find pleasure in the body's delights. It was therefore high time for her to undergo physical trials for her mental and spiritual improvement: she must learn how to get along without touching gold and silver.

Prem Swami's credo was repeated, and I was told more than once: 'God is more important than one's wife.'

It was hopeless to argue with such a man. To change the subject I told him that I was going to spend a few days at Jater Dol near the Sagar Island to watch the celebrations in honour of Manasa.

'So you have turned superstitious,' he sighed loudly like an actor on the stage. 'I am disappointed. In spite of all that I have told you during so many years you want to behave like the ignorant pilgrims. This is a shame. I hope you will change your mind.' He gave a further exposition of Prem Swami's theology and ended with a quotation from Kabir, the saintly weaver of Benares:

> Not ambrosia, but water will you find in the sacred bathing-places;
> And I know they are useless, for in them have I bathed.
> Not life, but mere brass will you find in the sanctified images;
> And I know they are voiceless, for them have I rated.

VII

I went to Jater Dol all the same. For I was longing for the countryside, for the whisperings of the grass, the murmurings of the trees, and for the sight of the open horizon.

Sitting on the verandah of my bungalow I made a general survey of the land and the sea. The place was so different from the other seaside resorts known to me. The marine view was not dissimilar from what one would find everywhere, but it was the shore that gave Jater Dol its distinctive peculiarities.

Perhaps my bungalow enhanced my liking for the place. It was said to have been there more than a hundred years ago when General Cunningham was exploring the region for Buddhist relics. He used this very cottage as his headquarters. Later, another orientalist, James Burgess, honoured it with his stay, and subsequently it received from time to time other renowned visitors. Some of the entries in the Visitors' Book seemed to me unaccountable, for example, those of James Prinsep who died in 1840 and John Leyden who died some thirty years earlier. Strangely enough after 1890 no one (with the solitary exception of Emile Sénart) seemed to have signed the register or stayed in the bungalow. Perhaps the exploration of the region was completed, and that was the reason why the Archaeological Survey was willing to let me rent the cottage for a mere song—one rupee a month. I could buy it, I was told, with all its contents for fifty rupees. For the Survey it was no longer worthwhile to incur the expenses of maintaining the cottage in repair. They were only too willing to get rid of it. It would, however, have been wicked had I accepted their offer about the purchase; for the bungalow contained a number of stone and bronze objects, which alone must have been worth many times fifty rupees, to say nothing of a box full of manuscripts of James Prinsep and some odd volumes with handwritten corrections by Louis Mathieu Langles. There was also a detached bas-relief of an 'ass curse' brought from some island in the Ganga Sagar.

The bungalow stood by itself, somewhat outside the village of Jater Dol, on a promontory commanding a wide view. From its verandah I saw the wide expanse of the Hooghly flowing into an arm of the Ganga Sagar. The river itself looked like a part of the sea as its other shore was lost beyond the horizon. At high tide the sea reached halfway up the flight of steps that led to a palm-fringed atoll almost below my bungalow.

The whole area was covered with a low vegetation, chiefly consisting of dwarf palms and pygmy mangroves; fan-palms and toddy-palms ran along the water's edge. In the riparian region of mud and sand—between the levels of the high tide and the low—grew twisted Nipa palms which flourished even under water to throw up from their thick stems pale yellow-green tufts of leathery leaves bearing at their base great heads of small nuts: millions of such nuts floated in the waters and germinated in the mud-banks. There was also an abundance of dwarf screw-pines and curious ferns of vivid green in certain areas of the beach.

The earth—grey on the river bank and reddish on the seashore—was covered with turf: Neptune-green *dhob* grass Spartina—excellent for the prevention of soil erosion, as it tenaciously clings with its roots in layers to the earth, hence the adage: 'Where the *dhob* groweth the goat frisketh.' What the goat cannot destroy water cannot erode. A *dhob*-covered promontory of earth can be as lasting as a ridge of granite running into the sea.

How old was that headland on which my bungalow was anchored? And how ancient was the village Jater Dol? Nearby, was discovered by Emile Sénart, an inscription in Brahmi characters dating from the third century before Christ. There was, I thought, every possibility of unearthing still older relics in the neighbourhood. 'Was not this locality associated with the stories and legends of the mariners who sailed from Tamluk? Jater Dol furnished the helmsmen of Singha-Bahu, and of Vijaya Singha, and his followers who sailed to Ceylon long before the time of Asoka. When did Kapila live? Long before Buddha's time. Why was he honoured in that area? Was it simply owing to the fact that legends associated him with the descent of the Ganges to the earth?

I mused on these and other questions as I walked up and down the covered verandah of my historic bungalow. Its ridiculously low rent made me smile: one rupee a month!

The view over the waters—the many-mile wide river and the limitless sea—was for me a new vision of infinity, very different from the hilly landscapes with which I was more familiar. The grandeur of the scene before me was enhanced by the presence of distant tree-clad islands, coppice-covered shoals, and shell-strewn sandbanks, and of sailing ships, steamers, boats and barges. From where I stood they looked no bigger than the decorative figures on a painted map: it was a wondrous sight, surrounded on three sides by the expanses of water—of the river and of the sea. The bowl of the horizon appeared infinitely wide-stretched and the canopy of heavens much higher than it looked when examined from the streets of filth-sodden Calcutta.

I turned my gaze towards the village of Jater Dol. The landward prospect was equally attractive. Beyond the beach, further inshore, throve isolated groves of tall bamboos and still taller clumps of coconuts and palmyras. It was a picture of green felicity. It reminded me of the view obtained from the Falcon's Rest in Chandernagore; though it was so dissimilar its quality was the same: it was soothing as a caress.

Soaring above the forest of foliage and the barriers of bamboos and palms, rose the proud dome of the Kapila Muni temple. Dignity and sublimity were the attributes of the sage Kapila: the master from whose teachings Buddha, son of Kapila-Vastu, derived the first truth, 'Without knowledge there is no deliverance from suffering.' It was fitting that the cupola of this sage's shrine should be stately and severe. The western sun painted its crest in gold.

The curvilinear roof of a smaller shrine which stood near the Kapila temple was just visible above the canopy of green tree-tops. In between the clumps of bamboos I caught glimpses of the cone-shaped cottages of Jater Dol: some of them stood on piles like the houses in Tibet and in the Penhari Parganas.

In an open greensward the villagers were busy giving the finishing touches to the conical roof of the temporary shed put up for the dances and mystery plays to be given in honour of Kama Deva—the Lord of Love, Manasa—the Mind-born and other deities.

Patches of crimson-and-orange cannas and of violet irises as well as the light-green of the plantain groves heightened the colour effect of the general scene. While the flowering trees and shrubs made the air fragrant, the sea breeze enhanced its balmy effect.

I recalled the affectionate terms my English tutor, Major Arnott, used in this connection. 'At Jater Dol,' he told me, 'the peculiar aroma of oleander, sweet scent of jasmine, exotic perfume of frangipani, nostalgic reminder of gillyflower, spicy fragrance of carnation, and indescribable wholesomeness of leaves all have their appointed time, and the gardens there are scented calendars.' As for the perennial nasturtiums of the headland, they rightly deserved the praise of my patroness Sarojini Naidu:

> Poignant and subtle and bitter perfume,
> Exquisite, luminous, passionate bloom,
> Your leaves interwoven of fragrance and fire
> Are Savitri's sorrow and Sita's desire,
> Draupadi's longing, Damayanti's fears
> And sweetest Sakuntala's magical tears.

Near the palm-lined atoll naked children were playing in the shallow waters of the creeks. Some were gathering sea-shells and some rolling themselves in the sand. They were laughing. The waters of the streamlets flowing into the sea were laughing too.

There was general rejoicing.

All the birds of the air were loudly voicing their delight. How infinitely more attractive they were compared with their harshthroated compeers in the towns. I noticed now the presence of some new varieties of brightly plumed birds: the blue magpies with their long feathery tails, and the *koklas*—wedge-tailed green pigeons—as brilliantly coloured as the parakeets, with green head and neck and bright yellow about the wings, possessing the gift of melodious warbling, which recalled to me the sound of yodelling in the distant Penhari mountains; and the *jantris*—or nutcrackers—with a peculiar trilling call like the playing of rattles; and finally, the orioles: this bird is at once a beam of golden light and a note of sweet music resembling the tinkling of silver bells.

The more gorgeously plumed the bird the greater was its predilection for roosting in the brighter flowering trees, like the silk-cotton plant or the asoka or the suriya, or the champak. For its fragrance the champak with its pale-yellow blossoms is justly far-famed and our myths tell us that the Lord of Love tips his arrows with its blooms; the asoka tree with its orange and crimson flowers has received its due mead of praise from our poets. But somehow the *koklas* showed their preference for the less lauded—but certainly no less beautiful—suriya trees bearing tulip-shaped flowers of pink and purple, with panicles about two feet in length. The blue magpies, on the other hand, nestled in the silk-cotton trees: the flowering silk-cotton tree is a heavenly sight; its branches stand at right-angles to the bole like the yards of a ship's mast and shed their leaves with the changes of seasons; and at each season, long before the arrival of the new leaves, come the glorious bell-shaped blossoms in wild profusion; the ground is carpeted with fallen petals, a crimson rug, many inches thick, which remains fresh for days.

Why have the poets ignored these magnificent trees? And overlooked the butterflies as well? Rarely had I witnessed so many of them all in one spot. They avoided the sun and fluttered about in shadowed places where light had a deep green quality. Their variety seemed to be endless: the largest species being an enormous velvet black with scarlet spots at least eight inches wide, and the smallest, of a lustrous peacock blue, measuring no more than the tiniest cornflower. They all seemed to share the joyousness that pervaded the atmosphere.

Unknowingly I found myself breathing the prayer:

> O Earth, auspicious be thy woodlands,
> Auspicious thy hills, rivers and ocean.
> O earth, bountiful be thy blessings
> A mother unto me thy son.

It was a boon to be there, far away from Calcutta's asphalt and filth, where dehumanized men—jostling crowds of beggars and traders—lived like ants. It was a still greater boon, I thought, to be a participant in the festivities connected with the entry of the sun into Capricorn. I was conscious of my role and very happy about it. Apart from acting as a flautist in the village orchestra I was accorded the part of Vasanta in the mystery play, and over and above I was entrusted with the task of releasing the porpoise, Sisi-Magar.

There stood at anchor in the atoll my bamboo barge painted bright vermilion and bearing the pennant with a porpoise on it. Sisi-Magar was examining the wooden framework that barred its way from the atoll to the open sea. It suddenly changed its mind and dived underneath the Vermilion Boat to hide itself.

I was waiting for Mug, and wondering if he would join me in a trial sailing of my Vermilion Boat.

VIII

Mug was born under the sign of Pisces—the fish. His second name was Panada.

Who on earth had the idea of giving him such a ridiculous name I never learnt. Mug was bad enough for a Furtado, but Panada was the limit. Panada, as we know it, is milk-sop or chicken-feed, a variety of paste—stale bread mixed with buttermilk—destined for poultry. Perhaps his second name was responsible for his occasional moods of prostration, preceded by frenzied fits of religious outpourings. In circumstances which would have driven any other student to run amok, Mug ran to the nearest church only to rush out of it cursing his eyesight and bad luck.

'Can you tell me where is the nearest church?' Mug would babble.

'You have just come out of one.'

'No, no,' Mug would wail. 'Not this sort of a church. I want a Catholic church. I want to confess.'

What the enormity and diversity of his sins were I never knew. I did, however, come to learn from the Goanese family he lived with that the padre of the Catholic Church in Armenia Bazaar was pretty sick of Mug. It was rumoured that apart from the purpose of administering the extreme unction the much harassed priest was no longer prepared to face my friend. This gossip might have been an exaggeration. But I was willing to accept it as wholly true. For I knew that no priest, however patient and understanding, could cope with my friend—Mugdagh Panada Furtado—when he had his paroxysms of piety. He was then like one possessed: he wanted to be chastised—mercilessly scourged for his failings, real or imaginary—and his confessions lasted for hours. It was a matter of surprise to me that he had not during one of his fits accused himself of being an accomplice to all the murders and outrages committed in every part of the world.

~

Once in such a mystic mood Mug gave away his much-prized violin to a street-corner musician who was twanging on a single-stringed mandoline—the *ektara*—to entertain passers-by.

'Brother!' Mug sobbed as he embraced the ragged beggar. 'Thy necessity is greater than mine. Take this, and praise the Lord.'

'Mug,' I murmured, as I tried to drag him away. 'Mug, you must not part with the gift of your great-uncle. A dead man's present ought not to be given away.' It was a rare violin. I did not know the exact date of its make, but I recalled that it was considered to be far more precious than another violin Mug's great-uncle obtained from his Excellency Dom Fernandes of Goa. This second instrument—the less valuable one—was made in the same year as that in which Job Charnock founded modern Calcutta, as could be judged by the text of its engraved label: ANTONIUS STRADIVARIUS CREMONENSIS ALUMNUS NICOLAI AMATI, FACIEBAT ANNO 1690. 'There are at least a thousand genuine Stradivarii,' Mug's great-uncle had declared when he divided up his treasures for his legatees. 'But not a hundred violins by Guarneri del Gesù of Cremona. So Mug shall have the Guarneri. I don't care for girls. But as Mug's good-for-nothing gadfly of a sister is not bad with her violin, I shall leave the Stradivarius to her.'

I tugged at Mug while the surly beggar with the mandolin muttered curses at me: I was the evil genius trying to prevent an act of generosity: a violin would be so handy to him, as there were pawn-shops in the neighbourhood.

'Your great-uncle's gift, Mug!' I repeated. 'You must not sacrifice it in this way. Think of your sister, Anita. She may like to exchange her violin for yours.'

'A poor man's need counts more than Anita's wishes,' Mug replied firmly, and the violin was gone. The rascally mendicant disappeared without uttering a word of thanks.

Though I am only a flautist—and my instrument is a plain bamboo flute—and my knowledge of fiddles is very limited, this much was obvious to me—that a violin by Guarneri del Gesù—once the most treasured heirloom of the Tartinis and later the object of pride of an Italian prince living in Via delle Botteghe Oscure of Rome—was not to be easily picked up even in Cremona. All remonstrance was useless. Mug was adamant.

Had I forcibly prevented Mug from carrying out his act of charity or bribed the beggar to leave us to ourselves, there would have been murder that day, or suicide, or perhaps both: Mug would have killed me and then hanged himself.

~

Though liable to attacks of amnesia when confronted with question-papers, he obtained extraordinary visions of lucidity when he had his fits: he remembered with great precision every sin since he was born. This memory weighed Mug down whenever anything went seriously wrong. Occasionally, in the laboratories when he failed—within a certain self-imposed time-limit—to make a nice cross-section, dye it, and mount it on a slide for examination under the microscope, he knew (he muttered), the cause of his clumsiness. 'It must be due,' he would sigh, 'to my failure to attend early mass three weeks ago. I ought to have confessed that at times I feel too lazy to attend the Sunday services.'

Gradually his mystic mood would gain upon him. Like a gramophone record playing backwards he would then start accusing himself of ten million sins—committed in word, thought and deed—from the hour the spirit seized him to the day of his birth. It was a marvel, some of us thought, that Mug never bothered about confessing his ante-natal crimes, infamies, and lapses. This sort of mental distemper lasted for about a week, followed by a couple of days' silent recuperation from general exhaustion, and Mug would re-emerge as his usual self.

'I must not take part in this year's *Holi* festivity,' Mug spoke falteringly. 'I don't want to squirt anyone with red dyes nor do I want anyone to do the same to me. I must not have anything to do with the Hindu carnival of the vernal equinox.'

'Mug, don't be crazy,' I protested. 'What harm will it do to have some fun like the others?'

He shook his head, and declared in a solemn tone that as a Catholic he should abstain from pagan ceremonies: his inner self told him that his failure in the examination papers on plant physiology was due to his participating in the *Holi* feast of the preceding year.

'That settles it,' I sighed. I realized that nothing in the world—not even a threat of torture or murder—could make Mug change his mind for the coming seven days.

IX

Mug was in one of his mystic moods when he threaded his way through the gathered company of musicians seated under the *pandal*—the temporary pavilion—put up for the dances and plays in connection with the Ganga Sagar festivities. He was pale and trembling. I watched him coming; he was evidently looking for me. But why was he alone? He was expected to bring with him both Anita and Roma.

'Sorry, Brother,' Mug whispered. 'I am extremely sorry. But I can't stay with you in your bungalow during the three days of the Manasa festival. I must not watch any pagan ceremony. Forgive me for letting you down.'

I tried to calm him, and thanked him for helping me to make the bungalow neat and tidy. But he became more nervous.

'I must leave the place before the musicians start.'

It was, I realized, useless to argue with him. The best course was to let him have his own way for seven days. I asked him anxiously if he had brought Anita and Roma with him.

'I can't let Anita take part in this pagan affair. I left Calcutta without telling her a word about my journey to Jater Dol.'

'And what has happened to Roma?'

'She has come on her own. You will find her in the outer circle of spectators.'

I gave a sigh of relief. Thank God, I said to myself, she has not let me down.

Before leaving me Mug told me that there had been wireless announcements about a coming typhoon towards sunset. The loudspeakers, I understood, were issuing warnings to the pilgrims and there would be no illuminated boat-races. 'You would do well,' Mug counselled, 'to release your porpoise as soon as you can. In any case before sunset. Don't go far with your Vermilion Boat. It is not seaworthy.'

I did not pay much attention to his warning about the coming storm. My mind was taken up with Roma: it was good to know that she was there. Did she know that I was taking a small part in the mystery play about the Birth of the Warrior God?

'Why don't you release your porpoise now?' asked Mug.

'I will go as soon as my role is over.'

'Give me your word of honour.' Mug insisted. 'You must not go far with your boat. The Vermilion Boat is not seaworthy. And remember what the English sailor at Kidderpore told you: "The sea is a bitch. Keep out of it. It isn't meant for one like you." Let me have your word of honour.'

He did not, however, stay to receive my promise! At the first sound of the tuning of the musical instruments he rushed out as though chased by the devil. His precipitate departure made me smile.

~

I craned my head and looked in all directions for Roma. There was a sea of faces, and I was right in the centre of the circular pavilion squatting on the ground with other members of the improvised orchestra. The spectators sat in rows and rows surrounding us on all sides. Perhaps Roma saw me, but I failed to identify her in that huge crowd of pilgrims and visitors.

It was a pity she was not sitting next to me. That would have helped me to explain the broad outlines of the mystery play in which I was taking part. Apart from being one of the flautists in the orchestra I was appearing as a Companion to the Lord of Love—Vasanta, whom the Greeks called Lycoris.

To appreciate an Indian dance or a Mystery Play with its ballet interludes one must know the Hindu legends. I had my doubts about Roma's knowledge of Sanskrit epics as modified by our different local traditions. Hence I regretted very much that I had overlooked recounting to her in Calcutta some of the incidents connected with the descent of the Ganges to the earth, and of the birth of the Warrior God, Skanda.

This legend, like most of our myths and traditional lore, is difficult to recount in a few words. The episode in which I was appearing with a number of Pahari performers may, however, be briefly described as follows:

Uma, Daughter of the Mountains, aspires to be the consort of Siva, who, immersed in his meditations, takes little notice of her till the Lord of Love comes to her aid and brings Siva's austerities to an end; the Lord of Love has been moved by Uma's beauty and also by the supplications of the other minor deities engaged in combating the demons of Darkness who cannot be overcome till the heavenly host obtain as their commander the issue of the union of Uma and Siva; the offspring of Uma and Siva is found to be no other than the Lord of Love reincarnated as the Warrior God, Skanda.

'The nuptials of Uma and Siva,' our commentators point out, 'serve as the prototype of human union and sanctify with divine precedent the forces which make for home life and carry on the race of men.'

Our dancing is as intricate for the uninitiated to follow as our legends—particularly our religious dances, which are never given on the stage; they are so unlike 'Les Biches' and other Western ballets because they do not consist of rhythmic movements of the feet and the arms only. Every minute gesture—even the slightest movement of the finger-tips, the *mudra*—has a symbolic meaning. Our performers—they all come from the country and not from the towns—are not glamorous in the sense Comrade Chumchicke Adhikari's hula-hula dancers are. They need no limelight nor darkened atmosphere to create a world of make-believe. Our dances are the most spontaneous and at the same time the most conventional: like the traditional attitudes and postures in our acts of worship. How can they possibly appeal to all? People who find garish posters aesthetically satisfying will not care for our delicate miniatures.

'To admire well-known prima donnas and ballerinas,' Profulla Babu told me, 'is a cult in the West. Even when these good ladies have lost their voices and their capacity of moving with ease they attract admiring crowds.' Perhaps he was joking and exaggerating the fact that our town-dwellers, being confirmed admirers of everything Western, do love to admire professional successes. However that may be, our up-country dancers are not professionals and they do not appeal to townsmen and cinema fans. I was, therefore, surprised to see a large number of camera-carrying spectators from Calcutta in the crowd that gathered to witness the religious mysteries at Jater Dol.

Calcutta's indigenous inhabitants have little feeling for religion. What brought them there? Was there something below their crude, unconscious mind which urged them—in spite of themselves—to participate in a collective act of adoration?—Some hidden earnestness about which they themselves were unaware. Or was it just prying curiosity?

'Their curiosity is pardonable,' I finally concluded, 'provided they bring with them the spirit of reverence. Our dances are prayers. Those who do not believe in prayers have no business to be here.'

But why did they bring their cameras with them?

None of the dancers gathered at Jater Dol had at any time been photographed. They were not of the category of our cinema artistes, being simple and humble folks—many of them did not even know how to read and write. Dance to them was a ritual to which they had been trained from their childhood in the same fashion as they had been taught their parental calling or craft. Some of the men were corn-grinders while others were potters or weavers, or cowmen or ploughmen, while the women were matrons or neatherds or milkmaids or simple village girls. All of them, however, regarded dancing as a part of the expression of holiness. Their attitude towards dancing was so different from that of the overwhelming majority of the townsmen that the mere sprinkling of Calcutta's tourists irritated me.

I feared the townsmen's ironic—or even well-intentioned—clapping at the end of the performance; for I recalled that some of the well-meaning fools cheered lustily when the Sistine Chapel Choir from Rome ended one of their recitals in Calcutta with the 'Benedicite'. That was a disgrace.

If someone were to ask me: 'What is the most treasured possession of inhabitants of your part of the world?' I knew what would be my immediate reply; 'Our religious dance.' This has been transmitted from generation to generation—from father to son, and from mother to daughter—throughout the ages. This is the philosopher's stone which transmutes our dross of life into hallowed gold. Thanks to it our hard existence has been transfused with the sustaining sense of beauty. It transforms one's toil and travail into joy; it makes a poor man wealthy—a thousandfold richer than factory-workers or industrialists who have the benefit of easy access to cinemas, cabarets, prize-rings, and grog-shops and to cheap literature and other forms of readymade pleasure.

Tradition, let me repeat, plays a big part in these performances, and I suspect many of the camera-swingers found the Pahari dances as boring as Daoud Benisraeli found the Indian legends. I wonder if they understood the symbolic value of the setting where the dances were given.

Each religious ceremony demands an arrangement of its own. For the festival of the sun entering Capricorn, the people of Jater Dol had done their best to adhere to the time-honoured plan and procedure. A large, circular area on the greensward was marked out by transplanted plantains whose trunks were stuck into the ground. In its centre stood the conical roofed pavilion covered with palm fronds. Beyond the area marked by the plantain trunks was a wider circle bordered with neatly cut white leaf-sheaths. There was an outer enclosure of bamboos ornamented with festoons of flowers, strings of gaily coloured paper lanterns, and brightly tinted flags bearing the images of parrots or peacocks, or porpoises, or pigeons. The ground of the innermost arena was marked with bands of purple and white—of *avira* dust and powdered chalk—indicating the area reserved for the musicians and mimers. The rest of the place was, of course, for the spectators. Everyone sat cross-legged on the ground. Some visitors from Calcutta, especially those with cameras, preferred to remain on their feet and stood at the extreme edge of the outermost circle. A few of them had provided themselves with 'shooting-sticks' proclaiming in this way that they were not country folks and sitting cross-legged like Buddha was liable to lower their dignity.

~

The chorus was sung or recited as the tradition demanded by the musicians, either in unison or in canon. (A word about these songs and recitals: they never end in the usually accepted sense of the term; they slowly die away as if the singing should only make audible for a while a continuous silent melody. The effect is haunting: it has vivid evocative powers.) Occasionally a single voice chanted the main features of a forthcoming scene or commented on the action. This might be judged from the following verses, informing the audience of Uma's approaching womanhood:

Single voice:

As pictures waken to the painter's brush
Or lilies open to the morning sun,
Her perfect beauty answered to the flush
Of womanhood when childish days were done.

Chorus:

Soft the blossoms of Sirisa,
Softer Uma's rounded arms,—
Were they chains young Love had fashioned
For the God who owned her charms?
On her neck and heaving bosom
Hung the pearls in graceful cluster,
Did they lend her brighter beauty,
Did her bosom lend them lustre?
If the lotus oped its petals
In the beauty of the night,
Moon-lit blossoms then might rival
Uma's face serene and bright!

Flautists began piping softly, while the lightly touched cymbals imitated the jingle of the anklet-bells. I noticed some of the visitors from Calcutta getting their movie-camera ready, thinking Uma was due to appear soon. They had to wait a long while for that! The poetry and the music were to prepare the mind, to attune it to the proper appreciation of the greater mysteries to be revealed later through dancing and acting.

I lowered my head to avoid being distracted by the flashlights which some photographers were using. However, once the voices restarted the chant, I forgot all about the people of Calcutta and listened spellbound as though translated to an unknown grove where there was no one but I:

Single voice:

Suppose a blossom on a leafy spray:
Suppose a pearl on spotless coral laid:
Such was the smile, pure, radiantly gay,
That round her red, red lips for ever played.

And when she spoke, the music of her tale
Was sweet, the music of her voice to suit,
Till listeners felt as if the nightingale
Had grown discordant like the jangled lute.

Instead of Uma, I found I was thinking of Roma. Was I paying any attention to my flute-playing? I fear I was responsible for a few false notes that afternoon. (That did not, of course, matter much so far as the dancing was concerned; because the music of the flute was not so much an accompaniment as a stimulus and a background. All the same, I felt ashamed of myself.) 'I must shake myself up,' I rebuked myself, and shifted my position.

The second reciter now led the chorus:

Chorus:

And her glances! Did the wild deer
Learn the dark charm of her eye,—
Did she from the deer of the forest
Learn that secret mystery?

Arched eyebrows darkly shaded
Thrilled the gazer's beating heart,
Were they young Love's bow of prowess
Quick to send the fatal dart?

And in dark and clustering ringlets
Fell her ample wealth of hair,
Did the long-haired mountain Chowrie
Hide in shame within her lair?
Fairest forms and shapes in nature
Richest tints and softest shade,
Were in harmony united
To create this mountain maid!

Roma wore her hair short, or rather, comparatively short. Her ringlets came down in thick clusters to her shoulders (like the hair of the Santal dancers in the Penhari Parganas). Otherwise, I thought, the above description fitted her perfectly. I shifted my gaze from the point of my nose to the ground. I did not dare look up because Uma of the Pahari dancers came into the arena just then, and I was terribly afraid that she might prove disappointing. 'I am crazy,' I muttered, and wanted to chastise my irreverent thoughts.

Apart from the soles of Uma's feet, which were dyed red, I saw little of her. I did, however, notice that her toenails were lacquered saffron and the braids that tied the clusters of bells round her ankles were also saffron. That was all, and she danced right in front of me! I could have touched her by stretching out my arm.

I kept staring on the ground. Uma's exit was followed by the entry of Urvashi the Coryphæa and her companions, the Apsaras.

I saw nothing of them and barely heard the verses in connection with their arrival and departure. Only a few snatches of songs clung to my mind, and these referred to Kama-Deva—Lord of Love, Eros:

The first voice: Wind-borne Eros—you are fleet of foot, fleeter than the forked shaft the lightning throws.

The second voice: Wingèd Eros—you are more beauteous than beauty.

Chorus of Apsaras (aside): We are only less than he, because we bear no arc and arrows.

My immobility, or perhaps my indifference to what was going on in the arena might have led my neighbour to think that I had fallen asleep. He gave me a good nudge. I looked up, and judged it was time for me to get ready for playing my role of Vasanta, the Lord of Spring.

Kama-Deva, the Lord of Love, was already on the scene. He was unarmed. The only weapon he carried was his flute: on this he played, demanding the presence of the nymphs and dryads, the goddesses and maidens, and all others desirous of knowledge about love and joy. They responded to his call and rushed towards the arena from all sides.

There was no greenroom. The artistes sat, as customary, with the musicians or with the spectators wherever they found room to squat without being squeezed. They threaded their way through the serried rows of seated men, women and children till they reached the circle of the arena marked by a border of purple *avira* dust. There they stood for a few moments so that all of them could step in at the same time.

Some thirty or forty women answered the summons of Kama-Deva. They were of all ages and all heights: purposefully chosen to form well-balanced groups during their performance.

Their hairstyle indicated their status. Those representing the divinities wore their hair rolled and done in an Elf-knot, while others—semi-divinities and mortals—had their long tresses coiled in different ways round their heads. But whether personating heavenly or earthly nymphs, they all carried, fixed to their floral diadems or jewelled crowns, transparent veils of various hues symbolizing different feminine qualities. Their main garment was the many pleated bell-shaped skirt of vividly coloured gossamer silk shot with gold, which covered them from the hips to the ankles; over this they wore sash-wise flowered kirtles, while a narrow band of diaphanous muslin, delicately dyed, swathed round the body and kept in position across their bosoms by a simple knot, heightened the scintillating colour effect of their costumes—each hue alive, luxuriant and quivering like the landscape under the afternoon sun. As for their ornaments and jewellery, these were very different from those worn in the Penhari Parganas: some of them had a broad baldric passing over the right shoulder and under the left arm, on which hung gold and silver chains, clusters of berry-shaped bells, strings of corals and pearls as well as braids sewn with minute bits of mirror. The unveiled face was unadorned, but for the mark of vermilion *tilka* in the middle of the forehead and the collyrium paint on the eyes. The neck—as well as the chest—was bare except for carcanets of gold and silver. Their honey-coloured arms carried wreaths of flowers—with symbolical bearings—entwining slave bangles and manacle bracelets of gold, silver and lacquer. They wore no rings, neither on their fingers nor on their toes. Their unshod feet, however, bore anklets fitted with tiny bells similar to those fixed to their baldrics. The palms of the hands as well as the soles of the feet were dyed red with Henna. Their nails also were brightly lacquered.

The nymphs acknowledged the supremacy of the Lord of Love with a prostration in his honour. Immediately afterwards, keeping him as the centre of the circle they formed, they greeted the audience with a slow curtsey and the *anjali* salutation: the prayer with the stretched palms joined together. They then spread out their arms to touch each other by the finger-tips, and slowly advanced step by step—making their circle increasingly larger—till their feet trod on the purple band of *avira* marking the border of the arena—or the stage, for our purpose—allocated for their performance. This is known as *treading the stage* or *walking the floor*.

Its purpose was solely to measure out the exact space at their disposal for doing their gyrations, roundels, lavoltas, cotillions, and other more complicated steps and tableaux. This treading the stage was so cleverly carried out that none of the visitors from Calcutta, except those well acquainted with this particular mime and dance—*manadala nritya*—guessed how a minute later, when most intricate and rapid movements were made, not one of the dancers overstepped by a fraction of an inch the inconsiderable limits of the circular space allowed to them for their mimes and dancing.

It is hardly necessary to mention that none of the Pahari dancers nor I nor any other participant in the performances had had any opportunity for rehearsing. In this respect we were no worse off than other groups of dancers from different parts of the country at the *mela*.

Rehearsing for religious dances is simply not done. For secular dances it is deemed unnecessary. Rehearsals are looked upon as almost abhorrent, just as our image-makers hate the idea of making use of immobile models. A moment's glance, a single measurement, one rapid survey ought to suffice a true artist: that is the belief of our country folks.

As soon as this measuring of the arena was done—artfully, yet with artless ease—the dancers pirouetted round to face the Lord of Love once again, and with the movements of their hands they introduced themselves to him, collectively and then individually. All the time they were in movement, in a clockwise fashion, never allowing both their feet to rest on the earth at the same time; before taking a step the free foot was swung backwards and forwards, keeping time with the music of the drums. They moved in the clockwise way because for circumambulating an altar or an image of a deity, as has been said before, one should always have the right hand nearest to the incarnation of holiness.

At a given signal from the musicians the circle round the Lord of Love ceased to be one; it became two: those of short stature formed the outer ring facing the audience while their taller sisters crowded round the central figure to recount to him the trials of Uma, their most beloved and loveliest companion.

The Lord of Love wanted to know more about Uma. Each one of the nymphs had some secret to impart to him, which could be breathed to him alone. The deity held out his hand. Who would be the first to take it and dance with him and tell him of the secret while dancing? As the nymphs were timid, the Lord of Love chose his partner, the one nearest to his left hand. In dancing with her he guided her movements as he himself whirled round and round, and so did the others. While revolving in gyrations—now slow, now fast—the Lord of Love changed his partner—not once, nor twice, but some thirty or forty times—till he had danced with every one of the nymphs, and gathered from each all that he wanted to know. Then came his sudden realization that Uma was not in the throng of his worshippers.

Where was Uma? They searched for her, but she was not in the arena.

Kama-Deva, Lord of Love, played on his flute once again to send his message to his companion Vasanta (Lycoris): Vasanta, Lord of the Season of Spring, was bidden to fetch Uma.

Vasanta was, of course, none other than I. But so absorbed was I with watching the dance that I had ignored a number of nudges from several of my neighbours in the orchestra. Now I got up in a flurry, and instead of following the indication given by the man who played the *sitar*—the long-stemmed lute—I made a wrong move. A minute later I found I was tugging hard at Roma's hand: she was far back in the outer circle of spectators, and I do not even now know how I automatically sought her out without knowing where she was sitting.

The situation was fortunately saved by the timely appearance of Uma in the arena without Vasanta to introduce her to the Lord of Love.

As might be guessed, the rest of the performance was but dimly seen by me. My eyes smarted, my ears tingled. Suddenly I felt I was going to have a severe attack of cold. I just avoided having a breakdown in the middle of the performance.

X

Had I followed the way of traditional story-tellers I ought to have kept back up till now that Roma slapped my face soon after the Pahari dances were over: when I came out of the arena and took her to the bungalow; there I offered her the five jewels—tiny bits of diamond, emerald, topaz, and coral with a pearl in the centre—mounted on a brooch, wrapped in the scarf bought in the kiosk of the Sacred Precincts of the Golden Pagoda. It was the scarf that bore the magic formula:

With longing feathered, tipped with love,
Its shaft is formed with fixed desire:
With this arrow levelled well
Shall Eros pierce thee to the heart.

'You have managed the affair pretty well,' she remarked enigmatically, and refused to listen to me. I could not get in a word edgeways. 'You are a fine boy! Now I know why you wanted me to appear in a sari. So that I may remind you of your Mahajantooli lady friends. Or perhaps some of the inmates of the Golden Pagoda district.'

Mug's sudden fit of mysticism, Anita's failure to join Roma, my undertaking the task of releasing Sisi-Magar, the offer of the scarf bought in the Golden Pagoda, and even the very words printed on the scarf, all these and a hundred other things were interpreted by Roma as parts of a long-thought-out sinister plan for compromising her.

'Aren't you clever?' she went on. 'You have arranged things in such a way as would force me to spend the night alone with you in your bungalow. I am not going to be under the same roof as you all by myself. Where is Anita?'

It was not her cuffing that mattered so much as her words. I was deeply hurt when she accused me of behaving in a dishonourable way, and what was worse she declined to let me explain the situation. She waxed angrier and angrier when I told her that Sisi-Magar had to be released before I could take her to one of Mug's relatives in Jater Dol or see what might be done about her return journey to Calcutta.

'Go and look, after that porpoise,' she stormed without paying the least heed to the fact that it was my duty to set Sisi-Magar free in the Ganga Sagar. 'Does that porpoise belong to one of your lady friends? Naturally, it is more important than my night's lodging. I shall sleep under the stars.'

This was the second time that I saw Roma in a strange light. The first occasion I shall never forget, when she pulled me about by my hair before the mob near the Prince Ghulam Muhammed Mosque: she then behaved like a hysterical woman. 'A common tart' was the epithet that had inadvertently come to my mind then. Now she seemed to be a spiteful viper spitting out poison: accusing me of being a 'deep one', a mean, sly rogue—worse than Naga Gangoo the Lady-killer.

What had I done to deserve all this? Why was she mad with rage? What had her wearing a sari to do with her reputation? Why at the sight of Sisi-Magar had she suddenly flared up and told me that no man had ever insulted her as much as I had done? When had I insulted her? What right had I at any time to utter one unkind word against her? Was I not remorse-stricken for my unjust thoughts? Did I not recognize that she was the only person with whom I could talk freely? Was she not the one who made my life bearable in Calcutta? She was for me sweeter than the goddess Uma. How could she think that I had a deep-laid plot for humiliating her?

~

At first I was angry—angry with myself, angry with Kolej Huzoor, angry with Mug, angry with Anita, and angry with Roma—and then I became terribly depressed. I wrote a few lines for Mug and left my message for him on my table, and walked out of the bungalow. It was absolutely no use talking to Roma. Moreover, she was nowhere to be found. So I went towards the atoll to get my Vermilion Boat ready for Sisi-Magar.

Pretty women, they say in the Penhari Parganas, are whimsical and bound to be more erratic than other women. The Second Master of the Ranigunj School used to say: 'A woman's mind—be she pretty or ugly—is a bottomless pit, which you think you have explored; but it has depths beyond any man's experience. Search as deep as you will, you will never find logic in it.'

Perhaps, I thought, there is more than a grain of truth in all these sayings.

The first time I was slapped on the face by a woman, I did not get so upset. It was the hula-hula dancer at Kidderpore who struck me when I had protested against her costume. 'Go back to your mummy's lap,' she screamed as she boxed my ears. 'Go home and don't spoil other people's pleasure with your grumbling.' A few minutes later when I was thrown out of the dancing hall the same woman came running after me and asking me to wait for her. 'Don't be a fool!' she whispered. 'Wait till the show is over. We shall go home together.' Her behaviour was highly illogical. But as I did not know her it mattered little to me whether she was logical or illogical. If I was depressed on that occasion it was for reasons other than being smacked by a woman.

Between a hula-hula dancer and Roma there was a world of difference. When she behaved like a mad woman before an infuriated mob it was not improbable that she did so on purpose: perhaps she wanted to distract the gangleaders and divert them from their objective of murder and arson. If that was the case, she could not be accused of being illogical. Far from it: there was, on the contrary, a method in her madness.

But what made the same—clear-thinking, intelligent, kind and witty—Roma behave so differently.

'No,' I spoke to Sisi-Magar. 'There must be some reason for her getting angry with me. This is not the first time I have offered her a present. It is not my gift which has upset her. She is not only angry with me, but with you as well. You have not offered her a scarf. All the same, she is furious with you. Now let us get ready.'

Sisi-Magar splashed about joyously as I busied myself with the Vermilion Boat.

~

Some fishermen shouted something to me from the distance. I noticed among them the powerfully voiced, one-eyed boatman who had sung a Bhatiali song for me on the day of my first visit to Jater Dol. He was a friendly soul. I had given him in return Roma's favourite piece: *Ami chini-go, chini*—I know you, O Daughter of alien shores.

I waved my neckcloth to them.

The anchor was raised.

The one-eyed boatman pointed to the signal-mast showing gale warnings. Of course, I knew about the coming storm. It was, however, difficult to believe that there was some lurking danger in the atmosphere. Everything looked so placid and so calm.

The sea was smooth like polished silver. The sky was bare of clouds; it shimmered like a burning opal: argent and white. The dunes and the mud-banks glistened in the sun: silver grey. A pearly haze filled the atmosphere. The sun was blazing, yet I could not see far. The bowl of the horizon seemed to have shrunk considerably.

No breath of air stirred the fan-shaped leaves of the palmyras: The trunks of the coconuts and palms were immobile as though they were petrified.

The boat slid along the surface of the water as on a glassy lake. I left the current to look after its course. I was no longer going to bother myself with anything: certainly not with the land; I had had enough of my bungalow and Jater Dol. My gaze was now fixed on the sea. I wanted to go beyond the curtain of haze that hung over the waters: beyond the Sagar Island, beyond the horizon.

~

After releasing Sisi-Magar I realized that I was free to do what I liked. I had no further responsibility to anyone.

I was alone.

Alone? Not quite. My sombre thoughts were keeping me company. How were melancholy reflections possible under a firmament that glowed opalescent? And was not the sea as gleaming as translucent moonstone? And my boat a thing of beauty, painted in vivid vermilion? In the midst of so much brightness how was I invaded by memories blacker than night? I do not know.

I sat with my back to the sun and watched the shadows flung far by the spars of my boat, and mused with my eyes half-closed. I did not feel the movement of the boat. So far as I was concerned it was not the vessel that drifted, but the land and the islands and the promontories: they simply receded. The tentacles of the ridges running into the sea grew smaller and smaller till they ceased to be anything: no more than insignificant pencil marks on a silver sheet; finally the curtain of haze hid them for good.

The atoll, the palm trees, the bamboos, the mangroves, the screw-pines, the mud-banks, the shoals of sand, and everything else connected with the land vanished long before I bothered to raise my head to discover how and in which direction my Vermilion Boat was bearing. My back, as I have said, was turned to the sun, and that was all that mattered. I did not want to get the sun on my face. It was coursing westwards and its beams shone smoothly on the waters. I was reminded of the reflection given by a polished plate of enamel to a slanting stream of powerful light. There was not the slightest glimmer anywhere to reveal the smallest ripple. The sea might well have been a burnished mirror of quicksilver or a sheet of glistening glass.

Where was I going? I did not know and I did not care. Only one thing was clear to me: I was not returning to Jater Dol.

~

And now even if I had wished to do so that would have been impossible. My bamboo barge was not destined for sea voyaging, and I had thrown away the rudder long ago. I had no compass with me, and the sky had grown black many hours before sunset. Imperceptible specks of clouds—minute scraps, hardly deserving notice—rose from the brim of the horizon to climb the vault of heaven; as they rose higher and higher they knotted themselves into dark contortions, and finally they blotted out the sun to change the day into night.

My boat was no longer gliding. Its movements were now like a drunkard's. With the total veiling of the sun, the wind rose, and the sea chafed. My bearings were completely lost.

It was high time for me to settle my reckonings.

The only person concerned with my fate was no other than I myself. Therefore I had delayed till then—what I thought to be the last hour—to do my reckoning.

I was accountable, so far as I could make out, to none but myself. But that account had to be settled. Otherwise, I had no right to depart in peace, nor had I any right to aspire for that last peace which, my villagers say, is every honest soul's legitimate portion. So, I started cross-examining myself: I became my own accuser and my own defender.

Did I bear any resentment to anyone?—Certainly I did, and to very many.

Was I prepared to be reconciled to them? Was I ready to admit my mistakes, and to ask their forgiveness?—My answer was most emphatically in the negative. I should feel humiliated if any miracle rescued me from the jaws of death on condition that I was to ask forgiveness of those I despised, those against whom I bore resentment.

Who were they?—Those who taught untruth, preached untruth, practised untruth, and pretended to be truthful. Those who talked in terms of saving humanity and refused to do the least service to their brothers. Those who deliberately misled young people like myself. Those who repeated cant, and discoursed on virtues in which they themselves had no faith. Those who were bent on destroying the beautiful because they were incapable of appreciating beauty. Those who proclaimed that the voice of the mob was the voice of God.

Should I not have pity for them, instead of resentment?—Pity for the demons! No, certainly not. I was not prepared to waste pity on rogues and rascals.

What good was I doing to myself by getting drowned?—No good, save this: no one could accuse me of trying to do anything dishonourable. At least Roma would understand me better from now on.

Would that be of any help to her? Would she not accuse herself of being the cause of my drowning?—I did not know my answer.

Did I then owe no one anything? Did I not want to be forgiven by those wronged by me? Did I claim that I had wronged no one in my life?—I owed nothing to anyone. No one had ever been wilfully wronged by me: not so far as I could remember.

~

I saw a flash of lightning in the distance: it was far, far away. And suddenly I remembered one face and burst into a stream of hot tears.

~

I was unmanned by the canker of remorse. I was haunted by a face: the face of someone I had injured: someone I had wronged greatly and whose forgiveness I had never asked; someone with every right to impeach me before the Judgment Throne.

Who was this person?—It was a woman: a woman with a frightened face.

But who was she?—I did not know. I searched my memory in vain. I clutched my head in my hands, and tried hard to remember. I asked myself a thousand questions to find some clue as to when, where, and how I had come across that face. Alas! I failed to elicit anything from memory: there was no help forthcoming for the solution of the mystery.

The Vermilion Boat was now continually turning and twisting. Occasionally it took to twirling as though caught in the whorls of the sea. It began groaning. It was never meant to be seaworthy. It was built for a single voyage down the river. The fact that it had so far withstood the battering of the waves was a near-miracle. Now it looked like breaking into two any moment unless it was sucked down to the bottom of the sea before that.

The sea had long ceased to be the moonstone pool of the afternoon. It was now a swirling mass of seething pitch. Its billows coiled and curled angrily around me to spin my frail vessel before disintegrating it.

I looked overhead to avoid the terrifying spectacle of the swell and fall of murky waves. The sky was like a black panther that snarled viciously. It was gloating over the groaning Vermilion Boat. It stooped low to watch every detail of the doomed victim's agony. It wanted to crush it under its weight. It crouched lower even as I watched it and came down to press upon the main mast which bent like a wand of willow and finally snapped into two.

My defiant mood was gone. I was trembling. My teeth chattered. I was in anguish lest the creaking boat split up before I had settled my accounts with my conscience—with the woman whose face floated back to my memory all of a sudden at that last hour.

'I must obtain her forgiveness,' I cried. 'Before I drown I must recognize the injury I had done to her.' There was no expiation, I knew, without acknowledgment of the sin committed. And at the same time my memory did not help me to recollect the precise circumstances in which I had seen that woman's face and injured her.

Whose was that face? And why did its memory torture me? Why did I see no details of that face save its lustrous black eyes? Those almond-shaped eyes were widened with fright.

~

It was impossible for me to concentrate my thoughts. How could I think clearly when I was being swept about like an empty seat in a whirligig. The wind wanted to whisk me off the deck into the sea, and then it pressed me down like a weight of lead: I felt like a grain of corn in a corn-grinder. The milling waters now began once again spinning the boat in a circle, and the circle grew narrower and narrower every minute.

There was not much time to waste. 'I must be at peace with myself,' I sobbed. 'But how can I have peace when I have not made myself worthy of forgiveness? Help! O Memory, help! Come! O Mind-born! Come and help me!'

Suddenly I remembered the *pitcher posture*: the crouching position which enables a yogi, they say, to resist the blast of Shani, the Demon of Misfortune, because it helps him to gather all the reserve of his inner resources. I stooped down and squatted on the latticed framework of the deck clutching at the stump of the broken mast; my bent knees reached my ears, and my two hands, grounded between my feet, embraced the remnant of the mast still adhering to the boat. There I remained with my eyes closed and my head bent. My crouching saved me from being swept overboard. I was comparatively safe for at least a few more minutes. Thus I had time to think again.

~

In my mind's eye I saw once more the pair of lustrous black eyes and a pair of beautifully moulded hands trying to cover them: the fingers were long and tapering; there were dainty bracelets at the wrists; the eyes were full of supplication. 'For pity's sake,' they begged, 'do not hit me.'

How could I have ever thought of hitting this unknown woman? 'No,' I protested to the raging wind. 'Not I. Not one man of the Penharis has ever hit a woman. No man of Chandernagore can ever hit a woman. No sane man—even of Calcutta—will dream of hitting a woman with such beautiful eyes and such delicate hands.'

Yet the face remained before my mind's eye. I disavowed ever having wronged her. But her face did not vanish. The language of her anguish-filled eyes was clear enough: 'For pity's sake, don't hit me. For mercy's sake, don't insult me.'

I struck my forehead against the stump of the mast and cried. 'Tell me, O unknown one!' I supplicated. 'When and where did I meet you? And why should I have given you the impression of being a brute?'

The pair of black eyes vanished, and I imagined a different scene: a tiny dog jumping into the circular basin of a fountain for a swim and then running away at a bound at my approach; the fountain was of the familiar pattern, found in most town squares and public gardens; it consisted of a number of bronze dolphins gurgling out water from their open mouths and nostrils. I saw once again the pair of tormented eyes.

The vision filled me with dread. I shrieked. I was no longer ready to die.

This knowledge did not, however, help me to identify her.

~

My failure to establish her identity led me to think that perhaps there were many others like her, whom I had injured and insulted—wittingly or unwittingly—in Calcutta as well as in other towns known to me.

Certainly there were many to whom I had not been kind. My memory brought back to me a score of other faces—dozens of people—to whom I ought to have brought succour, but brought nothing—not even a kind word. My indifference to them was as bad as deliberate cruelty. Cruelty, I knew, was the most abhorrent of all human failings, and I accused myself of having practised it unwittingly. What plea could I put forward to justify any prayer for forgiveness?

All thought of being at peace with myself was gone. More visions rose before me to augment my suffering.

What association of ideas shifted my thoughts to Padre Johan of Jamtara, I do not know. Padre Johan was the man whom my hostel mates called crazy because he once addressed them a sermon in which he dwelt on the theme dearest to his heart: 'If material prosperity is to be bought at the price of spiritual bankruptcy, let my people remain poor.' I admired Padre Johan. He wanted me to learn Danish to read Kierkegaard with him, yet during my stay in Calcutta I had not bothered to master a word of Danish. I felt ashamed of myself, and at the same time I longed for his blessing—the blessing which I did not deserve. I yearned for the sound of his sonorous voice which was like the peal of deep-toned bells. I recalled his corrugated iron chapel at Jamtara and the enthralling beauty of the language of his predications. I repeated to myself some of the words of his open-air address at the foot of the Ochterloney Monument: 'Satan is stalking the earth. He is talking through the mouth of demagogues. An honest man's duty is plain: he must combat Satan.'

'Padre Johan!' I cried, though I knew he would never hear me. 'Forgive me for forgetting your precept. God is the taskmaster, but I have bowed to Satan.'

A thousand things flashed back to my mind. Words vaguely heard long ago, and scenes barely seen: they came crowding back before my tightly shut eyes.

I recalled Profulla Babu's answer to my question: 'What can one man do to stem the flood and undo those who want to cover the earth with ugliness?' 'Forget,' he counselled, 'what the crowds should do. Think about yourself. If instead of marching in the wake of those who talk of paradise round the corner, you keep your head steady and succeed in producing something perfect—or as near to perfection as your disciplined goodwill and trained ability will permit—your life will be well-lived. You will attain your spiritual redemption, and make the world better by your attainment. Forget all about the professional patriots and professional world-betterers: they are like crows eyeing charnel heaps.'

'If you understand,' the village Punditji exhorted, 'the truth about the smallest grain of sand, you are well on your way to the understanding of the truth that concerns the whole earth.' 'But what is the truth?' 'The truth that concerns you,' he expounded, 'is for the time being the correspondence of idea and experience. It is the absolute value for all human beings, irrespective of time, space and civilization. But remember, the Absolute Truth is with God, and with Him alone.'

'What am I on this earth?' once I asked Kumar the image-maker. 'What am I good for?' 'If you have faith,' he replied, 'you are good for anything that your hands can mould. If you have faith in yourself, you will inspire faith in everything you touch, in everyone you meet, and you will then be able to keep faith with others. Think of your Didi-Ma, and her trials.'

~

The more I thought of the past the more I yearned for a longer span of life.

The image of Didi-Ma made me hold my breath. What infinite trouble did she not take to produce her thornless roses—Bourbon Zephyrine Drouhin—the beautiful silvery blossoms? Their musk-like heavy scent filled the whole house in Chandernagore.

'If I perish now,' I reflected, 'no one will perhaps miss me. But I shall then make my exit without fulfilling any of my duties. I have not even begun on them. Didi-Ma's thornless roses and brambles have remained neglected ever since her death.'

This began a new train of thoughts: my dues to the dead, my debts to the living, and my duty to the yet unborn. There is, I believe, no feeling more galling than that of being a traitor to one's friends, and of being a betrayer of their trust. And I discovered that my friends were many, both among the dead and among the living: there were some to whom I had not given the least thought for a long time.

Red-belly the pony: the chief delight of my boyhood days. Red-belly was sold a long time ago. It was no longer mine. But whenever I revisited my village Red-belly made it a point to call on me. The poor, ageing animal plodded over ploughed fields, hobbled over stony ridges, and swam across rivers solely for the fun of being patted by me. It came unasked and returned to its present master equally unasked. How did Red-belly know about my arrival at the village? 'It sniffs the air,' Ramdas the village watchman explained. 'And the air gives away the secret of your presence. If a pony could read I would have said Red-belly had a glance at the postcard announcing your arrival. But here most men do not know how to read, not to say anything of our animals. They are as illiterate as their masters, but they have good noses.'

Mohan the pygmy elephant who befriended me when I was a child: where was Mohan now? I did not know.

Boka Buk the silent stork that came from nowhere to settle down on the banks of the canals of Rani Nilmani's Estate and to guard the washing of Moti-Didi the laundry woman. It used to stand sedately on one leg and keep an eye on troublesome boys. Whenever any of them tried to pelt Moti-Didi's things with mud the stork knew what to do. 'My Treasure!' Moti-Didi begged of me when I left Rani Nilman's Estate, 'Don't forget Boka Buk when I am dead. Do revisit the corner where it lives and see how it gets along.'

Then there was Daftry-Chacha, the bookbinder. He too was one of those unforgettable figures of Rani Nilmani's Estate. And many others too.

I had not bothered to revisit the area which was once Rani Nilmani's Estate. This in spite of my long sojourn in Calcutta. I was disgusted with myself.

What was I to do?

'It is too late,' the wind replied. 'You can do nothing now. You were given the chance, and you did nothing.'

That being the case, all that was left for me was to await the inevitable.

'Why must you wait?' the wind asked. 'You will gain nothing by waiting. Come and join the waves. Moreover, it is going to rain and hail. You will be drenched through and through and pelted with hailstones. Why not make a swift end now?'

'No, I will not listen to you. I shall stay where I am.'

'Are you afraid of getting drowned? Better face the worst and be done with it. Why are you sitting with your eyes closed?'

I opened my eyes. I was no longer afraid of dying. The pride in my self-righteousness was gone; my remorse loosened the shackles of paralysing fear. I was submissive to Fate. But there was no reason for me to be servile to the wind and the waves.

'Why prolong your agony?' the wind and the waves asked in chorus. 'Come down to the bed of the sea. It is strewn with corals and pearls. You will find peace there.'

I did not bother any more to listen to these voices.

~

A quarrel among the sea-birds helped me to ignore the howling of the wind and the roars of the waves.

A wounded *puyati*—a foul-smelling petrel—dropped over me. Its claws grazed my back. It hopped about the deck of the Vermilion Boat believing perhaps that my presence would save it from the attacks of its fellows. The silly bird, however, jumped overboard of its own accord as soon as it had recovered its breath, and I did not see any more of it. Its wings were remarkably long and narrow, white underneath, otherwise all black. Though it went overboard it must have closely followed the boat, for very soon a number of other petrels came to flutter round about me. In spite of the terrific violence of the wind they flew about like seagulls in calm weather. They were engaged in a fight, or perhaps a mock fight, among themselves, emitting strange cries and filling the boat with a sickening stench.

What were the fulmars wrangling about?

Was it over the possession of the Vermilion Boat or of a phosphorescent body which was swirling round my vessel. This phosphorescent thing might have been a human corpse still wrapped in its swathing. Or perhaps it was a shark—a living one or was it dead?—I could not judge. It floated just underneath the surface of the waters. Only when the waves formed a trough had I flitting glimpses of it.

The noisy discord among the malodorous *puyatis* was not, after all, due to the gleaming object or creature, for it suddenly drifted underneath the boat to disappear for good, while the sea-birds kept on their quarrel. Strange as it may sound they brought to my mind the memory of the crows in Profulla Babu's lawn. Whom were they judging? And for what?

Gradually a strange truth dawned upon me, and I felt like a schoolboy ready to jump up with the raised right hand and shout: 'Now I know the answer.'

The putrid-smelling petrels were certainly not concerned with the fate of the phosphorescent object nor with mine. They were passing judgment on one of their fellows who had sinned—committed the gravest sin imaginable in my land—the crime of seeking pleasure in love. They were discussing the gravest problem affecting the Indian subcontinent from the Himalayas to the sea: frustration in love and frustration in life; frustration brought about by the constant inner conflict between the desire to possess and the yearning to renounce; the longing to win the saint's crown of heavenly glory and to relish the rake's cup of vicious delights. This perpetual struggle, I was now convinced, thwarted the creative capacity of my people, especially of those dwelling in the towns, and it was the root cause of our mob violence, absurd recklessness, unbelievable squalor, constant feuds, and demoniacal jealousy, and of extreme asceticism.

The reason why the rapacious storm-birds had lamed one of their fellows—the wounded petrel that sought for a brief minute refuge on the Vermilion Boat—was, I was ready to swear, jealousy. It was jealousy again that had driven the crows on Profulla Babu's lawn to destroy one of their own kind. 'The animals of a land,' the Punditji affirmed, 'take up the qualities and the defects of its people.' As our people are jealous by nature, I reflected, it is obvious that the birds are suffering from the same distemper.

'That crow was pecked to death,' I spoke to the wind, 'probably because it was smarter than the rest. Therefore it had to be punished. That's the fate, my fellow-students have told me, of all smart ones.'

~

'Who are the smart ones?'

I recognized the voice. It must have been the wind, and I did not bother to explain that in the jargon of the students of Calcutta a smart one meant somebody adroit with women. 'Others are jealous of such a man,' they told me, 'and do their best to run him down.'

'Are you never jealous?'

I was not going to talk to the wind any more. In fact just before the evil-smelling petrels came to befoul the deck of the Vermilion Boat I had definitely decided to ignore the voice of the wind. But the question worried me. I thought over it, and recognized the fact for the first time that I was capable of unreasonable jealousy. I was jealous of Roma's success, her gift of brilliant repartee in large companies, her quiet self-assurance, and, of course, of her admirers—real or imaginary—past and present.

'Is not Roma also jealous?'

This question led to my making a new discovery, which made me sadder still. And momentarily my anger rose against Sisi-Magar.

It was that silly, harmless porpoise, at long last I found out, that had caused Roma to blaze against me, and Roma's caustic remarks led to my scrawling a few lines for Mug and then launching myself upon this mad adventure. 'For whose benefit are you releasing that porpoise?' she asked sarcastically when I brought her to the atoll to examine the surprise—the porpoise Sisi-Magar—I had in store for her. She gave me a curious look as she murmured: 'Is it for the benefit of one of the gay ladies you know? Setting a porpoise free is supposed to bring success to a courtesan.' 'What do you mean?' I was totally flabbergasted. 'Do you think that the acolyte of the Golden Pagoda is a gay lady?' Roma mocked at my surprise, and told me about my visit to a house opposite the Fountain of Porpoises in the Mahajantooli district of Burdwan.

The rest was simple: it was as plain as the palm of my hand. Viewed from a new angle it was like this:

Some four of five years ago, when she was staying in Burdwan she had gone out one afternoon for a stroll with her dog. Her pet was enjoying a swim in the basin of the Fountain of Porpoises when a long-haired, bumptious young cad in his teens came out of the house opposite to frighten her dog away, because the fountain was not meant to be a dog's bath! He then walked up to her and offered her a gold-and-silver filigree rose and demanded to be entertained in the same fashion as he had been regaled by the gay ladies. She had forgotten all about that impudent rascal till the sight of Sisi-Magar reminded her of the Fountain of Porpoises.

'Is it not late in the day to make this discovery?'

'Perhaps,' I cried, unable to contain myself any longer. 'But it is better to die knowing the truth than living under a cloud of misapprehension. Now at least Roma will know that I am not a rogue.'

'Much good will that do to her!'

'Don't speak to me.' I shouted. 'I don't want to listen to you.'

'You will have to listen whether you like it or not.'

I tried to fix my gaze on the distance to distract myself.

~

It grew darker as the rain started.

The raindrops were like hot glass splinters. They pierced my body. But I did not mind: I deserved my ordeal. I had a new burden on my conscience. I ought to have told Roma everything about my visit to the Mahajantooli quarter. It was imprudent of me to have left a letter in the bungalow which told about my decision to drown myself because of Roma's harsh words.

Now I recognized my foolishness from the beginning to the end.

The petrels suddenly stopped their clamour and flew away in a body. I tried to follow them in their flight. But it was so dark that they soon disappeared beyond my range of vision. With their departure the boat was freed of the evil stench they brought with them. Where were they rushing? How did they manage to breast the gale which was blowing at a tremendous speed?

Now I discovered what attracted them. All the birds flocked towards a large luminous patch in the midst of the sea.

XI

A circle of lambent flame on the surface of the storm-tossed waters! It was a weird spectacle. It must have been very uncommon, otherwise the sea-birds would not have been attracted to it. The sight made my flesh creep, but I got over that as the vision persisted. My new paroxysm of fear and awe was due to the belief that perhaps I was witnessing visions with my eyes open. However, as soon as I discovered that it was neither my fancy nor a sea mirage visible only to distracted mortals, I regained once again my composure—or rather, comparative composure.

In spite of the wind and the rain and the waves, which now twirled and now tossed the Vermilion Boat and forced me to shift my angle of vision every second, I judged that it was not a circle of flame that I was watching, but a shaft of light springing from the bed of the sea and rising straight to heaven. It was a dazzling wonderwork! Soon similar slender shafts of brilliance—recalling the hue of the flame-of-the-forest trees in full bloom—shot up in profusion on all sides. They were straight and lithe as the trunks of mountain *deodars*, graceful and tall. The wind failed to shake them and the rain went through them, they remained unbroken and unscattered. Soon they grew in girth and in solidity; they steadily rose higher and higher, lifting on their heads the ceiling of the sky. They finally set up a luminous pavilion of soaring height and immense dimensions—inconceivable to the imagination of man. It was a sight that my wildest dreams could never have devised. It robbed me of my power of thinking; all my consciousness was concentrated in simply seeing.

The enthralling vision became more awesome when the sable roof of the sky was rent asunder and a cataract of fulgurant flame poured upon the sea. It was like a mighty cascade of luminous waters tilted out of a gigantic vessel of burnished brass. The brightness was almost blinding. My spirit bowed in deep reverence to that glory in the sky.

Why was this ethereal pillared temple of heavenly resplendence raised upon the tumultuous Stygian waters far, far away from the gaze of all human eyes save mine? Was the stage being set for the dance of Urvashi the Coryphæa and her company of Apsaras—nymphs born out of the churning of the sea? Why was I accorded the supernatural spectacle denied to others of my kind? Was the vision of glory granted to me as a boon because I was doomed to perish soon?

The contemplation of the awe-inspiring vista absolved me of all my fears and sorrows. 'To die,' I whispered to myself, 'all mortals are destined. But to depart with my eyes fixed on a heavenly sight would be bliss.'

XII

The murky waves grew jealous of my happiness. They wanted me to cower and cringe, and became more fiendish than anything ever imagined in my most ghoulish nightmares. To distract me they put forth tongues of greenish flame. They hated my watching what was not meant for human eyes.

The wind became jealous too. It drove the boat in a trough whose sides seemed high as hills and as sable as shrouds. It lashed the fuliginous billows till they became maddened seahorses wearing flaming crests and breathing fire.

They were bent on destroying me before I had my fill of the vision beatific.

The sea-horses tossed their fiery manes. They pressed on one another; they clambered over each other. They tried to frighten me with their snorting. They breathed liquid fire and burning frost. They spewed and spat. Bitter spumes of congealed phosphorescence began covering the deck.

The crackling Vermilion Boat became, by and by, as luminous as the flame-crested waves surrounding it. With malicious delight the chargers of the sea then clambered over its sides to come closer to me; they tried to hypnotize me with the fixed glare of their unblinking, glowing eyes. More and more of them crowded on the deck, and under their weight the frail vessel began to founder.

Nevertheless, I stayed where I was: I did not move an inch. I was no longer crouching, but was sitting in the poised pose of proud Kapila Muni when he faced the wild hordes of Sagara's sons. Like him I watched the frenzied herd and challenged them to do their worst.

The water rose to my waist, but the boat was still under me: I could feel it, though but vaguely. Then all of a sudden my mouth was filled with brine, which burned my tongue and blinded my vision, and the boat was gone: the sea-horses were trying to smother me under their weight.

In spite of all logic and common sense I found I was engaged in buffeting the jealous coursers of the sea. I knew it was a senseless combat to struggle against the waves. Where was the least chance of victory for me? The moment I overcame one, another came to take its place, then yet another. They were an infinity, whereas I was but one: alone against an innumerable horde.

What pleasure did they get by dragging me into that unequal fight before my eyes had gazed their fill? Their triumph over a lone person in a frail boat was a foregone conclusion. Yet why did they show unseemly haste and rob me of the bliss of witnessing Urvashi's dance? It was cruel of them to press on their helpless prey.

XIII

Perhaps the waves were endowed with perception, and they knew what was till then unknown to me: they were aware of the fact that I was not alone and friendless in that wilderness of weltering waters.

In the squall-driven chaotic sea the Vermilion Boat was followed by an unknown ally, who was unafraid of the raging elements. The incredibly ugly but infinitely lovable Sisi-Magar was all along on the vessel's track. It was following it about like its shadow, and when the shadow vanished it swam underneath its keel.

And when I thought all was lost its slimy body rose from the waters and stood between death and me. There was no further need for me to wrestle with the fiery stallions of the angry sea. That porpoise in spite of its silly expression and cumbersome movements outwitted all the swift-racing coursers of the deep.

Sisi-Magar became my boat, and straddled on its back I was transformed into a sea-god—one who defied the elements and to whom the wind and the waves paid homage. They no longer raved about death, but spoke of abundant life.

XIV

How long it took Sisi-Magar to bring me back to the palm-fringed atoll at Jater Dol I do not remember. Rightly or wrongly, I concluded—not then, but next day—it was a short trip. But without the porpoise's help this journey back to land would not have been undertaken, for I had completely lost my sense of direction. And without Roma's help it would have been equally impossible for me to ascend the ridge and get to my bed in the bungalow. My body was sore and the joints stiff: I was more dead than alive when Sisi-Magar shook me off its back in the atoll.

Poor Roma! Her vigil must have been most exhausting. I found her waiting for me at the foot of the steps. I guessed what she had gone through on account of my foolishness.

We did not exchange a word. We sobbed in each other's arms: we instinctively recognized a great fact that we had lost and found each other.

~

The warmth of Roma's body brought new life to me. The taste of her lips was like ambrosia, and her embrace was a balm. She instilled new strength into me. Enfolded in her arms my frame stiffened like a bow held taut before loosing its shaft, and it then learnt the bliss of uttermost repose: the bow unstrung, and the target transfixed with the arrow. A sea of harmony flooded through our veins as our hearts and limbs fused into one. We became one body and one soul.

I blessed my stars for the first knowledge of a joy known only to one who has ceased to be a youth: the joy that comes through winning a woman's heart and hand; the proud privilege of attaining manhood; a felicity whose existence I never knew before. I blessed the gods: in embracing Roma, I knew I was worshipping Uma. I remembered the saying: 'Even the things you do after the flesh are spiritual. For you do all things in Him when you aspire to the fullness of joyous existence.'